THE CURSE
OF GANDHARI

Aditi Banerjee

BLOOMSBURY
NEW DELHI • LONDON • OXFORD • NEW YORK • SYDNEY

BLOOMSBURY INDIA
Bloomsbury Publishing India Pvt. Ltd
Second Floor, LSC Building No. 4, DDA Complex, Pocket C – 6 & 7
Vasant Kunj New Delhi 110070

BLOOMSBURY, BLOOMSBURY INDIA and the Diana logo are
trademarks of Bloomsbury Publishing Plc

First published in India 2019
This edition published 2019

ISBN: PB: 978-93-88002-00-4; eBook: 978-93-87863-99-6

2 4 6 8 10 9 7 5 3 1

Typeset in Bembo Std by Manipal Digital Systems
Printed and bound in India by Thomson Press India Ltd.

Bloomsbury Publishing Plc makes every effort to ensure that the papers used in the
manufacture of our books are natural, recyclable products made from wood grown
in well-managed forests. Our manufacturing processes conform to the environmental
regulations of the country of origin.

To find out more about our authors and books visit www.bloomsbury.com and sign
up for our newsletters

To those who preserve and nurture the Mahabharata tradition — the keepers of manuscripts, the custodians of the oral tradition, the translators, the artists, the storytellers, the grandmothers, the gurus and rishis who keep alive the stories and bring us again and again to the churning of this sea of wisdom, otherworldly and earthly alike. I bow to them repeatedly.

A NOTE TO THE READER

The most frequent question I received while writing this book was, 'Why Gandhari?' Why write a novel about Gandhari – a legendary, yet ambiguous, enigmatic character – when there were more obvious heroines like Draupadi or Kunti, colourful personalities like Satyavati or Hidimba? But I have always loved Gandhari.

As a child, I idolized her for the grand sacrifice of blindfolding herself for her husband, the blind prince. It appealed to the romantic in me, this noble gesture of devotion. As I grew older, my fascination grew for the paradox of Gandhari. She was a queen virtuous and powerful enough to curse Krishna, the greatest of the gods, and yet there was more to her than mere virtue. There was her bitter defiance of and challenge to Krishna, the anger and pathos behind that infamous curse, gathering together the outrage and grief of all the women who lost their husbands, sons, fathers, brothers to war and confronting the divine one who allowed it to come to pass. I also marvelled at the strength of will in a woman who, upon hearing that her rival had given birth to the firstborn heir of the kingdom, struck her own belly so hard that her foetus was expelled, whose grief was so deep that she blackened the toenails of Yudhishthira with a mere glance of her eyes. What an incredible queen!

In writing this story, my main source has been the English translation of the Critical Edition of the Mahabharata by

Bibek Debroy. Parts of the book, of course, are products of my own imagination. I do not conceive of this as being the 'true' story of Gandhari. I would frame it as a meditation upon Gandhari, a focus on those essential qualities and ethos of her personality that can be gleaned from the sparse lines of the Mahabharata and improvising on them to conjure a speculation of what her life may have been or could have been. There are limits in interjecting oneself into the sensibilities of another civilization dating back thousands of years. There are limits, too, in writing on the Mahabharata. It is a clever text that tricks, traps and eludes you: sly, subtle, mischievous very much like the Krishna who is at the heart of the story – the more you chase it, the further it retreats; the more you think you understand, the more riddles come your way.

Gandhari has traditionally been depicted either as a devoted, self-sacrificing wife or a bad mother who was unable to control her sons and was therefore partly responsible for the great war. She has been reduced from a complex, nuanced woman to the symbol of her blindfold. So much of the discussion about her centres on whether blindfolding herself was an act of devotion or spite, as if answering that would be enough for us to understand and judge her. Such caricature does disservice to Gandhari and to the poetic greatness of Veda Vyasa who with exquisite sensitivity and nuance depicted this enigmatic woman, who remains a mystery in some ways to the very end.

Gandhari is not a conventional heroine. She was never beloved to the people nor did she win the titles and accolades that Draupadi and Kunti attained. Yet she was someone who even Krishna respected. She won the blessings of Shiva and Veda Vyasa, and even Krishna accepted her curse with a smile. She may not have been *good*, the way we traditionally define a 'good' woman. But she was great in her own way. And it is so uncommon for us to find female personalities in world literature who are fully fleshed out human beings, complex and ambiguous, who are not easily relegated to categories of 'good' or 'bad', virtuous or sinful. In that sense, Gandhari broke the mold. An inherently noble woman of great devotion, iron will and power, bold and brave enough to challenge Krishna himself – she may not be a conventional heroine, but she is someone who commands and deserves our respect and empathy.

PROLOGUE

*T*housands of years after he died – if gods can die – and for thousands of years more, until the end of time, when the mountains dissolve into the stillness of the cosmic sea, they will sing the songs of Krishna's pastimes in the forest.

How he glittered like sapphire against the green trees and swaying grasses muddied black by the night. How he would slip away from all the young girls who chased him, flute dangling from his hand, a plain yellow silk cloth wrapped around his waist.

How his friends – the cowherd boys who played pranks with him and the cowherd girls who longed to dance with him – would pursue him across the forests to the moonlit banks of the Yamuna river, hungering to be as close as possible to him, the all-attractive one. Radiant white cows would trail behind him by the hundreds like a swaying tail of moonlight across the dark night. Even trees would bend towards him longingly as he wove his way through the forests of his boyhood, leaves shedding their branches to touch his blue skin.

But there was once a time when Krishna was the one in pursuit; once, he was the one chasing a woman, in a different forest when he was much older; when a gem-encrusted crown had replaced the peacock feather in his hair. The woman he chased was emaciated and old, yet elegant still, despite the white gauze bandage wound tight around her eyes, blindfolding her. She was running away from him, desperate to avoid him.

But he would not relent. He had come to confront her – Gandhari, the erstwhile queen of Hastinapur – one last time, to prepare her to die.

1

IN THE FOREST, NOW

Gandhari woke up on the forest floor, and the first thing she tried to do was quieten her hunger. It had been over a year since she had eaten food. She told her stomach to behave itself. She knew it would obey her. She touched the earth beneath her. Her first prayer was to the earth for bearing her weight and the weight of all the humans who trampled upon her and destroyed her. Her fingers brushed against the straw pallet carpeted with leaves that served as her bed. She preferred the bare earth, but the men in the hermitage denied her that austerity, seeing in her still the queen she no longer was.

Where are you?

This is how she oriented herself in the world every morning since the day she had blindfolded herself, the day she could no longer see.

I am in the forest ashram of Veda Vyasa, fifteen lengths of a bow from the river. She tested herself. Yes, now she could hear it: the chants of the yogis finishing their morning prayers; the hiss of oblations being poured into the sacrificial fire, the murmur of water being poured into clay pots for cooking the day's meals.

Listen more closely. What is different today? What is missing?

The wind.

The wind had fallen silent in the trees looming above her. So many nights, for years, she had lain on this forest floor, blindfolded and bored, counting the leaves by their individual sounds as they rustled through the wind, numbering them, leaf by leaf, high above her where the topmost branches of this giant canopy of trees met and mingled. She counted them as she had once counted the lives lost in the great war. Eighteen million leaves, that's how far she had counted. How long it had taken to count to that number, how many nights spent awake in this forest, an insomniac. But there had been even more lives lost, lost by her, because of her. That unsettled her. She stopped counting then. She was afraid that if she counted more, if she counted all the leaves in the forest, it still would not add up to the number of lives lost on her account. Just the thought of the war that had cost her all her sons, all her kin, the kingdom that should have been her sons' – stirred up the dormant anger, the fury.

Focus. What else do you hear? What else is missing?

The insects had fallen silent too. The forest that had always hummed and vibrated as termites gnawed through trees, as cicadas hissed, as innumerable creatures feasted on sap and pollen and rotting vegetation – it had become deathly still, as quiet as a cave.

It was then that she started to worry.

She touched her face, pressed her palms over her eyes, warming them through the coarse white bandage. Her gnarled fingers combed through her hair. This, and the splashes of water across her body in the cold river where she would now go to collect water, would be her only grooming for the day.

Once upon a time, it had taken several hours and two serving girls simply to dress her hair for the day. They would waft the smoke of *sambhrani* incense through her tresses and thread gems and flowers into the strands of her long hair, as straight and strong as black iron. She had always insisted on tying the bandage herself. She would screw her eyes shut as her deft fingers loosed and retied the bandage after her wash so that there was no chance of inadvertently casting her eyes on the world.

She had spent years cultivating her physique, smoothing her skin with creams and scrubs that stung her sensitive eyes. She had learnt to drape her dresses at an angle that made her appear taller, to suggest the dip of a waist where there was none. She had sketched elaborate coiffures for her hair, wreathes of braids, cascades of curls like a carefully sculpted waterfall, artful scatterings of pins and shells. Her hair was so heavy when tied up that her neck hurt, but she practiced her gait, the soft, measured tread, the slight elephant-like sway to her hips, the butterfly fluttering movements of her hands. She did this not out of vanity but with the miserly fastidiousness of a merchant hoarding his wealth, carefully investing and growing it.

Beauty was one of the few assets young princesses had.

She wondered how grey her hair had become now.

She rose from her makeshift bed and listened to her own measured tread, the deliberate footfall as she picked her way down to the river. The others had taken to being barefoot but she wore bark sandals to keep her feet clean and supple. They thought it an indulgence perhaps, the act of a spoiled queen. But she needed to be surefooted. She was determined that no one think her weak, that the only sign of her self-imposed infirmity be that white strip of cloth bound elegantly across her eyes. She was adamant in each step to not trip over a pebble or bump into an unexpected tree.

In the beginning, it had taken her two hours to walk that little distance to the river, one slow step at a time, so careful was she not to err. The young boys studying in the ashram had taken pity on her and marked the path from the river to the ashram with spiked posts and a rope hanging between them that she could hold as she walked.

She knelt at the edge of the river, and despite her best efforts, it was an ungainly movement as she lowered herself onto her creaky knees on the pebble-strewn ground. The sharp wind pierced her belly like daggers under her thin, pale yellow cotton sari. The wind invaded her body, clawing at her throat and stinging her eyes through the bandage. Her hands trembled, spilling water from the copper vessel she filled for her husband.

What kind of cold is this? This is the not the cold of winter.

She leaned over the surface of the water to wash her face. As she was about to dip her hands into the icy water, a blast of cold air pushed against her from beneath the water and her eyes flew open beneath the bandage. She could not see; but she saw now. She saw the broad surface of the river frozen white, rippled with stiff waves stuck in mid-motion. Her death was etched across that blank white mirror of the river. There was no lettering, no image, no vision, yet she saw it with certainty, as if the guardian spirits of the water had whispered this to her:

Gandhari, it is time for you to die!

They did not seem particularly disturbed at the prospect. Why should they be? She was an old woman now.

She rose and made her way back to the ashram. The wind clung to her, clasped her behind the neck, played with her hair. It would not let her go. She wrapped her sari around her more tightly but the wind was relentless. It mocked her, howling against her skin. The way back was slow. She gripped the rope a little too tightly, fraying her skin against its rough knots. *I am going to die, I am going to die,* she told herself with every step. A sickly dread settled in her stomach.

She finally reached the hermitage and detected through the sounds of conversation that the others had already gathered in front of the sacrificial fire. She had often thought what an odd sight they must make: these four elderly guests from the royal court of Hastinapur, uninvited guests living among the hermits. They wore the garb of hermits but held themselves awkwardly, stiffly, as if presiding over a court at which they no longer had authority or power, a place where they were now just tolerated guests.

Kunti, her sister-in-law, the widow of her husband's brother, the one who had taken it upon herself to look after Gandhari and her husband.

Sanjaya, the king's erstwhile charioteer and trusted advisor, the closest thing the king had ever had to a friend, who had also accompanied them to the forest to serve them.

The old king himself, her husband, Dhritarashthra, blind from birth. Even now his blindness did not sit easily with him. While the others sat ramrod straight and still, his hands flailed in his lap, grasping at empty air, for something solid to hold. His head wobbled from side to side like a bird, groping for sounds to tell him what his eyes could not. Especially here in the forest, bereft of the whispers of courtiers and ministers, he felt himself vulnerable. He agitated the air all around them.

Gandhari approached Dhritarashthra with the cup of water that she knew he would refuse. He had taken to refusing water in the last few months along with food, but she insisted on serving him. When he waved away the cup, she poured it onto a nearby plant with a feeling of perverse satisfaction. It was hard carrying out the duties of a devoted wife to a renunciate. These rituals that had become meaningless were all that she had left.

The hermit currently in charge of the ashram lowered himself down to the forest floor, sitting next to the four of them. The morning worship had ended. He said gently: 'My revered ones, I must share certain bad omens with you. You know that the sacred fire speaks to us. It tells us of inauspicious tidings. Death hovers nearby.'

'For whom?' Kunti's voice was as placid as the slow ebb and flow of the river where Gandhari had just bathed.

'For us all. Danger hangs over this forest for all of us in the next few days.' He paused to let them take it in. They continued to sit motionless. Even Dhritarashthra's movements had stilled. 'Of course, we will look after you and protect you with our lives.'

'We will die tomorrow,' Gandhari said flatly.

Dhritarashthra gasped. 'So, it is really true then? I have also seen it this night in my dreams! Are we to die? At long last? Is the day finally here? Have we foreseen our own deaths?' His voice trembled with excitement.

Gandhari rolled her eyes behind her bandage. What was so surprising about that – that they should be dying and that they should foresee it? Those who did penance acquired *siddhis,* supernatural powers born of spiritual practice, the ability to curse and bless, to see and manipulate the future. There was nothing remarkable in that. It was just another form of capital. She had been a princess once, a queen; she knew how to build and spend capital, whether it was financial, political or spiritual. Her years of sacrificing her eyesight and devotion to her husband had given her powers, powers she had exercised, capital that she had wasted, foolishly.

'My lord,' the hermit said. 'There is no need for you to worry. You have done so much penance all these years. Surely, you will go to the heavens.'

'Yes,' Dhritarashthra's voice brightened. 'I – I think, even if I have not lived well, perhaps I can at least die well.'

Even now, the smugness. Her husband felt entitled to the heavens. He had been raised all his life to know the greatness of the Kurus, the valour and glory of the dynasty into which he had been born. Whatever else he had done, whatever grievous wrongs, could not affect the essence of what he was, his heritage and his birthright. He was born into a dynasty of heroes and should have earned the afterlife of heroes, in his own mind.

It was so unlike her to lose control over her speech, but suddenly Gandhari blurted out: 'I am not ready to die.'

She immediately felt foolish. The protest of it surprised her. She had never protested before, not when she had been married to the blind king, not when her sons committed perfidy after perfidy, not when her sons had died, not when they had exiled themselves to the forest. It felt almost illicit to protest such a small thing now, the passing of her life when it had already become so dried and hollow, a dead leaf simply waiting to fall off the branch.

'Gandhari, what is left for us to see in this world? We who will never see our son be king? We who will never see our children again?' Dhritarashthra's hands groped for her face, her hands, for comfort; to take, not to give. He had never learned how to be blind gracefully, to mask his disability, and his movements were clumsy and feeble.

Gandhari thought she heard a snicker, or was it the rustling of the leaves, the rush of the river? Then Kunti said: 'I have no fear or worries. Krishna is my refuge. He will protect me here and hereafter.'

Gandhari imagined the self-satisfied smile on her sister-in-law's face. It was so like Kunti to make a contest out of this, out of being the one to die the most virtuously. They always had been rivals after all.

Gandhari knew, too, that Kunti had purposely brought up the name of Krishna, the name Gandhari most dreaded.

Well, she was not dead yet.

'Sister,' Gandhari said sweetly, 'I'm surprised that you want to die so early. You begged your *nephew* to send you unending pains and sorrows the last time you saw him. Have you had enough already?' She emphasized the word 'nephew', knowing how Kunti hated hearing Krishna referred to in mere human terms. Krishna was a god, no doubt, but there were still those who puzzled over his ancestry, his status as a divine king and a true avatar of Vishnu. For some, he was just an exalted politician, a brilliant ruler and diplomat, a wily player in the game of thrones who had masterfully made his way from a cowherd to powerful king through his wit and charisma.

The hermit excused himself with a murmur and hurried away, probably desperate to escape the type of squabbling he had become a celibate to avoid.

Kunti's prayer to Krishna had already become famous across Bharat. The last time they had met, as Krishna was taking her leave after the war had ended, Kunti had requested the strangest of boons. She had begged him for an unending string of sorrows, because it was only in times of sorrow that the *devas,* the divine beings, could be remembered; it was only in sorrow that humans could remember to pray. And so, Kunti had asked for a lifetime of sorrow to bring her closer to Krishna.

You and me, sister, we've already seen enough to remember the devas for a hundred lifetimes. What was the need to pray for more? Gandhari thought.

Kunti replied, 'Sister, do not worry for me. If the *devas* wish to test me further, then through tribulation I shall remember them and them alone. If I am to die, may I die with Hari's name on my lips.'

She paused: 'I know the source of your bitter words and I shall not be goaded. You are worried for your own fate. Well, it is not too late to seek refuge with the *devas*. It is not too late to ask for Krishna's mercy.'

Sanjaya had long ago assumed the role of mediator between Kunti and Gandhari in the face of Dhritarashthra's passivity. He intervened, 'The queen has undergone the most rigorous of penances. Even the *devas* bow to her chastity as a wife. She has accumulated the merits of the three worlds due to her devotion to the king.'

Gandhari hid a smile. Sanjaya could not know how it riled Kunti, a widow, to be reminded of Gandhari's devotion to her husband, a virtue Kunti could no longer accumulate.

Kunti's voice was as corrosive as the iron wedding-bangle that adorned Gandhari's wrist. 'What penance can protect a queen who has cursed a *deva*, Sanjaya? Who can say what kind of afterlife awaits she who cursed Krishna?'

Dhritarashthra murmured weakly in protest but said nothing.

Gandhari retorted, 'Perhaps the same afterlife that awaits the mother who abandoned and renounced her own firstborn son.'

She heard the indrawn breaths and gasps of shock from the young students who had been eavesdropping. Of course, they would be shocked and scandalized. They had probably heard the rumours – the Kurus were famous by then, the royal family whose feud had killed millions in the Great War – these young ones must have heard about Kunti's first son, Karna, whom she had abandoned at birth as he was born out of wedlock.

They would have heard the stories but perhaps not expected it to be true, at least not expected it to be hurled in Kunti's face like a weapon. These young untested boys would not match the sordid story with that virtuous woman who served the king and queen respectfully and silently, whose face had turned into stoic stone.

What did these boys know after all? What did they know of the hardness of our world? Who were they to be scandalized by Kunti or me? thought Gandhari.

What would these boys say if they knew Krishna's last words to Gandhari, after she had lamented the death of her sons, after she had wept and wailed and beat her chest, after she had cursed him to witness the destruction of his own clan and die an inglorious death, after Krishna accepted that curse with a smile, that she had no reason to mourn, that princesses like her gave birth to sons for the purpose of being slaughtered?

Kunti left in a huff and Sanjaya followed her with a sigh, leaving Dhritarashthra and Gandhari together alone. The young acolytes of the ashram ran off to their morning studies and yoga practices. He turned to her and implored, 'Let it go, woman, let it go at least now, now that the end is coming.'

'What are you talking about?' Her voice was smooth and controlled.

'All your bitterness. Against Kunti, against me. A man can never be content if his wife is unhappy. Your unhappiness has been the curse of me for all these years. How long will you hound me with your hate? Even into the afterlife? Let it go, woman! Your resentment, your spite, has been a shadow over the family ever since we were married. How long will you punish me? How can I go to the heavens when your displeasure is so strong?'

'You are being ridiculous. I am not angry. I am not unhappy.' Her voice grew harder, as she tried to convince herself.

He scrabbled the ground at her feet with his hands, trying to make a place to bow his head at her feet, to prostrate before her in supplication. She felt his tears fall on her toe. 'Please, Gandhari, I beg you.' His voice was trembling and wet. 'I beg you, please, forgive me. Please let go of your anger, now, before it is too late. Or else I will be cursed in the afterlife as I have been on earth. Please let me go.'

She drew her feet away, refusing his pleas, and left him. It was unbecoming for a husband to bow to his wife. Always he had been so insipid, so weak. It came back to her now, the initial disgust, the contempt, the shock, the fury, the disbelief that she would be married off to this pathetic failure of a man. It sprang back at her now, when it was definitely too late – those suppressed wonderings of what her life could have been without him.

Gandhara, Then

The journey from Gandhara to Hastinapur had taken weeks in a caravan across rivers and through dense forest. It was a slow, cumbersome journey with her full entourage of counsellors, maids and her childhood ayah, Ayla, who had come to nurse her eventual babies. Subala, her father, had added three more maids to the entourage when Gandhari had chosen to blindfold herself.

It had all started with Bhishma's surprise visit to Gandhara. The only visitors to Gandhara tended to be barbarian invaders from the Western steppes, hoping to raid the wealthy kingdoms of Bharat. Gandhara was one of the most remote kingdoms in the northwest corner of Bharat and a constant site of battle with foreign marauders, seeking to make it past the border kingdom to the wealthy territories of the mainland ripe for plunder. And now one of Bharat's most revered and feared rulers was at their doorstep. King Subala posted spies everywhere in his territory, ever on guard. Thus, they learned of Bhishma's impending arrival a few days before he actually appeared.

Other than when Gandhara was at war, Pushkalavati, the capital of the kingdom, was a sleepy frontier town. The court lacked bards, musicians, dancers or even astrologers to keep them entertained. Instead, the royal family played dice, wagering each other with apples gathered from their vast orchards. The king would hold forth discussions on war strategy and the history of heroic battles fought in the past. His one hundred sons were usually not interested and instead congregated in the horse stables to drink fermented grain alcohol. Gandhari, his only daughter, listened, enraptured, at the feet of his throne, and citizens thronged from all over to learn from the wise king.

Bhishma's visit jolted everyone into action. Gandhari's mother took charge of whitewashing the palace walls, faded and dull from the onslaught of dust in the summer and snows in the winter. She hung freshly embroidered tapestries in the audience hall and had the wooden walls of the palace freshly polished. Goats were herded and killed, and herbs snipped from the royal gardens to make meals fit to match the sumptuous fare of the mainland courts.

Others speculated in fear and excitement. Bhishma was a living legend. He was the son of Ganga, a river goddess, and the late king of Hastinapur, Shantanu. The *devas* themselves taught him the rules of governance and warfare, ethics and justice. He was one of the most valiant princes the world had ever seen, a fearless fighter and conqueror, as famous for his stern righteousness as his mettle in battle.

The court was flooded with whispers, whether Bhishma had come for battle, to invade and conquer their kingdoms, or had come to hire soldiers from their forces. Gandhara's soldiers were venerated as some of the fiercest soldiers in the realm. They reaped wealth as mercenaries in between Gandhara's wars. Or, had he come to bear some dire warnings or other ill tidings, perhaps that Gandhara was on the brink of being attacked?

Subala took Gandhari aside. 'Madhu, my daughter, what do you make of all this?' Madhu, literally honey, was his pet name for her.

She tilted her head carefully, considering. Her mother had taught her to be deliberate in all her movements. Economy of movement expressed regal upbringing. She replied with confident succinctness: 'He has not come here for war.' She jabbed at the air to make her point. They were in the audience hall, even though there was no one else there. Subala liked to have Gandhari take the seat of one of the ministers, to practice statecraft with him. 'The kingdom of the Kurus is already stretched too thin. And ever since his nephew Vichitravirya passed away, Bhishma has had to spend more and more time at home, governing alongside the regent queen, his mother.'

'Stepmother,' corrected Subala softly.

'Oh, yes.' How could she have forgotten one of the most salacious pieces of gossip to have come out of Bharat in generations, although it had happened well before her time.

'Not just to rule, daughter, but also to raise — how many princes, Madhu?' Subala slipped into calling her by her pet name when nobody else was around. His wife thought a princess should always be addressed by her proper name. She was from a prestigious mainland kingdom, married off to Subala in exchange for a military alliance to bolster the dwindling treasury of her father's kingdom. She had been trying very hard to elevate the standard of etiquette at this backwater court, including by persistently nagging her husband and daughter to become more civilized.

Gandhari racked her memory. She practiced for hours with her private tutor, memorizing the lineages, boundaries and intersecting dynasties of the dozens of kingdoms that comprised Bharat. The Kurus, with Bhishma as their scion, were particularly confusing. 'Three?' Before her father could shake his head, she corrected herself. 'No! Two princes.' The third brother was born of a maidservant and was therefore ineligible to be prince.

'And what do we know of the current princes?'

'One is weak, the other blind.'

'And who is the crown prince?'

'The weak one – Pandu.' His pallor caused concern among the kingdom, but it was still deemed better than a blind king. And thus, it was Pandu who was the crown prince.

Subala nodded, pleased. 'Bhishma has raised them well. Despite their ... infirmities, it looks like they may be competent enough to govern. But that is not enough to guarantee them a good reign. Madhu, what else is needed?'

She averted her eyes shyly with a small smile. 'A strong bride.' One who could produce a strong heir to the throne that has proved so slippery.

Subala smiled at her slyly, with a wink.

♋

That night, Gandhari went to bed, blushing. She inventoried all she had heard about Pandu. Her father taught her that information was the most valuable currency that they had. They were not invited to the typical tournaments and *swayamvaras,* where women chose their husbands based on feats of strength. They missed out on those royal congregations where they could gather gossip and size each other up through tournaments, assessing princes by their individual prowess at archery, mace play and the show of force they brought with them. Spies were their substitute for direct observation.

Pandu was supposed to be handsome and skilled at fighting. He was pale and though physically strong, there was a fatal weakness in him. No one quite knew what it was. Yet another secretive mystery of the Kurus. It was as if, say, one pushed him too hard, he might shatter into a thousand pieces. This is what they heard.

Gandhari imagined being the wife of Pandu and ruling as the Queen of Hastinapur. She felt a rush of affection for the crown prince, tenderness for the precarious position in which he found himself. He was the only chance of the Kuru line surviving after the last king had died, childless.

'Don't worry, my sweet prince,' she whispered into the starry sky where the thirty-three million *devas* would hear her. 'I will protect you and keep you safe with my life.'

So, this is what a vow of celibacy does to a man.

Gandhari watched Bhishma as he approached the palace from afar across the undulating valleys bordering River Panjkora. Everyone in Bharat by now knew the story of Bhishma's vow. In old age, Bhishma's father, the king Shantanu, had fallen in love with a fisherwoman. The fisherwoman's father refused to marry her to Shantanu without the guarantee that their sons, and not Bhishma, would inherit the throne. To assuage him, Bhishma not only renounced the throne but vowed lifelong celibacy so there would never be a rival to the throne. That was when he became known as Bhishma, the one who had made a terrible vow. Conches had sounded from the heavens and the gods showered flowers of blessings upon him.

A vow like that changed a man. Gandhari observed how tautly he held himself, like a finely strung bow. His shoulder-length blunt cut hair had started to silver. Yet he was still broad in chest, his muscles roughly hewn. His face at one time would have been smooth, softly etched like the son of the river nymph and a besotted king that he was. The austerity of his vow had engraved deep lines bracketing his lips and slashes above his low-set, perpetually frowning eyebrows.

Gandhari shivered at his form riding towards the palace, reins tightly gripped in his powerful hands. He was a man cruel to himself in penance if not to others.

Last night, Subala had gathered together his various ministers and counsellors to confer about Bhishma's visit. They were refreshing their intelligence about Bhishma. Gandhari was concealed in the darkness of the back of the chamber to learn from their deliberations. When the others were expressing admiration over Bhishma's vow and sacrifice, Subala had demurred: 'Can a prince afford to put the emotional yearnings of his father above the security of the lineage and the continuation of the dynasty? What if Satyavati had turned out to be barren?'

The others had fallen silent.

Subala had stared directly at the back of the audience chamber, where Gandhari was concealed. 'This is why one must carefully choose one's vows, to contemplate the consequences, not just for one's self but for the family, the kingdom and the nation.'

Gandhari chafed at her father's cynicism. The tales of all their *devas* and heroes were full of glorious vows. She loved

the tales of Rama, his vow to remain banished in the forest
before claiming back his crown, his vow to never wed another
woman after Sita, the vow of fasting undertaken by Parvati to
win Shiva as her husband. A vow, a sacrifice, could alter the
course of destiny.

Her maid, Ayla, gently pulled her back from the window
where she was watching Bhishma's approach. 'Come, princess,
it is time to come downstairs. He is almost here.'

After Bhishma arrived at court, Gandhari's mother was
fastidious that all the etiquette and protocols be scrupulously
followed. His feet were bathed in milk, scented water and
flowers; he was offered the customary food and drinks; he and
Subala exchanged the customary questions about the wellbeing
of their respective kingdoms and subjects.

It was awkward between Subala and Bhishma, as was
often the case between two men who had heard much about
each other but never met. There were long pauses in between
the stilted conversation, and Subala's one hundred sons grew
restless and fidgeted in their cushioned seats on the floor.

Bhishma smiled at the sight of them. 'How fortunate you
are, king, to have so many healthy sons.' He turned his head
to give a kind smile to Gandhari, seated demurely next to her
mother. She wore a pale orange sari, deliberately suggestive of
bridal red. Her hair was braided with combs formed of ivory
coloured shells and encrusted with small orange gemstones.
'And, of course, a lovely daughter. One hundred and one
children! You are truly fortunate!'

Subala laughed: 'One good child outweighs one hundred
(and one) brats.'

Bhishma smiled politely, then became solemn. He set down
the silver tumbler of fruit wine. 'Subala, it has taken me weeks
to get here. And I must return back to Hastinapur tomorrow.
We had better get to the business at hand. There is something
of utmost importance I wish to discuss with you.'

Subala inclined his head. 'Of course, although we regret you are leaving so early. We would have liked to enjoy your company for a longer time. Please proceed.'

'It would be better addressed in private.'

Subala frowned but conceded. He liked having all of his children around for such meetings. He used them as lessons in governance. Afterwards, he would quiz them on their observations and how much they had been able to read between the lines. Gandhari felt anxious. Her heart started pounding. To not even be in the chamber when her very future would be decided! It was intolerable for someone as curious and inquisitive as she was.

Everyone other than Subala's wife was dismissed. Gandhari lurked behind one of the pillars near the entrance to the chamber, where the door was left ajar. Bhishma fascinated her. There was so much lore and knowledge that he carried inside him, so much exoticness from his conquests of far-off kingdoms, so much brooding concealed below his hard exterior. His accent was different, and, for the first time, she understood the sophistication her mother missed, her sense of isolation and disconnect.

Shakuni, her brother, hid next to her. He was different from Gandhari's other brothers. Where they were rambunctious and carefree, Shakuni was brooding and intense. He rarely said a word, just watched all that was going on around him like a hawk and filed it all away. His brothers enjoyed hunting and riding horses, but Shakuni hated to move. Speed and action distracted from the spider web of thought he wove in his concealed mind. He was short and already potbellied before he had reached twenty years of age.

The voices from the chamber were muffled through the thick walls. She could not see them, but she could hear. Bhishma said, 'Subala, your kingdom may be remote, but your daughter's fair reputation has spread far and wide.'

'Ahh. And what is it that is being said of her?'

Gandhari's heart started thumping. Since last night, she had been imagining herself as the Queen of Hastinapur.

'It is said that Shiva has given her the boon that she will bear one hundred sons.'

Subala did not respond. Gandhari knew he was displeased with the answer. That was not what he wanted his daughter to be known for.

Her mother jumped in hastily. 'Yes, it is true. Our daughter is so devoted. For a full year, she had worshipped Shiva, fasting every Monday. After one year, Shiva appeared to her in a dream and promised her one hundred sons.'

Gandhari still remembered that night. Ever since she had heard about how Parvati had spent years in the forest, subsisting on nothing but air, meditating on Shiva and praying to become his wife, Gandhari had desperately wanted to do the same. As a young princess, she could not run off into the forest, but she had worshipped Shiva steadfastly. On Mondays, she woke before dawn, chanted his one thousand names, offered a stream of water from a copper vessel vibrating with the power of her chants, and repeated the mantra of his name over and over again from sunrise to sunset, without stopping to eat or drink. At sunset, she would sit on the bank of the River Panjkora, gaze into it, intent upon meditating on Shiva until she would catch a glimpse of his form in the rippled water beneath her. Sometimes it would be his *trishul*, his trident; sometimes the ash-smeared complexion of his body, sometimes his tawny matted locks. Only then would she eat.

When Shiva had graced her with his presence in her dream – this beautiful ash-grey *deva* clothed in deerskin with matted tawny locks of hair crawling down his broad back, a trident gripped in one hand, fierce yet kind and gentle – she had felt too shy to ask him for the boon of winning a husband with his qualities who would make her as happy as Shiva made Parvati.

Instead, he promised her the one hundred sons she had not asked for.

She suddenly wondered now if he had done that because it was the only boon he could give her, that perhaps she was not fated to have a good husband.

She wrung her hands inside the orange folds of her sari. Dread knotted her stomach, even as her heart pounded in hope.

Bhishma said approvingly, 'A girl who is so devout, so virtuous, so blessed by and dear to the *devas*, from such an illustrious line – well, let me come straight to the point, it would be an honour to have her marry my nephew and become part of the Kuru clan.'

Gandhari clasped her hands so tightly that her nails dug into her skin. Shakuni watched her intently under hooded eyes. His body was held tensed and still.

Subala said probingly, cautiously, 'We have, of course, heard how valorous and talented Pandu is–'

'Oh! Not Pandu!' Bhishma's voice was adamant and decisive. 'I meant my eldest nephew, Dhritarashthra.'

Gandhari's mother exclaimed, 'But he is blind!'

Blindness along with other infirmities was considered inauspicious. He may have been the older son, but he would never inherit the throne.

Bhishma said stiffly, 'He may be blind, but he has been educated and trained in all the arts and sciences just like Pandu. He is an exceptionally skilled archer notwithstanding his lack of sight. He will still be the scion of the Kuru clan. I should think your daughter would be blessed to have a husband like him.' There was the hint of smugness and condescension that a man as blunt as Bhishma could not disguise. 'She could not hope to make a better match.'

'We had thought this may be the reason for your visit. But we had thought for Pandu. She would make–'

Gandhari imagined Bhishma waving his arm dismissively. How she wished she could see them with her own eyes! 'No, we have someone else in mind for Pandu. It will not be Gandhari.'

Another ruler would have been more diplomatic, employed charm and grace in the refusal. But austerity had made Bhishma hard and stern with others as he was with himself.

This is what a vow does to you, Gandhari repeated to herself.

It was Shakuni who saw his sister's face crumple in front of him, the soft whimper that escaped between her trembling lips, her eyes that turned upwards in accusation at the *devas* for letting her down.

It was not that Dhritarashthra would not be king. Well, not just that. There were troubling rumours of his feebleness, of how he cried out in the middle of the night, his paranoia that assailants were lurking around intent on murdering him. His bitterness at being passed over in favour of his younger brother was ill-disguised and he had become a piteous unpleasant man, so it was said. She could not tolerate the idea of him as her husband.

Shakuni punched his fist into the wall. He hissed: 'Marry our one princess off to a blind man? Never! How dare they insult us like this!'

Gandhari was sobbing silently, careful to not make a sound that could give them away. Shakuni reached over to awkwardly pat her shoulder. This was the first time she could recall this odd brother of hers touching her. He ordinarily shrank from human contact.

Shakuni became jumpy and started pacing.

Subala requested time to consider the proposal. Bhishma said he needed an answer before he left the next day and, all things equal, he would prefer to take Gandhari back with him in the morning.

Shakuni lost control then and tore into the audience chamber, yelling hoarsely that his sister would never be married off to the blind prince, that she and their family would not be insulted like this. Gandhari ran after him.

Subala had to physically restrain his son who was now ranting incoherently, frothing at the mouth, trying to claw at Bhishma's face. Gandhari pleaded with Shakuni to back down. She threw herself between Bhishma and her brother, turning her tear-stained face, coloured red in embarrassment to Bhishma beseechingly, pleading with him silently to forgive her brother.

Bhishma had a look of such undisguised contempt on his face that all the tears in Gandhari – behind her eyes and clogging her throat – froze and hardened into iron.

I will never be shamed in front of him again, Gandhari vowed to herself.

His lips had curled in disgust, his eyes reflecting his shock and outrage. It was as if to say he had expected them to be uncouth but not this wild, not so unpredictable. As if he had not quite bargained for this.

Well, Gandhari thought to herself, *maybe his spies are not as good as ours.*

♋

Some hours later, after Bhishma had been placated, fed and put to bed, after Subala and his wife conferred at length in private, Gandhari and Shakuni were summoned by their parents into their private bed-chamber. Gandhari knew her fate as soon as she saw the sad resignation in her father's face and the quiet triumph in her mother's.

Shakuni snarled: 'You cannot possibly consider it, *Matashree*, You know what they say about the blind, Respected Mother! How can you give her away to such an inauspicious man? He will doom her life! How can you send her to that snake pit of a palace, ruled over by a fisherman's daughter and the bastard princes who were not even sired by the king?'

Gandhari's mother shook her head. 'Whatever you say, the Kuru lineage is one of the most prestigious in all of Bharat. Well, even if not queen, at least she will be part of a good dynasty. And anyway, what choice did we have, after your disgraceful little outburst? How could we let such an insult to Bhishma stand? We will be shunned if we do not make amends. She will marry the blind one. That is it.'

Gandhari looked at the floor as she walked over to her father. She swallowed hard so that her voice would not waver as she addressed him. She looked into his face that was beginning to wrinkle, his hair that was mussed and greying, his sudden frailty and helplessness. His eyes darted from hers like an anxious rabbit.

She placed her hand on his forearm, her eyes fixed on his hand. That hand that had held her protectively against him as they rode on horseback through the forests on hunts. That had pointed out to her on the map all the kingdoms of Bharat, teaching her patiently their history, culture and geography as she sat on his lap. That hand that had patted her to sleep on so many nights as a child. He was not a usual father.

She lifted her eyes to gaze at his face steadily: '*Pitashree*, Respected Father, this is not what you trained me for.'

'Everything I have taught you, you have learned well. You will use your knowledge well.'

'Just as we are in the hinterlands here, I will be banished to the hinterlands of Hastinapur.'

It was rumoured that Dhritarashthra preferred to sit in the darkened rooms in the most remote recesses of the palace at Hastinapur. Too many voices, too much activity, too much light overwhelmed him.

'Madhu, it is for the best. You will be the most virtuous and devoted of wives. You will be his strength and guide him through his infirmities.' The steel of command had re-entered his voice. 'You will be all that I have raised you to

be, and you shall be his wife, bringing honour to our name
and clan.'

Gandhari looked away. She had known the gods were
fickle. She had known she could not trust her mother. But
she had not expected betrayal from her father. Her hands and
stomach turned cold. It was as if the blood had stopped flowing
in her veins, as if she had stopped living, as if the Madhu she
had once been was no more.

It was the night of the full moon. The palace, the sandy banks
of the river where she worshipped every dawn and dusk, the
gardens with the hardy plants, the only ones that could cling
to life in this desert region, the dirt trails she rode horseback
with her father, they were all limned in silver moonlight. At
midnight, Gandhari slipped out from her chambers, where the
maids were packing her belongings and gathering together the
jewels, costly garments and other gifts that would constitute
her bridal trousseau.

She slowly wandered the grounds. She touched the blooms
of the rose bushes that her mother had planted when Gandhari
was still a child, her fingertips lingering on their petals, so
easily crushed and bruised. She visited the stables and patted
the heads of her favourite horses, careful not to wake them.
She walked by the river, listening to the murmur of the waves
as they bid her farewell. She listened intently for messages or
clues. But if they were there she could not decipher them. She
turned to the rippling water that had once carried to her the
form of Shiva, the blessings of the *devas*. She stared hard into
its moonlit surface, but all she saw was her own reflection, dim
in the dark night.

She walked back to the palace and tried to remain hidden
from view as servants scurried to prepare for her departure.

She walked the hallways that were remote and deserted. She trailed her fingers against the wooden walls. Wood always felt frail to her, easily splintered, susceptible to burning and breaking. She watched the flames from the oil lamps, how they flickered and danced against the painted walls and thought how easy it would be for them to consume the walls, the whole palace, her family, the kingdom. It was her father who taught her how to identify weakness, how to root it out and replace it with iron strength. Iron. When she was a child, when she lay down to sleep while her father and brothers were away in battle, when she feared the invaders would invade her palace and home, her bedchamber, she had dreamt of iron castles. Castles so strong their walls could never be breached.

She had heard that in the south the palaces were built of stone. But stone walls could not protect you from your husband, from his family.

I will be my own iron fortress.

She had made her way to the furthest reaches of the palace. Here even the sounds of the bustle in the main chambers did not reach. Here her path was shrouded in darkness, as the maids forgot to light the lamps or simply did not bother. No one of import came here. Here she could walk more freely, allow the tread of her feet to carry noise. She moved faster.

There was a chill in the air. It climbed up her spine. She would not hurry, not betray that sign of fear. But as she made to turn around, the sound of high-pitched chanting and sputtering caught her ears. Despite herself, she drew forward. In the corner, at the bend of the hallway, was a room that had no door, not even a curtain for privacy. Soot had blackened the walls and the smell of damp chopped wood stacked haphazardly in the corner of the room, and burnt offerings of substances she could not identify, singed her nostrils. What should have been auspicious, repelled her.

In the middle of the room sat a half-naked wild man, tending to a sacrificial fire. But this was not the fire that she knew.

The fire of *yajna,* of the sacrificial rites, was bright and benevolent, emanating warmth and light, sinuously undulating into the forms of the *devas* to whom the offerings were being carried. This fire was a dim, sickly orange that hunched over the smouldering logs and dried cow-dung cakes in the bottom of the fire pit, forking out its limbs, like an old humpbacked woman. It sputtered and sizzled angrily, protesting when offerings were dropped into it rudely by the man, like a serpent turning on its master.

As her eyes lifted to the man tending the fire, she found he was staring at her intensely, even as he continued pouring the ghee and strange herbs she had never seen before into the fire. His hands were coated with powders of crushed substances emitting unpleasant odours, and he flicked them carelessly into the fire, not bothering about the powder that spilled over around the fire pit, dirtying the floor.

The fire priests of the palace were always so meticulous that not one drop of ghee, one pinch of herbs or seeds, should miss the fire pit. The offerings were meant for the *devas*; to be so clumsy and careless was to disrespect and deprive the *devas* of their due.

Finally, she recognized him. He had come to the palace years ago, a wandering ascetic, in search of shelter and appointment. Gandhara did not have a local population of brahmanas who could perform the yajnas and present the teachings to the royal family of Dharma, philosophy, statecraft, rites, yoga and other matters that were the province of brahmanas. The brahmanas had to travel far and wide to attend gurukulas where they could be properly taught, and they rarely returned. The frontier kingdom was too wild for their liking.

This was a cause of dismay to Gandhari's mother. Those few who stayed in Gandhara were the dregs of the brahmana class, some of whom never finished their education or were expelled from gurukulas for perhaps unsavoury reasons, although there were a rare few who stayed in Gandhara because they preferred to be there, because they wanted to continue their studies of arcane texts and rites undisturbed. When this one had come, he had wandered straight into the audience chamber where Subala was holding court – it was the day of the month when any subject could approach the king and present their requests to him – so the guards were unable to keep him from entering the chamber. He was dressed only in a loincloth; his buttocks visible. He had not bathed in weeks and the rank smell and sight of him made people turn away in disgust, recoiling from his very presence.

Gandhari's mother swooned and was ushered away by her handmaidens.

The man approached the throne and addressed Subala in a rough dialect, the words rumbling like an uncomfortable cough in his throat. His voice was rusty and in disuse, almost feeble, as if he had not talked in months. Perhaps he had not.

The man, who offered no name, rattled off that the palace had no astrologer, no *rajpurohit*, no *rajguru,* no royal priest or teacher. Subala scoffed that he had no need for such men, that he relied on good governance and his own battle-earned wisdom. Then, in a flash, so fast that even Subala's bodyguards could not hold him back, the man climbed up the ten steps that led to the platform on which Subala's throne sat and leaned over the throne and whispered something into Subala's ear. As the guards pulled him back, the man snarled a laugh and his eyes gleamed in victory. Subala had paled, his fingers that rested on the lion heads carved onto the arms of his throne trembled and his eyes widened, searching the room until they finally landed on Gandhari. Subala stared at her while the guards dragged the man away. As the man passed her, he winked at her lewdly.

All thought that he had been dispatched, far away from Gandhara, that the bodyguards had thrown him out or maybe even had him killed. But later that day, Subala had visited Gandhari in her bedchamber as she was about to sleep, something he had not done since she was a child. He paced the small room, deeper in worry than she had ever seen him. Finally, he sat down next to her on her bed, and held her hand.

His face was framed in a square patch of moonlight and as his eyebrows scrunched together in deep thought, his eyes intent on his daughter's face, his hand gripping hers tightly, Gandhari thought he had never looked so dear to her.

'Madhu, you are a good girl, aren't you?' he asked softly, weighing the words as if he were weighing her virtue.

'Pitashree, what do you mean?'

She had been so young then, less than ten years old. She thought about it, how she finished her lessons on time, how she did not waste food that was served to her, how she woke up as soon as the maid roused her, how she repeated all her prayers. She examined the situation carefully in her mind, as her father had taught her to do. But she could not find any evil within her. Her brothers sometimes hurt small animals, often beat on each other and lied to their parents. But she never did.

Subala suddenly shook his head, as if ashamed of the question, as if to shake off the doubt that had been nagging him since the wild man had come. 'Nothing, Madhu. Do not mind me.' He rose and walked to the window, peering up at the night sky, at the faraway stars, as if he could divine them, as if to search out the *devas* who resided there.

'Madhu.' He did not meet her eyes now. 'The *devas* are not your enemy.'

'Of course not, Pitashree!'

'They are not your enemy. They are not your enemy.'

The first was a statement of fact, the second a command.

Before he left, he told her the wild man would be staying in the palace, to conduct rites for protection of their home and kingdom, that she was never to cross his path or to tell others of his presence. Since then, she started even more rigorous worship of the *devas*.

A peculiar power started to grow around the palace since the wild man began living there. More and more brahmanas started leaving, driven off by an unsavoury magic that started to take hold of the palace. Gandhari's family grew stronger and more invincible, yet there seemed to be a darkness that hung over them, too, that protected them like a dark, clinging shadow.

For so many years, more than ten years, she had not seen him. But she saw him now. She felt a powerful urge to run but refused to be a coward.

'So, girl, you have come now just as you are about to leave.' His voice was wheezing and guttural all at once.

'What did you tell my father that day?'

He laughed. 'I told him what I saw in the fire that day. What use is it if I tell you that today?'

Her voice was haughty. 'Fine. Then, tell me what you see today.'

He did not move a muscle but it seemed suddenly his face was only an inch away from hers, wet and smelling of sweat and blood that was not his own, swarthy and wild-eyed. His eyes were wide and unblinking as if they would devour her. His hair was twisted into matted locks that hung like limp ropes down his back and cast fierce shadows against the walls.

'Are you sure you want to know, princess?' His breath was foul, like a rotted animal carcass.

She nodded.

He turned to the fire and glowered at it. He picked up a staff made of knotted tree bark lying next to him and pounded the ground with it. With each thump that shook the wooden floorboards, the flames leapt higher, snarling and sputtering. The skinny tendrils shrieked like hungry ghosts and flickered blue and black before diving down to the blackened wood and burnt offerings at the bottom of the pit and jumping up again. Finally, he held out his hand into the fire pit and the flames pooled and stretched in his palm, hovering above his flesh just barely, like a tamed wildcat curling up into itself. He tightened his fingers, and the fire folded itself into a glowing orange ball. He tested the ball of fire in his palm by moving his hand up and down, side to side. The ball obeyed his hands instantly, then suddenly, he drew back his hand and threw the fire into the opposite wall hard and fast. The fire splattered against the wall with a sickening thud and spread its tentacles even as it extinguished into oily blackness that started dripping down the walls.

Gandhari and the man stared at the wall, the dripping oil that spelled out a script on the wall that Gandhari had never seen before. The characters were runes, mesmerizing and bizarre in shape and image. Each rune was a stick figure bent in different ways, standing in different poses, carrying different items. For long minutes, the wild man read the wall intently, so close that his nose touched the soot and became blackened by it. Finally, when the oil was dried and indistinguishable from the rest of the wall, he returned to her.

'You will be the mother of one hundred sons. You will be powerful beyond measure. Even the *devas* will bow down to you. Your power will be enough to shake the world and rotate it off its axis.'

His voice was full of foreboding.

She raised an eyebrow. 'Well, isn't that a good thing for a princess?'

He spread his hands to indicate his disfigured body. He so cleverly disguised his deformities that she had not noticed them before. His left arm was shrunken and shrivelled; networks of fine white scars and angry red welts crisscrossed his torso. His teeth were black and shrunken, crooked and broken. He was unable to stand straight properly; his body swayed this way and that, lurching just to stand upright.

'Power always comes at a cost, princess.' He spewed the last word with venom.

'Power is the currency of royalty. It is only meet that I should accumulate as much power as I can. If I am that powerful, then it means I have done my job well.'

He turned away and returned to the fire. 'And how shall you spend that power, princess? How?'

As she walked back, his words echoed down that cold, long hallway, following her.

Gandhari walked back to her bedchamber. Ayla was packing her saris and other belongings into a trunk. Vials of scented oils, worn copies of maps and texts, heaps of jewellery, her strings of beads with which she prayed to the *devas* – all these were packed neatly into trunks. Ayla offered to leave and come back later so that Gandhari could rest. She did not mention Gandhari's absence in the middle of the night; Ayla was too accustomed to the eccentricities of the royal family. Gandhari waved at her to continue. She perched on the side of the bed covered by satiny fabrics of all hues and colours. She held them one by one, letting the sheer fabric run through her fingers. She loved colours and was a constant annoyance to her maids, who carefully picked out her outfits for her, because she would whimsically decide after her bath to wear another dress whose colour better suited her mood that day.

Gandhari spent hours watching as Ayla carefully packed away her life and belongings, until the bedchamber was stripped to just the bed. In the morning, even that would be dismantled and follow her to Hastinapur. Her parents did not want her to be in any way a burden to Hastinapur, even when it came to furniture.

'Ayla, will you come with me?' Gandhari asked softly.

'Yes, princess, the king has ordered it so.'

'Won't you miss it here? Your family is here: your parents, your brother.'

Ayla shook her head a little too quickly. Gandhari watched her closely, the downward twitch of her lips before she smoothed her expression. *This is what I will have to become, a woman of iron strength and fortitude*, Gandhari told herself as she unclenched a fistful of saris from her hand and let them fall to the bed.

Gandhari did not bother to move aside her clothes once Ayla closed the door behind her. She made a heaping pile of them, laying down upon them, burying her nose in them, smelling her mother as she always did in her saris – the mix of cloves and rose petals and sandalwood. Her mother often mixed scented oils and other fragrant powders to imbue a pleasant smell into their clothes and living spaces. Gandhari breathed deeply and tried to hold her breath, to keep in the fragrance.

She looked out the window, to the river in the distance, the stars in the furthest reaches of the sky. How would she survive in Hastinapur? How would she hold her own, as the wife of a blind prince, in a court full of strangers and foreigners? Was her fate to be nursemaid to the infirm prince who would not be king, to tend to him, to share in his inauspicious fate, relegated to the dustbin of the palace and history? *Dhritarashthra*. Even the sound of his name was sour.

Her sleep was disturbed with dreams of the wild man playing with hissing fire, morphing into the form of her future husband, a dark shadow that invaded her, pressed upon her, passed through her, violated her, until she became as dark and insubstantial as soot drifting through air.

The next morning, the palace was filled with people come to wish the princess farewell. Citizens from far and wide across the kingdom of Gandhara came to see off the beloved princess. She was known to them. She would ride for days at a time to the furthest reaches of the kingdom to see how the subjects fared, to meet with them and talk with them, to learn of their lives, their struggles, their priorities, and she would come back and report to Subala and the ministers so they could address the needs of the people. Subala bragged that she would have made a fine spy, better than those under his command who were already the best in all of Bharat.

All the furniture was cleared out of the main audience hall to make space for the crowds. There were still thousands of people more in the grounds, stretching all the way to the banks of the river, eager to throw sanctified raw rice and flowers dusted with vermilion at her as her caravan made its way out of Gandhara.

Gandhari was carefully dressed and decorated that morning. It took hours. Her mother bathed her with her own hands, fastened the jewellery tenderly around her neck, hands, fingers, forearms, upper arms, ankles and waist, combed the thick tresses of her hair slowly with an oil-rubbed comb. The sari she wore was a deep green colour, studded with diamonds and gold thread. It was so heavy that the part tucked in around her hips would surely have fallen out had there not been two maids behind her to gracefully help her carry it as she walked. *This is too much,* Gandhari protested to her mother. But her mother scoffed with a grin, excited to send off her only daughter in such style. The word 'gaudy' would never have occurred to her.

Gandhari was the last to appear in the audience-hall with her mother and Ayla in tow, slowly picking her way down the stairs to avoid tripping over the heavy folds of her sari. The crowd quieted to watch her. She knew she was a remarkable sight. She was not conventionally beautiful, but there was an austere strength to her face – unflinching eyes, lips that never quite smiled – a face that was *striking*, that left an impression,

and in the other sense of the word, too, striking a blow, always
on guard, always at the ready to attack. She could hold a room
without saying a word.

She made her procession in front of the ministers,
exchanging nods and receiving their blessings with downcast,
demure eyes. Their advice, too, would now be lost to her. She
would have to rely on the counsel of her husband's ministers.
She walked past her brothers lingeringly. Ordinarily unruly,
they were uncharacteristically solemn that day; a tribute to
their only sister. Finally, she met Bhishma and her father by the
altar, where she would make her last offerings before leaving
home.

This was the altar where offerings were made to the
ancestors, the rishis and the *devas*. Here she had offered marigold
blossoms that she had picked herself from the gardens. Here
she had placed in tiny bowls flavoured rice pudding and other
sweetmeats she had made herself for the immortals to eat. Here
she had prayed, every morning, after her bath, with hair still
wet, for herself, for her family, for the kingdom, before her
maids would drag her away to get suitably dressed.

She turned away from the others to face the altar, an empty
space into which was invoked the deities, the spirits of the
ancestors, the holy sages. It was a roughly hewn plank of wood,
undecorated, other than a small white chalk yantra drawn by
her mother's hand, the residue of cone incense stubs and oil
from the lamps marring the pale-wood varnish. The smells
lingered, of camphor and incense and ghee and the sugary
essence of the food offerings. This was the smell that gave her
succour and comfort, and she tried to breathe it in now.

She did not know when the idea came to her or when
she had decided for sure. Years later, even at the end of her
life in the forest – those few times she permitted herself to
think of it – she could not recall, she could not identify it with
precision. Was it as soon as her father had told her she was to

marry the blind prince? Or had she been driven by the fury of her brother, Shakuni? Was it that last night, when she had seen the wild man, when she had looked into the fire and that black spidery writing on the wall? Or an answer given by the *devas* as she slept on the pillow wet with her own tears? Was it just now, when she heard Bhishma sigh behind her, and she thought of that man, his vow? Was it her bitterness against him, or the one who stood silently by him, her father?

Or, was it something different, was it all those tales of sacrifice and great vows, the stories of her heroes, of the great ones, the immortals, this desire to be great in one way if she could not be great in another? Was it a yearning to be good, to prove herself good, to answer her father's troubled eyes from all those years ago, as he begged her to remember that the *devas* were her friends? How could she ever defy the *devas* she had worshipped so devotedly? Was this her way of proving it?

Was it an impulse or something she had really intended to do? Was it a mistake or a choice? She did not bother asking herself this, not until the very end of her life, when it was too late.

She did not know what it was that made her look at her wrist, to the hem of her upper cloth as it hung above her clenched fists. But she did. A dress as ornate as hers had to have a plain upper cloth for balance. That made it easier. She picked up the hem of her upper cloth and held it between the fingers of her left hand, bruising the delicate fabric with the sweat of her hand. She held the fabric with her right hand, pulling at it, testing the weight, the strength of the fabric. It was flimsy. She carefully tore it in a straight line, tearing off a plain green strip of the cloth.

In the quiet of the assembly at court, there were gasps and indignant whispers at what she was doing. Subala whispered loudly, *Madhu!* But none dared to disturb her. One's time at the altar was inviolable, sacrosanct.

Gandhari placed the strip of cloth on the altar and smoothed it into the wood with her fingers. This was to sanctify it, to make it auspicious and sacred. She whispered her prayers, invoking the *devas* one by one – Indra, Varuna, Mithra, Agni, Surya, Narayana, Rudra – asking them to bear witness to and bless her vrata, her sacrifice, her vow. She offered her obeisance to the forefathers, vowing to bring only honour and fame to their line and name. And then it was time.

She wanted to do it at the altar. This way she could face the *devas*. She wanted to face the divine ones, not the humans behind her. She wanted them to be the first to bear witness. Her hair was so elaborately coiffed and tied on top and at the back of her head that it was nearly impossible to tie the cloth in a way that would not cause her hair to become loose and in disarray. But she managed it and tied the cloth around her eyes.

She took her time about it, did not rush. None could stop her now. There was a queen called Kalavati once who had been singing a hymn to Vishnu when her palace started burning down. But she refused to leave her spot until the hymn had ended, and the servants and her family knew better than to drag her away. She walked away just as a flaming beam from the rafters fell down and would have killed her in the next moment.

When Gandhari turned around, she was blindfolded. Bhishma spluttered in rage, 'What is the meaning of this, young woman?'

'I will not see the world my husband cannot see. He will never be at a disadvantage to me. As his wife, I will be deprived of sight by the choice of my vow, as he has been deprived by the fate of his birth.'

Bhishma sighed but did not say anything further. Who was he to interfere with a vow?

She could hear choked sobs from her father next to him. Her mother was gushing at the sight of it, the quiet drama of devotion that would finally make Gandhara famous, give the kingdom its due. Gandhari would have to become a better listener now; there was no other way of understanding the tumult that was going on around her. Thus she began her lifelong practice of picking out the threads of sounds around her, attributing them to the people making them and interpreting their meaning, now that she could no longer see their faces, the language of their bodies.

Subala touched her with trembling hands. The only relief was that she did not have to see his face. 'Daughter, what have you done to yourself?' His voice cracked with anguish.

'I will be the most devoted of wives to Dhritarashthra. I will be the most virtuous and best of wives. I have done this as my first act of a good wife.' And it was true. From that moment, she never even thought or spoke of another man. Since the day she met her husband, she did not let any unspoken desire or need of his go unfulfilled. She would not eat until he had eaten, sleep until he had slept, argue or utter one disagreeable word to him. She became as quiet and loyal as a shadow.

That was the day Gandhari became famous. The news of this astonishing act of sacrifice, this woman of extreme piety and devotion, travelled far and wide. She received adulation even as she walked out of the palace; the ministers, the elderly, her brothers, falling at her feet to receive her blessings. She continued walking without pause.

But there were no conches that sounded, no rain of flower blossoms from the skies. It was deathly quiet in the heavens.

It was Bhishma who led her out of the palace. Bhishma who had once been Devavrata, before he had taken his vow. And then he had become known as Bhishma, the one who had uttered the terrible vow. The conches had sounded for him; flowers had fallen from the sky for him. His name had changed. He became someone else. But she was still Gandhari, the princess of Gandhara, before and after her vow, before and after her marriage.

Perhaps for a man to do something so extraordinary, he became different and transformed by it. For a woman, to do something extraordinary was just an attestation of the powers of womanhood, her inherent femininity. Extreme piety, purity and devotion were not extraordinary to women but inherent to them. Perhaps for women such acts were not transformations but rather affirmations of who they were.

Perhaps, thought Gandhari, that was why the *devas* did not garland her, why the flowers did not fall.

2

THE FOREST. NOW

Dusk was falling in the forest. The boys in the hermitage were preparing their evening food. Despite herself, sometimes the smell of food still gave Gandhari hunger pangs. Her body no longer craved food but sometimes her mind did, not for physical satisfaction but as a distraction, as a break from the routine drudgery of daily life, as a way of not remembering. It should not have mattered anymore, not in the *vanaprastha* phase of their lives, when they had renounced their worldly life and retired to the forest for quiet contemplation.

Perhaps she had not lived enough already, Gandhari acknowledged, and now, at the end of her life, this craving for life, this hunger she did not know how to quench, was rearing its head. Sometimes she dreamt of mangoes, of the spicy pickles her mother used to make, of meat and fish, of astringent mustard leaves fried crisp and bitter. When they had taken to eating roots and leaves, the vegetation on the floor of the forest, when they lived off that which they could forage and did not kill, the penance had been a relief to her. It felt cleansing. But now it was its own weight, its own burden. Now she felt like a ravenous woman.

She used her willpower to tamp down her appetite. The gods knew, she had reserves of willpower beyond mortal ken. She did not bother praying to the *devas*, the way Kunti and her husband did. She wanted neither their help nor their remembrance. It was easier for her to see her own death foreshadowed in the water of the river than to see the apparition of Shiva or the other *devas* come to accuse her, to remonstrate with her.

She sat at a distance from the ashram, away from the chanting of the evening prayers, the gentle laughter and chatter of the young boys. There had been a time when the chants of the names of the *devas* gave her pleasure, when she was drawn to them eagerly morning and night. But now the thought of the *devas* troubled her. She did not want to see their accusing eyes, to feel them weigh the merits and demerits of her life as they determined her fate in the afterlife. She wanted quiet.

Kunti approached and sat down next to her, on the thin mat Gandhari had spread under a large tree, without asking whether her company was welcome. Gandhari stifled a sigh. Could not she at least die in peace?

They did not speak of the harsh words exchanged in the morning. They never spoke of the past. How trivial it would be to dwell on these squabbles, on sharp words, when it was Kunti's sons who had killed Gandhari's sons, when it was Gandhari's sons who had killed Kunti's grandsons. And yet they bickered and poked at each other without ever letting it turn into an open confrontation. What could one do against the mother of her children's murderers?

Kunti was always matter-of-fact. 'Sister, we need to make arrangements if we are to die.'

Gandhari said nothing. Kunti was always so very practical.

Kunti continued, 'Sanjaya should be saved. He should live a long and fruitful life. He should be there to tell news of us to the others.'

Gandhari acquiesced with a nod. She should have thought of it herself. Sanjaya had been a good aide to Dhritarashthra and her. It bothered her that Kunti had thought of it first.

It made her feel one-upped. She became irritated at Kunti's sanctimony and her own callousness.

'Yes, your sons would want to know what happened to you,' Gandhari paused. 'There is no reason for you to stay with us anyway. Why don't you leave with Sanjaya? Death must be coming to claim my husband and me. You could return to Hastinapur.' Even as she uttered the words, she knew Kunti would not do it. Kunti had made her decision to follow Dhritarashthra and her into the forest and would never back down. It was like asking Gandhari to untie her blindfold. Gandhari had wondered what it was that drove Kunti to come with them to the forest in the first place. Perhaps there was something about that long terrible war, the loss of her firstborn son at the hands of her other sons, that made her feel more comfortable with the grieving parents of one hundred sons lost, than her own sons, the victors. Perhaps, she could no longer bear the presence of youth, to be in a palace whose halls would feel forever hollow, bereft of her grandsons, her husband, her firstborn who should have reigned over it.

Kunti continued: 'That was the other thing I want to discuss with you. I will not be deprived of death this time.'

Gandhari knew immediately what she meant. When Kunti's husband had died, Madri, her co-wife, had jumped into the funeral pyre, leaving Kunti behind to take care of Madri's two sons in addition to Kunti's own three sons with Pandu, their husband. Kunti had acquiesced and stayed back to care for all of them. She had never treated Madri's sons as any less than her own three. They were forever the five Pandavas, the five sons of Pandu.

Gandhari inclined her head, 'I understand.'

'Sister, do not let them stop me this time.'

Sister, so many choices about our lives were taken away from us. At least we will die on our own terms. That much they cannot take from us.

'I will not,' promised Gandhari. She meant it.

They sat together in silence. Crickets chirped, and the birds sang a mournful song as the sun set. Still Kunti remained. Gandhari wondered what more she wanted of her. Unable to bear the silence any longer, Gandhari pressed, 'Do you not want to at least send word to Hastinapur? Perhaps your eldest could come to at least perform the final rites.' She still could not bring herself to use Yudhishthira's name, the one who had become king instead of her own son.

Kunti said decisively, 'No. I walked away from Hastinapur. I have renounced my past. They are no longer my sons. I am no longer their mother. My work is done. Let my corpse decompose or be eaten by vultures or be burned by fire. It is of no matter to me.'

Gandhari turned away. How was it so easy for Kunti and Dhritarashthra to have severed all connections, to have cut asunder all bonds and attachments and memories? At least they still had people to be connected to, who cared what would became of them. Dhritarashthra still had his other brother, his nephews, his illegitimate son. Gandhari had no one, but she felt mired in the mountain of corpses of her sons and brothers, all those who had fought and died so her son could have been king. She had no one left to renounce but was unable to let go of the phantoms that haunted her still.

They sat together in uneasy silence.

Gandhari could feel the darkening of the day on the other side of the blindfold, the shadows crawling over the tall trees, slowly draping themselves over the forest. Even the chanting of the hermits could not ward them off. The night animals began stirring themselves for the hunts they would undertake that night. The birds flew away to the nests where they would sleep and wake again in the morning. The leaves rustled and whispered to each other, indifferent to the passage of time.

Gandhari felt the play of the dance of shadows across the blindfold. How they climbed up and stole across the forest, invading the daylight, snatching to themselves all that was in sight, silently and steadily devouring and growing into the blackness of night. When she closed her eyes, she could feel the corpses from the war claw their way out from smouldering funeral pyres, reaching for her with bony fingers, grasping at her feet, trying to pull her down. She drew her feet under her and scrunched herself into a ball, tight against the tree, not caring how undignified she looked. Tears leaked from underneath the blindfold, and she hoped it was dark enough for Kunti not to see. She felt the insects from the tree crawl down her back, slip in between her garments and her skin and start to bite at her, drink her blood, puncture her flesh. Better them than those ghosts, those corpses. She clasped her arms around her knees, trying to keep herself intact.

Gandhara, Then

Shakuni insisted on accompanying Gandhari to Hastinapur. He was paranoid that she would come to ill during the long journey, that Bhishma was not up to the task of protecting her. It was irrational and implausible, yet Subala was too aggrieved once Gandhari had blindfolded herself to disallow it. Gandhari did not share her brother's fears. She knew that she was useful so long as she could provide heirs.

In the beginning, Shakuni rode with her. It was stifling hot and stuffy in the chariot. The blindfold chafed at her skin and was itchy. Her eyelids sweated beneath the constricting fabric and sometimes she longed to tear it off, for coolness if nothing else. But she dared not remove it even when she slept.

Ayla had argued with her about that. Ayla worried about not letting the skin around her eyes breathe. She pointed out that in sleep her eyes would be closed anyway – what was the need for the blindfold then? But Gandhari worried that she may accidentally wake up in the middle of the night and inadvertently open her eyes. She was scrupulous about her *vrata*, her vow of austerity, that there not be a single break in it.

Bhishma said nothing as Shakuni, Ayla and she argued. How easy his vow was, Gandhari thought. It was easy to control not having sex. The logistics of blindfolding, of retaining the physical ability to see but not actually seeing, were much more complicated.

Shakuni's temper stayed at boiling pitch ever since Gandhari had blindfolded herself. He was barely civil with Bhishma and when he did speak with him, he spat out words incoherently. Gandhari kept him by her side to separate the two of them. Shakuni punished her for her sacrifice by remarking upon all of the beautiful scenery they passed. She could hear the roaring of the five rivers that they crossed, and he audibly gasped at their beauty, the drop of crystalline waters over round black boulders. He named all the birds and flowers they passed along the way, describing the different trees of the forests. It was sparsely populated terrain they travelled through, a remote wilderness Gandhari would dearly have loved to take in, to ramble through, to ride horseback on her favourite horse, Shalva.

Instead, she trained herself to hear things properly. She quickly learned to distinguish voices from each other, memorizing the cadence and inflection that identified the speaker, so she knew who was around in the general vicinity even if she could not decipher their words. She learned to tell the passage of time by differentiating the intensity of the sunlight falling upon her blindfold. She learned to eat by smell. She learned how to walk anew. She refused to take a stick, to look disabled. Instead, she learned how to balance, so when the ground beneath her feet gave way, when the ground was not level, when she tripped over a stone, she could immediately catch herself, like a cat who always fell upright. She learned to mask pain. Every time she bumped against an object, walked into something hard, she refused to wince or cry out. She simply remembered where it was and how to avoid it so that it did not happen again. She walked on as if nothing had been amiss.

She counted on Ayla to make her appearance decent. She learned to pray blind, to offer the *arghya*, the water offerings, gracefully, without seeing where the water fell, to memorize the texts she had once read. When there was no one else around, when she was certain no one would overhear, sometimes she would ask Ayla to read her stories, to allow herself that small entertainment since she had always been a voracious reader.

Shakuni kept taunting her again and again until, finally, Gandhari ordered him to keep quiet. He started sulking but did not say a word. Instead, he started playing dice, throwing them against the walls of the carriage, rolling them everywhere and all the time. Even as they slept on the hard ground near the campfire, he would throw them onto the dirty ground, read them, pick them up, and roll again. He was like a madman. But Gandhari did not dissuade him, so long as he kept quiet.

Now that Shakuni had been somewhat neutralized, Bhishma joined Gandhari in the carriage. After asking after her health, he offered, 'Now that you will be joining the Kuru clan, daughter, it is time you learn our history.'

'I already know much of it.' Try as she might, Gandhari could not keep the haughtiness out of her tone. She knew she should be demure to this stalwart who was, after all, in a sense, her father-in-law but she still smarted from being married off to the inferior brother and she wanted Bhishma to know she could have succeeded as queen.

She could imagine Bhishma raising his eyebrow. 'I am confident Subala has taught you well.'

'And our spies.'

'Hmm. Then, tell me, princess, what is it you know?'

She knew how the dynasty had started. She knew that the ancient king Kuru had come to a barren field in the dusty plains in the heart of Bharat. He had performed such intense austerities and sacrifices that the place itself had become sanctified and known as Kurukshetra. He founded the Kuru dynasty that had become the premier lineage in the land. But she did not start there. She started with Bhishma's grandfather, who once sat on the bank of a river, in quiet contemplation. A river goddess emerged from the waters, dressed in diaphanous white, sheer and flimsy, like a curtain of frothy bubbles. She was as effervescent as the waters from which she emerged, laughing and flirtatious, settling herself on the king's knee. She asked him to unite with her, to become her husband, but he demurred, intent on his life of renunciation. She was the great river goddess, Ganga. He said that she had sat on his right knee, which was the knee reserved for daughters and daughters-in-law, and it was only the left knee on which wives and lovers sat. Therefore, he said, she belonged to him as a daughter-in-law and was meant to marry his son.

She agreed and in time she met his son, Shantanu, who became Bhishma's father.

They were on a bumpy trail over rocks and mud now and Bhishma grunted, either at that or at Gandhari's words. Gandhari thought he would have preferred talking of the great battles they fought, the territories they had claimed, the kingdoms that had become their vassals. But this was the interesting stuff for her.

'When Ganga met your father, Shantanu, she made him promise that he would never question her, that she would always be free to do as she pleased, and if he ever challenged her, she would walk away forever, leaving him behind. He agreed. So it is said.'

Bhishma affirmed with a gruff grunt.

Gandhari paused. She was not cruel enough to talk about the next part, when Ganga gave birth to seven babies, and after each birth, she took the new-born baby to the river to drown each baby, again and again, until Bhishma was born. Shantanu was aghast but too besotted with her to protest. The citizens of the kingdom were horrified and started whispering against this otherworldly woman and the strange sorcery she must have woven over the kingdom and their beloved king. Finally, when Ganga gave birth to Bhishma, their eighth child, Shantanu protested and stopped her from killing him, calling her a mad evil woman.

Ganga had turned to him with a sad smile. She explained that these babies were the eight Vasu deities who had been cursed to be born on Earth. Before taking birth, they had asked Ganga to be born to her and for her to deliver them from earthly life as quickly as possible. That is why she had drowned them right after birth. Because Shantanu had tried to stop her, she left in his arms the eighth baby, Devavrata, and went on her way. 'He is meant for you, king. He is meant to stay with you and be your family even as I must leave you.'

Shantanu was heartbroken, but he had no choice but to let her go.

That is the hard price of breaking a vow. Sometimes you cannot understand what you have entered into, what you have cost yourself by a sacrifice, a vow. And if you break it, you cannot know how everything may be lost. Everything.

Yes, Shantanu had eventually remarried but he had never recovered from the loss of Ganga, that ephemeral, elusive river beauty whose grace and charms had won over his heart and that of the kingdom despite her eccentric behaviour.

Gandhari resolved to never falter from her vow. Never.

Desperate to change direction from these dark thoughts, Gandhari asked, 'Venerable one, they say that you learned from Brihaspati, the guru to the *devas*, himself. That you went to the heavens and learned from the *devas* how to wage war, how to rule, the codes of righteousness.'

'Yes, it is true.'

Gandhari said wonderingly, 'How lovely that must have been! To learn at the feet of the *devas*, to while away the years with them. Truly, you have been blessed.'

'Perhaps. Or perhaps I have been cursed, to have been sent back here.'

'It is a matter of perspective.'

'Yes, princess. What is a curse is often a blessing and what appears a blessing is often a curse.' He paused, 'I hope one day you will learn to look upon your marriage as the blessing that it is for you and for us.'

Shakuni's dice rattled against the carriage windows loudly, as if he was playing for their lives, to get them out of there. But they were almost at Hastinapur now. The air had changed. It had grown hotter, dustier, the sun scorching her wherever she sat, her legs sticky with sweat. Every few minutes, she shifted position, trying to shrink back away from the sun as much as possible.

Her father had taught her to look at situations in permutations, to examine the range of possible outcomes before making a decision. During those weeks traveling and camping along the way, there were many times she had fantasized about escaping or even being abandoned by Bhishma. If he found her unworthy, then perhaps she could go back. She could perhaps tear off her blindfold and run back home with her brother. She could gallop away on a horse; she could win herself a different fate.

But they were so far away from Gandhara now, in foreign lands, where the dialect was smoother, more urbane, unrecognizable to them, that even if they evaded Bhishma, they would be hard pressed to find their way home. And how could their parents accept them now, how could Gandhari make them lose face like that? This was how Gandhari convinced herself that the path to Hastinapur was the only road forward, the only option left to her.

But the truth was that even if the circumstances had allowed it, even if Bhishma forsook her, she would not have been able to go back. Her vow bound her now to Dhritarashthra and it was a bond that did not permit her escape. Even if she walked all the way back to Gandhara, the power of that vow would have drawn her all the way to Hastinapur again, to this stranger, to this man for whom she felt nothing. When she had blindfolded herself, she bound himself to a man in a way that was more deep and profound than the rite of marriage, than the power of seven circumambulations around the sacred fire. This was why Subala had cautioned her that day to be careful in choosing which vows to take. In those vows, one loses one's willpower, one's heart. Even if she was a world away, she would be drawn to Dhritarashthra again and again, like a calf who finds her mother even in the midst of a great herd unerringly. All paths led to Dhritarashthra now, and she had better accept it.

Navaratri: the nine-night festival in honour of Devi, had begun by the time they reached Hastinapur. Combined with welcoming Gandhari, the first bride of the Kuru princes, the city was at peak festivity. Ayla described to Gandhari how the wide avenues and brick walking paths were swept clean, doorways festooned with green mango leaves, bulls and cows garlanded with bright marigolds. The chariots of Bhishma's entourage slowed as they entered the city gates. Even Shakuni remarked in awe at the towering stone elephants that stood guard at the doorway to the city.

Bhishma was at the forefront of the procession and was forced to slow their progress as the citizens rushed out onto the roads to throw rice and brightly coloured flower petals at their beloved regent. He stood proud and graciously acknowledged their adulation with pronouncements of blessings, as stern and methodical as if he were reading aloud an ordinance. Despite his stiffness, it was clear the kingdom adored him and even Gandhari had to admire the standing he commanded among his people. *How happy they would have been*, she thought to herself, *if only he had become king.*

She could smell chickpea flour fritters frying in sesame oil, the scent of ghee lamps burning, the simmering rice puddings being cooked as offerings to Devi, the crush of flowers being torn into petals for worship during this holy period. It was hot here, hotter than she was used to, and she could feel the sweat pooling beneath her armpits, staining the red blouse of her outfit. She could feel her hair growing damp and untamed, the sheen of sweat that would make her face look oily and shiny. She was desperate to compose herself before meeting anyone else in the royal family, not trusting Ayla to do complete justice to her toilet in the chariot, but she didn't know whether Bhishma would extend this courtesy to her. She ran her hands up and down her arms and necks, checking her earrings and other jewellery to make sure Ayla had put the right ones on her for today – she wanted the flaming ruby set that sparkled and glowed even in the dimmest of lights. She had a feeling that Dhritarashthra's chambers would be dim indeed.

Finally, the chariot drew to a graceful halt. Ayla whispered, 'We are here,' and took her by the elbow. Gandhari descended from the chariot, heart pounding. She did not want to seem weak, so she did not dare ask Ayla how many people, if any, were standing there in front of the palace entrance, to have their first view of her. Was it just the servants, or had others come, too, citizens from the city, from far and wide? Her senses were not yet sharp enough to discern this on her own.

Best to act as if they were there in the thousands. She held her head up regally, picked up the edges of her sari delicately and moved forward in small, graceful steps. The driveway was pebbled, and it was difficult to keep her balance atop the hot, shifting gravel. But she managed. She shook off Ayla's hand, not wanting to appear incapacitated. The Kurus should not think they had gotten a burden with her as a bride. They should feel grateful and honoured.

Bhishma was greeted by an onslaught of ministers and commanders, pestering him with updates and questions, eager for his counsel and decisions after his time away. Bhishma walked away with them, barely paying Gandhari a second thought. Gandhari did not move or turn or in any way betray the slightest uncertainty or inquisitiveness. She would wait until someone came to fetch her.

In a few moments, Gandhari caught her smell. She smelled her before she heard the tread of her footsteps, before she saw her shadow fall across her line of vision through the blindfold. It was Satyavati, Gandhari realized, the Queen Regent of Hastinapur, whose grandsons were Pandu and Dhritarashthra. She was known as Yojanagandha, one whose fragrance spread for over a *yojana,* approximately twelve or fifteen kilometres in distance. Finally, Satyavati stood still before her, even her shadow imposing and haughty.

Gandhari bent down to prostrate in front of her, aiming to touch her feet but she missed by half a foot, touching the stones of the driveway instead. She reached forward again until her fingers felt the cool softness of her grandmother-in-law's feet. She touched her own forehead with that hand in respect and then rose, a sign of respect due to her elder.

Satyavati drew a finger lightly across Gandhari's blindfold: 'So. The reports of the blindfolded princess are true. Well, it sounds like something someone from Gandhara would do.'

Her voice was steely and rough, a contrast to the urbane refinement of her stepson Bhishma. Gandhari's heart pounded as she followed Satyavati into the palace. Of all the people she was to meet in Hastinapur, it was Satyavati who intimidated her the most. Nervous and on guard as she was, Gandhari was also careful to count the steps she took from the entrance, along the marbled floors of the palace to the chamber where Satyavati led her. She wanted to build a map in her head of the palace, of every wing, chamber and seating area, so that she would never be lost or dependent on others.

Satyavati instructed one of the maids to take Gandhari to a chamber where she could bathe and refresh herself. She told Gandhari to come to her personal audience chamber afterward, so they could converse privately. Gandhari quickly washed herself and straightened out her clothes. She did not want to keep the queen waiting. It was late afternoon when she arrived, the period during which most of the household was resting at the height of the heat and humidity of the day, and by the time she was ready to meet the queen, dusk was approaching. Gardenia-scented breezes wafted through the heavily curtained doors and windows. The marble floors had become cool to her feet's touch. She could hear the ringing of bells and drones of Vedic chants as the evening prayers commenced. There was a full retinue of priests here, performing all the rites to ensure the well-being of the kingdom and royal family. Her mother would have been envious.

The maid took her into Satyavati's audience chamber, seating her on a bench right next to Satyavati's cushioned chair, at a small but noticeable height above hers. The queen entered, sat on her chair and swung her legs up, reclining back on the cushions. Satyavati commanded the maid to offer Gandhari refreshments. A heavy silver tumbler of flavoured sweet hot milk was placed in Gandhari's hands. She sipped at it politely, the milk scalding her tongue and coating her throat chalkily.

She did not care for heavy dairy but didn't dare offend the queen. When the maid placed a plate of foods in her hands, Gandhari, however, demurred.

She explained to the queen, 'I fast during Navaratri. I will only take milk and fruits.'

Satyavati sighed: 'Girl, you've been on the road for weeks. As it is, you've already blinded yourself. No need to starve yourself, too. We cannot have any more weakness and infirmity in this family than we already do.'

'I assure you, revered mother, I will not be in any way weak or frail. My body is used to fasting.'

'Have it your way then.'

Satyavati waited until Gandhari had swallowed some more of the milk. 'Now, tell me what is this *nautanki,* this melodrama, with the blindfold. I had not expected such histrionics and melodrama from Subala's daughter of all people.'

Gandhari kept her voice even. 'It is not melodrama. It is part of my pativrata, my vow of marriage and devotion to my husband, to sacrifice my eyesight in honour of he who has been blind since birth. I am sure this sacrifice of mine will bring blessings for him and the entire family.'

Satyavati popped some nuts into her mouth, munching them loudly. Gandhari was taken aback at her brazen manner, until she reminded herself that Satyavati was a woman of low social standing originally. She was the adopted daughter of a fisherman, after all. In her youth, she had helped her father ferry passengers back and forth across the river in his boat.

'You know what a disaster my daughters-in-law were, I presume.'

'I'd always heard how virtuous they are, queen mother.'

Satyavati snorted. 'One grandson ended up blind because one daughter-in-law couldn't bear the sight of my son; the other ended up a pale weakling because my other daughter-in-law shuddered in fright at my son's countenance.'

Gandhari said nothing. To disagree would be an affront to Satyavati. To agree would be an insult to her mother-in-law.

Satyavati leapt up and began pacing the floor of the small chamber furiously. 'Fools! Their inability to deal with reality ruined our lineage. I did not want the next bride for this family to be another such simpering miss. That's why I told Bhishma to go to Gandhara. I had thought you would be bred of sterner stuff.'

'Is that why? I thought it was because of the boon that I would bear one hundred sons.'

Satyavati chuckled and resumed her seat. 'Well, that helps, I confess. You must realize how precious the guarantee of sons and a continuing lineage is for us, especially in our circumstances.'

Gandhari simply nodded.

Satyavati appeared to be studying her for some moments. When she spoke next, her voice was quieter, more thoughtful. 'I know what they say about me. How I schemed and tricked my way onto the throne and my sons into the succession. The tricks I used to keep the dynasty and my bloodline going after my sons died. But the thing is, daughter, while Bhishma and the others are out winning wars and conquering kingdoms, and winning fame and glory for our name, it's we women who keep the kingdom intact.'

Her voice hardened: 'So, girl, what is it you've heard about me and our family? I know of Subala's spies and I know of the gossip that has travelled the furthest reaches of Bharat.'

Gandhari smoothed the sari over her lap. When Bhishma had tested her, it had been cerebral. This was different and far more nerve-wracking. She replied diplomatically, 'Many things are said, queen mother. It is difficult to separate fact from fiction.'

She laughed. 'Probably the truth is even more bizarre than what you've heard. Don't worry, girl, I won't quiz you. I believe if you're going to be part of the family, you should be privy to its history and secrets and all the skeletons in the closet, including mine. How else can you do your duty to the Kuru clan? But are you really one of us now?'

Gandhari carefully got off the bench and knelt at Satyavati's feet. She placed her hands in the queen mother's elegantly shaped, soft as satin, be-ringed hands. Satyavati's hands stayed as they were and made no move to curl around hers. Gandhari said slowly and steadily, 'This blindfolding was not an act of pique. I am a girl of devotion and penance. If not, I would never have won the boon from Shiva for one hundred sons. Yes, it was a shock to me when Bhishma asked for my hand for Dhritarashthra, but when I stood in front of the altar on the morning before coming here, I knew this was my destiny. During the journey here, I felt myself more and more bound to him. He is my life, my family, my husband, my fate. I will never utter the name of a man who is not my husband or entertain the thought of any man in my mind. You will never find a more devout or chaste bride than me. In the name of all the thirty-three million *devas*, revered grandmother, I promise you this.'

Satyavati murmured in satisfaction and pressed her hands gently, placing her right hand on the top of Gandhari's head for a few moments in blessing. She herself led Gandhari back to her seat on the bench and then resumed her seat. 'My daughter, now I shall tell you my story and the story of this family since I married into them.'

Satyavati murmured for the maid to bring sliced mango for Gandhari to eat. Then she began in a confiding tone, as if she were narrating a tale from long ago and not her own life story: 'It is true that I was raised by a fisherman, but it is said that I was the daughter of a *Chedi* king. Once, the king had travelled deep into the forest for a hunting trip. He had been away from his wife, the queen, for days, perhaps weeks, and one night in the forest, he — hmm, how shall I put it— released a nocturnal emission, and did not want it to go to waste.'

Gandhari did not blush at the queen's frank language. It was true that a man's *virya* held his life force and was not to be wasted; his semen was to be carefully preserved and used to further the family and lineage, to produce the progeny who would ensure his and his family's immortality, to please the ancestors and the *devas*.

Gandhari could feel the queen shrug, felt her strong perfume disperse afresh through the cool air surrounding them in the small chamber. 'Well, who knows the truth of the matter, but it is said that he placed it in a leaf to be carried back by an eagle to the queen for insemination. The leaf – err – dropped when the eagle started fighting with another eagle mid-air and was eventually consumed by a fish and then the fish became pregnant. Then the fish was caught by the head fisherman, my adoptive father. When he sliced open the belly of the fish, he found me there and I became his daughter.'

Satyavati did not say so but Gandhari knew that Satyavati also bore the smell of fish since the day she was born. The acrid, gagging smell of cold raw fish clung to her like scales. Satyavati laughed: 'What a beginning I've had, and now look where I've ended up! A widowed queen who has outlived both her sons – is there a more inauspicious fate? And yet, by tooth and nail, I've kept Hastinapur intact! I've held onto this throne for my grandsons and no one knows how many prying hands I've had to fight off, desperate hands who have longed to hold my body as much as they longed for the throne of the Kuru kingdom, men who wanted to make me their wife and become king of this throne that has for so long been empty of a proper king.' She swallowed hard. 'I may not be conventional; I may be an outsider forever and always to this court. But, princess, I have done whatever has been needed to keep our lineage going. Mind that, Gandhari.'

Your lineage, perhaps. But you also saw fit to end the lineage that would otherwise have continued with Bhishma.

There was a long silence as crickets chirruped and in a chamber some distance away, far removed from the women's chambers, voices were droning in debate, a council of ministers perhaps plotting a war strategy or debating a tax policy.

Satyavati waved her hands. 'I've been rambling, and the night is fast approaching. You have to still meet the others. Well, let me make it quick. I know you have heard about my sons, Chitrangada and Vichitravirya, the heirs to the throne, each of whom was crowned king albeit for too short a time. But probably you have not heard of my first-born.' Satyavati's voice softened with affection. It was the first time that Gandhari sensed the mother in her. 'Dvaipayana, the island-born one.'

'No, queen,' Gandhari said softly. 'I have not.'

Satyavati's voice took on the fond tone of an old woman given to reminiscing; the queen giving way to the inner woman. 'As a girl, I helped my father, whose job it was to ferry passengers from one bank of the river to another. Sometimes I would ferry customers on his behalf. One day, oh, I shall never forget this day, this giant of a man came on my boat. He was toweringly tall, his face sunburned and fierce, covered with a beard. He was a rishi, there was no doubt. The fires of his penance emanated from his body. He was so fierce in form that all the other customers were scared and ran off as soon as he appeared. He was the most fascinating man I'd seen in my life.

'He did not say a word, merely grunted at me, and got in the boat. He stared at me so intently, unblinking, that I almost lost my grip on the oars. Suddenly – we had hardly left the shore – he grabbed my right hand.'

Gandhari lifted a brow. To hold a woman's right hand meant one wanted her sexually.

'I tried to snatch my hand back. I told him a brahmana of his stature should not desire a lowly woman like me, especially a woman who stinks of fish. But he would not listen. He moved towards me again and again, so forcefully, I thought the boat might tip over. I was so out of my element; no one else had ever desired this fishy girl and I didn't know how to handle him. But I've always kept my wits about me, girl; there's no other way of surviving in this world. So, I told him to keep a hold on himself and wait until we reached the bank on the other side of the river.

'He obeyed and then reached for me as soon as we stepped on dry land.' Satyavati laughed heartily. 'Isn't that always the way of these ascetics? They spend years and years denying themselves food, warmth, women, civilization, and then desire comes on them like a storm and they cannot stop themselves.

'Anyway, I told him that my body stank and our time together should be enjoyable to both of us. That powerful rishi, Parashara – he finally deigned to tell me his name – wove a spell removing my bodily odour and replacing it with a beautiful fragrance of musk. That fragrance has stayed with me ever since, enchanting men even now. He approached me again, and I insisted that he wait until night. How could my reputation survive if my father and others saw me? He was too impatient even for that. Out of his powers, he created a dense fog that shrouded the land. He touched me again, but again I dissuaded him until I got from him the following promises: that our liaison would remain a secret and that my virginity would be left intact; that the child of our union would win fame and glory; and that the fragrance he bestowed on me would stay with me forever.

'He agreed eagerly and… afterwards… he bathed in the river and left. The same day, I gave birth to the dark-hued Dvaipayana. He was born practically an adult and left for the forest to do penance shortly after. Too much like his father, I suppose. But he agreed to come to my aid whenever I needed him. Imagine that! He only ever saw me on the day he was born, and yet, every time I need him, he appears. In some ways, he has been dearer to me than the sons I raised with my own two hands.'

Her voice softened to a whispered longing for this strange child of hers who by now must have been a man verging on old age himself. 'I think, one day you shall meet him, too, Gandhari. Oh! I wish you could see his face. I do not think you would be repulsed as my weak-kneed daughters-in-law were. He looks like a wild man, barbaric, orange tangled hair and dark, swarthy face and features. But I think you would not be scared of him.'

Later, much later, Gandhari would remember these words, when Kunti shared her anguish over the son she had abandoned, and she would wonder at the intensity of love that ripens in absence, the brew of guilt, regret and longing that went into these women whose first-borns were taken away from them because of their impossible situations, both of whom were the hardest, toughest women Gandhari knew. Maybe it was something about that kind of love, that kind of longing, that kind of loss, that hardened a person, made her impervious to all things, made her ruthless and reckless, a dire sense that after giving up one's own blood and flesh, there was nothing left to lose.

'That was it. The rishi saw to it that no one ever came to know of the indiscretion. He went on his way and I on mine. Only Bhishma and now you know of this. Now tell me what do you think of it?'

Another woman may have commented on how blessed Satyavati was for having attracted the attention of such an eminent sage, or sympathized with her plight at having to deal with such a difficult personality. But Gandhari was different. She said thoughtfully, 'I'm glad to be married into this family under your wise stewardship, queen mother. In that difficult situation, you kept your wits and you protected your interests time and time again, to ensure he did not take advantage of you. Another in your place may have ruined her life unwittingly by not taking the precautions you did. You protected yourself and your family.'

Gandhari could feel Satyavati nod vigorously, through the gentle chime of her bobbing earrings and the fresh waves of fragrance bombarding Gandhari's nostrils. Gandhari admired the power of Parashara's spell that had devised this fragrance that was ever charming, never cloying.

Satyavati continued, 'It is always different with rishis, you know. They take care that no harm is done to the woman or others involved. He left me with the most wondrous son I could have dreamt of. But one has to take care of oneself these days with other men, human men. It was different before. Before, women could go freely where and with whom they wished. Since then, since the time of Shvetaketu, it has all changed. Now one has to be careful.'

Gandhari nodded soberly. Chastity was now a woman's greatest strength. Chastity was now something different than what it once was.

Satyavati sighed airily. 'You know about my wedding to the king, of course, and Bhishma's vow?'

'Yes, queen mother.'

'Well, Shantanu and I had two sons. The first died in a stupid battle he picked against the king of the Gandharvas. The second, Vichitravirya, died heirless. Bhishma got him three brides – the sister princesses from Kashi: Amba, Ambika, and Ambalika. So like a man, Bhishma thought he could get three brides in one go. Always so efficient. He brought home all three sisters, or tried to.'

'What happened?'

'The eldest, Amba.' Satyavati's voice soured. 'She did not like that Bhishma had won her hand in the *swayamvara* through defeating the other suitors. She was in love with another man who she had thought would win her hand at the *swayamvara*. But he, like the others, was defeated by my stepson. Bhishma returned her to her home when he realized her heart was set on another man, but that man would not have her. Nor would Vichitravirya, once he learned of her attachment. Then, she asked Bhishma to marry her as a last resort. But, of course, he refused. She went away to the forest then, for penance. I would say, for revenge. We will yet sow the karma for that, I am sure.'

Gandhari shivered with sudden foreboding.

'Vichitravirya died heirless – so besotted with his wives, yet unable to produce a child. It seemed then that our dynasty had come to an end. Oh! The proposals I got. You can well imagine, how hungrily others eyed the kingdom and me. But I would not give up so easily. Shantanu would not see his line come to an end like that; not when he had entrusted the future of this family to me. He would not regret from *Swarga*, the heavens, that he had married me. Never!' Satyavati gritted her teeth. 'There was still the path of *niyoga*.'

Gandhari knew immediately what she meant. Niyoga was the practice of requesting and appointing a man to sire a child with a woman whose husband was either incapable of fatherhood or had died childless. The man was often the husband's brother or else a revered person of elevated spiritual stature. In niyoga, the child would be considered the child of the husband and not the biological father. The biological father would never seek any paternal or other relationship with the child. The man was permitted to perform niyoga only a maximum of three times in his lifetime. It was considered a sacred act of Dharma and not one of passion or lust.

'First, I asked Bhishma.'

Gandhari gasped. She could not help it. She had not guessed that even this daring queen would have had such temerity. Satyavati acknowledged stiffly, 'Yes, well, he did not take kindly to that suggestion either. He was not ready to sacrifice his vow of celibacy.'

'How could you think he would? Especially when he had taken that vow at your father's behest!'

'Well, you tell me! What choice did I have?' Satyavati rose and paced. 'The lineage would have died without his intervention. He put his vow above his duty to continue the lineage and safeguard the kingdom.'

'The vow he took for your sake,' Gandhari could not help snidely pointing out.

Satyavati paused. 'He did not have to take the vow, you know. His father had agreed to not pursue me if it meant Bhishma losing his right to the throne. No one forced Bhishma into that vow. He should have thought about it more carefully in that case. And what was I to do? Or my father? Did we not have to look after ourselves? How was I to compete with the ghost of Ganga, the goddess? Or my son with Bhishma? Our position would have been precarious at best, once Shantanu had had his way with me, once we were married and he had passed. Who would take care of me then? My father and I also needed to secure our own future.'

Gandhari murmured, preferring to stay non-committal. Bhishma would never have abandoned her. There was security, and then there was naked ambition. She would have liked Satyavati all the more had she admitted it openly.

'In any event, Bhishma refused; but then I called upon my other son, Dvaipayana. He came instantly. He took after his father, that ferocious rishi, in his fearsome, dark appearance. His radiance was even more bewildering than his father's. To city folk it was intimidating, perhaps. At least it was to my daughters-in-law. They reluctantly agreed to the *niyoga* with him. But one was so terrified, she closed her eyes at the mere sight of him. The other shrank bank from him. Thus, one grandson was born blind – your fiancée – and the other a pale, nervous thing, Pandu. *Hmmph!* Pampered princesses! Milk instead of blood coursing through their veins.

'Then there was the maid who happily took to my son. She gave birth to the wisest of my three grandsons: Vidura. He, born of a maid, shall never inherit. But, mind you, girl, he will be the best counsel you can ask for, the best advisor.'

Gandhari stored that information carefully.

'And now there is you.'

'Yes,' repeated Gandhari sardonically. 'Now there is me.'

Satyavati slid closer to her and leaned forward to lift up Gandhari's chin. Even blindfolded, Gandhari could feel the intensity of the queen's eyes boring into her. She steadied herself resolutely.

Satyavati said slowly, 'I think, princess, you are like me. We know how to survive, how to be tough, how to be ruthless in this world when we need to be. We are strong.'

'That's a good thing, isn't it?' Gandhari could not quite keep the tremor out of her voice.

'I thought so. I thought so, daughter. I prided myself on it, all these years. I endured and prevailed where others would have been smothered into the dust. But, sometimes I think – Satyavati was lost for some moments, struggling in thought, and Gandhari could feel the weight of her memories pressing down upon her, the desire of two powerful men who wove her into their destinies and how she wove them into hers, the sons who disappointed her, the one who surprised her and came to her in her hour of need, the strange relationship with her stepson who outlived her own blood, the gossip ever-swirling about her, the ghost of her husband's first love who lingered in the hallways of the palace long after the river goddess had disappeared.

'–Sometimes, I think, did I do it the right way? Or was there a better way? My son,' her voice filled with tears as she remembered him, 'My son, Dvaipayana, when he had come to perform the *niyoga*, he looked at my face, and said: "Mother, there is strength, there is sharpness of intellect in you and that has always served you well. But there is something even more important, more elusive, something you have lost. Subtlety of wisdom, the soft fluidity of water that goes where rock cannot enter." That softness was gone in me long ago. And my hardness has become something brittle, frail.'

Gandhari shivered. It was a warning that perhaps she should have heeded.

Then Satyavati rose abruptly. 'Come, the others are waiting. It is time to meet the rest of the family.'

Satyavati led her to a formal audience chamber. She was suddenly pressed on all sides by the Kurus and their ministers, plying her with prying questions and morbid curiosity about her blindfold. None dared to touch her or it as Satyavati had, but she felt naked and vulnerable in front of them, all the same. Despite her best efforts, Gandhari could not remember the names and titles of all who surrounded her in the small audience chamber, which felt claustrophobic with its stifling heat and thick stone walls. The only voice she could distinguish was the kind, gentle, wise tone of Vidura; aloof from the others, removed, yet who reacted with sharp alacrity to the words of others. Gandhari privately agreed with the queen grandmother that he was one whose counsel should be heeded.

It was Pandu who rescued her from the crowd. Nearly an hour after Satyavati had relinquished her to their custody, a laughing Pandu entered the chamber and told the others to back off. He shooed them away so he could escort her to finally meet her betrothed. Dhritarashthra was not present with the others. He was resting, she was told.

Pandu had brought along a chambermaid to hold her hand and guide her along the hallways. Gandhari hesitated, torn between wanting to appear self-sufficient and not wanting to embarrass herself by falling or stumbling. She reluctantly took the maid's hand. Pandu slowed down his pace to keep up with them.

He asked after her health and the wellbeing of her family and the kingdom she left behind. Then he said affably, 'I cannot tell you how excited my brother is to meet you.'

Gandhari blushed. 'Is that so?'

'Oh, yes! For weeks, he has been asking me about you, to describe the portraits we received of you. Word has spread of your charms and he was eager to know what I've heard. I have never seen a man more excited about the prospect of matrimony. He is thoroughly besotted just with the thought of you.'

'I see.' Gandhari's heart thudded in her chest. She supposed she should have been flattered, but there was something unsavoury and sinister in what Pandu was describing. She shook her head slightly to dispel the niggling doubts about this man she was going to marry.

'Not much further now. This palace is a maze of hallways, chambers and secret chambers. I still find myself getting lost.'

'Never mind, prince. I shall learn my way around in no time at all. Even the secret chambers.'

Pandu laughed. 'I do not doubt it.'

They stopped in front of a chamber with a locked door. It was cooler here, the torches dimmed to keep it darker than the rest of the palace. Here no other sounds of the palace were decipherable. It was as reclusive as could be. Pandu rapped on the door lightly.

In a few minutes, a squeaky voice asked, 'Who is it?'

Pandu grunted. 'It's me. Open the door now. I've come with the princess of Gandhara. Make sure your master is in a decent state, and open the door. Do not leave the princess waiting.' By Pandu's tone, it seemed that he had been kept waiting by this person at this door more often than not.

There was a rapid shuffling of feet, and then the door opened. Chapped, rough, sand-dry hands reached out to grab

Gandhari's arms, holding her painfully tight, and then dragged her into the oppressively dark and hot chamber. She squeaked again, 'Ah! So, the princess has come.' The speaker seemed to be a short elderly woman, judging by the sound of her voice that emerged somewhere at Gandhari's chest level and the gnarled fingers wrapped around her arms.

It felt like the chamber of an invalid, as if her husband were a dying man.

Pandu exclaimed, 'Kutili! Unhand her at once. Show some manners for once, woman. Give some respect.'

Kutili quieted down and politely but firmly pushed Gandhari down into a cushioned bench.

From a distance, a feeble male voice called out, 'Pandu? Is it you? Have you brought my bride?'

Pandu sighed. 'Come, brother, you are not deaf or lame. Come forward to meet the princess of Gandhara.'

Gandhari heard him get up out of bed – *how could he be sleeping at such an hour?* – and shuffle with the help of Kutili towards her. Gandhari bowed her head deeply at his approach, although she knew he could not see the gesture.

'Pandu,' he called out weakly, 'I cannot see her. Describe her to me. Is she beautiful?'

Gandhari gritted her teeth. She despised weakness in any form and though she understood his physical disability, she found it hard to respect someone who relied on his brother for courtship. It disgusted her – a man who had to depend on his brother for romance, who was content with second-hand accounts to form his opinion of her, who was not man enough to fall in love with her on his own.

Pandu was a little short with him: 'Brother! Get hold of yourself. You shall get to know her for yourself and discover how blessed you are by this union. Her beauty is matched only by her intelligence and grace. She has blindfolded herself in honour of you, as a token of her regard for you.

You should be grateful to have won the hand of such a noble woman.'

'I am, Pandu, I am.' His voice was tremulous.

Pandu headed towards the door. 'I will let you get to know each other on your own. Honoured to have met you, princess.'

Pandu left, and Gandhari found herself wishing he would have remained. He was so friendly and gregarious that he could make up for the silence and passivity of his brother. An awkward silence ensued. Gandhari wondered what Dhritarashthra looked like. How odd that she would never see the face of her husband. Perhaps she should ask Kutili to describe him to her, Gandhari thought to herself bitterly, and ask whether he was handsome.

Kutili spoke again in a wheezing voice. 'My master is of very delicate health. I do not know how you will ever manage to do for him what I do, but I suppose you must learn. Well, I will teach you, there's nothing else for it. No one else in this household knows how to keep him happy but me. Now it is up to you.'

'It is true,' Dhritarashthra said. 'She is the only one who has ever bothered to take care of me.'

So, this is how it is, Gandhari thought to herself. Distaste shivered down her spine. Perhaps she was being overly fanciful and letting her imagination run riot, but she kept envisioning Dhritarashthra in the care and at the whim of Kutili, ensconced in darkness in the furthest reaches of the palace where none dared to trespass. She wondered what kind of poisonous words Kutili may have been pouring into the ears of Dhritarashthra, perhaps even about Gandhari.

Gandhari bit her tongue. She slowed down her breathing and silenced herself as she began listening and taking mental notes from his servant on how to care for him as his wife.

Now was not the time to say anything.

♋

The wedding was a blur to Gandhari. She felt the heat of the fire, she felt her hand being pressed by her brother Shakuni into her new husband's; she felt the heaviness of her sari and jewellery; heard the droning of the priests; smelled the burnt coconut and herbs offered into the sacred fire to bless their union. She remembered the richness of the food – the plates heaped with cuts of fish and meats, vegetables simmering and sizzling in succulent gravies, flatbreads of barley and millet. It was so rich that it turned her stomach inside out. But she had to eat. She did not want to be fed by her maids, to appear weak and dependent, so she had Ayla whisper into her ear what had been placed on her plate and where on her plate and fed herself by hand.

Then it was night. Her wedding night. Her mother had not prepared her, but she knew what was to come. She was not dumb. But how to go about it blindfolded? With a blind man? Gandhari's throat turned dry. She had not considered this logistics.

It was a peculiar night. For a long time, for almost an hour, Dhritarashthra reverentially touched her face. His fingers were tentative, groping, yet eager. He traced her eyebrows, the curve of her hairline, her cheekbones, the lines of the bandage newly wound around her head, the shells of her ears, the contours of her lips. He stroked her chin as gently as if she were a child, chucking it like her father once had. It had made her almost cry.

He had marvelled at her hair, weighing it in his hands, sifting it like sand through his trembling fingers, crying out with pleasure at the feel of it. He had leaned into her neck and inhaled deeply for several breaths, before sighing in contentment.

For months, he did not even want sex. She was impatient for it, not out of desire for him, but out of desire for children who would be their heirs. But he did not even want to talk of such things. He became a child around her, a petulant child, tugging at her as if she were his mother rather than his wife.

Dhritarashthra kept Kutili around, and it was often just the three of them in the dark chamber. He would ramble and ruminate about whether someone was trying to poison him; whether a light cough he had developed was a sign of a terminal illness that would soon kill him; whether Pandu was hiding treasure and information from him, not that he ever showed curiosity about the goings on of the kingdom. Kutili delighted in indulging his paranoia and Gandhari was constrained in how dismissive she could be of his paranoia without seeming a disrespectful wife. She did not even have the power to dismiss Kutili. She still had to earn the trust of her husband; of all the Kurus.

Gandhari longed to be out in the audience chambers of the palace, in the side chambers where the ministers deliberated, debated and decided, in conversation with Bhishma and Satyavati, as they governed over the kingdom. But Dhritarashthra would not let her go. He was too enraptured by the idea of her as his wife, a coveted plaything he dare not let anyone see. It was a miracle to him simply to have someone in his bed, someone who bore his touch, someone who did not push him away, someone who had blinded herself for his sake, someone who belonged to him alone. It made him greedy for her; it made him hoard her.

For weeks, they barely emerged from their chambers. Finally, Gandhari convinced him that for their own survival they needed to be visible to the court, the royal family, the citizenry. He was petulant at first, but she persisted. She told him that he, too, was prince, that he had his duties towards the kingdom, that he had to be ready to serve were Pandu incapacitated.

That piqued his interest. 'Well, Gandhari, you know, he has always been a weak sort, my brother. You are quite right, my wife. One must always be prepared.'

From then on, he started seeing in his dreams the throne of Hastinapur and himself atop it. He confided these dreams excitedly to Gandhari, rousing her in the middle of the night, tugging her hair, to share his increasingly wild visions. Gandhari had originally meant simply to prod him out of inertia, to motivate him to take seriously his responsibilities and get him out of the darkness of his own chambers. But she wondered if she had pushed too far, if he was harbouring dreams that would never come true, whether she had catalysed in him the flowering of a dark, sinister plan that had been festering in his mind for long.

She did not back down or retreat, however. The truth was she was so desperate to get out of the recesses of the palace, crazed with boredom and restlessness, that she would have said anything to get out. So, one day, Dhritarashthra and Gandhari finally emerged into the main courtyard. She had chosen the day of the week when the palace was open to all the citizens. Anyone with a grievance could appear and have audience before the king, currently Bhishma, who presided as regent over the court. It was a solemn obligation of the court to address the grievances of all citizens. The reign of Sri Rama, the ideal king, had long passed but it was still the duty of kings to emulate his reign, during which even a dog had won the audience of a king. This was the duty owed to all the living subjects of the kingdom.

Gandhari had carefully dressed herself in a bright orange sari, inlaid with fine gold embroidery. It shone as bright and fervent as the sun, and that is how she wanted to appear to her new people. She described it to Ayla in detail so that she would pick the sari that Gandhari had in mind. When she brought it to her, Gandhari carefully touched the fabric, running it through her fingers, yard by yard, before she was convinced that it was indeed the correct one. She patiently waited while the maids took hours to oil, wash, comb and dress her hair.

She prepared speeches in her mind of what she would say to win the hearts of the citizens and the royal family. She instructed Dhritarashthra gently, so skilfully and diplomatically, that he did not know he was being commanded.

It was a sunny winter morning when they came out to the courtyard. Gandhari could feel the sun-warmed slate stone beneath her feet, the rays filtering in through the gauze bandage. It was crowded to the hilt – lusty cheers and cries of joy and welcome filled the courtyard. Throngs of people pressed upon them in waves and waves. Gandhari was delighted. Perhaps this would work out, after all. Perhaps they could be the royal couple they were meant to be. She beamed and let a rare smile slip out onto her face.

Making her way to the centre of the courtyard, dragging her husband with her, Gandhari opened her mouth to begin her prepared remarks. Suddenly, Satyavati swooped down on her, grabbing her by the arm and interrupting her: 'What are you doing, daughter?'

Gandhari was flustered and stammered, 'I – I was just going to address the people.'

'Address the people? What is there to address? Come with me. You must take your place next to me. She is almost here!'

Gandhari stumbled as she tried to keep pace with Satyavati. 'Who is almost here?'

Satyavati grunted. 'Girl, you better learn to keep up. I thought you had more wits than this. Have you been so oblivious to what has been happening? Has Dhritarashthra not told you?'

Gandhari cursed herself for having allowed to herself to be secluded away with Dhritarashthra for so long. They had not heard of any important news, or if Dhritarashthra had, he had kept it from her. 'Forgive me, queen mother. I was not aware.'

Satyavati snorted. 'In a honeymoon mood, are you?'

Gandhari blushed furiously.

'Stand here now. Stand straight. Was it necessary for you to dress so flamboyantly today?'

'Flamboyantly? I'm hardly a widow!'

'No, but you don't want to overshadow the new bride.'

'I thought *I* was the new bride?' Gandhari worked to keep her voice diffident.

Satyavati laughed. 'You were, but now Bhishma has fetched a bride for Pandu. Kunti. She will be here any moment and you will bless her as your new younger sister.'

Kunti.

The word sliced through her like a dagger. From that very moment, from before she had heard her voice, felt her touch, knew anything at all about her, Gandhari hated her. For stealing her moment, her limelight, her position in the family and at the court in Hastinapur. Gandhari may have been the senior princess, but Kunti was wed to the prince who would be king. Kunti would be queen. Kunti had been deemed worthy of Pandu, where Gandhari had failed.

The bitterness rose like bile in her throat even as Kunti arrived and prostrated at her feet. Gandhari went through the motions of blessing her with a long life, with a hundred sons, even as she inwardly fumed at this unwelcome stranger – her sister-in-law, her companion, her greatest rival, with whom she would rewrite the pages of history.

3

IN THE FOREST, NOW

It was night. Gandhari lay on a bed of straw and leaves under the same tree she had lain under for years now in this forest hermitage. Kunti's words, her voice, her sanctimony, rattled around in Gandhari's skull, rankling her. She had never seen Kunti's face, of course, but she imagined it as a squeezed lemon, perpetually sour and dour, always self-righteous and judgmental.

I will not go to sleep on my last night on earth thinking of that bloody woman.

Gandhari tossed and turned. The others were still awake; talking amongst themselves, but Gandhari had wanted to escape. She had wanted solitude. But now that she was alone she felt troubled and restless.

So what if I am going to die? I am an old woman. This is precisely what I have retired to the forest for, in order to die. What is surprising about it? Why does it affect me so? Why am I weak now after having been strong for so long?

She cried out for Ayla before realizing that Ayla was no longer there, had been gone for years, decades in fact. *Feebleness of mind! The one thing I cannot countenance and now it plagues me.*

Despite herself, tears trailed down her cheeks. *This is for drinking the water in the morning. Had you not indulged yourself, your body would not have had the capacity to produce tears. Your weakness in will has produced this weakness in your body, in your emotions. Get a hold of yourself!*

Yet, she found it impossible to stop the tears. Ayla! She had not thought of her maid in years. Ayla brought back memories of her childhood, of Gandhara, her parents, her brothers—

No! Do not think of that. Not ever!

Gandhari drew a deep breath. In the past, she perhaps would have recited the names of the *devas*. But now the sound of their names was like poison in her throat; a bitter, acrid thing that burned her from within.

'Sister? Are you troubled? May I be of help?'

And there she was again, her sister-in-law, Kunti. Gandhari gritted her teeth. 'I am fine. Let me be.'

But Kunti did not. She never did. Kunti seated herself next to Gandhari, the pile of branches and leaves creaking under her weight. She was thin enough but there was a solidity, a heaviness, a weight to her that made her seem denser than she really was.

'Why do you always insist on serving me? I do not need anything. Look after yourself. I am fine.' Gandhari did not intend her voice to sound as irritated as it did.

Kunti suppressed a laugh as she whispered: 'I suppose I am used to it. I have always been serving others. Even in my father's home, I was a servant.'

'Hmm.'

Gandhari had not meant it to sound inquisitive, but Kunti took it as a prompt to say more. Perhaps it was the notion of impending mortality that made her so talkative now, so fixated on the past. Gandhari sighed inwardly as Kunti kept talking. 'By father, I mean my adoptive father, Kuntibhoja, after whom I am named. Did you know my biological father sent me away?'

'Hmm.' Gandhari tried to sound sleepy, as a hint to quieten Kunti. She had enough demons of her own to contend with; she did not need to hear about Kunti's, too.

Kunti continued, unperturbed. 'He had made a vow to send his first-born child to Kuntibhoja, his cousin, who was childless. I was called Pritha, but after he adopted me, I became known as Kunti. He had a large kingdom and was forever entertaining wise men and rishis. I was given over to the *devas* and the guests who frequented my home. It was my responsibility to serve them. So, I'm used to serving people, I suppose. Trust me, you are easier to look after than Durvasa rishi.'

Gandhari snorted in amusement. 'Well, that is not saying a lot.' Durvasa was an irascible yet revered rishi (literally, one who sees, a sage, a person of wisdom and high spiritual attainment) . He was quick to lose his temper if he was not served food promptly or if it was not salted or spiced to his taste. And when he lost his temper, bad things happened. He was prone to uttering curses, causing people to be reborn as animals or trees, and though he often felt remorse after cooling down and offered a blessing as an antidote, it rarely was sufficient to overcome the initial curse. A rishi's words always carried power, and a curse once uttered, could never be fully negated.

It was said that Durvasa had been inordinately pleased with the ministrations of the young woman Kunti had been at that time. It was then he had given her the boon of being able to invoke the *devas* at her will and bear a child of the invoked *deva*. That was how she had borne all her sons.

Kunti replied softly: 'Well, he may have been difficult, but his blessing saved me and my family.'

And destroyed mine.

Kunti remained silent for so long after saying this that Gandhari almost finally fell asleep. But then Kunti asked softly: 'Sister, do you think I will find him in the afterlife, in the lands where my consciousness will wander after departing this earth?'

Gandhari did not have to wonder to whom she was referring. It was the anguish of a mother, the harsh remorse only a mother who had abandoned her child could feel. Kunti was referring to Karna, her first-born son.

Gandhari did not answer directly. 'To imagine what happens after death is to enter into murky waters. The rishis tell us this. They tell us to die well, and we will attain the heavens on the basis of our merits. They describe to us the different worlds, but are they other planets, are they faraway heavens and hells, or are they the lives that await us back here on this very planet? It is impossible to tell. It is not wise to dwell on such matters when we cannot know the truth.'

'Will I not meet my son again?' Kunti's voice was choked with tears.

'It is said that we find our ancestors and forefathers in the heavens.' A ghoulish laugh escaped Gandhari's lips. 'Even our rishis did not contemplate that a woman's children would predecease her. There is a word for orphan, but no word for a mother who has lost all her children. At least, you still have your other sons.'

'But your sons did not die hating you,' Kunti pointed out bitterly.

'Well, I did not abandon them to die when they were born, either, woman!' Gandhari could not resist snapping back. She could not understand how Kunti could feel sorry for herself when she had been the one to abandon her new-born.

'Did you not ever consider it, sister? Really?' Kunti sneered. 'I heard about what you did when you heard my Yudhishthira had been born. You were so jealous, you almost aborted your own children.'

Gandhari bristled: 'Once they were born, once I held them in my arms, I could not bear to be parted with them. Even when I was told by Vidura and others to abandon Suyodhana, that he would be evil, that he would be the source of destruction of our house, even then, I kept him.'

Kunti whispered, 'When Karna was born, he was golden and radiant, just like Suryadeva, the sun god who fathered him. He was born with small golden armour around his chest and golden earrings. Oh, he was so beautiful!'

'Yet, you floated him down the river.'

'I did not even know if he would survive,' Kunti confessed. 'But what choice did I have?' For a woman like Kunti, it would have been social suicide to have kept a son born out of wedlock.

'I couldn't do it. Even when I was asked to abandon my eldest, even when I was told to do it for the sake of the kingdom, I could never let him go.'

Kunti's voice was leaden. 'And now we are both paying for our sins. You for keeping your child, me for abandoning mine.'

'Now and in the hereafter.'

The shadows of the night passed across their faces. A cool air chilled their bones and spread through the forest, silencing the insects and night birds that otherwise kept them company.

Gandhari asked curiously, 'Did you never tell Pandu about Karna?'

'I dared not! My position was precarious as it was. He was so besotted with Madri, I thought he may abandon me if he knew the truth.'

'He would not have done that. He was too noble and righteous.' Gandhari loyally defended him; she still remembered he was the first to have been kind to her in Hastinapur, her first and perhaps only friend in that foreign kingdom.

Kunti laughed. 'Yes, of course he would not besmirch his reputation by kicking me out. But he could have banished me to the furthest reaches of the palace and made Madri the senior ruling queen in effect. He could have made me irrelevant.'

'Like me.'

'No, sister, you did that to yourself.'

Gandhari did not respond. Some minutes later, Kunti rose to leave. Gandhari hesitated, then said softly: 'He was a brave man, your son. He safeguarded my son with his life and his blood. There was a nobility to him; I was glad, always glad, that he was part of Suyodhana's life. And he came to you in the end. He did know you as his mother. There is some peace in that, surely.'

Gandhari could imagine the bitter twisting of Kunti's lips as she replied: 'Oh yes, what a wonderful mother I was, to come to him begging him to spare my other sons' lives; revealing myself to him only to ask him that he spare my lawfully born sons. He died knowing me as the mother who abandoned him and then who begged him for a favour. Who was I to ask him anything when I had given him nothing, left him with nothing?'

'You had to do it, for your other sons.'

Kunti laughed bitterly. 'And what thanks did I get from them? Yudhishthira cursed me and all women that womankind will no longer be able to keep any secrets, so angry was he that I kept Karna's identity from him.'

As Kunti walked away, Gandhari said, 'When a great one is cursed, a *deva* or a parent or a rishi, it is the one who pronounces the curse who suffers, sister, not the one who has been cursed.'

Kunti said nothing

Finally, when she was alone, Gandhari gave in and did what she had done every night for eighteen years after the war had been lost, after her sons had died. She had stopped afterwards, once they had moved into the forest. She had tried to renounce it all then: her past, her attachments, her grief, her regrets. She had pretended she had no identity, that she had never been queen, that she had never been mother, that she was just a renunciate with no past. It had not worked, but she tried.

Now as the tears flowed, wetting the leaves and branches that were her pillow, she gave in. She recited the names of her children, one by one, like a prayer, slowly, lovingly, in a murmured whisper so soft no one else could hear her:

Duryodhana, Duhshasana, Duhsaha, Duhsala, Jalasandha, Sama, Saha, Vinda, Anuvinda, Durdharsha, Subahu, Chitrasena, Dushpradharshana, Durmarshana, Durmukha, Duhshkarma, Karna, Vivimshati, Vikarna, Sulochana, Chitra, Upachitra, Chitraksha, Charuchitra, Sarasana, Durmada, Dushpragaha, Vivitsu, Vikata, Urnanabha, Sunabha, Nanda, Upanandaka, Senapati, Sushena, Kundodara, Mahodara, Chitrabana, Chitravarma, Suvarma, Durvimochana, Ayobahu, Mahabahu, Chitranga, Chitrakundala, Bhimavega, Bhimavala, Balaki, Balavardhana, Ugrayudha, Bhimakarma, Kanakayu, Dridhayudha, Dridhavarma, Dridhakshatra, Somakitri, Anudara, Dridhasandha, Jarasandha, Satyasandha, Sadahsuvak, Ugrashrava, Ashvasena, Senani, Dushparajaya, Aparajita, Panditaka, Visalaksha, Duravara, Dridhahasta, Suhasta, Vatavega, Suvarcha, Adityaketu, Bahvashi, Nagadanta, Ugrayayi, Kavachi, Nishangi, Pashi, Dandadhara, Dhanurgraha, Ugra, Bhimaratha, Vira, Viravahu, Alolupa, Abhaya, Raudrakarma, Dridharatha, Anadhrishya, Kundabhedi, Viravi, Dhirghalochana, Dirgabahu, Mahabahu, Vyudhoru, Kanakadhvaja, Kundasi, Viraja, Duhsala; the last her only daughter.

It brought her no peace, only the churning of grief and anger and torment. She knew they would trouble her dreams tonight, haunt her and chase her through the labyrinths of her consciousness. But she did not resist. She was drawn to them, her children, her sons, her dead, evil sons, as a moth was to flame.

Hastinapur, Then

'Well, this one is even stranger than you.'

Gandhari repressed a smile at Satyavati's exasperation.

'What do you mean, queen mother?'

They were taking a stroll in the gardens. Although Gandhari could not see the flowers, she enjoyed feeling the soft petals between her fingers and lifting the scent from her hand to her nose. She enjoyed the drone of bees and birdsong swarming around her. They were better company than the sullen paranoia of her husband.

'I had thought a blindfolded princess would be eccentric enough. But this Kunti is even stranger!'

'How so? I heard she is beautiful and virtuous.'

'Well! In features and form, yes. But I have yet to see her smile or her jaw unclench. She is so stern that even poor Pandu has become quiet.'

Gandhari replied diplomatically, 'I am sure she is a fine match. Kuntibhoja is a valuable ally, surely.'

Satyavati snorted: 'Who knows why Bhishma chose her? Can't trust a celibate to pick a good bride, that's what I say.'

Gandhari asked curiously, 'Were you not in favour of the match?'

Satyavati plopped down on a bench and Gandhari sat next to her. Some maids walked by, collecting flowers for the evening worship, wafting cones of incense to keep away the mosquitoes. 'The more time that goes by, girl, I think it's not so much the house, the lineage, the pedigree that matters. I think it's the stock, the breed of the person, the strength of their stomach and will. Bhishma plots marriages like he's looking at a map, picking territories over each other for their political value. But is that what holds up a family? A kingdom? Or is it character?'

'Ideally, it should be both.'

Satyavati snorted again: 'And what in this world is ideal?'

Satyavati rose and began pacing again. 'Well, I have to say, even my other son Dvaipayana was in favour of the alliance. But for a different reason.'

'Why is that?'

Satyavati drew in a breath. She paused. 'You are the daughter of Subala, you tell me, girl. What do you think?'

Gandhari sighed inwardly but neither her face nor her voice betrayed her exasperation. She was constantly being tested on her political acumen and recall of the history and geography of the diverse territories of Bharat by members of the royal family and their ministers. It was grating to be perpetually under examination, but she bore it. 'Kuntibhoja is a powerful ally and Kunti is renowned as a virtuous woman.'

Satyavati tut-tutted. 'Yes, so are many other princesses around Bharat. Come, princess, think harder.'

Gandhari warmed to the challenge. She racked her mind and rattled off more statistics about the size of Kuntibhoja's forces, the strategic import of his terrain, the pedigree of his bloodline. But she was missing something. Satyavati kept grunting, no, no, no, at each of the reasons Gandhari volleyed.

Finally, Gandhari gave up and admitted, 'I cannot think of the reason then, queen mother. Please tell me.'

Satyavati sat next to her, sending up a cloud of perfume that filled Gandhari's nostrils. She had been growing increasingly fond of that smell, associating it with the eccentric, always fascinating persona of Satyavati. She had never been particularly close to her own mother and she felt an unfurling of love for Satyavati that she had never felt for her own. She leaned close to Satyavati, breathing in the soft fabric of her sari, artfully and elegantly folded yet slightly tousled, too, a little dishevelled and careless, to show how unaffected she was by her own appearance. Gandhari did not want to appear so weak as to lean into her for an embrace, but she did sidle a little closer.

Satyavati's voice changed into something softer, more measured, wise – the voice of a woman who had been with a rishi, who had been mother to one, who had earned her wisdom the hard way. 'You see, daughter, you have infinite intelligence when it comes to the hard facts, that which can be gleaned from numbers and recitation of history and lineage. But there is an insight that goes deeper than that, that understands power is not gained through war and politics alone, that there are more mysterious forces at work in the universe. Forces that if we tap into them can alter the course of our destiny forever.'

Gandhari swallowed. A nervousness started twitching in her fingers and palpitating her heart. Her throat grew dry, her breath short. There was nothing ominous in what Satyavati was saying but she felt a frisson of foreboding.

'Daughter, do you understand what I am saying?'

'Yes, queen mother,' Gandhari replied, her voice cracking from the dryness in her throat.

Satyavati rose and began her habitual pacing again. 'Do you know what is the most important thing that Kunti brings to us, girl? Her most valuable asset? The whole reason behind the alliance with Pandu?'

'What?'

'Not what. Who.'

Gandhari lifted a tumbler of rose-scented warm milk to her lips. A puzzled frown creased her brow. 'Who?'

'Her nephew.'

Gandhari began tracing through the dynasty maps she had drawn in her head but she could not identify this suddenly important nephew.

Satyavati inhaled deeply and pronounced, 'Krishna.'

At the very sound of his name, Gandhari was seized by a sudden dread and existential fear. She could hear the howls of jackals and cries from a distant battlefield. The tumbler of milk fell from her suddenly lifeless hands. She shivered violently.

The very sound of his name inspired horror and revulsion within her, as if he would be the source of destruction of herself and all she held dear. She moved to cover her ears as if that futile gesture would remove the sound of that name from her consciousness, eradicate it from her memory.

'What on earth, child? What has happened to you?' Satyavati exclaimed, wiping off the spilled milk from her wet dress.

Gandhari's voice was fainter than the heart hammering loudly like a kettle drum in her chest. It was barely a whisper. 'Krishna? Who is that?'

Everyone else of import in the kingdom had to be referred to by his full name, his father's name, the name of his kingdom, his title, his lineage. The more flourishes one had, the more powerful he purportedly was. Yet, the very name 'Krishna', shorn of all ornamentation and embellishment, was enough to thrill the heart, in desire, fear, attraction or hate. Who must this figure be if his very name was this powerful?

Satyavati called for a maid to clean up the spilled milk. Gandhari dabbed ineffectually at the droplets of milk staining her blouse. Satyavati continued, 'As of now, he is nobody. A young boy of mysterious origins, tucked away in remote forests, where he sings and dances, plays with cows and seems to be slaying an endless slew of demons sent by the evil king Kamsa to kill him. He is said to be utterly charming, a mischievous, blue-coloured lad who has stolen the hearts of Vraj.'

'I hardly see the value of that for our kingdom.' She took deep breaths and willed her pulse to slow down.

Satyavati lowered her voice so that the servants could not hear. She whispered, 'They say he is a god, child. They say he is Narayana incarnate, the next avatar of Vishnu after Sri Rama.' An avatar was a manifestation of a deity in human form, an incarnation.

'A cowherd boy as a god?' Gandhari was incredulous. 'That's not possible!'

'As I said, a boy of mysterious origins. Even my son Dvaipayana travelled many, many weeks to have sight of him as a baby. He – the great rishi my son is – bowed down at his feet, the feet of a baby! Can you imagine?'

Gandhari forced herself to shrug nonchalantly, as if she was not deeply troubled within. 'Such tall tales abound. It is hard to know what is fact and what is fiction. It seems an awful lot to wager a marriage on.' *This is who they choose over me to marry Pandu? An aunt of a strange blue boy who is either a trickster or a god?* Hmmph, Gandhari thought to herself, the spies of Gandhara were worth more than that.

Satyavati was thoughtful. 'My son is not prone to superstition. And, I can feel it in the air. I have been around a lot longer than you, girl. I know the very air of the earth is changing. The book of history is turning a new page. One epoch ends, while another dawns. Such things only happen when the *devas* are here. It is better to keep them on our side.'

'Hmm.'

Satyavati's voice filled with amusement. 'And in any case, if there is nothing to Krishna, how come you were so affected by the very mention of his name?'

Gandhari admitted, 'I do not know. Something overcame me, some notion that my destiny is intertwined with his. And perhaps not in a good way.'

'I must tell you, I've met so many interesting people in my lifetime. Even Dvaipayana's father, who was a great rishi, one of the greatest rishis this world has ever seen – even he was nothing compared to what is being rumoured of this lad. I cannot wait to see him for myself.'

I never shall see him, not with my eyes, thought Gandhari to herself. *Imagine that, a once-in-a-million years event, the coming of an avatar and I have blindfolded myself, robbing myself of the sight of him, a vision that would surely bless me and my family.* Gandhari quickly changed the topic, unwilling to entertain the thought of what she had lost by blindfolding herself and even more unwilling to think more about this strange, perplexing figure of Krishna who made her hairs stand on end and sent trickles of dread down her spine.

♋

Satyavati arranged for Pandu, Kunti and Gandhari to go on an outing at one of the pleasure gardens nearby. It was a garden full of fountains and shaded groves with flowering rosebushes and a large lake at the centre for boating, built for the royal family as a retreat. Satyavati did not even bother inviting Dhritarashthra, who was convinced that he would die of fever if he were to step outside of the palace gates. Satyavati was keen that the brothers and their wives get along with each other, and this was her way of getting them to bond. Pandu dismissed the servants and rowed the boat himself. He liked to exercise to keep himself fit and robust. Gandhari thought he pushed himself a little too hard, perhaps defensive against the rumours that there was still a weakness in him, a pallor that robbed him of full health. She wished she were able to see him with her own eyes to judge his strength for herself.

He rowed near the banks of the lake, under the shade of tall trees, to shield them from the heat of the sun. Gandhari turned her face upwards to feel the breeze ruffle against her cheeks, to inhale the fertile scents emanating from the leaves. It reminded her of home, and she felt a deep pang of homesickness for the orchards where she would ride on horseback with her brothers for hours on end, pounding the earth beneath her feet, outpacing even her brothers. Now, it was a miracle if she could manage to walk ten paces without stumbling.

Pandu was trying desperately to make conversation with Kunti. He was such an affable person that it should have been easy for Kunti to warm to him. But she was so stoic and severe in response and countenance that Pandu gave up. Even Gandhari, out of pity for him, tried gamely to start a conversation. She asked what it was like to grow up with Kuntibhoja, how it was to serve Durvasa, the legendary rishi who was infamous for being impossible to please. It was said that Kunti had pleased him with her steadfast devotion and ministrations to his eccentric needs. Gandhari was genuinely curious but Kunti refused to share anything at all. When it came to Durvasa, Kunti simply said in a flat voice that brooked no follow-up: 'He is an illustrious rishi. It was the boon of a lifetime for me to have the opportunity to even serve such a great one.'

Pandu tried to soften her up: 'Indeed. And it is a credit to you, my dear, that you were able to win his favour. Most people earn his wrath. But he has always spoken so highly of you.'

Kunti's voice sharpened to a shrewish tone: 'I did not seek any favour from him! If he was moved to bless me, that was his greatness of compassion. The rishis always bless those who cross their path. There was nothing special about me.'

Pandu and Gandhari lapsed into silence at that point. They rowed and ate wordlessly. It was awkward for Gandhari to eat lunch out in the open without the plates and vessels she was used to. Kunti took to feeding her, briskly scooping up the thick lentil gravies mixed with rice and pressing them to her mouth. Gandhari's cheeks flamed in embarrassment as she tried to protest but Kunti persisted.

'You are my older sister,' Kunti told her. 'It is my duty to serve you. Now eat.' And she prodded the spoon so firmly into Gandhari's mouth that Gandhari had no choice but to comply, uncomfortable as she was.

Afterwards, when they came back to the palace, Pandu accompanied Gandhari to her and Dhritarashthra's private audience chamber. He talked to her quietly as they walked. By now she had memorized the route to her chamber from all the various other chambers and sitting areas in the palace, so she easily kept pace with him. If one did not see her blindfold, one would not have guessed at her incapacity.

Pandu whispered to her, 'May I confide in you, as my older sister?'

'Of course, you should not even hesitate to ask.'

Pandu let loose. 'Of course, I know what a virtuous and admirable woman Kunti is. I am very fortunate to have her as my wife. But, you see, do you not, sister, that I cannot possibly connect with her? It is like being with a statue! I really do not think I have ever even seen her laugh.'

Gandhari tried to comfort him: 'Well, surely, she is shy. She was a lone child in Kuntibhoja's home, secluded in prayer and serving the honoured guests who came to his place. It must be a big change for her to suddenly be here in the midst of such a great family, to finally have companionship after being alone for so long. Try having some patience with her.'

Pandu sighed heavily. 'I have won so many battles, sister. Conquered so many kingdoms. Ravaged so many palaces. But I do not think I have encountered a fortress stronger than the one that she has built around herself.'

Gandhari was amused: 'Perhaps that is a good thing. It is a challenge you might enjoy.'

Pandu hesitated. 'Sister, I do not think I will like what lies inside the fortress.' The words fell from his lips like lead.

They had reached the audience chamber by then, and at Pandu's knock, a servant from within opened the ornate wooden door. Dhritarashthra was sleeping, so it was just Pandu and Gandhari inside the room. They sat while Ayla fetched them cooling hibiscus tea. Gandhari did not respond to Pandu's confession. There was nothing appropriate to say.

Pandu continued, 'Sister, I have come to seek permission from you and my older brother. Since he is – occupied, I will make the request of you.'

'Yes, little brother. Ask.'

'I would like to go to Madra.'

Gandhari hid a smile. She knew well that the princess of Madra, Madri, was famed to be a woman of uncommon beauty, coquettish charm and a giggly, exuberant nature that compensated for her lack of brains. She could imagine how appealing Madri would seem to Pandu after having been wed to Kunti.

'And what is it you wish from the kingdom of Madra, little brother?'

Pandu chuckled. 'Do not play dumb with me, sister. You know well exactly what it is that I seek. Do I have your blessing to bring you another younger sister, who shall be at your service and command, as the eldest wife of this house?'

Gandhari smiled but inwardly she fumed. She may have been the senior-most wife of the house, but Kunti was the one who was queen. Gandhari would be closer in stature to the frivolous Madri, an irrelevant queen who would not rule. The weight of the crown mattered more than the weight of age.

'You have my blessing,' said Gandhari to Pandu nevertheless. She sincerely wished that he would find happiness and fulfilment somewhere. It was so easy for princes like Pandu to simply go elsewhere when they were dissatisfied with their lot in life; if they tired of their first wife, they could find a second or a third or a fourth. Gandhari did not have that choice, but even if she did, she could not conceive of the possibility of it, of being with anyone other than Dhritarashthra, so complete was her devotion to him. So, there was no resentment in her, no grudge, when she leaned forward to place her hand on Pandu's head in blessing. She did, however, despite herself, feel a twinge of pity for Kunti.

The days that followed were miserable. Pandu's triumphant
return with the lovely Madri in tow made Kunti even more
sour and dour. Gandhari now felt overshadowed by both the
wives. The attainment of Madri appeared to embolden Pandu.
He began a period of intense warfare to show off his military
and physical prowess, as if to defy those who had said he had
been born with a deformity. The brighter he shone with
victory after victory, the more bitter and angry his brother
Dhritarashthra became. And, Gandhari, too, began to resent
being eclipsed by women who lacked her political savvy and
her intent eagerness to rule.

The lowest point was when they had to preside over the
city's celebration after Pandu's triumphant return from a string
of military victories over other kingdoms. He brought in tow
wagon upon wagon full of gems, pearls, coral and other glittering
stones – cows, artwork and even slaves. Then there were
multitudes of horse-drawn chariots, elephants, donkeys, camels,
buffaloes and some goats and sheep. The crowds went wild for
him. Gandhari's maidens oohed and aahed over the display.

Bhishma had arranged an opulent celebration ceremony
for Pandu. It was held outdoors to accommodate the thronging
crowds. He and Satyavati, along with Ambika and Ambalika, sat
on a high dais on an elevated platform so they could be visible
to the people. Sometimes Gandhari forgot that the two mothers
of Dhritarashthra and Pandu were even in the palace. They
were always in seclusion, perpetually, it seemed to Gandhari, in
hiding. Gandhari, Kunti and Madri sat to the left on a slightly
lower dais. Even Dhritarashthra had been persuaded to come
out on this day. It was perhaps part of his masochism to put
himself at the centre of his brother's glory. Vidura sat next to
him to tend to him and inform him of the happenings.

Ayla was the only one in Hastinapur that Gandhari dared
to fully trust, so she had Ayla sit next to her and be her eyes and
ears. Ayla had a quick mind, and she was able to rapidly relay to

Gandhari just how many wagons were in the caravan, guessing at the weight of the various barrels of golden coins and gems, the number of cattle being paraded through the streets of the city. She whispered in awe how Pandu was calmly at the front of the procession, leading it with a smile, pausing to wave and exchange pleasantries with people in the crowd who pushed closer to him. The procession was leisurely, giving Pandu ample time to soak up the adulation.

Eventually, as the trumpets and kettle drums sounded louder, as the priests began droning chants of blessing and gratitude, Gandhari heard the heavy thud of Pandu's feet ascending the steps up the platform. He bowed in front of Satyavati and Bhishma, offering them the first and finest of the treasures, and then reported in measured tones the string of victories he had achieved: he had travelled to the east and defeated the Dasharnas. Then, with his army in full force, packed with elephants, horses, chariots and foot soldiers, with colourful flags fluttering everywhere, he had attacked Magadha. His victories spread to Kashi and Pundra. Everywhere, he had brought kings to his feet, toppling them with flaming arrows and the glitter of his dazzling swords. It was a tribute to Pandu, thought Gandhari, that he was able to boast of his triumphs in such a humble, self-deprecating way. His voice betrayed no pride or arrogance, only the hushed reverence of a son reporting to his elders.

Bhishma wept openly. Gandhari had never seen such naked emotion from him. Ayla whispered to her how Bhishma embraced Pandu closely, his lips trembling and mumbling incoherent words, tears streaming down his cheeks and wetting his beard, his hand gripping Pandu's head tightly to his silver-armoured shoulder. Pandu comforted him, chuckling at his sentimentality, stroking his hair until finally Bhishma released him.

Then, Pandu made his way to Dhritarashthra: 'Older brother, all these riches have been won for you. I lay them at your feet. They are yours to do with as you will. Command me, and it shall be done.'

Ayla whispered that Dhritarashthra's hands shook as he bent forward to touch Pandu's head in blessing. He appeared to hesitate until Vidura leaned towards him, whispering to him the appropriate words to be said. Dhritarashthra nodded weakly – how grateful Gandhari was to Ayla's keen sense of observation and her forthrightness – and said to Pandu, 'Younger brother, these riches do not belong to us. They belong to our elders, to grandmother Satyavati, our uncle Bhishma and our mothers. Taking their blessings, let the treasures be distributed among our people, to the needy, to the brahmanas, to the widows. Let all of this be given as alms to our people!'

Satyavati cleared her throat loudly. Dhritarashthra added hastily: 'And, of course, we must share a portion of this with our brother, Vidura, without whom we would all be lost!' Gandhari did not need Ayla's report to imagine the daft smile Dhritarashthra would have turned towards Vidura at that moment, insincere in its affection and regard for his lowborn brother.

Thunderous cheers applauded Dhritarashthra's command. *Well, Vidura's command*, thought Gandhari. How different it all would have been if Vidura, the wisest and most competent of them all, had been permitted to rule.

In the days to come, Dhritarashthra's instructions would be followed meticulously. Vidura, too, was found a suitable bride by Bhishma. She was the daughter of King Devaka and a service woman. When Vidura had come to take Gandhari's blessings, she had smilingly asked him if he were pleased with the match. He confessed shyly that she was beautiful and cheerful, a virtuous and devoted woman, who was affectionate to him. Gandhari felt a rush of affection and gladness for Vidura then, that at least this one brother, the one who had been deemed ineligible to rule, the one who deserved it the most, would find some measure of happiness.

Before the celebration concluded, Pandu came to the platform where Gandhari sat with Kunti and Madri. Madri called out teasingly, 'O husband, what gems are you bearing in your hands for me?'

Gandhari swore she heard Kunti literally grind her teeth.

Pandu laughingly replied, 'Wait your turn, wife! My first offering belongs to our elder sister.'

Pandu knelt at Gandhari's feet. 'Elder sister, I have brought this specially for you as a tribute. Please let me place it in your hand.'

She opened her hand, palm up, and he carefully placed a delicate ring with a large elliptical stone, so large that it would extend over three of the fingers in her hand. There was a rush of indrawn air as Ayla opened her mouth to begin describing the jewel in detail to her, but Pandu cut her off.

'No, no, let me tell her what it is I have brought for her. Sister, I know you will never see this ring, but you will be able to feel its beauty. It is a rare form of sunstone, that captures the energy of the sun. Feel it.' Gandhari stroked it; it was smooth yet spiked with a glittery layer of stone. 'It is red like the dawning sun and sparkles when held up to the light. The more you rub it, the smoother and deeper in hue it becomes.'

Gandhari smiled, a teeth-baring, impulsive smile, and slid the ring onto her fingers, stroking the unique stone. 'Also,' Pandu leaned forward to whisper conspiratorially, 'I have been told that rubbing the stone helps one keep their temper and stay patient. I thought that may be helpful for people like us – who may be prone to losing ours, considering the difficult people we have to deal with in our lives.' Gandhari chortled. From a distance, she heard her husband ask Vidura what was going on at their platform.

She exclaimed, 'I can imagine just how red it is, little brother. I know the fiery red colour of the sun at dawn. I have

seen it every day of my life in Gandhara. Not only shall this
stone teach me patience, not only shall it adorn my hand
prettily, but it shall also remind me of home. It is the most
beautiful thing you could have brought me.'

'Now you must give me your blessing.'

She leaned forward with a smile and placed her hand atop
his head with affection. 'May you live a hundred years,' she
murmured the traditional blessing and added impishly, 'And
bring me a hundred more stones!'

Pandu chuckled as he moved onwards to his wives. Madri
whined coquettishly that the gems he had brought for her and
Kunti were dwarfed by the opulence of the ring he had given
Gandhari. Gandhari turned away to hide her smile.

♋

For the first time in her life, Gandhari felt irrelevant. There was
nothing for her to do at court. Pandu and Kunti took easily to
ruling the kingdom with the sage counsel of Satyavati, Bhishma
and Vidura. Dhritarashthra also ignored her. Pandu's military
victories drove Dhritarashthra further into bitterness and
resentment, a miasma of dark jealousy and self-pity covering
his chambers. Gandhari could not tolerate staying near him. He
seemed to prefer the company of Kutili, his maidservant, in any
event, and she commiserated with him more sympathetically
than Gandhari could. Pandu was too occupied with running
the kingdom and tending to his two wives to give her company,
and even Satyavati was more inaccessible. Satyavati was waiting
for heirs so she could finally retreat from active life in the
court, once the line of succession was ensured. She exerted her
diplomatic influence to keep firm the alliances that secured the
pre-eminence of the Kuru clan in Bharat.

Then Gandhari turned to that which had always given her
peace and solace in the past. The *devas*. She secluded herself in

prayer and fasting, and, once again, wasted away to nothing. It was when Ayla reminded her that she was a princess and how valuable a lovely figure was for a princess that Gandhari resumed eating. Dhritarashthra hardly noticed, so long as her hand was cool on his forehead, stroking away his headaches, her voice gentle as she lulled him to back to sleep between bouts of fitful tossing and turning.

It did not bring peace but a perverse pleasure in denying herself the comforts of palace life, in shrinking into a shadow by her own asceticism so that she could not be overshadowed by the other wives, neglecting her health and body in response to a court that increasingly neglected her. She was bitter, and her penance served only to drive her bitterness ever higher.

One day, as she sat in a bench, picking through grains of rice to be cooked by her own hand and fed to the *devas*, rice she would never consume herself, Satyavati stomped heavily across the mosaic tiles towards her and plucked the basket of rice from her hands. Satyavati said sharply, 'Enough! As if we do not have enough eccentrics wandering through this palace, now you are apparently trying to kill yourself through starvation.'

Gandhari protested weakly.

Satyavati snorted. 'Well, up you get now! My son is coming, and you will need to tend to him.'

'Dvaipayana?' Gandhari asked in surprise. He spent almost all of his time in the jungles and mountain caves, shunning civilization. In his adult life, he had only visited with his mother a handful of times.

'Yes, Dvaipayana! What other son do I have left?' snapped Satyavati. Then she sighed: 'Forgive me, I am cross. It is so stressful when he visits. I'm always worried that I will do something to annoy him and he will go away and perhaps never return. These ascetics are so finicky, you know.'

Gandhari laughed. Despite herself, her pulse picked up in anticipation of meeting this enigmatic figure she had thought about so much ever since Satyavati had shared his story with her. She offered, 'I'm sure Kunti will be able to manage him fine; after all she served Durvasa, that temperamental rishi, so well. No one has a worse temper than Durvasa.'

Satyavati hesitated. 'Gandhari, I want you to be the one to look after him. You are the eldest daughter of the house after all.'

Gandhari frowned behind her blindfold. She was sure that was not the real reason, but she could not decipher Satyavati's motive. There were always wheels within wheels spinning in that quick mind of her grandmother-in-law.

Gandhari acquiesced with a nod. A frenetic few days followed. Special chambers were prepared for him, shorn of all furniture, even a bed. He liked to be in the wilderness, so Satyavati had constructed a small hut at the edge of Hastinapur, bordering the forest. There was a beautiful flower garden there and she arranged for vats of water to be carried there daily, in case he would refuse to stay in the palace.

Finally, Dvaipayana came. No one was there to greet him other than Gandhari and Satyavati. Bhishma was wary of his wildness; Ambika and Ambalika were still too traumatized by their conception of their sons through him to face him; Dhritarashthra and Pandu were embarrassed to have been physically sired by him and wanted to keep their distance. Vidura alone among the three honoured him but was occupied with matters of the court.

Gandhari had never witnessed Satyavati so happy. She doted on her son, shooing away the servants so that she could feed him herself. She chattered away happily, telling him of all the gossip and news, while he grunted in between bites to show he was listening. She overexerted herself, unaccustomed as she was to such manual labour, and in the afternoon, after lunch, she retreated for a long nap.

It fell upon Gandhari to assist him in preparations for his evening worship. She did not let her blindfold deter her as she carefully washed all the vessels, drew powerful geometrical symbols of positive energies, yantras, with white rice powder, and snipped dried branches of various plants to be burned in the sacrificial fire. She worked silently and Dvaipayana appeared to appreciate that after the babble of his mother. He murmured his satisfaction at her handiwork and as dusk fell he began his worship. He invited Gandhari to stay and witness the ceremony, which she knew was a rare honour.

Gandhari had never been part of a yajna like this. His voice was fierce; when he chanted the Vedas, it sounded as if the Vedas issued forth from his lips as if they were his own words and not words he had faithfully memorized and recited. The very palace seemed to shake with the force of his *tapobola*, his spiritual powers, and a wind started stirring and whirling within the room, lifting the hairs off the nape of Gandhari's neck, rustling up the fire until she could feel the flames leap up to the ceiling. Scent after scent started unfurling from the fire – some beautiful, like musk, sandalwood, camphor, jasmine; others noxious like acrid charred flesh. She could feel all the negative energies from the palace being whirled into the room, summoned by him, and cast into the fire to be burned away.

That was just the first ten minutes. Then, there was stillness for a few moments before an eerie howling began, first as a faint hum in her ear, and then something shrill that grew louder and higher in pitch until it was a screaming whistle that made her want to cover her ears but Gandhari dared not move. The air became thick and weighted, heavy with presence. She could feel the *devas* congregating in the room, circling her. They were silent, shapeless, but she could feel them, how their eyes fell upon her, watched her, judged her. They sat next to Dvaipayana and wove in and out of the fire, as if wandering in and out of the chamber, as if it were a party. Dvaipayana sometimes laughed, sometimes grunted, sometimes said something in such rapid Vedic Sanskrit that Gandhari could not follow.

Finally, the ceremony ended. Gandhari was trembling from the overpowering experience. After the fire dwindled to embers, Dvaipayana softly called out to her. 'Come here, child.'

Gandhari lifted the skirts of her dress above her ankles and carefully walked towards him, winding her way through piles of firewood, metallic bowls filled with incense, turmeric, sandalwood paste, vermilion, things she could recognize by smell now, and crouched at his feet.

He smelled divine, literally divine. Gandhari had never been enraptured before, but she felt substance-less, a bundle of lightness, spellbound by his presence. She could not help her hands from fluttering above her waist, almost reaching towards him.

Dvaipayana was amused. 'What is it, child?'

Had it been anyone else, Gandhari would not have admitted it, but she was disarmed by the power of his presence, the depth of the worship he had performed, the lingering vibrations of the spirits he had summoned still swirling about in the chamber. So, she said in a girlish voice that she had not used in years, in a burst of words tripping over themselves: 'It is just that I wish I could see you. I am sure the very sight of you would have been a blessing for me. You are the most fascinating person I have ever met.' She concluded sadly, 'And now I shall never have that chance.'

Dvaipayana gave a low chuckle. 'This is why one has to be so careful about the vows one chooses.'

'I have heard that before,' she muttered in exasperation.

Dvaipayana said thoughtfully, 'I've rarely met a woman so steadfast, so devoted, so focused. It is a welcome thing to have such a one wait upon me and assist so ably in my worship and sadhana. If you wish, you may try to see me with your hands.'

Gandhari hid a sharp intake of breath. It was uncommon for an ascetic like him to allow himself to be touched. Even Satyavati did not dare to embrace him. Gandhari knelt, the oil residues from the offerings staining the soft satiny fabric of her sari. She had instructed Ayla to dress her in a yellow sari that resembled the watery sun on a winter day. She lifted her hands and reached out, tentatively with trembling fingers, first, to touch his feet and take his blessings, touching her fingers to her heart.

Then, she reached out to touch his face.

His cheeks were sunken, rough with a bristly untamed beard, like sandpaper against her hands; his forehead was weathered and leathery from endless days of baring himself to the sun; his eyebrows slashed down angrily as if he was always brooding, perpetually frowning; his skin was warm to the touch, as if the fire he had kindled for worship was nothing compared to the fire that burned within him; her hands dropped to his shoulders, his torso bared to the waist. His hair hung to his shoulders, matted and unruly, and his shoulders were broad and well-muscled. *He must have to be strong to survive in the jungle after all.* The sacred thread hung from one shoulder, and as her hand traced across his chest to the other shoulder, she felt the strong thumping of his heart, slow but pulsing so strong, it vibrated across his entire upper body. Finally, emboldened now, her hands dropped to his. His hands were hot from handling the fire, deeply callused from chopping the wood for his own sacrificial fires, from life in the jungle and caves, vibrating warmth and vitality.

Finally, Gandhari withdrew her hands. She breathed deeply, trying to absorb his strength and power into her being. Her bones felt liquid as if the simple touch of his face and hands had overpowered her completely. She was in awe.

'Satisfied?' he asked in exactly the kind of arch tone his mother used with her.

Gandhari blushed furiously. What must he think of her boldness, and what would he say of her to the others? How foolish it had been to be so impulsive!

Dvaipayana laughed, a great booming laugh that seemed to shake the very walls of the chamber, as Gandhari scurried away quickly.

$$\odot$$

Later that evening, Gandhari ran into Satyavati in one of the hallways as she was returning from the kitchens with dinner on a tray to feed Dhritarashthra. Gandhari would not let any of the maids or servants prepare the food for her husband and insisted on bringing it herself from the kitchens to his bedside. In so many ways, she could not connect with her husband or have intimacy with him, but this – the simple act of cooking for and feeding him – was her way of connecting to him. She ran into Satyavati almost literally, swerving out of the way just in time, a little bit of the different savoury broths, tomato sauces and rice pudding brimming in tiny copper bowls on the tray she carried spilling over the edges onto her fingers.

Satyavati was curious to know what Gandhari thought of her son.

Gandhari was unable to keep anything from her grandmother-in-law. She confessed, 'He's fascinating and so very – vital and strong, pulsing with life. I have never met anyone so alive. He's much – earthier than I realized.'

Satyavati laughed. 'Well, he's his mother's son, isn't he?'

Gandhari smiled. 'You both have the same laugh.'

Satyavati whispered, 'You did not find in him anything – repelling, did you?'

Gandhari was taken aback. This was the first time she had ever heard any insecurity or doubt in Satyavati's voice. She remembered what Satyavati had said about her daughters-in-law, how they had turned away in disgust and fear from the very sight of her son. Tears came to her eyes as she thought how hurtful it must have been for Satyavati to see her son so humiliatingly received.

Gandhari said gently, 'Not at all. He is the most spectacular person I have ever met. It is just that he is like the blazing sun. Some cannot withstand the brightness or heat of the sun; those who are weak will turn away from such light. It is not the fault of the sun.'

Satyavati affectionately kissed the top of head. 'Imagine if any of my simpering daughters-in-law had your nerves of steel, daughter. What a different tale this would have been! Sometimes I feel you are wasted on my grandson.' Satyavati chuckled, then whispered, 'I did not say that last part, child.'

Gandhari walked away with a shake of her head and a smile.

That night, Dhritarashthra was in an unusually talkative mood. They lay next to each other in bed, facing each other, with a long bolster pillow between them. His hand touched hers and he did not remove it. That was the most intimacy they had had in months. He was very curious to know what she thought of Dvaipayana. She honestly relayed to him all that had passed.

Dhritarashthra asked eagerly, 'Wife, do you think he is really that fond of you?'

She shrugged and said modestly, 'Such a great man is by nature merciful and compassionate. I am sure he is like this with everyone.'

He gripped her hand firmly. 'You know, wife, he is an inordinately powerful man. The spells he can cast! The power that lies at his fingertips! It is incredible.'

'Yes, I am aware,' Gandhari said flatly. So, this is why he was being so touchy-feely with her tonight, she thought to herself: he wanted to curry favour with Dvaipayana through her.

Dhritarashthra mused aloud: 'It has been months now since Pandu has been married. Two wives, and no heir yet!'

'Having two wives does not mean one can create an heir twice as fast,' she pointed out wryly.

Dhritarashthra waved his hands impatiently, accidentally swatting her face. 'Yes, yes, but what I mean is, we have an opportunity here, wife. A golden opportunity.'

Gandhari had a sinking feeling in her stomach.

He continued, 'An heir is everything, Gandhari. Yes, it is true that I cannot rule over the kingdom. I shall never be king. But why not my sons, Gandhari? I am the eldest son of this family and if my sons are elder to his – why should it not be their birthright to rule, to take up the crown that was denied to me? With the blessings of the *devas*, they shall not have my infirmity.' His voice became increasingly excited. 'Do you understand, Gandhari? Do you see what I am saying?'

It is the eldest son of the crowned king who would inherit, not the eldest son of the eldest brother. But she did not voice this aloud.

Ever since Bhishma had been denied the throne through his self-imposed vow, the succession to the throne had grown ever murkier. She could understand Dhritarashthra's resentment, his hope for his sons to acquire a better hand than the one that had been dealt him. 'Yes.' She hesitated but reminded herself that this was her husband and she should be open with him. She said softly, 'But I already have the boon that I shall bear one hundred sons. What more do we need?'

Dhritarashthra sniffed dismissively. 'That is something you saw in a dream, a vision. It is not very reliable. It is better to get certainty. If Dvaipayana grants you the boon, it will come true, I am sure of it. This is the opportunity to cement the boon, Gandhari, and make sure that we get the heirs we need.'

She almost snapped at him. He was so cavalier about her boon from Shiva, dismissing the one year's worth of penance she had done to attain it. Once her willpower had been enough to earn the attention of the *devas* themselves; now she wasted all of it controlling, or trying to control, her temper with her husband. She diverted her attention. 'One hundred sons?' asked Gandhari sceptically. 'Do we really need one hundred?'

'Yes!' cried Dhritarashthra. 'There can never be too many. It is so easy to lose sons in battle, to illness, to infirmity. And – I do not know whether this is something that is passed on to my children biologically, this blindness. I do not want to take any risks! It is better to have as many children as possible.'

One good child outweighs one hundred brats. Her father's words came back to her. She suddenly felt a shiver of foreboding but said nothing. She knew it was pointless to argue with her husband.

Dhritarashthra gripped her arm tightly. 'You will do it, won't you, Gandhari? You will obtain this boon from him? For me. For us. You will not let me down, will you?'

Gandhari swallowed. It was dangerous to play games with the great ones, to try to bend them to one's will, to try to pry boons and blessings that they were reluctant to offer. It went against everything she believed in, but it was not just her husband's words that stilled her tongue. She was bristling against the stifling life of the palace, where she had been firmly side-lined, where she did nothing but cook and tend to guests and her husband, where the only decisions she was charged with were what outfit to wear and how to dress her hair – and even that she could not do herself; she was dependent on servants by her blindfold and by her position as a princess. She was growing rusty in her studies, now that she did not read and could not ask Ayla to read dense, arcane texts of statecraft and espionage to her. The language and grammar in those books was too advanced and complicated for Ayla's basic literacy. Gandhari was not ready to fade into irrelevance quite yet and so the prospect of sons, heirs, who could have a greater role in court than she and her husband, who could achieve what they had not been able to on their own, lured her.

Around midnight, a knock came on the door. Gandhari carefully navigated her way to the door and opened it. Dvaipayana had dispatched a messenger. He requested her presence at his private worship before first light in the gardens, prior to his departure later in the morning.

Dhritarashthra was tossing and turning in his sleep but did not wake at the sound of the knock or the hushed conversation between Gandhari and the messenger. She came back to bed and was filled with wonder and excitement at the opportunity to once again sit for worship with the great rishi. Thoughts of boons and blessings slipped away from her mind as she recalled how it felt to sit with him in the afternoon, how transported and transformed she had felt. For the first time in a long time, she was looking forward to something and she fell asleep with a smile on her face.

♋

Gandhari did not take any servants with her on her way to her meeting with Dvaipayana. It was not quite morning yet. Torches were still burning interspersed throughout the gardens and courtyard. She could see the outlines of the flickering flames through her blindfold. It was hard going as she rarely walked this far out to the furthest reaches of the gardens, but she made her way slowly, tapping the ground in front of her with one foot before taking a firm step, gripping swaying branches from the trees even as the thorns pricked her palms. The grass was wet with dew, slippery, so that her feet and the bottom hem of her sari were sodden by the time she reached the furthermost corner of the garden where Satyavati had commanded a small hut be built for her son. This area of the land bordered the river and Gandhari could hear the hum of the waves lapping gently against the banks of the river. The sound of the river, the cool air, the sensation of night slowly greying into dawn, was soothing. No wonder the rishis called this the holiest part of the day.

Dvaipayana muttered crossly as Gandhari knelt before him in prostration. 'I should have realized what a hardship it would be for you to come here in this state. Why didn't you a bring a servant with you to lead the way, girl?'

Gandhari smiled. 'One should not take any luxuries when visiting a holy site or a holy man. Even emperors leave behind their golden slippers, their crowns, all ornaments, when visiting the ashram of a guru or acharya. One should come barefoot and alone when in the presence of the holy ones.'

'Hmm.' His voice was pleased. 'You have learned well, my daughter. Come, sit next to me.'

Gandhari sat next to him. He offered her a small deerskin mat on which to sit, as the ground was still chilled from the dew and the coolness of the night. They faced the river. There was no elaborate worship ceremony today. He told her nothing, simply commenced with the special breathing exercises of pranayama and then fell silent, so silent that it felt as if he had stopped breathing. He entered into a deep meditative state almost immediately and Gandhari could feel that he was inaccessible now, as if he were in another world; as if, were she to reach over and touch him, he would be like stiff wood, a dead corpse.

Gandhari did not know what to do. She simply closed her eyes and breathed gently, trying to hold herself still and calm so that she would not inadvertently disturb his trance. After some time, she felt lulled into a different space. The boundaries between her body and the outside seemed to fluctuate, to become fluid and wavering, until she felt her being expand into space, cover the earth and grow, grow, grow, to cover the whole universe, to become one with the light, to be nothing but light, white, radiant, hot light, the light of sun that gave birth to and nourished all life, and far below her, she could see all the sentient beings of the universe, all the cows, human beings, plants, birds, oceans, all the wildlife residing in the oceans, and all of it was blessed and nourished by her; she was mother to all; she was mother to the entire universe.

As soon as that word came to her mind – mother – Dvaipayana stirred and she felt the trance break. She had never felt anything so sublime, so wonderful. She did not want it to end, but it was Dvaipayana who had carried her into that meditation and now that he was stirred, there was no way for her to go back. She was forcibly brought back into the present moment.

He cleared his throat gruffly after some minutes. Then, he sighed. 'Was there something you wished to ask me, Gandhari?'

She swallowed hard. 'No, revered one. There is nothing I have to ask of you.'

'Are you sure?'

She recalled Dhritarashthra's words and her unspoken promise to him. Neither could she break that promise, nor could she bring herself to ask something so worldly, so materialistic, of this great man who had already blessed her in so many ways, indescribably more precious to her than the mere fact of bearing children.

She was so torn that she said nothing.

Dvaipayana chuckled gently. 'When I sit in meditation, if one sits with me as you have, their desires are imprinted so clearly on the slate of my mind, I can see everything. You do not even have to ask me, child.'

She bowed her head in shame. Why it should shame her, she did not know, but it felt like such a trite blessing to seek, the most common boon sought by all women, to become a mother. Yes, there was the desire in her for children, to give birth to a son who would sit on the throne denied to her husband and to her. But surely there were higher things in life for which to aspire? It felt a silly thing to bother such a great sage about – the trivialities of family life.

'Child, do you know what fate is?'

Gandhari shook her head slightly. She knew, of course, in a simplistic way, but nothing Dvaipayana ever said was simple. Every sentence was full of profundities that she repeated over and over in her mind until she could glean their complete meaning.

'Fate is nothing more than the play of karma. Through actions, equal and opposing reactions are generated. They do not bear fruit immediately, but the storehouse of those reactions, those karmic forces, is powerful. Strands of karmic debts and forces come together, born of one's choices and actions in lifetime after lifetime, and then they take a momentum all their own. They propel one's life in this direction, in that direction. A normal mortal is buffeted in the storm of their own karma. Fate, what we call fate, is that propulsion of karma, a standing wave, a current, a tide, pulling in one direction.

'But, for one who is strong in will, fate is nothing. Free will is everything. They can alter the course of their destiny, ride the waves of karma but steer their life on the course of their choosing. That is why fate is always only a probability, never an inevitability. Do you understand, child?'

Gandhari shook her head in uncertainty. She understood the principle of what he was saying, but there was a message for her, a warning, an omen, a gem of advice, that she was not able to discern. She remembered what Satyavati had said about his words to her once, that subtlety of wisdom was more important than sharpness of intellect. She felt sorely lacking in that subtle insight at this moment.

'Do you not understand, child?' Dvaipayana whispered. 'I felt moved to call you to my meditation this morning. I never do that. My morning meditation is the most peaceful time of the day for me. I enjoy it in solitude, just me before the river, with the *devas* standing in front of me, the sun shining above me, the birdsong and scents of forest flowers and foliage my only company. And yet I felt moved to call you. As we sat together, I felt impelled to grant you a boon, unsought. Somehow, motherhood came to your mind and then immediately it came to mine. The words came to my lips unbidden, the words that would grant you the boon of giving birth to one hundred sons. As soon as I was aroused from meditation, I almost said the words, pronounced the blessings.

'But I stopped myself. I made myself stop it. Even now, I am holding it at bay, by sheer dint of my will. The *devas* are compelling me; the force of your karma is compelling me; the desire of your husband is compelling me; the twisting path of fate is compelling me; yet I am holding them all back. Do you know why, Gandhari?'

She was sweating now, even in the cool watery light of dawn. Her stomach was twisting and lurching wildly, and she thought she would vomit or soil her dress. She was short of breath and her heart pounded, thudding with heavy slams against her trembling breast. She felt caught up in a game she did not even know was being played. She felt like a small pawn in a large chessboard, where all the other players dwarfed her in skill and size. She did not know which way to move.

Her throat was dry as she whispered, 'Why?'

'Because you are a woman of iron will, Gandhari. A woman of remarkable strength and intelligence, of deep devotion and virtue. A noble woman, a truly noble woman. I want to give you the choice. I want it to be your decision. Do I grant the blessing or not?'

Sometimes a blessing felt like a curse. She did not know why in this case, but it did.

Gandhari racked her brain, trying to think what her father would do in this kind of a situation. He would buy time, figure out all the options available to him before making a decision. She licked her lips and asked, 'What other options do I have?'

Dvaipayana said dryly, 'It is not a menu for you to pick from, daughter. Wrong questions will never get the right answer.'

Her palms sweated. She closed her eyes and tried to think but nothing came. All she could see was Dhritarashthra asking her for the boon. She thought of Kunti and Madri, whom she despised. She thought of Pandu, of how he had no time for her anymore. She thought of her father, how painstakingly he had taken the time to teach her so much, how it was all going to waste now. And what could she do, blindfolded, in this palace to rule when she was thwarted at all sides by Kutili, who jealously guarded Dhritarashthra, Kunti and Madri and Satyavati who were conspiring to shore up Pandu's rule, and Pandu himself, who sidelined her as an elder sister to be honoured but not one whose advice or guidance he earnestly sought? At least with a child – a child who one day himself may become heir to the throne through the vagaries of fate – who knew, after all, when a crown prince or a king could fall, when the crown would again be up for grabs? – at least with a child, she could finally put her gifts and talents to use. She would teach him to rule as she had never been given the opportunity to rule herself.

Somewhere inside, she knew this was pettiness. She knew there was something higher, a better boon to ask for, or the highest of all – to not seek a boon at all, to just be content with the blessings of a great one. But perhaps she was not as strong as Dvaipayana thought she was. And that made her eyes tear, to think of disappointing this great one, after all that he had come to mean to her.

'Is it not my dharma to ensure the continuity of the lineage, to provide as many heirs as I can? Is that not the best thing I can do for the kingdom, for the family, for my husband, my duty as a wife and princess of the Kuru clan?'

Dvaipayana snorted: 'Do you need one hundred sons for that?' She wondered if he knew that he was using her own words from last night against her.

'In this family, it is best to hedge one's bets,' she replied coolly.

Dvaipayana guffawed. 'You have me there. Can't deny that. Girl, I will certainly miss your wit once I am gone. You remind me of my mother, but different. More refined and elegant, I suppose,' he commented fondly.

His voice changed into something sombre and gravelly. 'So be it. Let us not delay. It is time for me to go, too.'

Gandhari knelt and placed her head at his feet. He hesitated for a moment, then placed his hands on her head, and pronounced the traditional blessing, that she be blessed with one hundred sons.

As Gandhari rose to leave, he lingeringly held her hand. 'Daughter, at the end of your life, come to my hermitage in the forest. You shall always have a home there, even if I am not there. It is your home, do you understand?'

Gandhari nodded wordlessly and walked back to the palace. She dismissed the thought of his hermitage. Why would she live in the forest at the end of her life? She would have one hundred sons there to care for her, to be her company, to keep her in comfort and love until she passed away peacefully from this earth. That much she had won with this boon. Hadn't she?

4

THE FOREST. NOW

Sleep eluded Gandhari. The names of her sons did not bring her peace, after all, but brought back terrible grief. Snippets of dreams tormented her – of cradling Suyodhana's head on her lap as he napped interspersed with memories of holding his cold corpse in her lap, wailing and beating her head with her hands until her glass bangles shattered.

She woke up crying. She could not help it. It was night now and she could hear the distant murmur of voices that told her it was not yet so late. She lurched to her feet. She stumbled her way to Dhritarashthra's sleeping place. He slept closer to the hermitage. He was afraid of being alone. When she reached his side, she heard his wheezy snoring.

'Sanjaya! Sanjaya!' she called out in a stage whisper. He slept near Dhritarashthra to tend to him and comfort him when needed. She was no longer able to do that for her husband herself; neither did he warm to her, nor did she feel capable of giving him solace. There was no response. An irrational panic fluttered her heart. She patted around the straw pallet on which her husband slept, but there was no trace of Sanjaya. She crawled all around, but he was not there.

She perked her ears and traced the far-off conversation she had heard from her bed to closer to the river, to the wooden edifice of the hermitage where the sacrificial fire was tended, where the boys studied and the hermits sat for their morning and evening meditations. She stumbled towards them. Usually, she was so sure-footed but the tears wetting the bandage around her eyes and her shaking limbs made her clumsy.

She approached them finally; she could hear the hushed tones of conversation between Sanjaya and the hermit in charge of the ashram in Dvaipayana's absence. She could sense the flickering flames of the sacrificial fire and it offered her some comfort to see that cheerful glow, to know there were others here to give her company. Dvaipayana had ordered that the fire never be allowed to go out, that it be constantly tended to and kept alive by the acolytes of the ashram. He himself was an infrequent visitor to his own hermitage these days. He spent most of his time wandering across the Himalayas. When he came back, it was to write – to compile and divide the Vedas, to pen the Puranas, the history of the times in which they lived. One day, he would write down this story, too, the story of Gandhari, Dhritarashthra, Kunti and Pandu and their sons, a story in which he played such an integral part.

Sanjaya was startled. 'Queen! What are you doing awake? What is wrong?'

'Sanjaya, I need your help.' Her voice broke.

Sanjaya rushed to her side and brought her closer to the fire, seating her on a log covered with a blanket. The hermit, after ensuring she was safe, walked away to give them privacy.

'Queen, what is wrong?' Sanjaya's voice was soft with concern.

Gandhari sniffled and was disgusted at her own weakness; to be a weepy woman went against everything she was, yet she could not help herself. The existential terror of what was to come made her tremble with fear and paranoia. Her nightmares brought to mind visions of hellish after-worlds, of an afterlife full of punishment for her wrongdoing. Her voice was broken with hiccoughs. 'Sanjaya, you will stay alive as we discussed, yes? You will not die along with us, yes? You will carry our news to the others?'

'Yes, Kunti has told me to do so. I do not wish to abandon either you or the king, even in death, but I will not disobey a command, if it comes from you, Queen.'

Gandhari was still in enough of possession of her senses to hear the faint reproach that it had been Kunti and not her or Dhritarashthra who had held that conversation with him. Her cheeks flamed in embarrassment. Sanjaya had always devoted himself to her and her husband, and at the end, they could not even take proper care of him. He was their responsibility, not Kunti's. It made her feel even more ashamed that she had come now to beg him a favour. How ill he must think of her. Her face dropped. How ashamed Subala, her father, would have been of how lax she had grown in her duties.

Sanjaya prodded her: 'Queen, tell me. You know I will do anything for you.'

She took a deep breath and calmed herself down enough to talk coherently, 'Sanjaya, when I die, who will be there to light the pyre? To perform the shraddha ceremonies for me? I have no sons left. How can I have a peaceful passing and transition to the afterlife without a son to perform the funeral rites for me?'

'I am sure that Yudhishthira will do the needful. He has always treated you like a mother.'

Even Gandhari could not fault Yudhishthira. At the end of the war, it had been Suyodhana, defeated by Bhima in battle, as he lay dying, who had encouraged the last three warriors left on his side to go destroy the Pandavas, who had permitted their sons to be killed in their sleep. And yet, Yudhishthira never punished her for it. Bhima and the other brothers sometimes taunted Dhritarashthra and her after the war, after they were all living uncomfortably together in the palace, but Yudhishthira, never.

Yet, she could not bring herself to accept that honour from him. She owed him too much – the karmic debt was already heavily tilted towards someone who was not her own son, and she did not wish to be further in debt of one who her sons had wronged so grievously. And also, after all this time, it still smarted, that he should live and not her sons. The five sons of Pandu survived, while all one hundred of her sons had died. It still made her want to beat the earth and wail in protest.

'No, it would not be appropriate to ask this of him. Sanjaya, will you do it? Please tell me you will do it.'

Sanjaya assured her softly that he would.

Gandhari laughed bitterly, the gasps of laughter morphing into choked sobs. 'One hundred sons! At least one should have remained to do this much for me. What was the point of it all? For two years, I bore them; for two years, I nursed them. This was the blessing given to me, twice, by Shiva and by Dvaipayana. And yet what did I get out of it? Nothing! Nothing! What kind of a blessing is it that a mother outlives her children, that she eats and drinks and keeps living, keeps wanting to live, even when the reason for her life, her very flesh and blood, are gone?'

Sanjaya replied gently: 'Queen, they died by their own actions. You know that. It was not the gods punishing you. Blessings cannot outweigh karma, the choices one makes, the actions one takes. There is no shortcut to avoid that, Queen. You know this.'

The tears flowed down unchecked, dampening the faded cotton cloth at her breast. 'I should have known better! I made the wrong choice.'

Sanjaya said nothing.

Gandhari was feeling lightheaded. Her hands scrabbled the ground. 'Is this where he sat? Is this where he meditated?' The words tumbled forth in a jumbled mess.

'Who, Queen?' Sanjaya fretted in puzzlement at her non-sequitur.

'Dvaipayana? Are we near the river?'

Sanjaya tried to make his voice soothing. 'Yes, Queen. The river is right there. You can hear it.'

Gandhari stilled her breathing and cocked her ears. She could hear it now, the waves lapping the banks. She remembered sitting with Dvaipayana, near the river, in Hastinapur, when he had given her the boon that she would have one hundred sons. She remembered that feeling of peace, expansiveness, the lightness of being.

'Is this where he would sit in meditation?' Her voice was desperate.

'Yes, Queen. Why? What is wrong? Why are you so agitated? Please be calm, my Queen. All will be well.'

Gandhari inhaled deeply and tried to go into that state where Dvaipayana had led her. She tried very hard. She tried to summon his presence by will alone, to recall the sensation of sitting next to him, to relive that one moment of her past. But there was too much churning inside her, too many dark waves of memory and grief.

She remembered now the warning he had given her, the way he tried to offer her advice, to seek something else, but she had rejected it. She began crying harder, giving up the efforts to slip into meditation, as if meditation could enter a troubled mind like hers. 'I should have listened! I should have asked for something different. Peace! Clarity! Wisdom! Anything but this. Anything but this grief, multiplied by one hundred! Oh, why did he not tell me? Why did he not just tell me?'

She knew all the reasons why, why the great ones and even the *devas* could not interfere with the play of human life, that they had to let the great pattern of karma unfold for itself, but it did not tamp down her pain now. She dug her fingers into the dirt, seeking something she could not find, and her hands were so strong that great clods of earth came loose and she threw them aimlessly, trying to hit something, but what she did not know. She lifted her face to the moon and wailed.

The wail was enough to pierce the sky, to wake the sleeping birds and send them scattering from their nests. Even Sanjaya was frightened and shrank away. She had lost all dignity now; she was naked in her grief and rage. She began beating her chest, striking it hard with the iron marriage bangles, hoping to draw blood.

Then came Kunti, solid, placid, unstoppable, unfazed Kunti. She did not hurry. Her tread was measured and plodding. She did not say a word, simply sat on her haunches in front of Gandhari and planted her hands on Gandhari's arms, gripping them down her sides so she stopped clawing the dirt, beating her chest. Her grip was fierce, almost painful. For once, Gandhari was grateful for the solidity, the heaviness of Kunti, how she ground her down, how she was like gravity, keeping Gandhari's feet planted on the earth.

'Be still, sister,' Kunti commanded her sternly. 'You are making a spectacle of yourself and waking up all of the hermits and even the animals.'

Gandhari quietened, hiccupping and sniffling softly now. 'They are all gone,' she whispered. 'They are all gone.' As if eighteen years had not been enough to remove the shock of it, the loss of them, the absence of touching their hair, feeding them, embracing them, hearing their unruly laughter and loud voices echoing through the halls of Hastinapur.

Kunti folded her into her arms, hard. It was not an embrace, it was a hard grip meant to numb her, to physically stop the spread of the pain and the grief, to replace anguish with that dull pain of her hold. Neither did Gandhari lay her head on her shoulder, nor did Kunti offer any tenderness. But she was grateful for those two arms that pressed her like a vice, that held her intact.

Karma – the generation of an equal and opposite reaction. Once, just once, Gandhari had held Kunti like that, when Kunti was herself lost to grief, when Karna, her eldest son died near the end of the war, when her other sons could offer her no comfort for they did not know he was their brother and if they had known, they would not have forgiven her so quickly, so easily. Gandhari and Kunti never spoke of that moment, just as they never would speak of this – they never gave voice or name to the bitter enmity and the empathy that wove themselves together like two strands into the unbreakable bond that held them together from the time of their marriages to the time, now approaching, of their death.

Hastinapur, Then

The day began with an ominous rumble of thunder. Even though the monsoon season had passed, omens of foreboding abounded. Crows circled the main entrance of the palace, signifying death. While preparing the food to be offered to the ancestors and *devas*, Gandhari kept spilling spices. The first batch of rice got burned to a black crisp; the second did not cook properly, even after an hour. The milk soured and curdled. Even the flowers seemed to lose their scent as Gandhari picked them in the garden.

Late in the morning, one of the scouts who had accompanied Pandu on a hunting trip in a nearby forest dashed into the palace, skidding to a halt in front of Satyavati and Bhishma, breathless, where they presided over the audience hall. It was the day when the court was open to all constituents for the king to hear and address the grievances of all the people; the deliberations and decisions were made in public, in front of the people, whom ultimately the king served. Pandu, when he was there, and now Bhishma, in Pandu's stead, would take the advice of his ministers and various brahmanas on the spot.

They would bring in various law books, the *dharma shastras*, for citations and guidance for the decision to be made. There was healthy debate, and even when the ministers were in agreement, Pandu would, in the interest of fairness, often ask some of the ministers to play the other side and tease out the counter-arguments and multiple angles from which the issue was to be seen.

So, it was a full crowd in the palace when the scout suddenly appeared. Gandhari was sitting with Kunti and Madri, off to the side from Satyavati and Bhishma, the platform on which they sat a little lower from where the elders sat. Dhritarashthra was still sleeping in his chambers. Vidura was there, though.

Satyavati exclaimed, 'What is it, young boy? Why have you come in such a hurry like this? Is Pandu well?' She ordered one of the attendants to bring him some water, as he had clearly exhausted himself running here at full sprint.

'Your highness, the king has sent me. He wants everyone to be gathered together to hear him when he returns from the hunting party. He is a few hours behind me. He says it is important that *everyone* be here, including his brothers.' Gandhari noted that he must have meant that for Dhritarashthra, who was prone to sleeping the day away. 'He has an announcement to make.'

Gandhari twisted her sari in her hands. She thought she would be sick. It could not be a good thing, whatever the announcement was. That was why there were so many bad signs in the morning. Was he well? Had he been injured? Oh, why could the scout not speak more freely! Or, was it that Kunti or Madri were pregnant? She had a sinking feeling in her stomach. She pressed down on her own flat belly spitefully. When would she finally become pregnant?

Satyavati maintained her even composure, not betraying a hint of the anxiety Gandhari knew that she must be feeling. She announced: 'So be it. We shall finish going through the requests of the people in the *sabha*, assembly, first and then, when my grandson arrives, we shall listen to his announcement.' Gandhari understood that she wanted to clear as much of the crowd as possible before Pandu's return. Satyavati dared not break court; that would only spread panic and fear.

Vidura left to rouse Dhritarashthra and get him ready for court. *What would we do without Vidura?* Gandhari thought, this brother who had the wisdom and humility of someone who would have made a perfect king.

Finally, after two hours, the entire procession that had accompanied Pandu to the forest returned. It had been a pleasure trip, one of the occasional days of leisure Pandu allowed himself. Ayla whispered to her that Pandu was at the head of the procession, that he walked calmly, that he looked fine.

'Is he injured? Is he in pain?' Gandhari's voice was urgent.

'No, my lady, he looks his normal self. Just eerily calm.'

Waves of relief washed over Gandhari. Whatever it was could not be so bad, so long as Pandu was safe and in good health.

The court had half emptied, as the morning's business had been concluded. Many curious bystanders lingered, however, keen to know what was happening after the cryptic message delivered by the scout. Pandu approached the throne slowly, deliberately. Gandhari recognized his unique tread, the confident yet controlled march of someone who was more warrior than ruler. There was always something so militaristic and disciplined about him. He made his prostrations to the brahmanas of the court, to Satyavati, to Bhishma, to his brother and Gandhari. Ayla did not describe this to her. Gandhari knew this was his routine, and she could feel his body move from this side to the other as he bent his head at their feet. She imagined she could feel it.

'Revered grandmother, I have returned. There is something of great import that I must announce.'

'Shall we wait until we are in private to discuss it, son?'

As even as their voices were, the tension was so thick in the air that it almost crackled like a flame. Oh! How Gandhari

wished she could remove her blindfold to see for herself
what was happening. Even Ayla was so caught up in what
was happening that she did not remember to whisper her
observations to Gandhari as frequently as she usually did.

'No, Queen Mother. It pertains to all the people of the
kingdom. They will know of it eventually, so it is only meet
that they hear it directly from my lips as their king.'

Gandhari's heart began to thud. She heard Dhritarashthra
inhale sharply and sit up straighter in his chair. Her palms
started to sweat.

'Go on,' encouraged Satyavati softly.

Pandu spoke as if he were making a military report to a
commander, his voice bland and devoid of feeling, as if this
Pandu that he spoke of were some stranger of no consequence
and not himself. 'I had gone for the hunt. Everything was going
very well. Then I saw a stag. A beautiful looking stag. He ran so
fast. I chased him through forest after forest. He was the leader
of the herd, obviously, he was so strong and fast. I had lost him
for some time but then saw him again as dusk was beginning
to fall. He was mating with a doe.'

'I shot them both with five golden-feathered arrows. I had
hunted my fill; yet, they were so beautiful, I could not resist.'

A cold sweat slid between Gandhari's shoulder blades. To
kill them when they were mating smacked of bloodlust, of a
cruelty that was unlike the Pandu that she knew. It startled her.

'The stag was dying, and as it lay dying, it started speaking
to me in a human voice.' Pandu swallowed hard. 'It was not a
deer; it was a rishi, the great rishi, Kimdama. He had tired of
being in the human form and had taken the form of a deer,
along with his wife, to find peace and contentment within
the forest. He faulted me for striking them with my arrows.
He said that in earlier days, the hunter never unleashed arrows
against an unprepared prey. He faulted me for killing him in
the midst of such intimacy with his wife, reproached me for

undertaking such a cruel act.' His voice dwindled to a whisper. 'And indeed it was. It was a cruel act.'

Satyavati's voice trembled. She knew what it meant to displease a rishi, the powers they wielded, the curses that almost inevitably ensued, especially from one who lay dying. 'And then what happened, son?'

Pandu's voice was reluctant, but he mustered the strength to complete the tale. 'He told me that since I had been cruel to a helpless couple, the next time that I am overcome by desire, death will come to claim me at that very instant that I give into the desire to touch a woman. And, at that time, my beloved woman whom I reach out to, my wife, will also perish. The last thing he said before he died in great pain and anguish was, "You have now brought me into grief when I was in the midst of pleasure. Like that, you will be afflicted with misery when you have just found happiness."'

A great silence descended over the hall. Everyone was thunderstruck. It meant that Pandu could never be with a woman again, without drawing death for himself and the woman involved. If he did, Kunti or Madri would die, too. It meant Pandu would have to be celibate in order to preserve their lives. A rishi's curse, once issued, could never be retracted. A piercing wail emitted from Madri. Kunti quickly shushed her.

Gandhari longed to be next to Satyavati, to be able to hold her hand through this, even though she knew Satyavati would not permit it in public like this. *Karma*, Gandhari thought to herself, *the creation of an equal and opposing reaction. Even the kings, even the great ones, are not immune to it*. She shivered at the hardness of the world, the hardness of life, that allowed one single moment of error, a mistake, to ruin a life, multiple lives, ricocheting across the web of karma to irrevocably change the course of life for so many people in the space of a heartbeat.

Pandu continued, as if this were a matter of trifling news and not a disaster that had upended his life. 'This curse is a blessing in

disguise. My own father died prematurely due to his addiction
to desire for his wives. The words of the rishi are true. My lowly
mind has been spent on the evil chase of deer, on chasing my
wives, especially Madri. I have not made time for the higher
pursuits of life. I think of the greatness of Dvaipayana, by whose
merit my brothers and I have been born. He spends his life
performing austerities in the Himalayas. His is the example I
should follow.

'Like Dvaipayana, I will now live alone in the forest, spending
each day under a different tree. I will shave my head and live as
a hermit, begging for food, while roaming the lands. Once a day
only shall I beg for food, and never from more than seven families.
If I cannot live off what I have begged from these families, I will
fast. I will worship the ancestors and the *devas* with food found
in the forest, with water and with words.' This was the path of
austerity that dulled the hunger of the senses, the life in which
celibacy could be maintained. Bhishma had the force of will to
be celibate in the midst of palace life, surrounded by beautiful
women and luxurious surroundings and food that enticed the
senses, but Gandhari did not think Pandu was capable of it. That
was perhaps why he chose to exile himself into the forest.

Satyavati cried out softly. It was like Bhishma all over again,
when Bhishma had renounced his claim to the throne and
become a celibate. That time, it was for her, in her favour. Now,
her grandson was being forced to do the same, when she most
needed him on the throne, to continue the dynasty. *Karma; it
is inescapable. She is reaping what she sowed*, thought Gandhari.

Kunti spoke in a firm voice: 'We are your wives under
Dharma. If you go to the forest, we shall accompany you. Our
life is with you and with you only. If you will take *vanaprastha*[1]

---

1   The third stage of life, after the life of a married householder, when
     one retires to the forest for a life of contemplation and quietude, in
     preparation for the stage of complete renunciation, the last stage of life,
     sannyasa.

now, so shall we. You can spend the *vanaprastha* portion of your life with us and still perform great austerities.'

Madri echoed Kunti's words, although much more reluctantly.

Everything began to happen so quickly. Pandu made arrangements to depart immediately. Gandhari sat, frozen in place, too paralyzed by shock to even assist Kunti and Madri in their packing, to offer them any comfort or solace. The queen in her could not help but recognize the possibilities this opened up for her and Dhritarashthra, for their sons who would be born one day. Bhishma had so far served as regent when Pandu was away, but he was growing old and now it would be Dhritarashthra who would be the regent and, if Pandu's exile were to be permanent, the king in reality.

But those were thoughts scattered in the background of her mind. They brought her no succour. Her mind was too seized by grief, by a terrible empathy for the plight of Pandu, by the shock of loss of his company, the fear of being the only royal couple left in the palace, by feeling totally unprepared for what would be coming next. In a way, she had grown used to being in the recesses of the court and she no longer felt confident to sit on the throne reserved for the queen.

Pandu offered the jewels from his crown to the brahmanas, and Kunti and Madri gave all their jewellery away to the wives of the brahmanas. Kunti and Madri were mute and said nothing as they came to take the blessings of the elders before their long journey into the jungle. The onlookers at court and the ministers left the palace, to give the family their privacy. They went to the city gates to await their beloved king to accompany them as far towards the forest as possible on foot.

Pandu came last to take their blessings. Bhishma and Satyavati wept openly. Bhishma, especially, was distraught, his great body racked by loud sobs that boomed against the walls of the chamber. Gandhari wanted to plug her ears to never again hear such sorrow. The pain of elders was something far more terrible to bear than one's own.

No one grieved as dramatically and theatrically as Dhritarashthra, however. He wept and howled, fussing over his brother with words of love and sorrow. Gandhari was unmoved. She knew it was a farce. She knew that later, in the privacy of their chamber, he would cackle with glee at the throne that suddenly now seemed to be in reach. *Was this my doing? Did I catalyse this for Pandu, through my own desires, through the boon I sought from Dvaipayana?*

Pandu spent long minutes conferring with Vidura, as the wise brother offered him advice and comfort and as Pandu whispered to him instructions, probably to protect and look after Satyavati, Ambika and Ambalika. Finally, Pandu came to Gandhari and knelt at her feet.

She felt him look up to her as he whispered: 'Am I doing the right thing, sister?'

Gandhari did not know how to answer. It was a complicated business, this taking of vows, this game of blessings and curses. It was murky and led to unexpected outcomes. It was like walking a razor's edge. But her heart was full of tenderness and admiration for this brother of hers, who had taken what seemed like a most cruel and unfair curse and was making it into a noble pursuit for his own salvation. She placed her hand on top of his head as a blessing but also to give comfort.

'You are doing what is noble and strong, brother. You are following the path of the aryas. You will be the pride of your ancestors.' She paused and swallowed the tears clogging her throat. She tried to imbue as much of her virtue and meagre powers as she could into the words that followed, a traditional blessing. She said it not as a platitude but an earnest request from the *devas*, a true blessing an elder sister may pronounce on her brother: 'May you live one hundred years, brother. May you live one hundred years.'

But her powers had perhaps not yet matured. Her blessing did not come true.

☙

Dhritarashthra reached for her again and again in the weeks that followed. Every night, sometimes multiple times a night. Sometimes he did not even wait until she was in the proper season. There was nothing manly about it; it was a desperate clawing, a clambering desire for the throne, not for her, a grunting effete effort lasting less than a few minutes, shuddering onto her body. She remembered the mistakes of her mother-in-law and aunt-in-law; so, she never flinched, never even closed her eyes behind the blindfold. She was calm and collected and determined, deep in breath and slow in heartbeat. She did the work. When his hand fluttered towards hers, she was the one who gripped him firmly, who took him into herself, who made him impregnate her.

And then, one night, she felt a dull pain in her lower abdomen. It was a heaviness, like a boulder lodged in her soft underbelly, pulling downward. She gritted her teeth. She could bear it. She could bear anything. She closed her eyes in gratitude towards Shiva and Dvaipayana, who had blessed her with this baby, the first of many children to come. She prayed for the baby to be well.

She waited weeks to be sure before she informed the others. It surprised her that she was not showing yet, but she had missed her season twice now and she could feel life growing within her. Dhritarashthra was so overcome by the news that he fainted. Satyavati, withdrawn and cold ever since Pandu had gone into exile, exhaled a sigh of relief and brusquely patted her on the head with a blessing. Vidura became worried and quiet, not even mustering a congratulatory word.

Bhishma, for once, was the most exultant one. He had become busier than ever in Pandu's absence, picking up the slack on governing Hastinapur as Dhritarashthra still did not bother doing any of the actual work of ruling. When Gandhari pressed him to take upon himself the role of king, now that Pandu was in exile, Dhritarashthra refused petulantly, saying he would not until the throne was officially in his name. 'For that, Pandu would have to be dead!' she exclaimed in exasperation. Or abdicate, but she could not imagine Pandu doing that.

Her husband chortled, 'Knowing how fond he is of Madri, that could be any day now!'

She turned up her nose at disgust.

'I shall not play the role of king until the crown in officially put on my head, and that is that.' For once, his voice was firm. So, it was Bhishma who took on Pandu's role in fact even though Dhritarashthra was the regent in name.

Bhishma pulled Gandhari aside after he heard the news of her pregnancy. He intoned solemnly, 'Queen, now the entire fate and future of the Kuru clan rests inside your belly. You must take great care. We are all dependent on you now. You are the most important person in the kingdom; the honour and destiny of our lineage, the fate of our dynasty – all of this rides on you now. It is a heavy burden, yet a great honour, too.'

They were sitting in the chamber adjacent to the main audience hall, where the king gathered together with the ministers and other advisers to deliberate and strategize in private. Low cushioned chairs were arranged in concentric circles. Bhishma had taken a seat next to her; usually, he sat at some distance from her.

He is trying to curry my favour, to buy my loyalty to the Kuru clan. He is trying to make sure I will toe his line. Now is the time to press my advantage.

'It is as you say, revered uncle. The entire future of the family is in within my womb. Futures are best safeguarded when there is certainty.'

She could imagine his frown as he stuttered, 'Of course, you shall have the best of all doctors and *vaidyas*, Gandhari. You will be cared for to ensure you are in comfort always. Why do you even worry about that?'

She replied lightly, 'Oh, I am not worried about that in the least.' She deepened and hardened her voice. 'But if you understand now that my baby is the only future you have for *our* lineage, then you need to make it official.'

He became wary. 'What is it you want?'

'Declare that my eldest son shall be the heir to the throne, just as Pandu was so declared when he was born.'

'Pandu was declared *king* when he was born because there was no king at that time, only Dhritarashthra who was rendered unfit to be king due to his blindness. Even if you give birth to a son, Pandu will still be king.'

Gandhari put a protective hand on her belly. 'I will give birth to a son. I am sure of it. One hundred sons, in fact. Remember, that is the blessing I bring to you. It is what you brought me for. It is not so easy a feat bearing one hundred sons. You should at least make clear their status. Do not leave any further uncertainty.'

'When he is born, whatever needs to be clarified shall be clarified. Never fear. I shall not allow the throne of Hastinapur to go unoccupied by one of our own.'

'At least to me you could give me your word, that my husband's eldest son shall be heir to the throne. Pandu has renounced the royal life. He lives as a hermit, with shaved head, begging for alms. He is no longer king, in fact. The least you could do is clarify that even though my husband is not king, our son will be.'

Bhishma said pointedly, 'Pandu has not abdicated the throne.'

'You did not ask him to. You did nothing to clear up the state of affairs. You have left the fate of the throne uncertain, susceptible to outside claimants with no clear line of succession.'

Bhishma's voice became sharp and angry. 'Pandu shall be king until the day he dies or the day he abdicates the throne in favour of another. You shall not snatch it from him!'

Gandhari sneered, 'He is living in the mountains somewhere! He sleeps and eats in the forest, living a life of idyllic solitude. He has given up all the duties of governance. He knows nothing about what is happening with his subjects. He is king? A hermit, thousands of yojanas away, can be king, but not the blind man, the eldest son, who is living in the palace, amongst the people?'

He laughed contemptuously, 'My dear, I do not think you want to get into a debate of which of these two brothers has done more when it comes the work and duties of governance. Do you? When has your husband ever acted like a king?'

Gandhari bristled. This is why she had been admonishing Dhritarashthra to be more active. It would have strengthened their hand. She said stiffly, 'It does not matter. My son will never neglect his duties. He will be an able administrator. He will rule effectively and well. As the daughter of Subala, that much I promise!'

Bhishma replied softly, 'That much I do believe, Gandhari.' He sighed, hoping to draw the conversation to a close. 'If you are so certain about the turn of events to come, then why do you worry, Queen?'

'Because this family always keeps everything so vague. You think it is hedging bets to leave things open. I am telling you, too much ambiguity causes confusion and conflict. You will pay the price for it later. Make things clear-cut and official. Otherwise, there will be plots and conspiracies to take advantage of the grey areas, the questions you leave open deliberately. Too many strange things occur here. Too many clever schemes. I do not want my sons to fall victim to the vagaries of fate or to some calculated plot that would deprive them of their rightful place.'

Bhishma inhaled sharply. 'Watch yourself, daughter. I am the scion of the Kuru dynasty. The entire Kuru clan. That includes you. My loyalty is not to Pandu, not to any particular king or nephew. My loyalty is to the throne and the throne alone. I will safeguard the interests of all the Kurus, including your sons. With my blood, with my life. Do not ever doubt or question that!'

Gandhari shrank back from the offended rage of Bhishma. Perhaps she had pressed too hard. She composed herself: 'I request at least that you send word to Pandu and Kunti of the impending birth. They deserve to know.'

Bhishma scoffed, 'I had expected somewhat better of you, my dear. I had not thought you would want to flaunt your success and gloat before them, they who will be deprived of ever having their own children.'

She thought of Pandu and Kunti. Kunti. Strong-willed, determined, implacable Kunti. *She is capable of anything.* 'They should know,' she murmured. He assented with a sigh.

She thought of Kunti again. She was not the type to give up, ever. She was her equal when it came to willpower and fierceness. Fear flickered in Gandhari's heart.

Finally, at six months, Gandhari began to show. It was a small, hard protuberance. It was barely visible, and Ayla told her worriedly how everyone was watching her figure expectantly every time she appeared before the family, before the public. There were looks of concern on the faces of Satyavati, Bhishma, Vidura, and deeper frowns on the faces of the ministers. Kutili, Dhritarashthra's maid, stared at her belly obsessively and made whispered reports to Dhritarashthra, who shook his head sadly. All this Ayla reported to her.

What do they expect? Can I make the baby bigger in my belly somehow? I am doing the best I can.

Yet, the anxiety got to her, too. Her dreams were haunted by babies. She knew very well that she was married into this family because of the boon that she would bear them one hundred sons. It brought a sheen of sweat to her forehead to think of what would happen, how far she would fall, if she could not deliver. She was the only hope of producing a royal heir to the throne. She could not fail. She pressed her hands into her belly, willing that foetus to life, willing it to grow strong and healthy, willing it to be a boy.

All of her prayers she poured into that belly. Into producing the perfect baby, the perfect heir, the one who would one day be king. That mass inside her, that rock-like hardness that felt like a tumour, began to grow and expand, spreading tentacles across her inner flesh, feeding on her marrow and blood. She became progressively weaker but revelled in that weakness, knowing her strength was going into her son. It became harder and harder to walk. Her belly grew so heavy in mass that she could not keep her balance when she walked.

Now it was the doctors' turn to become worried. They had never seen a pregnancy like this. They could not detect anything about the baby, not even a heartbeat. But something was growing inside her. They worried that the baby would be stillborn. Whether she had already had a miscarriage. Whether it was a disease, not a child, that was ravaging her body from within. They worried it was a demon who had taken root inside her, that she was being visited upon by some evil ghost. They worried she would die.

Gandhari thought she would vomit from all the worry, all the speculation. She was careful not to vomit. She wanted to safeguard each morsel of nutrition for her babies – now she had started thinking of them in the plural. The mass in her belly had become hot and fiery, burning through the lining of her flesh like acid, sending streams of bile upwards. She was sweating all the time; even when she bathed in cold water, it was like a fever that suffused her skin, made it red and splotchy, unbearably sensitive, hot to touch. She began moaning, a low, guttural, whining moan, unbeknownst even to her, so out of sorts was she, that she did not even know she was making that noise. If she had known, she would have been mortified.

Fed up with the doctors worrying and fussing over her, Gandhari finally threw them all out, disregarding Bhishma's protest. As they filed out, one admonished her that she was at risk of delivering too early, before the baby was ready to be born, if there even was a baby. It was a female *vaidya*. Her voice was stern and she sounded experienced, a true expert. She warned her to stay on continued bedrest with her legs suspended above her head, to keep the baby in. She told her that was the only way. Despite herself, Gandhari believed her.

And so Gandhari shut herself into a dark chamber. Ayla tied her feet together and lifted them up on a stack of cushions so that her feet were elevated above her head. Ayla was the only servant who would remain with her. The others had become too frightened by what was growing in Gandhari's belly and by her terrible mood. She was like a woman possessed. Her parents wrote and wished to visit her, but she refused to see them. She could not bear that after so many years they would see her like this.

Ayla was the only one who could soothe her. She lay next to her, washing her forehead with a wet scented cloth, fanning her in the unbearable heat of summer, reading her stories of her favourite kings and queens, the ones Subala used to tell her when she was a child. With Ayla, Gandhari could weep openly, gasping in pain when she felt the baby beating against the walls of her belly with hammering fists, perhaps as impatient to enter the world as she was to welcome him into it.

One day, Gandhari complained to Ayla, 'It feels like I have one hundred babies inside of me, Ayla, all waiting to be born.

That would really be a fine mess, if I am to bear all one hundred sons at once!' Ayla clucked sympathetically.

It was Gandhari's intent to imbue her baby with education even while he was in the womb. She wanted to recite all of the hymns to the *devas* that she had learned, to surround him with auspicious vibrations, to give him the company of the *devas*. She wanted to teach him all that Subala had taught her, reciting the names of all the eminent dynasties and lineages of the ruling families of Bharat, the history of their kingdom, the glories of their ancestors, the conquests, the piety, the might and valour of the family into which he would be born. She wanted to tell him about the values by which to live, how to care for and win the favour of the people, the duties of a king.

But in this too she was thwarted by Dhritarashthra. He would lie next to her in bed for hours, whispering bitterly into her belly, how he had been deprived of the throne by fate, how all of his hopes were vested in him, this baby boy who would finally win for him the throne he was denied, how he would do anything to make him succeed and secure his interests; he would lie, scheme, steal, kill, if he had to, to make sure his boy sat on the throne of Hastinapur.

Gandhari sometimes tried to put her hands on her belly to protect the baby from these venomous outpourings, as if she could cover the baby's ears so he would not hear this poison. But she was so discombobulated by weakness and strain, by the pulsing mass of flesh that was eating away at her, that she lacked the strength to keep her husband away from her belly, to inoculate her baby from his spite. Every time she tried to talk, her teeth chattered uncontrollably. Her limbs shook like she was in palsy every time she tried to move.

Months and months passed. It had been a year now, over a year, and still no babies emerged from her womb. Gandhari grew weaker and weaker. She was on the verge of unconsciousness all the time but lacked the respite of sleep in this limbo state between being awake and unconscious. She was tormented by nightmares of hellish worlds full of fire and demons. In her visions, all she saw was a blazing fire spread across the entire horizon, scorching her skin as she walked through it, looking for her babies. Every time she opened her mouth to call out to them, she swallowed fire and her organs withered and died. She became a walking skeleton. But still she went after her babies. They began to cry out to her, like hatchlings. She heard their cries, faint through the din of the roaring fire, that howled as it ate more and more of the world, consuming and charring everything in sight. She never saw them, only heard their cries, crawling and groping through this world of fire. She lived more in this nightmarish world in those last several months of her pregnancy than in the world of her stuffy, dank chamber.

It was as if she had been left to die.

Bhishma stopped visiting; Satyavati stopped sending special foods to nourish her. Even Dhritarashthra shrank away and retreated to his own chambers. Only Vidura was regular in checking in on her, providing special herbs to cool and soothe her. Ayla never left her side.

Gandhari stopped counting the days, once her pregnancy exceeded a year. And so, she did not know whether it had been three years or five or just one day beyond the first year, that day, when Dhritarashthra came running to her chamber. It had been months since he had visited her, and Gandhari stirred in surprise, trying to wake herself into a lucid state. She tried to comb her hair with her fingers, to appear presentable, but she had grown so weak that her hair felt too heavy for her hands.

She was startled to hear Ayla throw herself against Dhritarashthra, trying to forcibly bar him from entering the room. Ayla cried out, 'Leave! Leave! She is not fit for you to visit. Do not bother her now!'

Dhritarashthra was ranting incoherently, trying to push his way in.

Gandhari cried out, 'Ayla! What are you doing? He is my husband. Let him in.'

Ayla sobbed but obeyed. Even Kutili appeared perturbed. She had escorted Dhritarashthra here but now urged him to go back. 'Sir, another time. Not now. She is too weak. She will not be able to bear it.'

Gandhari's heart began to pound in terror. How bad could it be if even Kutili was trying to protect her against Dhritarashthra? Had she miscarried without realizing it? Her hands groped towards her belly. No, that pulsing mass was still there, throbbing inside her belly. She twisted her head, trying to hear better what was going on, through the ringing in her ears that had grown constant in the past few weeks.

Dhritarashthra pushed both of them aside and leaned over Gandhari, snarling: 'You promised me! You promised me one hundred sons!'

She began to quake. 'That is what Shiva has promised me. That is what Dvaipayana promised me. Surely, it will come true.' It hurt her to talk, so parched was her throat, so long had it been since someone had spoken to her, since she had managed to drink a few drops of water. Even though he was yelling at her so bitterly that spittle fell from his mouth onto her chin, it was almost a relief to have a human interaction again, to feel like someone cared enough to visit.

'It is no use now. No use! One son or one hundred. You are too late, woman, too late. You have been in this room for over a year now. Over one year, and still no baby! Still no heir!'

'I am trying my best.' As dehydrated as she was, tears started trickling down her cheeks, thinking how long she had been locked away here, how desperately she had tried to bear and keep inside her the weight of the foetuses until her babies were ready to be born. *What more could I have done?*

He sputtered indignantly: 'Well, you need not bother anymore. Kunti has given birth to a boy. Pandu has an heir!'

She tried to lift her head, shock freezing the blood in her veins. 'Kunti? Pandu? H–how? And Pandu is still alive? How is it possible? The curse – i–it cannot be possible!'

'How do I know! I was not there to witness the act, was I? They sent word by a messenger. The messenger was a rishi, no less! So, no doubt could be cast on the truth of the matter. A hale, healthy son, as fair and noble as Yama, the god of death and righteousness, himself! That is what they say.'

'Our son was conceived first,' Gandhari whispered defiantly.

He laughed hollowly. 'And what difference does that make? He will be born last! We lose yet again. Woman, we are done for now.' And with that, he left.

For long minutes, Gandhari was shell-shocked. She could not believe it! Pandu had adopted the life of a hermit, a celibate living on alms in the forests far away in the Himalayas. He would not have turned back on his vow. How could he have sired a child with Kunti, then? Her heart hurt, literally hurt, at the image of Pandu and Kunti bent over their little baby boy, the very picture of a happy family. And look at her now, stuck in this dark chamber that smelled of sweat and blood for over a year, left for dead, abandoned by all except her maid, Ayla, with a raving mad husband who blamed her for not having gone into childbirth earlier. What had she come to? How low had she fallen?

For months and months, she had held that mass of life within her, protecting it with all her strength and will, gritting her teeth through the worst kinds of pain, defying the concerns of doctors and nurses, in order to keep that foetus safe. She had taken Bhishma's command to keep safe the future of the Kuru clan that rested within her belly very seriously. She had nursed it with her blood, her marrow, her very flesh, to make come true her husband's far-fetched dreams and ambition. She had taken in faith the words of Shiva and Dvaipayana that she would be mother to one hundred sons.

Fool! I have been fooled! Yet again! By the devas, by the rishis, by this family! I have lost to Kunti, again! No more of this!

A low, animal-like, primal scream started emitting from her belly, then her lungs, her chest, her dry throat, her mouth, finally emerging from her trembling lips. She screamed and screamed and screamed. And she began striking her belly. Hard. Again and again. With force she did not know she had left inside her. She bashed her belly until her bangles shattered and stuck in shards into the skin of her taut stomach, drawing blood. She struck her belly harder and harder, desperate to expel that mass of flesh from her body, that cancerous thing that had devoured and destroyed her. She hit herself again and again and again, grunting from the exertion, her teeth gnashing against her lips until they bled, but still she did not desist.

Finally, as Ayla ran back to her, hearing her screams, there was an immense heaving from within the deepest recesses of her and that mass of flesh dislodged itself from the lining of her womb and lunged downwards, like an iceberg ripping off from a glacier wall. As Ayla cried out in shock and worry, reaching out to try to save her, that thing came out of her in a burst of blood and strange fluids, a heavy mass of dead, dense flesh, as heavy and hard as bone, woven round and round into a tightly wound ball of flesh that smelled rotten and diseased.

Gandhari cried out in anguish, feeling simultaneous relief and grief at this thing having been dislodged and delivered of her at last, so overcome and overwrought that she slipped into a deep unconsciousness, into sleep, for the first time in many months.

♋

When Gandhari awoke, many days had passed. She sat up at once when she saw Dvaipayana at her bedside. He shook her roughly. 'Gandhari, what have you done?'

Her voice was feeble and reproachful. 'You had promised me one hundred sons. But there was nothing there! Just a mass of dead flesh.'

Dvaipayana growled: 'Foolish woman! You have no patience. My words can never be untrue! That which you aborted; that is your one hundred sons!'

Gandhari sputtered, 'What is the point? Kunti already gave birth. Mine are not even alive.'

Dvaipayana walked away for some moments and returned. He commanded Gandhari to open her hands. She placed them above the blanket covering her from the chest down, upturned. He placed a cold, rubbery ball on her palms. She recoiled, shrinking away from it. It smelled fetid and rotten and felt like something dead and cold. But he pressed it firmly upon her, and she could not avoid it.

'Touch it, Gandhari. This is what came from your belly. This is what you pushed out, tried to expel. Touch it!'

'No!' she cried out, horrified and repulsed. But he was persistent.

She reached out tentatively. It was hard in spots and soft in spots, like a marbled ball of meat, with a dense, hard core, covered in spirals of softer tissue that felt almost like the beginnings of little hands and little feet. She wondered now, if it would have gone faster, if she had asked for one baby instead of one hundred. What she held horrified her yet moved her, bringing tears to her eyes. It felt dead but heavy with the pregnancy of life. It smelled sterile, not rotten. The rot was from her own innards that had dripped out with it.

Her voice warbled. 'These are my babies?'

Dvaipayana answered gruffly. 'They would have been your babies had you not so foolishly and rashly killed them by hitting yourself so violently.'

Gandhari cried out. 'I did not mean to! I was not in my right mind. I was so desperate, so frightened and in grief. I did not understand what was happening. I was all alone.'

He sighed and then softened his voice. 'I had promised you one hundred sons. I thought you had faith in me, my dear.'

There was a trace of sadness in his voice that made her heart constrict. It was the first time she felt empathy, a connection with another human being, in the time she had been locked away. It was not even a feeling, really; it was just an echo of a long-ago held capacity to feel.

Her voice was small. 'I did. It all just seemed so long ago, part of another world, another life. I could not really believe in your promise anymore.'

'My words can never come untrue. They shall yet be born, daughter, if you still want them.'

Her heart seized as she thought of those nightmares during the end of her pregnancy, of wandering through that fiery hellish world in search of her sons. 'I do! I do!'

He told her to heed his instructions well. He removed the ball from her hands and with Ayla's help, he summoned one hundred small pots to be produced in each of which he placed one of a hundred parts of the ball to grow into one hundred sons. As he explained this to Gandhari, she shyly requested whether he could include one daughter as well. He laughed and agreed, 'So be it, one hundred sons and one daughter.'

The ball was separated into one hundred (and one) individual parts, each part placed into one pot and topped with ghee and other herbal ointments and oils. Dvaipayana warned that the pots had to be guarded and watched over until the babies were ready to be born.

Gandhari solemnly nodded and promised to obey.

Ayla prepared the adjoining chamber and carefully placed the pots in even rows of ten. Gandhari roused herself from the bed, and with Ayla and Dvaipayana's help, she moved in front of the other chamber, laying her body across the threshold to protect and watch over her babies. Dvaipayana put his hand on her head in blessing before leaving, and she pressed the top of her head into his palm, that warm touch the only human comfort she had received in the preceding year.

For months, Gandhari lay there, ears perked to hear a human cry from the room behind her. But there was nothing. She forgot to eat or drink, until Ayla would press some food into her slack mouth, lifting her head to swallow. It was a long, lonely vigil. No one else really believed these pots would bear anything to life; it was too bizarre a thing, this arrangement of small pots, for anyone in the court to believe in Dvaipayana's words. It was only Gandhari who clung to the thread of Dvaipayana's words. Many, many months passed, without her even knowing it, without anyone visiting, other than Ayla.

One day, Gandhari, half drowsing, detected the noise of the faint cry of a baby. It sounded far away but she was sure she heard it. She cried out weakly to Ayla, who rushed to her side. 'Ayla! Ayla! I hear it, the sound of a baby crying. It sounds so far away, though. Please check. Please see whether any of my babies have come alive. It must be one of them. Who else could it be?'

But Ayla was not there. Gandhari frowned. This was the first time she could ever remember Ayla not being there when she had called out for her. In the past several weeks, she had been so tired that she had not called out for anyone. Someone wordlessly had placed food and water next to her head that she sometimes forced herself to consume. Now she wondered if that had not been Ayla after all. She felt a frisson of sudden worry. *Is Ayla all right? She has to be all right!*

Eventually another maid came and went into the chamber to inspect. The few minutes that she was gone stretched into the most anxious moments of Gandhari's life. She returned wordlessly and placed a small bundle on Gandhari's chest.

'He's alive?' gasped Gandhari.

The maid replied quietly, 'Yes, Queen, you have a healthy boy.' Gandhari missed Ayla all the more – how joyous she would have been at the news, how much sweeter the moment!

Gandhari sat up carefully, holding her son, cradled tight in her arms. She leaned against the doorway to support herself, bringing his body up to her face, sniffing him deeply. Oh! How she wished she could see his face, just once. *One day, one day, I will see you with my own eyes, my son, one day.*

Gandhari cried and laughed, cried and laughed, squealing with the delight of feeling his wriggling body in her arms finally, his fingers and toes warm and alive. He cried out lustily, and Gandhari heard the distant roar of thunder but paid it no mind as her fingers roved over her baby's body, inspecting each limb, each tiny bone and muscle, the dimple of his cheeks, the crease of his lips, the small button-shaped nose. She caressed him again and again, kissing his cheeks through the rain of her tears.

The maid held her to support her body which had become so frail and weak over the past two years. 'Take me to my husband. I want to present his heir to him myself.'

The maid murmured her assent and helped her up, the baby secure in her arms. 'Suyodhana. That shall be his name. Suyodhana. The Great Warrior. He fought so hard to be alive, and he shall fight hard his entire life for what is right, for what is his, ours.'

They walked slowly down the hallway to Dhritarashthra's chamber. It had been so long since Gandhari had emerged from seclusion, she felt herself coming alive, just as her baby had come alive from that pot and into her arms. She felt lightheaded and exultant. This one had been born, and so would all the others. Finally, they reached the chamber. A servant guarding the chamber stood up in surprise to let them in, announcing that Bhishma, Satyavati and Vidura were also inside.

Gandhari entered with her head held high, striding confidently into the chamber. She found her way unfalteringly to the bedside of her husband and placed their baby on his chest with a triumphant smile. She turned to face the other three, who stood on the other side of the bed. 'I present to you our heir, Suyodhana! There he is, the eldest son of the eldest son of the Kuru lineage.'

Dhritarashthra gasped and cried out. 'Finally! This is the second great news of the day!'

Satyavati rushed to bring Gandhari a seat. Gandhari was puzzled. 'The second?'

Dhritarashthra fell quiet and did not say anything. Satyavati said gently, 'Dhritarashthra was worried when you had not gone into labour for so long, while you were pregnant, that you would not give birth after all.' She paused to give him a chance to speak for himself, but he remained stonily silent, so Satyavati was the one to tell Gandhari that he had sired another child with one of Gandhari's maids, months ago. She had just gone into labour earlier this very day.

Which maid? But Satyavati did not say and Gandhari did not ask, even though she knew, in the marrow of her bones; she knew the answer. It was not something she could bear to hear today and Satyavati wisely held her tongue.

Bhishma said softly, 'But your baby was the first one to be born of Dhritarashthra's sons, queen. He is the first-born and the legal heir to your husband.'

Gandhari nodded stiffly, stifling a sigh, her cheeks flaming. Two years in the making and even this moment that should have been her proudest had been marred and defiled. She wondered whether it had been at the elders' behest that Dhritarashthra had done this, or whether it had been his own greed and fear that spurred him on. She felt suddenly vulnerable, wondering what would have happened to her had she not given birth after all. Perhaps her banishment would not have been so temporary. It was one thing to be a man who was impotent, such as Vichitravirya or even Pandu in his cursed status, but quite another to be a barren woman.

Dhritarashthra cooed over the baby. Gandhari could feel the weight of the gazes of the others in the chamber fall upon her child, sizing up his health, assessing his qualities and fitness. Before coming, she had rubbed her finger over his eyelids to feel whether they were normal, whether he could see. How could one tell from feeling eyelids? Yet, that's how desperate she was.

She should have known Dhritarashthra would have been too stupid to not ruin the moment. He said plaintively, 'I understand that Yudhishthira, the one who has been born to Pandu, will be the crown prince. He is the eldest prince and will inherit the throne. But will not this son of mine become the king after him?'

Gandhari gritted her teeth. Now was not the time for such speculation. Let them see first how healthy her baby was, how strong and mighty he would be, a fit ruler already at home in the palace, born in Hastinapur, with no strange curses attached to him or shadowy origins to his birth. It could have happened so naturally, his claim to the throne stronger than that of a strange boy who had never even lived in Hastinapur. But her husband had to force the issue.

Suyodhana wailed loudly. It was a howl, an outraged howl of protest and rage, so lusty and loud that it shook the rafters of the palace. Was he echoing his father's angst or fighting against even his father who conceded the right of Pandu's firstborn son to the throne? First the jackals joined the howling, then the carrion-eaters, then all the carnivores of the jungle. It was a deafening sound. It was as if her baby's cry had drawn out the wolves and predators of the jungles surrounding Hastinapur and called them to him, or spooked them, so that they howled and bayed at the moon.

Gandhari snatched Suyodhana from Dhritarashthra, tried to cradle him to her breast and soothe him. But he arched his back and became stiff like a drawn arrow on a high-strung brow. His little fists beat at her face and his tiny muscles strained, bending away from her. Gandhari was aghast to feel her new-born in such pain; she felt her heart breaking all over again.

Long minutes passed before he quietened. Gandhari collapsed against her seat, spent from the force of trying to keep him in her arms, sweat streaming down her back. It was Vidura who broke the silence, and Gandhari felt a shiver of foreboding as soon as he opened his mouth.

Vidura's voice was quiet yet resolute. He stood next to Dhritarashthra and addressed him, perhaps fearing her reaction. Vidura said, 'Brother, this son of yours will be the destruction of our entire family. There is great evil that surrounds him. This is the omen sent to us by the cries of the jackals and others from all directions. There is evil inside him. This is what we see on his face.'

Gandhari thought she had moved beyond shock with all that had unfolded today, but now her heart constricted anew. *How could Vidura speak like this? Gentle, patient, tender Vidura, always so wise and calm. How could he be afraid of her baby, how could he of all people pronounce him evil?* Anyone else Gandhari would have suspected of treason but Vidura was unimpeachable.

Gandhari choked back a sob but forced herself to remain controlled. She had felt her baby's face with her own fingers and all she had sensed was beauty, innocence. How could a baby be evil?

Vidura continued, 'He augurs disaster and a war so terrible that it will destroy not just our lineage but all the kingdoms of Bharat. This is what he carries inside him. You will find peace if you let him go; you will nourish evil if you nourish him. For the sake of the family, for the sake of Dharma, abandon him, brother. Leave him.'

To die?! It was a wonder that Gandhari did not faint. Her face turned ashen and she clenched her fingers on the cushioned seat to remain upright.

Dhritarashthra cried out, 'What are you saying? He is my son!'

Vidura kept on calmly. 'And you have one hundred others. One has been born already; the others will be born shortly. Let this one go for the sake of the family.'

Gandhari asked sharply, 'And how do we know you will not ask the same of the other ninety-nine? Perhaps they bear ill omens, too.'

'You heard his cry, too, Queen. You felt the baby in your arms. You know it is not normal.'

'He is my son.' Her voice was fierce. Strength was returning to her, flooding her muscles and limbs. She clasped Suyodhana even more closely to her body.

Satyavati tried to clear the air. She broached the topic no one wanted to address. 'It happened when Dhritarashthra asked about inheriting the throne. Perhaps that is what the ill-omens relate to, not this poor baby.'

Vidura exclaimed sharply, 'Dhritarashthra is too weak to do anything on his own. This boy has all of his mother's strength but none of her virtue! He has all of Dhritarashthra's desires but lacks his hesitation, his indecisiveness. Do you not see what a dangerous combination this is? Let us call in the brahamanas. Let us hear what they have to say.'

Bhishma brought in the brahmanas, who concurred with Vidura's assessment. Gandhari pressed them for their justifications. Was it there in his face? On his body? No, it was not just that, they told her. They could read it in the stars, in the quality of the evening sacrificial fire. It was in their gut. It was all around. It was not something Gandhari could argue against – a feeling, a certitude, the nebulousness of omens.

As the brahmanas filed out, Vidura intoned solemnly: 'It is said that one should abandon an individual for the lineage. One should abandon a lineage for the sake of a village. Abandon a village for the sake of a country. And one should abandon the entire world for the sake of one's soul. This is the path of dharma, dear brother. Think upon it.'

The words went through Gandhari like arrows. There was such conviction in his words, such wisdom, such power, that she could not even bring herself to disagree. Were it not for the fact that she was holding Suyodhana, she felt sure she would have collapsed into a heap upon the floor. She wished her father were there, to help her through this. She longed for his wisdom, his affection, his love for her. Here she was all alone at the mercy of these mercurial individuals who were still more strangers to her than family. She felt defenceless, helpless. She could not even count on her husband to not kill their son in deference to his brother. She could not count on anyone.

'I will teach him well.' Her voice was no more than a whisper, a grating of a finger against sandpaper. 'He will be good. I promise. I will watch over him. I will be a good mother.' Tears slipped down her cheeks. Two years she had borne him, waited for him to be born. Now this. She remembered how her father had worried over her when she was young, worried that she would be an enemy to the *devas*. Was there evil inside her? Had she contaminated her womb? She had always tried so hard to be good.

Vidura knelt beside her. He gentled his voice. 'Queen, I know you mean well. But Dhritarashthra has been filling your babies with poison, from when they were in the womb, his words of spite and longing for revenge, things he dared not act upon himself. But he has no compunction in commanding his babies to do this for him. I thought — I did not think this would happen, not until I saw your baby and heard him cry.

Until all the ill omens appeared. Until the brahmanas came here and agreed with everything I have said, every warning I have given. Queen, this is the truth. I am sorry, there is no other way.'

She flinched as if he struck her. Bhishma knelt next to them and reached out to touch Suyodhana. She recoiled and hunched over her baby, slapping away his hand. 'No! You will not take my baby away from me!' Her control slipped. After all that she had been through to bring him to life, she could not bear being separated from him. 'Your mother may have been happy killing her newborn babies, drowning them in the river, but I am not her!' She recalled how Bhishma's mother, the river goddess, Ganga, had drowned seven babies before Bhishma was born, delivering them from the misery of a human existence, leaving Bhishma the sole heir for his father, Shantanu.

Bhishma's voice was pained. 'You misunderstand me, Queen. I simply wanted to touch him, to feel him. This grandson of mine.' He chuckled softly. 'He is so handsome, so mighty.' Gandhari lowered the shield she had made with her hands and permitted him to pet Suyodhana. He whispered, 'Do you not remember what I had told you, daughter? My loyalty is to the entire Kuru dynasty, to you and your sons as well as Pandu and his. I will never see any one of us come to ruin. I will not forsake this baby. He is a Kuru and therefore he is mine and I am his. That is all there is to it. My fate is as attached to his as yours is.'

Gandhari exhaled in relief but knew there was no resolution yet, no permanent safety obtained for her son or for her. She wished Dvaipayana were there. He would have known what to do. He was the only one she would have trusted. But he had a trick for being there only at the opportune times, emerging from his Himalayan retreats only when necessary. Otherwise, he left them to their own devices.

Dhritarashthra sighed. 'What can I do, Vidura? I am helpless. He is my son and infinitely dear to me. And then you see my wife. She is so distraught. It is not possible. Ah! What will be will be. What can we mere humans do in the face of fate?'

Gandhari wanted to shake him. Even now, he was hiding behind her skirts.

Vidura asked Satyavati, 'Queen mother, what should be done?'

Satyavati said softly, 'It is not for me to tell a mother to abandon her baby. Leave it, son. We have rolled the dice and now we must wait for the game to be played. We wanted to make sure we had heirs and now it appears we will have plenty! We thought we were protecting ourselves with multiple options but did not stop to think that this creates rivalry, competition, doubt. We wanted Pandu to compensate for Dhritarashthra. We wanted Dhritarashthra's sons to compensate for Pandu if he could have none. We wanted the maid's son to compensate for both. Well, now we have to reap what it is we have sown. I do not see any other way, child.'

And with that, the discussion ended.

Suyodhana lived.

♋

Several weeks later, a shadowy figure entered the palace at Hastinapur. He was shrouded and slight, so silent and inconspicuous that he slipped past the guards unseen, like a stray cat. He approached the nursery, where Gandhari lay sleeping across the threshold of the doorway. Within a month of Suyodhana being born, all the remaining ninety-nine sons and one daughter had been born and were now healthy. No ill omens were found. Yet, Gandhari was too wary to trust her babies with anyone but herself. So, she guarded them with her body even as they slept.

The figure roughly shook Gandhari awake. 'Sister, I have come.'

Gandhari was startled. She reached out to touch him, to make sure it really was him. She felt the potbelly, the slight stature, the face habitually contorted in bitter anger. 'Shakuni!' she exclaimed happily and awkwardly hugged him to her, sitting up. The very day Suyodhana had been born, she had written a letter to her brother Shakuni, asking him to come and stay in the palace. Last time she had seen him was when he had escorted her here for the wedding. She had been so embarrassed of him that time, his maniacal playing of the dice, his frothing rage, his uncontrollable behaviour. It had been a relief when he finally left after the wedding.

But now she was eager to have anybody there who she could count on to be on her side, and that which once shamed her now gladdened her heart, that possessive loyalty that made him spit upon and insult others rather than see her disrespected. He had not replied but, somehow, she had known he would come. Now she felt safe. She picked up Suyodhana and put him in his uncle's arms. Shakuni chortled and Suyodhana gurgled in glee.

It should have been such an innocent sound but her brother's laugh and her son's eager response were so sinister to Gandhari's ears that it frightened her more than the howling of the jackals the night that Suyodhana had been born. She almost snatched the baby back from her brother's arms. But she did not. It had been years now since she had slept properly, since she had relaxed enough to let her guard down so that sleep could come and claim her. She felt out of her mind these days, wild-eyed and mad. It was so nice to have her brother here, to let someone else take care of things for a little while.

'Sister, get up off the floor. This is no way for a queen to sleep! Come, let me take you to your chamber. You will sleep properly from now on.' He held her elbow and lifted her up and walked her slowly to her chamber.

Gandhari mumbled sleepily as they entered her room, 'How is Father? How is Mother? How are our brothers?'

For a long time, Shakuni did not respond. Then he said stonily, 'I am here for them as much as I am here for you. They have sent me to be here with you, sister. It is because of them that I am here.'

Had Gandhari not been so sleepy, she perhaps would have frowned at that tone, those cryptic words, and questioned him further. She perhaps would not have ignored that tingle of foreboding that went up her spine at his too quiet, emotionless voice.

As she lay in bed, Gandhari turned towards Shakuni, reaching out to his face with her fingers. He dodged her. She remembered the revenge he had sought on her husband, on Bhishma, and now she worried that perhaps she had been too rash. 'Shakuni, why have you come? Have you come to do harm to the Kurus? I am a Kuru, too, now.' It was odd, suddenly feeling protective of those from whom she had sought protection with him. She was neither fully a Kuru nor fully of Gandhara. She felt stuck.

'I have come to make things right, sister. That is all. I have come to make things right.'

Gandhari mumbled sleepily, 'You will not hurt them, brother? Please. You will not hurt my sons or my husband or his family? I just want to be safe, that is all. I just want our interests to be safeguarded.'

She could almost hear Shakuni grin. 'I have not come to do anything at all, sister.' And then he shook in his hands a pair of dice. The dice sounded different from the ones he had carried with him before, as if they were made of a different material. These sounded harder, denser, yet somehow familiar. 'The dice have already been rolled, sister, before I even came here.' He shook them harder and harder; they rattled so loudly that Gandhari could hardly hear him speak. It was as if the dice were in her head, rattling inside her skull.

Suddenly he threw them against the floor and of course Gandhari could not see what had been rolled. She just heard the thwack of them against the stone floor and the clutter as they bounced and bounced before finally they landed and the play had ended.

Shakuni laughed, that maniacal laugh that hurt her ears. 'The dice have already been thrown, sister. I have just come to watch them fall.'

5

THE FOREST. NOW

Was it midnight yet? Gandhari stirred awake and all she could see through her blindfold was darkness. All she could hear was silence. Even the animals had fallen asleep or had been spooked away. Even the wind was silent. She sighed, and that sigh echoed loudly through the dense cluster of trees under which she slept.

'Sister? Are you well?'

Gandhari nearly had a heart attack at the sound of Kunti's voice. She was so quiet that Gandhari did not realize she was there until she spoke. She had not expected her. 'What are you doing here?' she asked suspiciously, already regretting she had broken her sleep only to encounter her sister-in-law.

'You were – distraught earlier.'

'I was, when I was sleeping,' Gandhari replied grumpily.

'I just wanted to make sure you were okay.'

'I am fine! You should sleep yourself.'

'Do we not have a very long sleep coming tomorrow itself?' Kunti laughed. She was rarely the type to make a joke but it seemed she had a penchant for gallows humour.

'You are certainly cheerful for one who is about to die,' remarked Gandhari drily.

'Do you know, we were so close to it once? So close, I could touch it. It was so beautiful. I longed for it then.'

'Death?' Gandhari was puzzled. *Oh no, is this going to be another story about how Madri robbed her of the chance to burn herself on Pandu's funeral pyre? Do I have to listen to this again? On my last night alive?*

'Not death. Not really. The heavens, the realm of *Swarga*. We had seen it – Pandu, Madri and I. When we were in exile. We went to the forest and lived on roots and fruit. We lived on a mountain called Nagasabha. We crossed the Varishena River and then we crossed on foot the snowy peaks of the Himalayas themselves. We reached Gandhamadana Parvata, the holiest of the holy mountains. For many months, we lived there. We lived among great men and women, realized sages, holy ones who blessed us and taught us philosophy and metaphysics. I had never known such peace.' Kunti's voice was full of longing and a softness Gandhari had never heard in her before. Despite herself, she was moved and listened intently.

Kunti continued, her voice faraway, 'We could glimpse distant lands in the north that led towards the heavens. These mountains were the playgrounds of the *devas*, the gandharvas, the bards to the *devas*, and the celestial nymphs, the apsaras. We caught the sound of birdsong, birds we had never even seen before. Gardens of brilliant flowers and foliage dancing in the wind wove colourful tapestries right before our eyes. Pandu practised intense austerities until he himself became a rishi, a brahmarishi, the highest kind of rishi. He wanted to take us with him, to cross the Shatashringa, to reach the heavens. We would leave behind everything, our families, the kingdom, our old lives, our very identities, so entranced were we with the world we glimpsed with our own eyes. If the path itself was so beautiful, who knew what lay beyond?'

Gandhari felt lulled into a reverie. After the war, she had forgotten the possibility of beauty, of pleasure, of something pure and sublime. Kunti continued, 'The great ones told us what lay ahead, beyond what we could see. The further up one climbed that mountain, the lonelier and more fantastical it became. Tracts of land covered with snow and ice, bared of trees and any vegetation, land so remote and barren that even birds could not venture there, nor insects. Only the air, only the rishis, the great ones, were permitted access there. Oh! How I longed to make that journey, with or without the other two.'

'Then, what happened?' whispered Gandhari. How different it all could have been had they made that journey and never returned – no competition for the throne, no war, no periods of exile, no bloodshed.

Kunti laughed scornfully. 'We prepared ourselves. Pandu was discussing with the great ones the routes to be taken, the precautions taken. They warned him against bringing us with him, but he insisted that he not go without us, his wives, when we had loyally followed him for so long. But then, Pandu, the one who had always been so decisive, the very morning we were to set out on our way, he was overcome with doubt.

'He was riddled with fear that he would never have sons. He discussed this with the sages who had kept us company for those long months. He said, a man is born with four debts, to the ancestors, to the *devas*, to the rishis and to men. The gods are pleased through sacrifice; the sages through studying and austerities; the ancestors through sons and *shraddhas,* the funeral rites; and men through kindness. How can I leave this earth without discharging my debts to the ancestors, without giving them a son to carry out my lineage, to make the offerings to them in my absence so they are never displeased or neglected?, he asked. The sages were quiet. They said not a word. Then my husband asked, as I was born to my mother through one who was not my father, shall I also have children in this way, through my wives bearing the children of some great man, like Dvaipayana did for me?

'Well, when he put it like that, what else could they say? If you ask the wrong question, you get the wrong answer. So, they all said, yes, having sons is the right thing to do. Then, that was it. No more journey towards the heavens.' Kunti's voice turned bitter. 'Those days were the happiest of my life. But then we had to come down, retreat from those lofty peaks, and go about the business of raising a family.' She sighed in regret.

'You would rather have gone to the heavens than had a child?'

Kunti snorted. 'I already had a child. One I had to abandon. I did not deserve or want the joy of having another.'

Gandhari knew the rest of the story. The use of Kunti's boon to call upon the *deva* of her choice to father her children. First, her three sons were born. Then, Madri requested of Pandu that she also partake of the boon, which Kunti allowed. Madri obtained twins, cleverly invoking the twin gods of medicine, to get two for the price of one use of the mantra. Kunti had gotten angry then and refused to use the boon further, although Pandu wanted more children. He was getting too greedy, she said.

'How was it when they were born?' Gandhari had never been able to bring herself to ask Kunti these questions before, to talk of the birth of their children. Always it was an affront to her, a travesty, of having given birth too late. Now, at the very end, the sharpness of those wounds stung less. It was other thoughts, other regrets that troubled her.

Kunti laughed softly. 'It was beautiful. They were born so easily, one year apart. I delivered them laying down on the forest floor. Conches and drums sounded in the heavens. The *devas* themselves perched on the clouds to bear witness to their birth, the birth of one of their own. They were beautiful and happy and strong.'

Gandhari noted wryly, 'It was a bit of a different experience for me. Well, what do you expect? My sons were merely mortal, born of a human father and a human mother.'

Kunti's voice was even. 'Perhaps, but they were strong enough to torment and exile me and my sons for all their lives.'

Gandhari swallowed and said nothing. She recalled Kunti's wistfulness about that trek towards the heavens, the completion of that journey denied to her by Pandu's sudden desire for sons. How different it all would have been had Pandu not changed his mind and not turned his back on the heavens.

Kunti sighed. 'I did not mean to upset you, sister. I meant only to check on you and offer some comfort. The heavens beckon to us. There are more welcoming worlds than the one to which we have born, in which we have lived and suffered so much. I have seen them myself, and perhaps tomorrow, we shall finally find our way there. And I will complete the journey I once began.'

Gandhari turned on her side, pretending to sleep. She was uneasy. She did not believe the heavens were the worlds that awaited her. She thought she was heading in the opposite direction.

Hastinapur, Then

It was harder to be a mother to one hundred sons (and one daughter) than one may have thought. Well, perhaps one hundred and one sons, if one included Yuyutsu, the son of her husband with Ayla, and he probably did count since Gandhari had summarily dismissed Ayla and sent her away, not back to Gandhara, but a distant forest far away for penance. That left Yuyutsu motherless and Dhritarashthra, too, never spared him much thought once his lawful heirs had been born. So, Gandhari deigned to include him in the count when she cooked for her children, to have clothes made for him as well when she had them tailored for her other children. But it was a cold formality, an unpleasant duty, and he was never in the line of children who filed past her every morning and night, for her to sniff their heads, hug them affectionately and bless them fervently with long life and good health. She never blessed Yuyutsu.

Perhaps then it was not a surprise that he started going to Vidura for affection and to be taught and effectively raised. Vidura, who was himself the son of a maid, wise, just, calm Vidura, who embraced him and taught him as he had never been afforded the opportunity to teach Dhritarashthra's other sons. Gandhari had jealously kept them away, never forgetting how he had asked for Suyodhana to be sacrificed. She did not trust her children in his presence. So, they grew up in the shadows of the palace, where Shakuni, her brother, and Dhritarashthra preferred to remain. Gandhari in any case preferred for them to learn from her brother than Vidura. She could trust Shakuni. Couldn't she? She did not let her memories wander to the sinister way he had spoken that night he had arrived. She told herself it was her fanciful state of mind in that period in which she had been delusional and half-crazed. She told herself she had imagined it all.

In any case, while the blessing for one hundred sons was a common one in Bharat, Gandhari wondered how much those who bestowed the blessing and those who asked for it had really thought through the logistics of it. Without maids, it would have been impossible, surely. Gandhari was adamant that every morsel of food that entered their mouths came from her hand and that it be freshly cooked off the flame.

She woke before night had ended and began preparing the grains and lentils, powdering whole spices into the unique mixes of cardamom, sesame and cinnamon she had learned from her mother in Gandhara, and began the process of cooking at least half a dozen dishes to accommodate the varying tastes of her children. It was done in batches. She fed them in batches of twenty. They would sit in a circle in their private chambers and she would sit in the middle, the vessels placed in a circle around her by the servants. She knew which one sat where, and when one of her children would cry out for more of this or that, she would serve them herself. And then she would begin the process again. She wanted each of the one hundred to feel special, so she never gave anyone leftovers from the earlier batches. She would remove herself to the kitchen and begin the process all over again.

In time, her daughter joined her in the kitchen, too, when she was old enough to stir pots and cut vegetables and measure out spices. Gandhari kept herself quiet then; she never bestowed on Duhsala the full force of her affection and love as she did for her sons. Her sons, she knew, would be with her always. Her daughter one day she would have to send off to marriage, to her husband's home, as Gandhari had been sent from Gandhara. The pain of that loss to come made her keep Duhsala at arm's length, even though she was the one child she had specifically asked for. Gandhari prayed hard for her daughter to have a happier life than she had been given herself. But in the end Duhsala's life and marriage were as painful and tragic as Gandhari's own and she was left to wonder whether there was anything good at all that came from her into her children or whether she had afflicted them with the curse of being born to her. Especially, this one, her daughter, the only one she had asked for herself.

Satyavati remarked to her wryly, 'Isn't this all a bit much? You do know, daughter, that this is a palace and you have a whole retinue of servants to help you with cooking.'

Gandhari had stopped finding Satyavati quite as endearing as she once did. She suspected scorn in each sarcastic comment and did not laugh back as she once used to. Instead, she replied stiffly, 'I am their mother. It is for me to feed them.'

Satyavati's voice sharpened: 'Feed them knowledge. Feed them virtue. That is what they need from you, daughter. Physical food is of less importance.'

'They are getting both. The tutors are with them daily. And my brother is also there.'

'Speaking of your brother, he really is staying quite a while, isn't he? Perhaps overstaying his welcome?'

Gandhari did not rise to the bait. She knew nobody else was thrilled with Shakuni's presence. They all found him repulsive, frightening even, a distinctly less than dignified and royal presence in court. That made her even gladder of his presence, a defiance against this court that had betrayed her. They dared not remove his presence for fear of her displeasure. Even Dhritarashthra was oddly frightened of him and never allowed himself to be in the same room as him alone.

Satyavati continued, 'Nourish their character, their soul, as much as their bodies, Gandhari. That is far more important.' There was an anxiety in her voice, one Gandhari did not hear often.

'What is it that troubles you, queen mother?'

'I worry about them, Gandhari,' she said in a whisper. 'They are so – unruly, always fighting, shouting, getting into fistfights with each other.'

Gandhari laughed dismissively. 'They are boys! That is what they are supposed to do.'

'All the same, I wish you would keep a closer eye on them. There is so much they could learn from you. Gandhari, they need you.'

'They have me!' Gandhari was offended.

'Daughter, all you do is feed them and kiss them and hug them. You never sit with them as they go through their lessons; you never tell them stories; you never ask them questions or test them the way Subala tested you on all the things you had learned.'

Gandhari was outraged: 'Have you been spying on me?'

Satyavati snorted. 'Of course, I have. What kind of matriarch would I be of this dynasty if I did not do that? You can choose to feel offended, or you can reflect upon this, child, and think upon whether there is some truth to what I say.' She sighed and softened her voice. 'Look, daughter, it is not an easy thing, raising one hundred children. It is too much to put on yourself. How can you possibly manage them well? Take the help of others in the palace. You do not have to do everything for them yourself. And it may be good for them to have exposure to others, too, to move out of the shadow of you and your husband.'

Gandhari's voice was stiff. 'I asked for the boon to have them. I asked for each of them to be my own. They are my responsibility and mine alone. I will care for them properly; do not you worry.'

But as she cooked the rice pudding that was Suyodhana's favourite later that afternoon, Gandhari did reflect upon Satyavati's words. She had too much affection and regard for her to dismiss her warning so cavalierly. There was truth to it, some truth. It was easier being in the kitchens, cooking for them. It was easier waking them up in the morning and tousling their hair, praying with them, watching over them as they slept. It was easier being with them when they were quiet, when they were at their most innocent, when neither could they question her, nor did she have to question or test them. She was perhaps too afraid that what Vidura said was right, that there was something wrong with Suyodhana, perhaps all of them, that they would wreak destruction over Hastinapur, that they would destroy their family.

What made it worse was she did not know what to teach them. Yes, she still remembered the genealogies, the aphorisms of the *sutras* on good governance and righteousness. She remembered every contour of topography of the map of Bharat.

But she did not know what to teach them, how to shape their dreams and goals, what direction to give them. How could she teach them what she did not know herself? Should she tell them to be patient, to not seek that which was not quite in their grasp, but could be, the throne that remained elusive even though there was no trace of Pandu or his mysterious sons in Hastinapur? The first role model of children should be their father, and what could she tell them of Dhritarashthra? Should she tell them to keep far away from him, to go to Vidura or Bhishma when they needed guidance; should she teach them to recognize his weakness, his senselessness? Should she not teach them to respect him as their father? There was unlimited strength in them, in her, but what was the use of such strength if it was unmoored, if there was no direction in which to channel it?

She did not have the guts to demand the throne for her sons. She did once, before they were born, before Suyodhana had been pronounced evil by Vidura and the brahmanas, but now she was unsure. And that was the worst curse of all. This doubt. This lack of resoluteness. Any decision was perhaps better than no decision. It was easier for her to simply leave it open, to pretend to leave it to fate and the gods, than to seize the mantle of motherhood seriously, to give her sons direction and firm guidance, to command them and be responsible for their upbringing. It was perhaps harder to be a mother than to be queen.

So, perhaps there was solace and respite in the kitchens, where her biggest decision was how spicy to make the gravy, how much quantity of rice was to be cooked, where her duty was circumscribed to cooking well, to the empty formalities of motherhood, that which was easy, which cost her nothing, which allowed her to abdicate those questions, those decisions, that haunted her from the day she was married off to Dhritarashthra. *Shakuni will guide them*, she told herself, *Shakuni will teach them well.*

From the day Dhritarashthra had come to tell her that Kunti had given birth, Gandhari knew the day was coming and she dreaded it. The day of their return to Hastinapur. She dreamed of all the ways it could happen. In some, Pandu's heir sneaked into the palace, sly and cunning as a thief, and stabbed her sons to death in their sleep. In some, there was a silent coup, as Gandhari and Dhritarashthra and their sons were all rounded up, drugged into sleep, and taken far away to some unrecognizable forest where they would have to live the rest of their days. How could a blind man and a blindfolded woman make their way back home on their own as declared enemies of the state? In some, Pandu's son came and sweet-talked his way into their hearts and affection, lulling them into thinking he was not their enemy. And then he would humiliate Suyodhana again and again, besting him at studies, in archery, in winning the favour of the people. Suyodhana became so decried and despised by the people that he ran away from Hastinapur. All this and more Gandhari saw in her dreams.

Yet when it happened, despite all of Gandhari's attempts to have prepared herself, she was taken completely unawares. They had all been in the audience hall, hearing the pleas of different petitioners from throughout the kingdom, some of whom had spent weeks traveling to reach the palace. Dhritarashthra was there but did not speak or guide the proceedings. He sat a passive witness, a regent who did not do anything but hold the throne ready for another – either Pandu or Pandu's son or his own son. Everything was led by Bhishma. Gandhari wanted Suyodhana with them, to begin at least hearing how such proceedings should take place, to listen and learn from his grandfather. Even Gandhari had to admit begrudgingly that Bhishma was a ruler par excellence and there would have been no better role model for her sons, not even her wily, crafty father, Subala.

But Suyodhana and her other boys were too busy wrestling and running around the gardens, whooping and chasing each other and beating each other up, to deign to sit quietly through hours of discussion and debate. They reminded her of her brothers. Perhaps it was impossible to tame children when you had them by the dozens. Gandhari did not force it either. She was afraid that Bhishma and Satyavati would find them lacking and judge them poorly. She wanted to shield them from that until they were stronger, better, prepared.

After there were no more pleas from the subjects of the Kuru kingdom, there was a pause and then a solemn procession of sadhus and rishis filed through the palace doors to stand before Bhishma and Satyavati. Gandhari did not even need to hear the announcement to know that it was a congregation of thousands of holy men. She could smell their holiness, detect how the vibrations of the environment subtly altered with their entrance, the faint smell of incense and sacrificial fire clinging to their skin, the otherworldly calm silence that marked their aura, the silence of their footfall, uncluttered by jewels or swords or sandals that would slap against the heavy stone floor. There were so many of them that it took longer than fifteen minutes for them all to enter the audience hall and it was not until they all arrived that their leader began to speak.

He addressed the queen mother solemnly, formally, as if these were words of a rite of worship that had to be accomplished meticulously and properly before they could arrive at the heart of the matter. He asked after the wellbeing of the royal family, the growth of crops in the kingdom, the health and happiness of the subjects, and Satyavati replied evenly, calmly, as if this were an ordinary exchange and not something that worried or surprised her in the slightest. Now Gandhari lacked the presence of Ayla to whisper her observations to her, so she did not know until hours later that there were six mysterious figures hidden under heavy cloths in the rear of the group of sages. The holy ones formed a protective arc around the figures.

Gandhari wished Shakuni could be there as her witness and informant but she was reluctant to call him into the hall. She did not want to draw attention to herself unduly at this moment, not when she felt she was the target of negative attention. She could feel the slide of the gazes of some of the men towards her, assessing whether she was a threat to what they had come here for today or not. She had not yet passed the test to earn their comfort, she felt, so she was doubly on guard.

Finally, he intoned in a solemn voice: 'Queen mother, revered Bhishma, all the peoples of Hastinapur. We have come as witnesses to bear you tidings of great import for the royal family and for the Kuru kingdom. We come bearing news that is both terrible and wonderful. Because of its import, we have all come together to bear witness together, to assure you of the truth of what we say.

'O people of Hastinapur, your rightful king, Pandu, passed away seventeen days ago, in the prime of his life, in the midst of his happiest days, with his family, his beloved wives and sons. His pious wife Madri has accompanied him to the afterlife.'

He paused for the gasps of shock, the cry of grief from Satyavati, the sobbing disbelief of Bhishma, the wails of the subjects for whom Pandu was a beloved king. Gandhari's heart had seized upon the word of Pandu's death, so that the reference to his sons did not even register in her mind. She was too shocked to grieve. Her blood and muscles and limbs felt frozen in time and place. Even as she heard Satyavati cry out and collapse from the throne upon which she sat, even as she heard Bhishma and the attendants rush towards Satyavati, to hold her up, Gandhari became immobile, paralysed. *Pandu. Dead. No! It is impossible.*

Later, Gandhari heard that upon deliverance of the message, the rishis had encircled the huddled figures at the back, to shield them if need be. They did not dare unveil the widow or the sons, to eclipse or undercut the news of the king's passing. The time would come for that later.

For thirteen days, all the royal family, all the subjects of Hastinapur, mourned in the forest and along the riverbanks of the city. The funeral rites were performed solemnly, the light of the pyre lit by Dhritarashthra himself. This time, even Dhritarashthra's wailing was real. It was one thing to long for his brother to be out of the way in pursuit of the throne, but quite another for him to die in reality, a brother who had always been good to him and kind, who never banished him to some remote outpost to keep the throne safe from his scheming jealousy, who comforted him as best he could, who shared the triumphs of his rule and conquests freely with him, who tried to make him happy, once upon a time. Dhritarashthra ordered full ceremonial grieving for his brother, above and beyond what was expected of him. He demanded that Madri be shrouded properly, to be kept safe from the sun and the wind. He stumbled, blind but refusing help, towards the pyre to light it for his brother. In that one moment, he was dignified, noble, a fitting older brother to the beloved king.

Even their one hundred sons were well-behaved for once. They seemed to sense the solemnity of the occasion, the loss that rendered the kingdom helpless and heartbroken. They were quiet and hung back in the forest, letting the elders mourn undisturbed. Kunti and her five sons sat apart from the rest, close to where Pandu and Madri's remains were being burned. None dared approach them. Kunti sat aloof and distant, her face a stony mask that revealed no expression, that did not soften with tears or a trembling lip. This Gandhari heard from the servants who marvelled at her calm and worried whether she was psychologically damaged, whether the trauma of it was too deep for her to ever recover from.

It fell upon Gandhari to comfort her sister-in-law. Vidura's wife was too shy to approach her, being of a lower social station. A dozen times, Gandhari made to approach Kunti. There were many things she wanted to tell her. She wanted to tell her that she had prayed for Pandu's health and long life, that she had wanted him happy, that he was the light of the kingdom of Hastinapur, how kind and good he had been to her when she had arrived alone and vulnerable in the palace to marry his brother. She wanted to tell her that it was not Kunti's fault for surviving, that she knew how hard it must have been to bring her sons on this journey, to feel all alone in this hard world with them, with the duty of caring for and protecting them. She wanted to tell her that she was home now, that she would be safe, that Kunti's sons would be safe with hers.

But every time she came close to Kunti, she fell back. Kunti was like a mountain of steel. There was nothing that relented within her. She did not respond to the outpourings of grief and comfort that were addressed to her. She did not embrace Satyavati or Bhishma when they came to her, mourning for Pandu. She did not acknowledge Dhritarashthra's pained offerings of comfort and solace. For thirteen days, she said not a word except when Bhishma pressed her for the details of what had happened.

She said it so matter-of-factly. That after their sons had been born, three belonging to Kunti and two, a set of twins, to Madri, they had been happy for years. And then, one day, Pandu was in the forest and forgot himself, so overtaken with desire was he for Madri, that he embraced her with lust and in that very moment he passed away. Madri, too distraught to live without him, asked Kunti to raise her sons as Kunti's own and consigned herself to death along with their husband.

Bhishma lamented, 'Oh, that foolish Madri! She should have protected him. She should have kept him safe.'

Kunti replied evenly, 'It was not her fault. Pandu wanted her and gave her no choice. She could not help it.'

Satyavati sighed, 'You would not have let it happen, daughter. You would have never let him die like this.'

Kunti replied evenly, 'I am not the one he wanted. I was never the one he wanted.'

And in those few words there was such suppressed pain, such suppressed grief, that Gandhari recoiled. It had been Kunti who had saved the dynasty by bearing Pandu children, by giving access to that same boon to Madri, so that she could also have children, and yet it had always been Madri that Pandu wanted and loved. Kunti was the senior queen, yet she was the neglected one.

Kunti continued, her voice firm: 'Madri entrusted her two sons to me. They are as dear to me as my own; the five of them are brothers and never shall any distinction be made between my three and her two. They are the Pandavas, the sons of Pandu, and shall always be united and speak and act as one. That is the vow I have made, that is the vow I will keep.'

There was something terrible in her words, something that awed and frightened Gandhari, and she lost the courage and willpower to approach Kunti at all during those thirteen days of mourning. She never offered her a single word of comfort, never reached out to touch her in those moments of the most awful grief.

As the thirteen days ended and everyone prepared for the return to the palace, Satyavati told Kunti that her old bedchambers had been prepared for her, the chambers of the queen of Hastinapur. Kunti said in a quiet but resolute voice that travelled through the forest so all who were there heard, so all understood immediately her will and resolution. She said: 'I have come here as the mother of the Pandavas and that is all

I shall be. I do not want the comforts of the palace. I have not come to seek alms as the widow of Pandu. I have come only to safeguard the interests of my sons, to ensure they are given their birth-right, that they live up to the duties and expectations their father had of them. I shall stay with them to watch over them, to teach them, to train them, to prepare them. I shall live in their chambers for as long as they need me. None and nothing will separate us again. I am the mother of the Pandavas now, nothing more.'

Gandhari shrank back and the sympathy and shared grief she had felt with Kunti evaporated. In those thirteen days, she had thought of Kunti as family. Now she remembered she was the enemy.

When they arrived back at the palace, when they had bathed and cleaned the palace top to bottom, to rid the kingdom and themselves of the ritual impurities of Pandu's death, only then were the Pandavas formally announced and introduced at court. It was left to Kunti to present them, as the holy ones had disappeared after bringing the Pandavas to the palace.

She brought them to the throne, one by one. First was Yudhishthira, the eldest who had preceded Suyodhana in birth. He was presented as the son of Yama, the *deva* of righteousness and death, the law-maker. Second was Bhima, the son of Vayu, the god of wind. Third was Arjuna, the son of Indra, the king of the *devas*. These three were the sons of Kunti. The last two were Nakula and Sahadeva, the twin sons of the divine Ashwin twins, the handsomest of the *devas*. These two were the sons of Madri. Gandhari thought to herself wryly that it was a fitting choice for Madri to have the prettiest of the Pandavas.

After the crowd of subjects finished oohing and aahing at the strapping young boys Kunti had brought back, Bhishma said gently, 'Daughter, you know that many questions will be asked of how these children came to be born after the curse that was pronounced on Pandu. Please explain their origins so that all doubts may be put to rest once and for all.'

Indeed, the palace was already rife with rumours about the mysterious appearance of these Pandavas and whether they were legitimately Pandu's sons and heirs. Gandhari heard that, other than the twins, the others did not resemble each other and very well looked like they could have been sired by different fathers. Was it a convenient excuse that each was from a different god? Others speculated that perhaps they were not Kunti's or Madri's at all, that after the death of Pandu, Kunti wanted to come back to Hastinapur and so she had adopted these sons in the guise of being Pandu's children to come stake her claim upon the kingdom. *Good*, thought Gandhari. *The more doubt that is cast upon them, the stronger becomes Suyodhana's claim to the throne.*

But it was not such an easy thing to fake being the sons of the *devas*. There was too much divine about them for the people to dismiss Kunti's story too quickly. Besides, her integrity was unimpeachable, her word sacrosanct. No one dared doubt her. And thus were the Pandavas accepted on the strength of Kunti's purity and nobility.

Gandhari had carefully kept Suyodhana out of the proceedings that day. She did not want an impulsive outburst from him to mar the occasion. She wanted to listen and learn carefully, and if he were there, she would have been too busy minding him to pay proper attention. Dhritarashthra also stayed back, unable to deal with being in the same room with those who had once again snatched the crown away from him and his sons. Gandhari instructed Shakuni to stay with them and keep them out of trouble.

Kunti reluctantly began her story: 'When I was a young girl, I was charged with keeping the guests happy at my adoptive father's house. He often had sages and other holy ones visit to discourse upon philosophy and metaphysics. Once, the great sage, Durvasa, had come. I was devoted to him and he was pleased with my ministrations. He granted me a boon.'

Satyavati interjected, 'That one is a hard man to please, daughter.' Durvasa was renowned for being of ill temper, prone to muttering curses and then their antidotes once his temper was restored. He was the angriest of all the rishis.

Kunti was unamused: 'Perhaps. But there is none as enlightened as he is. So much I learned from him. How I long for those days! Sitting at his feet with my father and others from the family, listening to him and the other holy ones spending hours in arcane debates over the metaphysical texts of the Upanishads and other spiritual sciences.'

'What was the boon, child?' Bhishma prodded gently.

Kunti hesitated. 'He gave me a mantra by which I could invoke any of the *devas* and they would be compelled to come and, should I wish it, leave me pregnant with their child.'

She carefully elided the question of whether or not there was physical consummation of the act of conception or whether it was simply a miraculous conception. Even Bhishma and Satyavati were too polite to ask about that.

A shout came from the audience of subjects. 'Had you used the boon before?'

Kunti inhaled sharply in consternation. However, even royalty had to answer the questions fielded by citizens. Kunti ignored the question with a noncommittal murmur.

Gandhari was immediately suspicious. It was the first time she had heard weakness in Kunti's voice. She was convinced that she was hiding something.

Kunti cleared her throat and continued: 'Pandu was very keen to have sons of his own before leaving this earth. When he learned of my boon, he immediately asked me to invoke it and to bear sons who would be his rightfully under the law.'

Under the laws of those times, a woman's children, whether born before wedlock, out of wedlock, or even after the death of her husband if born to men of high character and stature, belonged in name and law to her husband. 'The first three I gave him. When he wanted a fourth, I refused. It was being too greedy of the gods, I told him. And then Madri also wanted a son of her own. I shared the boon with her and she cleverly invoked the Ashwin twins, getting two sons out of the use of the boon once. When she requested more, I refused. She had cunningly gotten two out of me already.

'They were born one year apart, other than Madri's twins. As the rishi told you, the *devas* themselves rejoiced at each of their births. Garlands were thrown from the heavens and gandharvas sang and danced in the skies. It was a beautiful and auspicious thing. Surely Pandu's sons will bring only glory and righteousness to Hastinapur, to this best of families.

'For years, we were happy. The boys grew up happily, playing in the forests, learning from the holy ones. They were a delight to the sages, too. Then – I have already relayed the circumstances of Pandu's passing. Madri insisted upon dying with Pandu, as she was the one whom he had reached out to in his final moments and she could not leave him without her in the afterlife. She also told me that she would have been unable to raise my three sons as her own, and it was better that I be the one to stay behind, to raise our five sons as one. This I have vowed to do, revered uncle. This I have vowed to do.' Her voice had turned fierce.

No further questions were asked. One by one, the Pandavas, who had been wordless throughout the whole exchange, came up to offer their prostrations to the elders and take their blessings, beginning with Bhishma and Satyavati, then Ambika and Ambalika, their grandmother and grand-aunt, and finally Gandhari and then Vidura.

It was Yudhishthira who made Gandhari weep. She already did not care for Arjuna and Bhima; they were much too arrogant and restless for her liking. And the twins were too silent and passive to arouse her interest at all. But Yudhishthira left her completely undone. He touched her feet with humility and then embraced her as warmly and tightly as if she were his own mother, addressing her with affection and reverence. Unbidden, her hands traced the contours of his face and she found in his visage the same radiance and smoothness, the same nobility of features and warmth she had always found in Pandu. She wept even as he marvelled aloud at her devotion to his uncle, in wearing this blindfold for him. Again and again, her fingers stroked his forehead and cheeks, roving across his hair in spontaneous affection. She could not understand how anyone doubted this was Pandu's son – his character shone through him, his spirit. Through him, she felt again the pain of loss of Pandu but also the hope of his legacy continuing, his spirit being carried on through at least this one son of his, if not the others. It was as if he brought back Pandu to her, to this palace that had become so desolate and lost without his presence.

Yudhishthira stayed contentedly in her embrace until finally her tears subsided. She felt embarrassed at the spectacle she had made of herself and blushed furiously. She suddenly missed Ayla, who would have ensured she did not show such weakness in public. What must the others think of her? How scornful Kunti must be of her emotion when she, who had just lost her husband, had been so stoic throughout the weeks since her return to Hastinapur. But Ayla was not there to tell her how Kunti's face had softened momentarily upon seeing Gandhari embrace so warmly her eldest son, that glimmer of relief in her eyes at the hope of co-existence.

Afterwards, Gandhari went to find her sons and her husband. She walked calmly and peacefully, a small smile on her lips. She thought perhaps Yudhishthira would be a good influence on Suyodhana, smoothing out his rough edges. She felt less troubled than she had this morning. She felt a spark of hope.

Alas, when Gandhari finally reached Dhritarashthra's private chambers, she walked into an ugly scene. Her eldest son was snarling and growling, howling in rage, being forcibly restrained by her brother, Shakuni, as Dhritarashthra sought feebly to comfort and calm him. He was thrashing about, throwing things, smashing them against the wall. Gandhari was aghast. She rushed to her son, and he almost hit her in the face but stopped himself in time. She pressed him close to her body, holding him in a vice-like grip. Sometimes she was the only one who could calm him.

'Child, what has happened? Why are you agitated like this?'

'Those imposters! Those pretenders to the throne! I want them out of my palace. Now!'

Gandhari tried to soothe him by stroking his brow: 'Suyodhana, you should be kind to them. They are your cousins. They have just lost their father. This is the only home they have now.'

Suyodhana broke free of her embrace and sent a tumbler of water careening off a small table, splashing her with cold water. 'They are bastards! They are not legitimate heirs to the throne. Who knows what kind of men my aunt slept with to give birth to them?'

Gandhari gasped in horror: 'Suyodhana! Watch yourself and your language. How dare you say such things?' Had he remained within her grasp, she would have slapped him for such ugliness. But she could not see where he was; she could not reach him. She appealed to her husband, 'Husband, say something to him. He cannot talk like this!'

Dhritarashthra moaned and cried out plaintively, 'What can I say to our son, Gandhari? I understand his pain, his anguish. It is only natural. Why should he suffer so, simply because I was denied the throne because of my blindness?

Why should my sins be visited upon him? And really, how do we know the truth of what Kunti tells us? It is only prudent to be suspicious, to demand evidence before we welcome them into our home.'

'Pandu was the king. This is Kunti and her children's home. You know that Yudhishthira is heir to the throne and will be king. You have agreed to this yourself! Why are you allowing our son to be agitated like this? You have to tell him the reality of things. He is in anguish because he does not understand, does not accept the truth of the matter. You are his father! You must make him see right!'

Dhritarashthra said nothing, only sighed loudly and theatrically. Shakuni crossed the room to sit next to his sister. He placed his hand upon hers firmly and said, 'Now is not the time, sister. Let them be. Let your son be. He will be fine.'

'Another thing, mother,' Suyodhana whirled around suddenly to face her.

'Wh – what is it?' She was suddenly afraid of her own son. His mercurial moods, his extremes, his uncontrollable behaviour. Almost, almost, she felt for a moment happy that it would be Yudhishthira who would be king and not her own son. It was a shameful thought as a mother but perhaps the right one as queen.

'My name is no longer Suyodhana. I shall be known as Duryodhana.' There was such terribleness in how he pronounced the name that it sounded almost evil, a word signifying something bad and inauspicious. Years later, some would say that his name changed as a reflection of his character, that he was no longer worthy of an auspicious name, that his evil deeds had earned him this pejorative moniker. But they were wrong. It was a name he chose for himself.

'Why this name? Why Duryodhana?'

'Let my name be a warning to others to not mess with me. Duryodhana! It means the unconquerable one, the one with whom it is difficult to fight. Let not the Pandavas underestimate me.'

'You already have such a beautiful name,' whispered Gandhari. 'Suyodhana. The Great Warrior.'

He snickered contemptuously. 'Not good enough. There may be many great warriors, but there is only one me. There is only one who will occupy the throne of Hastinapur. That is Duryodhana. The unconquerable one.'

Gandhari turned beseechingly to her brother. 'Shakuni, what is all this nonsense? Talk some sense into him!'

Duryodhana snapped, 'Do not turn my uncle against me! Shakuni Mama was the one who suggested this name to me. It is his idea as much as mine. You are a weak woman, Mother. You do not know what you are talking about. Leave us to it.' He turned his back on her, walking off as if excusing her from the chamber.

'Shakuni! Is this true?' Gandhari was bewildered. She understood the delusions her husband and son harboured, but surely Shakuni must have known better. He was too wily and cunning to not realize that Suyodhana could not possibly expect to be king, not with the return of Yudhishthira. He would surely have known that it was for the best for Suyodhana to accept his place in the palace and make peace with his cousins. It was his job to teach her sons. That was why she had brought him back.

'Sister, we will talk of it later.' His voice was quiet but firm.

Gandhari was troubled. She was being ordered out of chambers which belonged to her. She was the one who should have been in charge here, but she suddenly felt vulnerable and out of place. She did not want the embarrassment of being defied, so she got up to leave uneasily.

'Mother!' His voice was sharp and strong, bouncing off the walls.

'Yes, son?'

'Say it. Say it once. It will only feel like it is properly my name when you say it. You are the only one who can name me.'

Tears came to her eyes. Only she heard the plea in his voice, the insecurity, the desperation to be validated and accepted, loved by his mother. She could never deny him. Never. She walked to him and stroked his hair, his forehead, kissing the top of his head as her tears fell into his thick curly locks. *Please protect him*, she screamed out internally to the gods, the ancestors, to Pandu who was now in the heavens. *Please keep him safe!*

Had she been stronger, she would have refused. And maybe a series of refusals would have been enough to change the tide, to pull back from the lure of war, the trap of inevitable destruction, the path that led them further and further away from Dharma. Love made her weak, though, made her murmur into her son's ears, 'Duryodhana, my son. You shall always be known as the unconquerable one, the one with whom it is terrible to fight. You are now Duryodhana.'

And with that bitter, sour taste of that name that felt so inauspicious in her mouth, Gandhari left the room.

♋

Satyavati was leaving. She was leaving with her daughters-in-law, Ambika and Ambalika, for the forest to spend the rest of their days in a hermitage before leaving the world. It was Dvaipayana who had come to her, after the news of Pandu's death had been announced, to comfort her in her grief and to instruct her gently that it was time to leave. He told her that dark days were coming, that the happy days she had known as part of the Kuru clan had come to an end. The earth has lost her youth, he told her, and days of darkness, of increasing evil and degeneracy were coming now. He told her she would not be able to bear witnessing the destruction of her family and the lineage.

In her customary way, Satyavati agreed brusquely and in the space of a day made ready to leave. Once she had decided upon a course of action, she set about executing it immediately. She summoned Ambika, Dhritarashthra's mother, and informed her that because of the evil acts foreseen to be performed by her son, that would result in the destruction of the Kuru clan, she was retiring to the forest along with Ambalika, Pandu's mother, and that she was welcome to join them if she wanted. Ambika consented meekly.

Gandhari was distraught at the prospect of losing Satyavati. Even in recent years, when they had drifted apart, she had found comfort and pleasure in Satyavati's presence and still saw in her the mother she had always lacked. She was tongue-tied now, devastated that it was her husband and her sons that were turning Satyavati away from what had been her home for so long. As they met for the last time, Gandhari expressed her wish that she could have accompanied Satyavati to the forest hermitage and looked after her there.

Satyavati dismissed her airily: 'No, Gandhari. You belong here. The time is not for you yet. One can only leave the world once one has finished one's work in it. I have seen it all, done it all. It is time for me to go, to leave the palace and the affairs of the Kuru family in the hands of the younger ones now. It is now your turn to guide the fate of the Kuru dynasty. One cannot go into renunciation until one has completed one's work.'

Gandhari bowed her head in acquiescence. She asked if her grandmother-in-law had any parting words of advice or instructions before she left. Satyavati sighed as if she were reluctant to say the words but since Gandhari had asked, speak them she did.

'How can I ask of you what I did not do myself? To honour the family into which you have been married, to treat those who are not your sons as your own sons? How long and loyally

Bhishma has served me and yet even now I cannot muster for him the affection a mother should have for her son. Still I am haunted by the memories of the sons I lost, who were pale shadows of men next to him, who did not deserve the throne upon which they sat, the throne safeguarded and protected by the honour and might of my stepson whom I never treated rightfully as my own. Never has he disobeyed or displeased me in anything, except the one time when he refused to break the very vow I forced him to take. I broke this family with my refusal to accept the rightful heir of the Kuru clan. From now until my deathbed, in the forest, I shall reflect upon this, commit penance for my past.

'And now here you are and history seems destined to repeat itself. But I am not so sure you will succeed. Shantanu wanted me more than he wanted the throne. Bhishma wanted his father's happiness more than he wanted to be king. No one wants your sons on the throne of Hastinapur. No one is concerned for your happiness, daughter. It is a losing fight your husband and perhaps you seek to pursue.

'But I will not ask you to turn away from the path you are walking. I will not ask of you what you cannot deliver. I will not ask you to put aside your interests for the good of the kingdom. I will not ask you to desist from the path of destruction your husband and son are on. I will not ask you to abandon them for the sake of the kingdom. I will not ask you to care for Yudhishthira or the Pandavas. I will not ask of you what I was unable to do myself. You are the mother of one hundred sons; I shall not ask you to be the mother of one hundred and five.' And with that, Satyavati kissed her on the forehead, not unsympathetically, and left.

6

THE FOREST. NOW

Gandhari stirred, reluctantly shaken awake by a nagging anxiety that did not allow her to be lulled into a deep sleep. This was not sleep; this was being held under water and sputtering to the surface, choking and gasping for breath before being dunked underwater again. In this way, she transitioned between sleep and the waking state, lurching from one to the other.

It must have been midnight. There was no Kunti beside her, no murmur of voices, only the dim orange glow of the eternal fire in the distance. Gandhari sat up. Sweat had plastered her hair to her brow. Voices hummed in her head. She had heard the voices of the *devas* once. In those days of her penance, she had heard Shiva, Ganesha, Durga whispering their approval to her, their acceptance of her offerings. She had yearned for their voices then, eagerly chased after them, delving more and more deeply into her penance. Even in the years leading up to the war, even as the *devas* receded into the background of her mind as she focused more and more on her sons, still they lurked within her consciousness and it was a comfort to know she could reach out to them at any time. She never lost the confidence that the *devas* were just one fast, one prayer, one act of sacrifice, away. Every vrata she had sought, ever boon, she had won, was reserved for that.

Until Krishna.

Krishna, her most despised enemy. Krishna, who thwarted her and her sons at every turn. Krishna, who defended and saved the Pandavas, again and again. Krishna stopped the voices in her head. Krishna took the *devas* away from her. Relentlessly, he had pushed them to the brink of war. That last day, on the battlefield, when she had cursed him, when he had coldly reprimanded her, she had stopped all worship. She banished the *devas* from her consciousness. What was the point anymore, after the judgment of Krishna, which had so obviously found her lacking? She accepted his judgment passively; she was resigned to her fate and never again sought to change it. She was stoic to the prospect of unending suffering. Indeed, she was. Even if they had stayed back in Hastinapur and suffered through all the taunts and insults by Bhima and the others, she would not have minded it. She would have accepted it quietly. She knew her fate and she greeted it dispassionately. Just as she had been fated to marry the blind prince, just as she had been fated to bear one hundred sons, just as she had been fated to give birth to the one who would destroy the Kuru clan, to see him die, so, too, had this become her fate. She had no protest.

The thought never occurred to Gandhari to turn to the *devas* now, to seek their comfort and guidance. Surely, they had abandoned her.

Sometimes, it shamed her, this insistence on survival. It was not desire. Desire meant the hope for something greater. Yet, she was not Madri, who consigned herself to the flames when her husband had died. She had lost all one hundred of her sons, yet she still persisted in living, when life had lost all of its joy and meaning for her. She felt lower than an animal, this clawing at existence, refusing to let go. There was still something she demanded of life, that life demanded of her.

She wondered if she would die in her sleep, if death would come like an insect, biting her unawares, spreading its poison slowly through her limbs and blood, without her realizing it, until it was too late. Would she know if she was dead after she died? Would there be a sleep before she woke again to don a new life, enter crying into a new world? Or would it be immediate, a yanking from this life to the next? Would she spend years and years in the realms of hell before the chance at a new life, at starting over? No, not even that, not a starting over, just a resumption of the life she had already started, a resumption of the burdens that weighted her even now. Death was not an escape – just a prolonging. The only escape was through the *devas* and that path felt lost to her now. She imagined praying to them and them laughing at her, scorn dripping from their beatific faces. She was too proud to risk such a rejection, so she turned away from them, resolute.

Maybe it would not be so bad, dying without knowing she was dying. Dying in her sleep – expecting to wake up but never again waking. She wanted to get it over with now, the business of death and dying. She wanted it to be done. *It is simple enough – how many times you have forced yourself to stay awake, to watch over your sons, to pray to the gods, to stay alert; now just reverse it, now just force yourself to stay asleep, to never again surface into consciousness, to slip into a slumber that will not cease. Do not think about it. Just do it.*

She closed her eyes, firmly vowing never to open them again. It was just one step away, from blindfold to blindness.

As soon as her eyelids closed, a gentle wind drifted through the forest, gentle yet powerful, lifting the fine hairs off her neck and whispering through the leaves, ruffling the grass. It made the forest sound like it was laughing and Gandhari, even as she screwed her eyes tight, curling into herself, into her pallet, was convinced somehow that it was Krishna, that he had come one last time, to laugh at her.

Hastinapur, Then

It had all started so innocently. That was what Gandhari told herself. In the beginning, it had just been roughhousing. They were boys after all. So what if they hit each other, beat each other up badly, her sons and Kunti's sons, transforming picnic outings into brawls. Always it was Duryodhana against Bhima, the strongest of Kunti's sons, and always Duryodhana was on the losing end of it. So, it did not surprise Gandhari, that he became more and more desperate, went to further and further lengths to fight back against him. That was why she did not bother to do anything about it. Boys will be boys.

Then came the murder attempts. Bhima was poisoned. Bhima was drowned. Only to come back from the verge of death, again and again, only to become a stronger and more popular hero in the eyes of the people of Hastinapur, only to make her son seem a weakling and a fool.

That was when Gandhari grew antsy. She went to her husband first. That was a mistake. Nowadays two others were always in his chambers – Sanjaya, the charioteer, who had replaced Kutili as his principal companion and advisor, and Yuyutsu, his son from Ayla. Kutili had left in disgust once Yuyutsu had been born, refusing to entertain the son of a maid (a maid like her) who dared to claim the status of being the king's son. Sanjaya, the gentle, wise charioteer, appealed to Dhritarashthra, a contrast to the volatile temperament of Kutili. He had had enough of women by then, in any event.

Yuyutsu was a sweet boy who preferred the company of his father to his rowdy half-brothers. He was gentle and good, and Gandhari hated him passionately. She hated him more than she had hated Kunti, more than she hated Kunti's sons – she hated him for being better than her own blood-born sons, for making her feel an inferior mother to her own maid even in absentia. What goodness there must have been in Ayla that had transferred to him and what badness must there have been in Gandhari to have produced sons who seemed bent only on killing their cousins. She bristled at his presence, and so she left the room whenever she found him there.

Having given up on her husband, Gandhari turned to her brother, Shakuni. He was hardly ever to be found on his own. He was always with her sons, principally Duryodhana, coddling them and ingratiating himself with them. They called him Shakuni Mama with as much affection as they called her Ma.

It was near midnight when she finally found him alone, in his chambers, strategically wedged between Dhritarashthra's rooms and Duryodhana's. The palace had grown quiet after dinner as the inhabitants, the royal family, the servants, the ministers who lived in the palace quarters, all retired to rest. This was when Shakuni was his busiest. Gandhari's new servants told her that the lamps were always burning in his chambers, that there were hushed whispers emanating from there even when there appeared to be no one else inside, that they could hear him muttering to himself late into the night and early into the morning. And always there was the rattle of dice, thrown against the wall, collected into his hands, and thrown again, harder and harder, faster and faster, as if he was throwing out every possible combination until he had worked out all the possibilities and could command the dice to fall as he wanted them to fall.

Her servants were in awe of him and in fear. They were mostly useless and did not catch half the things that ought to have been reported to her, the things that Ayla reported to her without fail. She felt even blinder than before, more helpless. She had thought Shakuni would be her additional pair of eyes, but now she felt he was yet another one that she had to monitor and suspiciously observe.

She knocked softly on his door and he opened it with alacrity, jumping up. 'Sister!' he exclaimed, not unhappily. 'What a surprise to see you here at this hour. Come in!' He unceremoniously yanked her inside the room and shut the door. He was wary of being seen.

His chambers were cramped. The air was heavy and smelled of sweat and mildew. It was hot and rank. Only one lamp was lit, and still and windless as the air was, the fire in the lamp jumped nervously, flickering and cowering in the dark shadows. Shakuni sat next to her, only a breath away. She felt his breath strike against her shoulder, an impatient, restless huffing, as jumpy as the fire in the lamp. He leaned closer to her and she resisted the urge to draw away.

'Sister, is something wrong?'

Gandhari cleared her throat. She was suddenly nervous, suddenly in dread of this conversation that she should have had with him long ago, long before her boys had grown into teenagers, old enough to cause real damage. She was suddenly afraid, suddenly sure, she would be hearing something that she did not want to hear, that by the time she left the room, something irrevocable would have happened, something ominous.

Her voice was so dry that it cracked as she forced the words out of her mouth: 'Shakuni, I am worried about my sons. I am worried they are on the wrong path. This fighting with their cousins, it is going too far. I worry that it will lead to their ruin. The sons of Pandu, they are too strong, too protected by the elders of the family, too beloved by the people. We cannot afford to be seen as their enemy. It is not safe.'

Shakuni said nothing. His silence was brooding, ominous.

Gandhari's voice turned plaintive. She hated sounding weak, yet worry for her sons was making her desperate. 'Brother, you must know this. You know Father, he would not approve of this—'

Shakuni's voice turned rough, sharp. 'Oh, you remember him now, do you? You remember him now?'

Gandhari frowned. 'Of course, I do. I always remember him.'

'When is the last time you heard from him?' His voice cracked like a whip.

'There have been letters–'

'And what do the letters say?'

'They ask how I am, how the children are, what is happening in Hastinapur.' They were always bland, full of pleasantries and formalities. Gandhari thought her father no longer felt connected with her after she had blindfolded herself, that she had become a stranger and martyr to him, that she had forever killed the daughter in his heart.

Shakuni's voice turned eerily quiet. 'And how do you know they are from him, from our father?'

Her heart started thumping so loudly that she could not hear her own breath. 'Who else would they be from? It – it sounds like him. Whenever I write, he responds.'

'Yet, you cannot know for sure, can you? You have not seen his handwriting, you have not felt for yourself the seal.'

Gandhari whispered, 'They open the letters for me and read them to me. You know that I cannot see.'

'I know you do not choose to see,' he sneered.

'What are you saying, brother? Has something happened to our parents?' she cried out.

'I said too much. Leave it. It is late and I am preoccupied with other matters. Go to bed.'

Gandhari racked her brain, trying to recollect the contents of all the letters she had received from her parents, trying to find one stray piece of information that no one else would have known, to prove to herself that those letters had really come from them. Her voice grew in urgency. 'Shakuni! Tell me the truth. What has happened? Are our parents all right? Is the kingdom safe?'

He was unperturbed. 'You should have come home when you were pregnant. A bride always comes home to deliver her baby. You never came back.'

Her voice broke. 'I could not. I had to stay here – to make sure that the royal heir was delivered in Hastinapur, to stake my son's claim on the throne.'

Shakuni laughed. 'And how did that work out for you?'

'Tell me what happened. If something was wrong, you should have told me at once. No more games, Shakuni. Tell me.' She drew into her voice the command of the queen.

He sighed. 'I thought not to worry you with all this. Very well if you insist. What do you think happened?'

She shook her head helplessly, imagining all the possible disasters that could have taken place in Gandhara. 'Was there an illness? A war? Was there trickery by the ministers? A rebellion by the army?'

Shakuni scoffed. 'Look closer to your new home, dear sister.'

Gandhari swallowed hard. She did not want to follow that train of thought further. 'H-has there been trouble between my family and the Kurus? Has there been a fight?'

'Do you not know your husband at all, dear sister?' His voice was as light and smooth as butter and all the more sinister for it.

'D-did he offend them?'

'This innocent lass act does not suit you, dear sister. Be your father's daughter and start thinking for yourself and ask better questions. What is your husband like?'

Tears started falling down her cheeks. She could not bring herself to slight her husband, even now. She could not bring herself to disparage him, even in thought or speech with her brother. She said nothing.

Shakuni took pity on her then. He said, 'You know he is a man of spite, of insecurity, of deep paranoia. You know that he cannot brook disrespect or insult. You know he cannot tolerate the thought of rejection. And then you came along, a strong princess from a strong kingdom. How insecure must he have felt? You can just imagine.'

Gandhari shook her head. 'I never gave him reason for doubt or insecurity. I have always been loyal to him; I have always been devout and faithful to him in every way. There was no reason for him to worry about anything.'

'When has that man ever needed a reason for his delusional fantasies and suspicions?' It startled Gandhari to hear her brother so dismissive and scornful of a man whose favour he so solicitously curried, into whose company he forced himself so regularly.

'What do you imagine your husband capable of, Gandhari? When he has free reign? When there is no one to oppose him or stop him? When he is fuelled by fear and incorrigible power?' Gandhari shivered despite herself. Her hands were shaking now. 'Did he hurt them? Is that what you are saying?' *But would I not have known? Would I have not felt it if he had harmed my family? Would I not have perceived it? Could I be so close to evil and not recognize it? I could not be so blind, so foolish, so gullible. Could I?*

His voice was flat and unemotional as he told her, 'A band of Kuru warriors came to kidnap us in our sleep. We had welcomed them as our guests, as our in-laws. They slaughtered the palace guards and took us away into a fortress where we were held prisoner. For years.'

Gandhari gasped and shook her head, recoiling. 'That's impossible! I would have heard it if it were true. Such a thing – others would have come to their rescue. Others would have protested it, they would have come here and demanded their release. You are spouting tales, brother.'

Shakuni waved his arms dismissively. She could feel the disturbance in the air. 'Who cares about a remote kingdom like Gandhara? A kingdom full of barbarians and strange mountain folk? No one cared, sister. I tell you, we were held hostage for years in a dark dungeon. Our parents, our brothers and me.'

She shook her head wildly, as if that could shake off his words.

He said quietly, 'You do not believe me. Here then.' He reached out and took her hand in his. His flesh was clammy and cold. He pressed her hand into his belly. It was hard and protruding. 'Do you feel this? Do you feel my stomach? Do you know what is in my stomach?' Gandhari moved to draw her hand away but he would not let her. 'They meant to starve us to death. Just one portion of food they gave every day, one portion for one hundred of us. Do you know what happened to that food, Gandhari?' She shook her head, trembling. 'Father remembered that I had been the one to oppose the match, that I had seen the true nature of these dastardly Kurus. He commanded everyone to give their portion to me. They all starved themselves so that I could live. I took all of their food and ate it and survived and lived. I lived in that dungeon until they became skeletons, until I was the only one left alive. And even then I did not leave. I did not want to be caught again. I stayed there, with the rotting corpses of our family members. I kept taking the food. They dropped it in through a hole. And I kept eating, and that is how I have this plump belly. And do you know what I did, sister, all those days I was alone in that dungeon?'

Gandhari whimpered and bit her hand, shoving her fist into her mouth to keep from crying out in horror, in revulsion, in agony at what he was describing to her. It was only through force of will that she did not soil herself. She wanted to cover her ears in disgust but did not want to appear weak before him.

'I played dice.' He laughed softly, a choking laugh that convulsed into an ugly sound. 'And I plotted revenge. I had already vowed it for you. But now it would be more spectacular than anyone could conceive. Oh! The plans I have, sister. The vision! It will be a wreckage like nothing you have ever seen or imagined.'

Gandhari collapsed to the floor, folded onto her knees and swayed against his squat legs, kneeling in front of him. She was sobbing now, loudly, snot running down her face and tears wetting her sari. 'This cannot be true, brother. Revenge against whom? Who sent the soldiers to take you? Who knew about this? What are you saying? Was it my husband? Was it Bhishma? Say it clearly, brother, what is your allegation?'

'I do not know. I know only it was Kuru forces who came to take us. I do not think the old man has it in him, the guts to pull off such a thing. He is too gallant. He would have fought in the open. Such sneakiness is not in *his* blood.'

Gandhari was shaking like a leaf. Shakuni patted her shoulder. He whispered conspiratorially, 'Do not worry, sister. I have plans.' He reached into his pocket and pulled out the dice, rattling them in his hands. Gandhari stilled his hand, holding her palm over the dice. Just as they had the night he had come back to Hastinapur, the dice felt oddly heavy and dense, a peculiar texture, that sent chills down her spine.

Shakuni whispered: 'Do not fear the dice, sister. They will never let us lose. They listen only to me. They follow only me. We will never lose with these dice. These dice are blessed.' There was a foul stench in his breath and Gandhari shrank away from him. He leaned towards her eagerly: 'Sister, I'll tell you – these dice, they are special dice. Very special dice. Do you know why?' Gandhari shook her head reluctantly. 'Sister, they are made with our father's bones! I made them myself!'

Gandhari cried out and crawled away from him. 'You're mad! You're mad and delusional and you made all this up! Stop playing these mind games!' The door was wedged shut and she could not open it. She leaned against the door, as far away as possible from her brother. She drew her knees to her chest and kept whispering, more to herself than him: 'You're mad. You're mad and a liar.'

She began shaking, because a part of her believed him. The part of her that had lain next to Dhritarashthra for all those years believed him capable of something this awful, that man who had spurned her in her maternity for her own maid, who had gleefully watched his brother driven into exile, always

covetous, of the throne, of her, of their children. The part of
her that guarded the threshold to the nursery fiercely, knowing
there were those among her in-laws' who would gladly see
Suyodhana and maybe even her other sons dead and out of the
way of the gods-born Pandavas.

Shakuni stood, towering over her. He said gently, almost
tenderly, 'Do not worry, sister. They will not get away with
what they have done to you. This I have promised you
from the beginning. They will rue the day they thought
they would marry you off to that blind prince, that weak,
pathetic fool. They will rue the day they ruined your life
and mine. The Kuru clan will be destroyed from within.
This I promise you.'

Gandhari cried out, 'The Kuru clan includes my sons! Your
nephews! You cannot destroy them. They are our blood!'

'They have been contaminated with *his* blood.' Gandhari
could feel his teeth-bared sneer.

Gandhari was unable to bring herself to her feet. She
dragged herself on her belly across the floor to touch his feet,
to supplicate herself at his feet. 'Please, brother, I am begging
you, do not hurt my children. They are all I have left. Please
protect them and watch over them. That's the reason I asked
you to come here, all these years ago. Oh, Shakuni! You are
beholden to protect them and watch over them! Please spare
them from your games.'

He said nothing.

'Shakuni!' she shouted. 'Do not hurt my sons!'

'He has used these sons to bind you, he is using them for
his own games and ambitions. They are nothing but pawns to
him, and so they must be nothing but pawns to me. Do not
blame me for it, sister. Blame him, the one you married, the
one you blindfolded yourself for!' There was petulance in his
voice and jealousy. Suddenly, Gandhari wondered if this had
not been his plan all along, from the beginning.

Gandhari's lungs were burning now from having cried herself hoarse and dry. 'You must know they will destroy themselves in their quest to destroy the sons of Pandu. The sons of Pandu are the sons of the *devas*. My sons stand no chance against them. Yet you are forcing them again and again to fight the Pandavas. You are prodding them on, encouraging their father's flights of fancy, his delusions about the throne, their dreams for the crown. You are pushing them on the path to their destruction.' Her voice grew ragged. 'They call you uncle! Yet you are killing them.'

Shakuni sniggered.

'I will kick you out of this palace! I will tell my husband. Oh, I should have listened to Satyavati when she warned me about you. I will banish you. You are a madman, you are poison to this family, this palace.' Yet, even as she denounced him, her voice faltered. She was torn by disbelief and denial – neither could she believe his wild tale, nor could she trust the family into which she had married, the family that had tried to take from her arms her new-born eldest son. Even as she chastised him, deep within, a part of her welcomed his fierce protectiveness, so long as he would protect her sons in the madness of his schemes. That was her concern.

'So, you are one of the Kurus now.' His voice was leaden with disdain.

'I am the mother of my Kuru sons! They have and will always have my first loyalty.'

'How quickly you have abandoned us, sister, your first family, the family of your birth. Even if your husband is a murderer, the murderer of us all, still you will side with him, is it?'

She shook her head decisively. 'I do not believe you. You are a madman.'

'And how is it that you will have thrown me out? What will you tell your husband? That you suspect your own brother of wanting to kill your children? Then who will be the mad one, sister? Who will be the one banished? Me, who is helping your husband's and sons' dreams come true, or you, who are thwarting them?'

Gandhari was quiet and resolute. 'I will defeat you. I will stop you from destroying my family. They are my sons. They will listen to me. I will guide them correctly. They will be safe and they will be protected.' She found the strength to stand up and twist the knob on the door to let herself out.

'Very well, sister,' he said in an even tone. He shook the dice and threw them brutally hard against the door, narrowly dodging her body, grazing the edges of her sari. 'Let us see how the game unfolds.'

♋

Perhaps that would have remained the end of it; perhaps it would have persisted as a stalemate – Duryodhana's plots, the Pandavas successfully thwarting him again and again, a nagging thorn in their side but not the cataclysmic war that erupted. Perhaps it would have been contained, embers of a fire that never quite combusted into the ravaging firestorm that was the war to come, had not the balance between the two sets of cousins been irrevocably altered by he who was Kunti's other son, the unacknowledged one, the illegitimate one, the son of the sun himself, Karna.

The boys had finished their training. Drona, their teacher, wished to show off their prowess. A tournament was arranged with great fanfare. An arena was built from scratch and filled with thousands of eager citizens from the kingdom. Kunti's sons and Gandhari's sons displayed their skills at archery, piercing targets with their names engraved on them to cheers from the crowds. Yet, the tension was obvious. When Bhima and Duryodhana entered, half the crowd shouted out for one, the other half for the other. The tumult grew deafening until Drona ordered for quiet, asking the crowd to not become angered over them.

Then he announced the entry of Arjuna. Drona fairly gushed over him: 'Now behold Arjuna, who is dearer to me than my own son. He is Indra's son himself, the protector of the Kurus, the supreme one among those who are skilled in the use of weapons, the foremost one in good conduct.'

The crowds roared their approval for Arjuna. Gandhari could hear Dhritarashthra from a distance asking the source of all the tumult. Vidura told him it was the sound of the crowd applauding for Arjuna. Dhritarashthra said politely, 'I am indeed fortunate that I am protected by these Pandavas, the sons of Kunti.' Only Gandhari detected the bitterness and resentment in his bland voice.

Then began Arjuna's turn to enthral the crowd. And enthral them he did. He created fire with an 'agneya' weapon, water with a 'varuna' weapon, created rain with a parjanya weapon, entered the ground with a bhoumya weapon, created mountains with a parvata weapon, made everything disappear with an antardhana weapon; appeared tall, then short; appeared yoked to his chariot, then in the middle of his chariot, then on the ground again. All these were celestial weapons conjured by his mantras and fierce concentration, erupting in puffs of coloured smoke and disappearing in a whiff just as quickly after the weapon had been used. It was Kunti who reported all of this in excruciating detail to Gandhari, her voice full of pride for her son. Gandhari politely murmured in approval, repressing the desire to tap her feet impatiently. She was bored of hearing of the feats of her rival's sons. Duryodhana never earned such glory. How could he? How could he or any of his brothers, those human-born sons, compare to the sons of *devas*?

Gandhari remembered how she and Satyavati had laughed at Bhishma once, for being such a poor picker of brides. But maybe he was onto something after all with choosing her and Kunti. Maybe he knew of Kunti's boon, that she would bear for the throne the sons of immortals who would be invincible while Gandhari would bear one hundred mediocre suns, enough to be a good insurance policy but never a real threat for the throne, never an even match for those who would clearly inherit the throne. Perhaps Bhishma was more worldly-wise than they had given him credit for.

The tournament was winding down when there was a sudden stir. The very earth seemed to shake and the sound of two arms slapping against each other echoed through the arena like a thunder clap. Gandhari frowned. 'Who is that entering the arena, Kunti?'

Kunti's voice faltered. 'He is a mighty warrior. He is radiant, as brightly golden as the sun. His shoulders and chest are massive. He is wearing a natural golden armour and earrings – just like –' with that, Kunti gasped sharply and collapsed onto the ground with a small cry. Vidura rushed to revive her and she was soon swarmed by attendants who brought her back to consciousness. She insisted she was fine and the others went back to their seats.

But Gandhari was frozen still. She knew that cry. It was the cry of a mother, a mother who had lost a child and found it alive again, as she had when Duryodhana was finally born. Gandhari frowned behind her blindfold. *Could it be? This mighty warrior who seemed so godlike? Could he possibly be a son of Kunti?*

The mysterious warrior cried out, 'O Arjuna! Don't be too smug about your skills. I will perform feats that will surpass everything that you have done.' Karna proceeded to repeat Arjuna's demonstrations with aplomb. Kunti was still in too much shock to speak, so it was a maid who whispered into Gandhari's ears. But Gandhari could hear it for herself, in the eager applause that met Karna's every move, in the encouraging shouts coming his way from Duryodhana. After he finished, Duryodhana ran to his side to embrace him and formally welcome him to the tournament. He professed admiration for Karna's prowess and asked what he could do to honour him properly. Karna said starkly that he only wished for Duryodhana's friendship and the opportunity to duel with Arjuna.

Kripa, the other preceptor of the Kauravas, interrupted to ask, 'Karna, we have already announced Arjuna as befits the occasion, with a complete presentation of his ancestry, lineage and titles. You must now do the same – tell us who is your mother, your father, what is your lineage, to which royal dynasty do you belong? Only then could Arjuna deign to decide whether he wishes to fight you – or not.'

Gandhari inhaled sharply. The veiled insult was obvious. Sons of kings did not fight with those of an inferior lineage. Kripa was calling Karna low-born.

Despite her own misgivings about Karna (and, in particular, his connection with Kunti), Gandhari felt a stirring of sympathy for him. To be so valiant, so talented, and yet spurned for one's birth. It struck a chord of indignation within Gandhari.

Karna sighed and looked upwards at the sun bitterly. The maid sniggered as she relayed this, as if it were an odd thing to do. It struck Gandhari, though, and she suspected what she later learned to be true, that he was indeed the son of Suryadeva, the god of the sun. His whole life, not knowing he was the son of Suryadeva, nevertheless something attracted him towards the worship of the sun and he had spent hours each day, worshipping the sun, standing on one foot, with his head and arms flung upwards, until the skin peeled off his back from sunburn. And the sun, too, was partial to this magnificent warrior. Even now, it shone proudly upon him. Gandhari could feel the strong rays striking against her blindfold.

It was Duryodhana who interceded. His voice was hot as he retorted, 'It is stated in the sacred texts that there are three ways to become a king – through noble birth, through valour and through leading an army. If Arjuna is unwilling to fight with someone who is not a king, I will immediately crown Karna the king of Anga.'

And just like that her impulsive son had Karna coronated on the spot, then and there, in the arena itself. Usually Gandhari was vexed by her son's impulsiveness, but on this day, she was proud. Yes, she knew he was goaded by the desire to humiliate Arjuna, to befriend the only person capable of defeating him, but part of her wanted to believe that he did this for a nobler purpose as well.

Karna, overcome by Duryodhana's gesture, asked, 'What can I give you that is comparable to the gift that you have given me? Tell me and I shall do as you wish.' There was in his voice a hint of servility that saddened Gandhari, the sound of one dependent on pleasing others higher in station.

Duryodhana replied, 'I wish for your eternal friendship.'

Bhima jeered at Karna, 'O son of a charioteer! You don't have the right to be killed by Arjuna in battle. You should hold a whip, not a bow, more in fitting with being the son of a charioteer. O worst of men! You have no right to enjoy a kingdom.'

It was Duryodhana who spoke: 'Strength is the most important virtue of Kshatriyas and even the most inferior of Kshatriyas deserves to be fought with. The sources of warriors and rivers are both always unknown and not to be investigated. It is said that the birth of the illustrious god Guha is a complete mystery. Our preceptor was born in a water pot, Kripa in a clump of reeds. And we also know how all of you were born. Can a deer give birth to this tiger, equal to the sun, with natural armour and earrings? He deserves to be king, not only of Anga but of the entire world, through the valour of his arms and my obedience to him. If there is any man to whom my action seems condemnable, let him fight me.' The crowd erupted in a mix of howls and cheers.

The sun set before the anticipated duel could begin in earnest. Perhaps it was the work of Suryadeva, intent on protecting his son. The tournament drew to a close and everyone left the arena happy, except for Gandhari. The Pandavas and their teachers were pleased at their strong demonstration of prowess; Duryodhana and his brothers were happy with the entry of Karna; the teachers were proud of their students; and even Kunti was happy to know that her long-lost son was now a king, however uneasy she may have been otherwise. But dread and worry gnawed at Gandhari. Only she knew how reckless and dangerous her son Duryodhana would be now that the chance of victory had crept into his hand, from the very brother of the enemies he wished to defeat.

It was said that there was no such thing as a bad mother, only a bad son. Gandhari had believed that once. Once, she had imagined that she was a good mother. She had borne her hundred sons in her womb for longer than a year, suffering through the most excruciating pregnancy. And for one more year she had nursed them, protected them as they grew in their pots. She had clutched back from death her eldest son when they had wanted to take him away, to kill him, to keep him away, to quarantine them from him. She had cooked for them and fed them and nourished them with her own blood and marrow as they grew inside her, that cancerous mass of flesh that had devoured her from within.

She thought she had taught them well. Always they were obedient to her, as unruly and incorrigible as they were with others, they disciplined themselves in front of her, listened patiently as she read to them, endured her caresses and good night kisses. When her head ached and the blindfold irritated her, they soothed her with their fingers.

Yes, they hounded their cousins, the sons of Pandu; yes, they attempted murder; yes, they exiled and taunted and oppressed the sons of Pandu until the Pandavas were forced to build a separate kingdom in the wilderness into which Duryodhana had forced them. But such was politics. Such was the life of royalty. Kill or be killed. Why should her sons have suffered, why should they have been held back, just because their father had been blind?

And the people did not complain about Duryodhana's reign. He was an able administrator. He was generous in opening up the coffers of the treasury for the delights and entertainment of the subjects of Hastinapur. No one clamoured for Yudhishthira, who was now ruling over Indraprastha, the neighbouring kingdom, partitioned from the Kuru territories and given to the Pandavas by Dhritarashthra as a veiled banishment, to take over the throne from him. Things had perhaps reached an unsteady truce, unsteady yet sustainable still. That was what she told herself.

But it was not to be. Not while Shakuni still bayed for blood. Not while Duryodhana chafed with jealousy at whatever Yudhishthira possessed – if Duryodhana had all the heavens and Yudhishthira owned a swamp, gladly would her son have divested himself of the heavens to greedily claim the swamp. And not while Karna, the unacknowledged son of Kunti, the loyal friend to Duryodhana, goaded him on, determined to help her son have everything he wanted and demolish his half-brothers (whom he did not yet know were his half-brothers) who gave Duryodhana such grief. All that was needed was a spark to kindle the fire that would burn everything down.

It was the wife of the Pandavas who provided that spark: Draupadi, who had unconventionally become wife to all five of the brothers through a trick of fate, after her hand had been won by Arjuna. She was the most beautiful, intelligent, brave, strong and desired woman in all of Bharat. She was born of fire and she was the colour of soot, her beauty so stunning that there was not a man in the kingdom who did not want her for his wife. She was fiercely loyal to her husbands, quick witted and sharp-tongued. She was also fearless – a lethal combination.

It had been a simple thing. Duryodhana had tripped and fallen into a pool, an illusory body of water created by the divine architect, Mayasura. Draupadi had seen this and had laughed at him scornfully. This slight was too much for Duryodhana to bear. For weeks afterward, he stewed and simmered in unquenchable rage. He closeted himself with Shakuni and Karna, plotting revenge amongst themselves.

That was how it started. That day of infamy, the day of the gambling match, the day that saw Shakuni's ambitions realized, the fate of the Kauravas, her husband and her sons, sealed into doom. Against the counsel of Vidura and others, Dhritarashthra consented to Duryodhana's request that the Pandavas be invited for a gambling match. He commanded the construction of an elaborate assembly-hall with crystal towers, filled with gems and beautiful sculptures that he could not see. Yudhishthira was reluctant to agree to the match, but the truth was, he was secretly addicted to the game of dice. It was his one vice. He agreed to the match.

A large assembly of royalty from all over the realm appeared, eager to watch this strange gathering. Yudhishthira played on behalf of the Pandavas and Duryodhana appointed Shakuni to play for the Kauravas.

And then the game began.

Yudhishthira made the first stake, announcing to Duryodhana, 'O king! This is a beautiful chain of gems, ornamented with gold. This is my stake. What is your counter-stake?'

Duryodhana replied indifferently, 'I also possess many gems and riches. But they serve no particular use for me. I will win this gamble.'

Shakuni rolled the dice. And Shakuni announced, 'I have won.'

Yudhishthira grew indignant and suspicious. 'You have won this gamble through deceit! Let us now play a thousand times. I have a hundred jars, each filled with a thousand coins. And then my treasury has inexhaustible gold. Let this be my stake.'

Gandhari heard in Yudhishthira's voice the rash impulsiveness that had once characterized Pandu. Her heart pounded. Despite herself, she was anxious for him.

Shakuni replied, with another throw of the dice, 'I have won.'

Yudhishthira said, 'My royal chariot is covered with tiger skin. It is adorned with nets of bells. This sacred chariot roars like the clouds and the ocean. It is drawn by eight horses that are famous throughout the kingdom. O king! These are my riches that I now gamble for with you.'

Shakuni threw the dice and calmly said, 'I have won.'

Yudhishthira's words grew louder and more desperate. 'O Saubala, the son of Subala! I have one thousand elephants that are in musk. They are adorned with golden girdles and golden garlands. O king! These are my riches that I now gamble for with you.'

Shakuni laughed and said, 'I have won.'

Yudhishthira did not hesitate. 'I have one hundred thousand slave girls. They are young and extremely beautiful. They are skilled in singing and dancing. O king! These are my riches that I now gamble for with you.'

The warm air of the assembly-hall tightened into tension, like a bow being drawn. It was one thing to gamble possessions, another to gamble people.

Shakuni threw the dice. Gandhari wondered if these were the same dice she had seen in his chamber earlier, the misshapen, odd ones, the ones he said were made of their

father's bones. She shivered. Maybe Yudhishthira was right –
even if not cheating, Shakuni may have worked black magic
into the dice, tricking them to respond to his call, like a snake
to a charmer. He said, 'I have won.'

Yudhishthira's voice grew high in pitch. 'I have thousands
of male salves. They are wise, young, intelligent and wear
polished earrings. With plates in their hands, they feed the
guests day and night. O king! These are my riches that I now
gamble for with you.'

Shakuni said, 'I have won.'

Gandhari's fists curled into her sari. Kunti was sitting
next to her. As Vidura relayed the unfolding of the events to
Dhritarashthra, Kunti did the same for Gandhari. But now
Kunti was wordless.

Yudhishthira staked in succession his chariots, his prized
horses, treasure chests made of copper and iron, each filled
with beaten gold. Each time, Shakuni threw the dice and said,
'I have won.'

It was then that Vidura leaned over to Dhritarashthra and
whispered urgently, in a voice deliberately loud enough to carry
over to Gandhari, 'O king! Duryodhana is gambling with the
Pandavas and you are pleased, thinking that he is winning, but
what you do not see is that this small victory is leading to the
disaster that will be the end of you and your line, a war that will
lead to the destruction of all men. As Shukracharya had said, as
I have told you the day that your son was born, "For the sake of
a family, a man should be sacrificed. For the sake of a village, a
family should be sacrificed. For the sake of a country, a village
should be sacrificed. For the sake of the soul, the earth itself
should be sacrificed." At least now abandon his cause, before it
is too late. Make friends with Yudhishthira. The Pandavas will
make peace with you, will treat you honourably and well.

'A terrible fire has blazed forth, yet you can extinguish it
still, you can extinguish it now before it is too late. The one

from the mountains, this Shakuni, knows how to cheat with the dice. O king! Let Shakuni go back home. He is fighting with black magic. He is casting his spell upon the dice, as he has on you and your family.' Vidura's voice was severe.

A cold shudder rippled down Gandhari's spine. Out of everyone in Hastinapur, it was Vidura she trusted. His scorn for Shakuni was like a dousing of cold water upon a flame of niggling doubt that Shakuni had lit that night, with his taunting accusations of their family's murder. The clarity of Vidura's voice, the depth of conviction, made her realize now that indeed Shakuni's words had been a lie. There had been no kidnapping, no murder of her family by her husband or by Bhishma. He had used those tricks of maya on her as he now wielded it on the Pandavas. She had been fooled, trapped by her own doubt and dark thoughts. She had let him go, had passively stood by as he had brainwashed her children, caught in the doubt that he was the only one from their family to survive, that he was the only link her children had to her family, that he was the one who could protect them and their interests.

But had he ever cared truly for her sons? No, they were just pawns in his endless game of dice – he played them as he played the dice. It did not matter if they bore the blood of Shakuni and of his sister; for him, they were contaminated by the blood of Dhritarashthra and for that he would destroy them as he intended to destroy all of the Kurus. Maybe he had grown so mad that he really did believe they had killed their family. Maybe it was revenge. Maybe he had just been bored.

She had yielded to him in doubt and insecurity, hedging her bets with the Kurus by keeping him around. What a fool she had been! Where she should have been the strong queen, stern and resolute, she had been weak and mired by doubt, giving him the entry to poison her family against their own good.

Duryodhana scornfully mocked Vidura and dismissed him, saying, 'One should not give shelter to someone who hates them and belongs to the enemy. O Vidura! Go wherever you wish. However well treated, an unchaste wife will always leave. We have done enough for you.'

Gandhari bristled at how insultingly he spoke to his uncle, who had always been so wise, gentle and kind, so devoted to the welfare of the family. With a dry throat, she remembered how Satyavati had admonished her to always take his counsel. And she had not.

Vidura fell silent, helpless.

Shakuni resumed with a chuckle. 'O Yudhishthira! You have lost the great riches of the Pandavas. Do you have anything left to lose?'

Yudhishthira took umbrage at the insult and replied, 'O, son of Subala! I know of unlimited riches that I possess. Why even ask me about my wealth?' He proceeded to stake his cattle, horses, sheep and goats.

Shakuni said, 'I have won.'

Yudhishthira then staked his city, his country, the land of his subjects.

Shakuni said, 'I have won.'

Yudhishthira pointed to his brothers – Kunti was so aghast, she could not report to Gandhari anymore. This Gandhari heard from a servant. Yudhishthira said, 'O king! These princes are resplendent in their ornaments, their earrings, the golden decorations on their chest. O king! These are my riches that I will play for with you.'

A terrible silence descended in the assembly-hall.

But there was no hesitation in Yudhishthira's voice as he said, 'This dark youth with red eyes, long arms and the shoulders of a lion, is Nakula. I stake him.' Nakula was one of the twin sons of Madri.

Shakuni chuckled and said brightly, 'O king! But Prince Nakula is dear to you. If you lose him, what will you have left to stake?' But he did not wait for a reply as he threw the dice and announced, 'I have won.'

Yudhishthira's voice grew thick with emotion and self-remonstration as he said, 'This Sahadeva is the one who administers dharma. He is renowned as a learned one in all the worlds. He is the one who maintains our sacrificial fire. He does not deserve it, but I will stake this beloved prince with one who is not loved.' That was as close to cruelty as Yudhishthira's voice could muster.

Shakuni said, 'I have won.'

Yudhishthira fell silent. There was not a noise in all the assembly-hall. It was as if the hundreds of kings gathered had forgotten how to breathe.

Shakuni's voice turned sly. 'I have now won both of Madri's sons, so dear to you. But I do think Bhima and Arjuna are even dearer to you, are they not?'

The prince replied hotly, 'You cannot create dissension among those who are one of heart.' Kunti had succeeded where Gandhari had failed. She had raised her five sons as one united front.

Yudhishthira was left with no choice, now that he had to prove that his four brothers were equally dear to him. He staked Arjuna, then Bhima, and lost them both.

Shakuni laughed. 'O son of Kunti! You have lost your brothers, your horses and your elephants. Are there any riches that you have not yet lost?'

He said steadily, 'I myself am left. If I am won, I shall do whatever deed I am asked to do.'

Shakuni rolled the dice with a flourish. 'I have won!' he exclaimed in a triumphant voice.

The kings began fidgeting, disturbed at the turn of events and the dark turn of the match. But none dared to say a word, too fearful to draw the wrath of the powerful Duryodhana.

Sweat trickled down Gandhari's back. She bit her lip. Should she have called down her brother and stopped him? Had it gone too far? Part of her was troubled by what was unfolding, but part of her felt relief, that maybe finally this rivalry, this enmity, could be resolved once and for all, through this nonviolent match. Maybe finally her son could be at peace and then there would be no more fighting, no more wickedness. It was a feeble hope but she clung to it desperately.

Shakuni's voice shattered the tense silence. 'O king! You have your beloved queen, who has still not been won. Stake Draupadi to win back yourself.'

No one believed that he would do it. Not Yudhishthira, this kind, gentle, noble prince so well-versed in Dharma and the Vedas. Not this prince who adored his wife, Draupadi, and revered her. Not this kind, young man who was the epitome of chivalry and honour. No one believed he would do it. Except perhaps Shakuni. He who had fallen so low could see that possibility of lowness in others, could see how easily and how deep they could fall.

Yudhishthira said slowly, in a voice thick with love. 'She is neither too short, nor too tall. She is neither too dark, nor too fair. Her eyes are red with love, and I will play for her with you. Her beauty is that of Devi. Such is her lack of cruelty, her wealth of beauty and the virtue of her conduct, that every man desires her for a wife. She retires to bed last and she is the first to wake up. She looks after the cowherds and the shepherds. She knows everything about what should be done and what is not to be done. Her waist is shaped like an altar. Her hair is long. O king! O son of Subala! I will stake the beautiful Draupadi of Panchala. Let us play.'

The assembled ones gasped. Kunti whimpered in disbelief. All the elders cried out, 'Shame! Shame!' The kings broke out in outraged whispers. Vidura sighed loudly and buried his head in his hands, sobbing softly. Gandhari was shocked, and yet some small part of her was relieved, relieved that it was Kunti's son who had become so debased, not her own, not yet.

It was Dhritarashthra who was unable to control himself, who kept asking, 'Has he won? Have the dice been rolled?' The eagerness, the excitement, was naked.

Everyone else was crying. Gandhari could hear their sniffles, feel the salt of their tears slide down their cheeks, their small choked gasps of breath.

But Shakuni was undeterred. He flung the dice with a loud clatter and announced, 'I have won.'

♋

Duryodhana commanded Vidura, 'O, son of a maid. Kshatta! Bring Draupadi here. Let her sweep the floors. It will be good to see her with the serving girls.'

Vidura spluttered with rage and refused, warning him, 'O evil one! You do not know that you are tying yourself in a noose! You are hanging over a precipice. Draupadi has not yet become a slave. It is certain that this will be the end of the Kurus, a terrible end that will lead to everyone's destruction.'

Duryodhana scoffed, 'Kshatta be damned.' Calling a servant, he commanded him, 'Go and bring Draupadi here. You have no reason to fear the Pandavas.'

The air had grown thick and ominous. Now Gandhari began to grow anxious. What was Duryodhana doing? Could he not see that the kings in the assembly-hall were turning against him? Could he not see he was taking it too far? Her stomach began churning.

The attendant returned. 'The queen told me to come back to the assembly-hall and ask the gambler from the Bharata dynasty whether he first lost himself or her. She wants to know, "Whose lord were you when you lost me? Did you lose yourself first or me?"'

Yudhishthira did not reply.

Duryodhana grew impatient. 'Let Draupadi come here and ask the question herself. Let everyone assembled hear what they have to say to each other.' Duryodhana commanded the servant to bring Draupadi to the assembly-hall. The servant refused, so afraid was he of Draupadi's wrath. With what outrage had she greeted him that he quaked in fear now, refusing a direct command from his master?

Duryodhana growled. He called out to Duhshasana, his younger brother, Gandhari's second son. 'O Duhshasana! This servant is an idiot. Go and bring Draupadi here yourself. Our cousins can do nothing now.'

Gandhari heard Duhshasana rise. She heard his menacing step as he marched across the hall towards the palace, where Draupadi was resting. Gandhari's body grew leaden with dread. Duhshasana was her baby. Even now, sometimes, he would lay quietly with her in bed, let her embrace him tightly, gently bringing her to laughter with his teasing jokes. Was this the son who would now forcibly drag a woman, his sister by law, to the court?

Her hearing had grown so keen that she could hear Duhshasana approach Draupadi, her daughter-in-law by all rights, and yank her out of her seat, dragging her by the hair towards the assembly-hall. She heard Draupadi make a run for it, veering towards the women's quarters, where she thought she would find refuge. And then Duhshasana roared, rushing at her. Gandhari heard later how he grabbed her by her long hair, that blue-back lustrous mane of thick tresses, wrapping his meaty fist in it lustily, and pulled her forcibly along with him towards the assembly-hall.

The servants, creeping behind Draupadi in horror and confusion, told her later how Draupadi had crouched, trying to protect herself from his prying hands, whispering, 'It is the period of my menses now. Do not take me to the assembly-hall like this.' That is why her hair was loose and dishevelled. That is why she wore only one piece of cloth, tied under her waist, for comfort and modesty.

Gandhari herself heard the roar of her son, Duhshasana. 'Pray to Krishna and Indra and Hari and Nara. Cry out for help, but I will take you, O woman born of the sacrificial fire! Whether you are dressed or undressed, you have been won by us and are now our slave. One can sport with a slave as one desires.'

Gandhari was paralyzed by horror. Breath had stopped and even her heartbeat had stumbled and collapsed. To breathe was an anguish burning her limbs. Her face was aflame, hot and burning, with shame and mortification. Was it her flesh and blood, was it her son whom she had reared, was it the descendant of her father, the proud king Subala, who spoke thus? Who uttered words so vile that the assembled kings were gasping and crying out in abject dismay even as they did not move a finger to stop what was transpiring as all this unfolded.

Had it been only a few moments that passed? Or long years? Gandhari had lost all sense of time. She heard only the leaden footsteps of her son as he dragged this daughter of the kingdom to the assembly-hall, the cries of Draupadi as still she resisted and fought. Draupadi cried out softly again, but now it was audible to all as they neared the entrance of the assembly-hall: 'My elders are gathered here. There are those in the assembly-hall who are learned in the sacred texts. All of them are my preceptors. I cannot stand before them in this fashion.'

Some small, distant part of Gandhari nodded in approval at Draupadi's words, how subtly she chided all the learned, righteous ones in the assembly-hall who even now did not come to her aid, how she built and strengthened her case even as she was physically helpless. Had she been her daughter, she would have trained her thus. *She is not your daughter. She is now*

your sons' enemy. One's victory shall be the other's ruin. That small
voice died.

Now they were in the audience hall and Draupadi no
longer restrained her voice, as she stood before her father-in-
law, Dhritarashthra, as she stood before the elders. And how
was it she appeared? Gandhari was desperate to know how
she looked. But no one could ever tell her, though they tried,
for weeks, years afterwards, as she begged them for the details,
they tried, but none could capture, none could persuade her
that what they recounted was how Draupadi appeared at that
moment. Gandhari knew she was in a single, flimsy garment,
that the upper cloth was slipping off as her son pushed
and pulled her, that her hair was long and dishevelled and
wrapped in her son's fist. Did she stand proud and defiant?
Did she cower in modesty? She knew, she had been told
later, the scornful and sidelong glances she had thrown in
the direction of her husbands, those who were her protectors
but did not protect her now. How did she look at the others?
With what eyes did she behold the elders – Bhishma, Vidura,
Dhritarashthra – who were beholden to protect her as their
daughter? With what eyes did she regard Kunti and Gandhari,
who were both her mothers by marriage – did she plead with
them with her eyes or did she scorn them as she scorned their
sons? Or did she not even bother looking their way, knowing
that they were as powerless as she in this court ruled over by
men?

Draupadi continued, her voice diamond-hard and emitting
sparks of rage. 'Shame! The descendants of the Bharata lineage
have lost their dharma and their knowledge of the ways of the
Kshatriyas! All the Kurus in this assembly have witnessed the
transgression of Dharma by the Kurus! What substance, what
vitality, is left in Drona, Bhishma and these other great-souled
ones, the elders of the Kuru lineage? Tell me! How could my
husband have staked me when he had lost himself?'

Draupadi cried out as Duhshasana yanked her even harder, laughing wildly and again and again taunting her by calling her 'slave'. Even Karna laughed, and Shakuni, too, applauding with their hands, with hearty claps, the molestation of the young queen.

Bhishma said sadly, 'The ways of Dharma are subtle and I cannot properly answer your question. One without property cannot stake the property of others. Yet women are always the property of their husbands. I cannot answer the question.'

Draupadi laughed mockingly. Gandhari's jaw nearly dropped. How was it that Bhishma, the scion of the Kuru dynasty, preceptor of Dharma taught by Parashurama, Brihaspati and Shukracharya, had fallen so low, had uttered words so feeble and unconvincing? Bhishma, who had let go of Amba, when she was to have wed Vichitravirya but had desired to be wed to another man. Bhishma, who had renounced the throne to placate the ambitions and dreams of a fisher-woman?

Draupadi was not fazed. 'How could it be said that the king chose to play voluntarily? He was tricked into losing by those in this assembly who are skilled, evil-minded and deceitful. Let all those assembled here today examine my words and answer my question.'

Duhshasana gnashed his teeth and growled at her with foul words.

Gandhari's breath caught in her throat as Bhima, the second son of Kunti, cried out, 'O Yudhishthira! Gamblers have many courtesans in their country. But they are kind even to them and do not stake them in gambling. You have committed a most grievous act in staking Draupadi. She did not deserve this! After marrying us who should have been her protectors, this innocent woman is suffering only because of your act. O king! I will burn your hands. O Sahadeva! Bring the sacrificial fire.' Gandhari shivered at the force of his words; she could imagine the sparks of rage emanating from his mighty body.

Sahadeva was the one who maintained the sacrificial fire for the Pandavas.

Arjuna sought to pacify him, to keep the five brothers united as a front. Bickering and debate ensued, and Karna grew impatient. Karna's voice boomed out hideously into the assembly-hall. 'It has been ordained by the gods that a woman should only have one husband. But Draupadi sleeps with many and therefore she is no better than a courtesan. There is nothing surprising at all in her being brought into the assembly in a single garment or even if she were naked.' His voice became guttural now, almost rumbling in his thick chest. 'O Duhshasana! Strip her. Strip Draupadi and the Pandavas, too.'

Later Gandhari heard about how the Pandavas immediately took off their upper garments and sat down on the floor in the middle of the assembly-hall, faces downcast, in abject shame and dejection.

Then all eyes turned to Draupadi.

And with what eyes did those assembled kings, those most mighty and powerful warriors of Bharat, look upon Draupadi then? With compassion, with sympathy, with guilt, with shame, or with unbridled lust? Gandhari knew that when Arjuna had won Draupadi's hand in marriage, in her swayamvara, when he had brought her proudly to the hut where the Pandavas and Kunti were living at that time in exile, when he had teased his mother that he had brought something special home and she had absentmindedly told him to share it with his brothers, as they shared everything equally among the brothers, those casual words of hers had been a sacred command, an adesha, that the brothers were then bound to follow. But Gandhari knew it was not so simple. Kunti was not so silly. She must have felt it, the charged air as soon as they had entered the home, Arjuna, the brilliant sun of the five brothers, always the hero in the spotlight, carrying this exquisite bride with such pride and joy, the silent admiration of his brothers. And perhaps their envy. And perhaps their desire. For, they were all struck by an inflamed desire for her.

And Kunti was too wise; she had spent too many years scheming to get them their due, to let a woman come in their way now, to pit one brother against the others. So, she had elegantly solved the problem by having Draupadi marry all of them. And how scrupulous Draupadi was. She divided her time among the brothers equally, allocating days to each in turn, and if any of the brothers were to intrude on another brother's time, he was to be punished. She was equal in her treatment of all of them, even if perhaps she favoured Arjuna, the one she had intended to marry, the most.

That Draupadi, who aroused such passion and desire, such love and awe, now she was in the middle of the assembly-hall, her garments held in the hands of Duhshasana, commanded by Karna to strip her.

Gandhari screwed her eyes shut even inside her blindfold. She shrunk her eyes into her eye sockets, withdrawing as far into herself as she could. If she could, she would have squeezed her ears shut, to have retreated and run away from the scene unfolding before her blindfolded eyes. She shrank into herself, cowering at the edge of her seat, holding herself away from Kunti, from the shame of knowing what her sons and their sidekicks were doing to Kunti's own daughter-in-law.

She heard the rent of fabric tearing as Duhshasana began pulling off Draupadi's dress. The gasps of disbelief from the assembly. The silence as no one did anything to stop it.

She heard Karna's low chuckle as Duhshasana pulled and pulled. Was she naked now? Were her breasts bared? Her bleeding, most private of parts? Her rear end? The body that all these men had at one time desired. Was it now open to their ogling eyes?

It was only because her hearing had grown super refined ever since she blindfolded herself that she heard it, that she heard the whispered name float from Draupadi's lips: 'Krishna.'

No one else heard it. In so many of the recountings of that day for the thousands of years that would follow, many would say she had never called his name, that he had never come.

But Gandhari heard it and then she saw it.

The name itself sent chills down her spine. It horrified her more than all the other horrors that had already transpired that day put together. She still recalled the day she had first heard the name of Krishna, from Satyavati's lips. *Krishna.* The name terrified her now as it had then. Gandhari almost ran away. She almost stood up and stumbled her way out of the assembly-hall, away from this disgrace being perpetuated by her sons. But an irresistible force held her down in her chair, not letting her rise. And though her eyes were screwed close, suddenly they flew open.

It had been twenty years since she had seen colour, since her eyes had beholden anything. Even in her sleep, she had been careful not to dream, since those days of her pregnancy when she had been haunted by those lurid nightmares. Even in her imagination, she did not let herself see, to imagine what her sons must look like, what she herself must look like all these years after she had last seen her own reflection.

Now it was as if her eyelids had been peeled back, her eyes pried open. She could not help but see. She expected to see horror, but she saw beauty.

She saw Krishna.

Beyond the periphery of her eye, the hand of Duhshasana was tugging at Draupadi's single rough-spun cotton cloth, pulling it away from her body, but before her body could be revealed, another garment took its place. The more he pulled, the more cloth gathered at Draupadi's feet, cushioning them like a soft carpet, while her modesty remained intact. Garment after garment slipped around that slender frame, hugging her body softly, in comfort and commiseration, and then slipped away to the ground as Duhshasana inexorably kept pulling.

There was a roar of astonishment in the assembly as they witnessed the miracle of Draupadi, the extraordinary sight of her being dressed in one garment after another. But no one else saw what Gandhari did. Not even Draupadi, who swayed like a sinuous flame, arms flung upwards, exultant and defiant, her eyes closed as her face was upturned towards the ceiling, towards the heavens, pleading for succour, even as she twirled and fine satin and cotton clothes spun themselves around her. Her hair was like a long, blue-black whip, whirling around and around, a weapon warding off the prying hands of Gandhari's sons.

But no one else saw Krishna.

They all saw the miracle, but they said she was saved by Dharma. And indeed she was, for what else but the force of Dharma could have drawn Krishna, the highest of the *devas*, the supreme avatar himself, to her side, to her rescue, as he had never come for Gandhari?

It was only Gandhari who saw Krishna. She had heard he had been a cowherd once, a simple farmer boy, with a peacock father tucked in his hair. She had heard that he was called an imposter, that he was taunted for not being a real prince, that his pedigree as a king, let alone as a god, had been challenged again and again, that Shishupala had insulted him ninety-nine times in a row, and this smiling, patient god, this Krishna neatly sliced his head off only on the hundredth time. Seeing him now, she wondered how anyone could doubt his divinity.

Each line of his sky-coloured body, draped in pale yellow silk, was graceful and elegant. The drape of the upper cloth as it fluttered atop his sloping shoulders, his bare chest bearing the Kaustubha gem, the blue-black locks of hair that fell over his forehead rakishly, the gold diadem crown atop his curly hair, that still bore a peacock feather as tribute to his boyhood, the cross of his right leg across his left, the arch of his right heel, reddish against his blue skin, how delicately and like a dancer it poised on the ground, leaning against the calf of his other leg.

Gandhari forgot everything as she drank in the sight of him like a woman mad with thirst. Whether her eyes were open or closed, she could not tell. She just *saw*. What tenderness was in his face, what love! His eyes were long ellipsoids the shape of lotus petals, lashes shadowing his dimpled cheeks flirtatiously, his shark-shaped earrings catching and reflecting the bright sunlight that still filtered in through the palace windows. He did not carry now the flute of his boyhood, but his very breath was music. To not have seen the world for decades and to awaken to the sight of him – she would have gladly blinded herself for hundreds of years for this magical sight.

Gandhari forgot everything – she forgot the assembly-hall, the disrobing of Draupadi, the misconduct of her sons – everything that was not Krishna and his beauteous form swimming in front of her eyes that had been opened as if for the first time. She could not remember the last time she had smiled – she had not even smiled at her babies. She had raised them sternly. She caressed them but without giggles, without the laughter and cooing that would have perhaps come naturally had she been able to see them crawl, see their fat cheeks, their once adorable, once innocent eyes. She almost smiled now.

She had thought she was beyond seduction. Since the time of her marriage, she had not even thought of another man beside her husband. But this was a god, this was the best of all the gods. She had once prayed to Shiva for a husband like Shiva. She had once fasted for a year for that boon. She would have fasted for a thousand years – forget blindfolding herself, she would have gouged her own eyes out – to have won this Krishna for herself, as Draupadi had won Arjuna. He who had come to the rescue of Draupadi, who could have taken her away from this miserable palace, this life that had become so rotten and hopeless.

A golden discus with a sharp, serrated edge rotated on the index finger of his right hand, the finger held up vertically to serve as the axis around which the discus spun. It was the Sudarshana chakra, the most powerful weapon in the universe. It could have cut through the core of the earth in moments, could have burned all the worlds into ash in the space of a second. Yet now it spun out soft cloths to drape Draupadi. With a gentle smile, Krishna sent yards of fabric out to cover and protect Draupadi, in soothing pink, yellow, orange tones, offering solace to her in every which way. The chakra spun them out like a loom and at the flick of Krishna's finger, the cloth flung itself to Draupadi, draping itself around her protectively.

It was a spellbinding sight, the love and tenderness in his gaze, the intent focus on Draupadi as she spun around and around, as Duhshasana tugged the fabric from one end and Krishna covered her from the other end.

It was the sound of her son's anger that broke the spell. There was a slapping sound and the grunt of Duryodhana as he grew frustrated at the failure of Draupadi's disrobing. Gandhari knew it was her eldest son. He made that same sound of impatience and hunger when he wanted seconds at dinner, demanding another serving of meat from her plates, growling until she served him. It was the same hunger, the same lust.

Krishna's eyes narrowed, reddened in anger and displeasure.

Now Gandhari heard the chortles of Karna and Duryodhana, goading Duhshasana onward, even as it was obvious it would not work; that they had been thwarted.

The chakra began spinning faster and faster, whirring with a high-pitched noise. He smiled. His smiles were legendary, so charming, so enticing, they drew cows and deer to his side, drew the flowers from the trees, made the waves of the river reverse course to come near him, turned women and men, boys and girls, the elderly, the sick, the royal, the poor, all to mush. But this was not that kind of a smile. This was a blood-curdling smile, a smile that promised war, total destruction, total annihilation.

Gandhari gasped, convinced that Krishna was going to decapitate her sons. Krishna's gaze slid to her and he raised an eyebrow at her challengingly, inquisitively. Gandhari remembered how he had severed Shishupala's head after ninety-nine insults. How could he be expected to bear this dishonouring of Draupadi, one of his favourites, one of his closest friends? Everyone knew of the special friendship between the two, how when once Krishna had hurt his finger, Draupadi had rushed to him, wrapping the wound with her own sari, how touched he had been, how he had vowed to one day return the favour.

Gandhari moved as if to lunge towards her sons, to fling herself in front of them protectively, to save them from Krishna. At that moment, all she could think of was saving her sons from his divine weapon, from his divine intervention, to protect them from his punishment. Krishna shook his head at her sadly.

It was then that Gandhari realized that it had not been her sons that were being tested at that moment; it was she. She had moved to save her sons when she had not moved to protect Draupadi. She had forsaken Dharma for her flesh and blood. She had moved to oppose Krishna instead of supporting him. She had chosen the vile deeds of her sons over the innocence of her daughter-in-law. She had failed.

She remembered now how her father had fretted and been so anxious after that wild ascetic had come to their court in Gandhara, how worried he had been that she would be an enemy to the *devas*, that there was wrong within her. She remembered how Dvaipayana had hesitated before giving her the blessing for one hundred sons. Had he known that this would happen? Had he known she would not be able to raise them well? That she would raise them with some evil, some evil that perhaps had been inside her all along? Had he tried to protect her from herself?

She had failed as a mother. She remembered now all the rules of etiquette that she had taught her sons, all the formalities, all the honorifics by which they were to address women, their elders, their teachers. But she had not taught them respect. She had not taught them to care for others, to feel compassion. She, who had been deprived of all of that for so long, had forgotten to endow them with that which had been taken away from her.

She had failed as a woman, a queen, who still had some authority in this court, moral if not legal. She moved her eyes desperately, looking for her sons, at least once, to see them for herself, to see if they were truly bad, if they had inherited that badness from her, to see once their eyes, their expressions, what their faces alone could tell her of their character. But everything else was darkness. Only Krishna was visible.

When her eyes found Krishna's face again, the love and longing was lost, subjugated by shame and despair. He was her enemy now. He would be the one to destroy her family, and by extension, her. Her body became leaden with dread and a terrible fear. They were now on opposite sides. An anguish and misery like nothing she had ever known before set firm inside her. That which had been hardened in her once now turned brittle, into something that would shatter into dust. For a moment, there had been possibility. For a moment, there had been hope that there was a different ending, a happy ending.

The whirring of the chakra became so loud it melded into the sound of a conch being blown, the conches of a war that was now inevitable, heralding a battle that would inexorably draw in all the kingdoms and families of Bharat, pitting them against each other, splitting families, teacher against student, generations against each other, a war that would tear apart Bharat and the only world they had ever known. The sound of the conches melded with the crying out of the people assembled in the hall, awestruck and horrified by the miracle and the debacle of what they had witnessed. And that sound melded with the low keening cry that came out of Gandhari's mouth, a cry of protest, too little, too late.

And then did Duhshasana finally give up, letting go of Draupadi's cloth and falling back to the floor in exhaustion with yards and yards and yards of fabric surrounding him. Then did Draupadi stop spinning, her feet carpeted by high mounds of soft silk and cotton saris, cushioning her. Then did the chakra finally stop spinning and the sounds fade into silence. And then all went black for Gandhari, once again.

Once again, she was without sight.

It was not yet over. Duhshasana collapsed wearily atop the pile of garments, the silken clothes flattening with a sigh. The assembly filled with cries of 'Shame! Shame!' and insistent demands that the Kuru elders answer the question of Draupadi.

Then boomed out the ferocious voice of Bhima, roaring, 'In battle, I will claw and break apart the chest of this evil Duhshasana and drink his blood!'

In the ensuing tumult of cries, Vidura spoke quietly bringing the hall to a standstill: 'Draupadi's question must be addressed. One in distress comes to the sabha. Those who are in the sabha pacify that person through dharma. When a person in distress asks a question about dharma, those in the sabha must answer, unaffected by desire or anger. O assembled lords! You must address the question raised by Draupadi.

'If one seated in the assembly-hall does not answer the question, even knowing about dharma, he incurs half the demerit that comes from lying. And if one is seated in the assembly-hall and answers the question falsely, even though he knows about dharma, he certainly incurs the complete demerit that comes from lying. As the great rishi Kashyapa has pronounced, one who knows the answer to a question but does not answer it out of desire, anger or fear, brings upon himself a thousand of Varuna's nooses. It takes an entire year for one of those nooses to be loosened. In a sabha where an act of censure is not condemned, half the demerit is attached to the head of that assembly, one fourth to the culprit and one fourth to those who do not condemn it. Let all those who are in this sabha reflect upon the supreme answer to Draupadi's question.'

Gandhari felt the sting of each word as an arrow aimed at her. *I should have known better. I should have acted.*

None of the kings uttered a word.

Still the debate continued, back and forth, back and forth. Draupadi challenged; the elderly men of the court prevaricated; Gandhari's sons pushed the Pandavas to disown their eldest brother or else accept their wife as a servant; it was a stalemate that prolonged itself in a descent into uglier and uglier manifestations, until her son, Duryodhana, bared his left thigh, inviting Draupadi to sit on it; the left thigh, reserved for lovers and wives, a thinly veiled sexual overture.

But Gandhari did not listen. She did not pay attention. She already knew she was doomed when she heard again the howling of the jackal. The same jackals who had howled the day Duryodhana had been born, who had warned them then as they did now, that her son would be the cause of the destruction of their lineage and the kingdom. It was the time of agnihotra, the kindling of the sacred fire in the household. It was twilight, dusk, when light met darkness, the dawning of the evening.

Donkeys brayed and terrible birds shrieked, birds she could not remember ever hearing before. Animals cackled and snakes hissed and the very earth seemed to rise in protest against her sons. Bhishma cried out, 'Shanti! Shanti!' It was then that Gandhari knew the time had come to put an end to things. It was then that she found her voice.

Gandhari whispered to her husband, 'Say something before it is too late. Our ruin is upon us.'

Dhritarashthra finally spoke. It was amazing that once he spoke, finally his words carried weight, finally they reflected some wisdom. It was only when it was too late that he realized the error of his ways, that he discerned right from wrong. That was the tragedy of her husband. He called out, 'O evil-minded Duryodhana! You have been destroyed. You have insulted a woman, not just a woman, but a lawfully wedded wife like Draupadi.' His voice choked, fearful of the fate of his sons. He addressed Draupadi and tried to pacify her: 'Choose from me whatever boon you desire. You are a chaste lady who follows the supreme dharma and you are the most special of my daughters-in-law.'

In an even voice, she requested two boons, the first to free Yudhishthira, the eldest of the brothers and the king, and the second to free the other brothers, together with their chariots and their bows.

Dhritarashthra offered a third boon.

Draupadi refused. She said, 'Greed destroys dharma and I am disinclined to do so. My husbands have been rescued. They will obtain riches and prosperity through their own sacred deeds.' *She does not need our charity.*

Even Karna marvelled at the composure of this extraordinary woman. He said in a voice of awe, 'Among all women in humankind, renowned for their beauty, we have not seen, nor heard, of the accomplishment of such a deed. When the sons of Kunti and the sons of Dhritarashthra were raging in anger, Draupadi brought solace. The sons of Pandu were immersed and drowning in an ocean without a boat. She became their boat and brought them safely ashore.'

Gandhari suffered a sharp pang of jealousy, more intense than anything she had felt before. Even when Kunti had come as the bride of Pandu, even when Kunti had borne a son before her, even when Ayla had given birth to her husband's son, even then she had not felt the jealousy, the burning fire within her heart that she felt now. This was who she should have been, someone like Draupadi. Someone strong, just and principled, fearless. Someone who could command respect and awe by virtue of her character. A true queen. Instead she had become this shell of a self-martyred woman, bitterness and a greedy, hoarding protectionism of her sons overwhelming what had once been her intelligence, her virtue, her strength.

She could have been a strong queen. Once. And how could she blame it on her husband? When this woman who had been betrayed by her elders, by her five husbands, by her own preceptors, still burned like a holy flame, still stood strong and proud, still commanded even when she was a slave, still brought to their knees the kings who lorded their judgment over her.

Yudhishthira approached Dhritarashthra, and Gandhari knew he would have approached in his customary humble demeanour, with his hands joined in salutation. 'O king! You are our lord. Command us as to what we should do.'

'O Ajatashatru, one without enemies! Go in peace and safety. On my command, rule your kingdom with your riches. O son! Do not take to your heart Duryodhana's harshness. Look at your mother, Gandhari, and me. We crave your goodness. Look at your old and blind father sitting before you. There is dharma in you, valour in Arjuna, strength in Bhima and respect and service in your twin brothers. Return to your kingdom. Let there be fraternal love between you and your cousins. May your mind always be established in dharma.'

It should have ended there but did not. Duryodhana and her other sons could not stomach the peace; that their ploy to once and for all destroy the Pandavas had failed. Duryodhana pouted to his father, cajoling him to agree to challenge the Pandavas to a rematch of the dice game. When Gandhari heard of this, she was aghast.

For even now, Dhritarashthra was soft, malleable clay in the hands of his son. Again he was deluded; overcome by his own greed. He was going to allow it.

Gandhari intervened. She came to his bedchamber, expelling Vidura, Shakuni and Sanjaya from his chambers. She knelt before him, as he sat fidgeting on the edge of his bed, and she placed her hands in his lap in an effort to soothe him. She gentled her voice, as if she were talking to a child. And, indeed, perhaps she was.

She said softly, 'When Duryodhana was born, your wise brother Vidura told us that it would be better to send this destroyer of the lineage to the other world.' Her voice caught in her throat and warbled as she remembered the feel of his warm new-born arms wound around her neck, the strength of his diaphragm moving in and out as he struggled to breathe and cry, pulling in as much oxygen as he could, always greedy, always covetous.

'He was right. As soon as he was born, he howled like a jackal. O husband, how can we deny it now? He will be the destroyer of the lineage. He will be the destruction of us all!

'Do not become the cause for our destruction, noble one. Who will reignite a dying fire? Who will breach a dam that has been built? Let peace, dharma, the counsel of others and your own natural intelligence guide you in making your decisions. Prosperity built through cruelty is destroyed. If it is gently nurtured, it grows old and passes to sons and grandsons.'

Dhritarashthra sighed, the ruffle of his breath tickling the tops of her hands, his knees trembling under her touch as if he were already an old decrepit man. And perhaps he was. Without sight, it was so easy to lose track of time, age, the passing of the years. He cried out in a feeble voice: 'Yes, Gandhari, you are right. It is indeed certain that the time of the destruction of our family has come. I cannot prevent it. What can I do, my wife? Let it be as our sons wish. We should not come in their way. Our fate is already preordained. Let them have their way. Let the Pandavas come back. Let them play one more time.'

When she was a child, Gandhari had been taught the various forms of karma. Her teacher had used the analogy of archery. Prarabdha karma was like arrows that had already been shot, that could not be retracted. And then, even within prarabdha karma, there were three types of karma. There was iccha prarabdha, the karmic fruits that came from one's own will, from the situations in which one placed oneself by their own volition. Aniccha prarabdha was that which could not be controlled, that which came from the elements, an earthquake, a thunderstorm, natural disasters, engulfing wars. And, finally, paraiccha prarabdha was second-hand karma, the smoke you inhaled from the fire lit by someone else, the contamination of your own field of karma by those who surrounded you.

Now she understood that which she had learned so long ago. Now she knew what it was to be trapped by another's karma. She was stymied by her husband and her sons, caught in the webs of their karma and ill intent. Even her own efforts, her paltry attempts to make things right, could not extricate her from the noose of destruction they tightened around themselves.

At that moment, Gandhari wanted to howl like that jackal, to weep in despair. Blindness was its own hell. But there was another pain, far deeper, far worse, that came from seeing that which those around her could not see, that which she could not convince others to be true. To see when others were blind. And for the first time she felt grateful for that bandage wound around her head, for that which protected her from the world she no longer wanted to see.

She did not bother to protest. Duryodhana and the others went off with Dhritarashthra's blessings. And then began the long hours of wait. She paced. She twisted her hands and fretted, muttering to herself. Dhritarashthra was there, too, in their private chambers, sighing again and again. She was not afraid that her brother would lose. She was afraid that he would win. Vidura, who was often a calming influence, had crept out quietly to witness the rematch, so he could report back to them.

The whole palace was on edge. There were bad signs everywhere. The flag-staffs had suddenly crumbled. Terrible winds blew. Meteors fell from the sky. The fires of the agnihotra had gone out, as the brahamanas refused to perform the sacrifice after Draupadi had been so dishonoured, so violated. As bad as what had transpired was, everyone could feel something much worse was about to occur.

But nothing prepared them for the terribleness of the return of the sons of Dhritarashthra and the sons of Pandu to the palace after the rematch. There was complete silence. A desolate silence that augured death. It was a silence so terrible that Dhritarashthra, who often hid in his chambers, shying away from the truth until he was forced to confront it, called out to his brother to come and report to them what was happening, as nothing could be worse than that silence.

Vidura approached them softly and sat next to them, gathering together carefully the words by which he should share the news with them. Gandhari winced at the memory of how insultingly Duryodhana had addressed him, treating him with the contempt accorded to a disobedient servant, insulting him, practically expelling him from their home. Her eyes clogged with tears. Where would they have been without Vidura? Bhishma was attached to the throne, but Vidura was attached to the inhabitants of the throne, of the palace of Hastinapur. Even when they were wrong, even when they were irredeemable, still he persisted, patiently, counselling them with equanimity, even when he had no hope of changing them or getting them to see, still he loved them, still he advised them, still he looked after them, even when he was kicked like a dog, still he was loyal to them, asking for nothing. And nothing was all he ever got.

Vidura said: 'Yudhishthira was unable to refuse your command, king, and he agreed to the match. Shakuni, your brother-in-law had designed the stakes to be twelve years of exile in the forest, with a thirteenth year of hiding in disguise, and then, in the fourteenth return; the losing party will return and regain their kingdom.'

Gandhari's fingers dug into her palm so hard that she drew blood.

Vidura continued in an even voice, 'Shakuni won.'

Dhritarashthra cried out in pleasure and exultation.

Gandhari's face dropped.

Thirteen years of exile meant thirteen years of reprieve, thirteen years of preparation for the war to come. Thirteen years for the Pandavas to become stronger, invincible. Thirteen years for her sons to become more degenerate, for Shakuni to sink his claws into them even more deeply.

Gandhari forced herself to ask, 'And then what happened?'

'Your son Duhshasana taunted Draupadi, goading her to choose a new husband now that her husbands would be forced to wear deer skin and live a life of austerity in the forest. When Bhima rebuked him, he danced around the Pandavas, challenging them, calling Bhima nothing but a cow.'

Dhritarashthra was sober now. 'And how did the sons of Pandu respond?'

'Bhima vowed to slay Duryodhana. Arjuna vowed to slay Karna. Sahadeva vowed to kill Shakuni, whom he called the deceitful one with the dice. Bhima vowed to kill Duryodhana with a club in battle, vowing to press down his head into the ground with his foot. And he vowed to drink the blood of Duhshasana.'

Gandhari shivered, remembering the righteous anger of Bhima at the time of Draupadi's disrobing. She did not doubt the truth of his enraged vow. She whispered, 'What did the others say?'

Vidura hesitated. 'Arjuna said, "Let the Himalayas move from where they stand, let the sun be dimmed, let coolness be removed from the moon, if I deviate from this vow. In the fourteenth year, if Duryodhana does not restore the kingdom to us with proper honour, all this will come to pass."'

Gandhari shivered. This was the son of Indra, the king of the gods. What hope did she and her sons have?

Vidura pressed on: 'Then Sahadeva grasped his own arms. His eyes were red with anger and he hissed like a serpent. He growled at Shakuni: "O foolish one! O destroyer of the fame of Gandhara! Your dice are not dice but sharp arrows that you have invited to battle. For you and your relatives, I shall certainly do what Bhima has said. O son of Subala! I will overpower you and swiftly kill you in battle with your brothers, if you choose to stay and fight with honour that you do not have."'

Gandhari's heartbeat tripped over itself. *Our brothers. So, they live! My brother was indeed lying to me. How foolish I have been! How gullible!*

Her voice was sandpaper rough as she prodded Vidura, 'And then, younger brother, what is it that the last one said? What did Nakula, the most handsome of men, say?'

'Nakula said, "At the gambling match, Dhritarashthra's sons used harsh and insulting words towards Draupadi. These sons of Dhritarashthra are evil and are soon to die. In great numbers, I will show them the abode of death. On Yudhishthira's instructions and following Draupadi's footsteps, I will soon relieve the earth of the sons of Dhritarashthra."'

They are all to die then. They will all be dead.

Tears slipped from Gandhari's eyes, wetting her bandage, leaving a taste of salt on her dry, cracked lips.

The Pandavas then divested themselves of their rich clothing, their ornaments, their possessions, after they had made provisions for the caretaking of their kingdom and property in their absence, after they had made arrangements for their mother Kunti to remain with Vidura and his wife during their long years of exile, now that she was too old to join them for this sojourn into the forest. Draupadi came to the women's quarters where Kunti and Gandhari and the other ladies of the court were sitting. The chamber filled with the sound of loud, gasping wails and cries of disbelief, the type of mourning the court had not witnessed since the death of Pandu.

Draupadi bowed to Kunti first. Kunti's voice did not waver, was iron in strength and tone, as she addressed her daughter-in-law. 'I need not give you instructions about your duties towards your husbands. Two families have been graced by your qualities and righteous conduct. The Kurus in the assembly-hall are fortunate that they have not been burnt down by your rage. Be blessed; may you travel on a route that has no obstacles. The minds of good women are not affected by what is inevitable. When you live in the forest, always keep an eye on my sons so that they do not lose hope.'

Draupadi murmured, 'So shall it be,' and took her leave, coming to stand in front of Gandhari, a scant few inches away from her. She had bowed to touch Kunti's feet but did not prostrate in front of Gandhari. She stood silently in judgment of her.

Gandhari was discomfited. She could sense the outlines of the cloud of Draupadi's dishevelled hair, surrounding her like a jagged black halo, like something wild, the shape of flames escaping from a fire. The warmth of her body, of a simmering rage that she would kindle constantly through the thirteen years of exile, was palpable, nearly singeing Gandhari with its intensity. She could smell the metallic tinge of her blood flowing, staining the thin cloth wound around her hips, just a

few inches from her nose where she stood in front of her. She
heard later that Draupadi had left her hair undone, that she
departed the palace in a single garment stained with blood and
marked by her tears.

Gandhari wanted to turn her head but did not do so. She
was shamed in front of this woman. What could she say to her;
what could the mother of the men who had molested her,
possibly say to her? Her whole life, Gandhari had been proud
of her piety. Her fasting, her prayers, her worship, her sacrifice,
her astonishing act of blindfolding herself, her devotion to
her husband, her virtuous and modest conduct. And now this
young woman, this new generation of woman, this daughter of
hers, made her feel so little, so inadequate.

It felt antiquated now, this act of blindfolding herself, that
had felt so radical then, so brave, so strong. Strength was what
Draupadi had done. Draupadi was the heroine; she was the one
they would write ballads about, who was able to inspire and
lead her husbands, who would invoke holy war when others
cowered and fled. She was the one who would be remembered
with honour and reverence; not Gandhari, not the mother of
molesters. Even now, as Gandhari sat in front of this woman
she had wronged, whom her sons had violated, she was full of
thoughts of herself, full of envy for this daughter of hers, full
of regret at what she could have been, the ways in which she
could have eclipsed the prestige of this daughter of hers if only
she had tried. And it was that self-absorption, that false remorse,
that shamed her more than anything else.

Draupadi turned away from her and walked out. As the
Pandavas left, Dhritarashthra asked Vidura to report to him the
details of their departure. The masochist in him was eager to
know everything.

Vidura's voice was quiet and terrible in its solemnity as he
described the situation to them:

'Yudhishthira is covering his face with his garment. He refuses to open his eyes in anger; he knows that he will burn these people down if he looks at them now with his terrible eyes. Bhima spreads his long arms to display the strength of his arms. Arjuna is scattering sand to show how he will release showers of arrows on his enemies. Draupadi is attired in a single garment; she is weeping, her hair is un-braided and her garment is smeared with menstrual blood. She has spoken these words: "In the fourteenth year, the wives of those who have caused my present plight will find their husbands dead, their sons dead, their relatives dead and their beloved ones dead. Their bodies will be covered with the blood of their relatives. Their hair will be unkempt; un-braided in their grief."

'Dhaumya, their family priest, is chanting terrible hymns from the Sama Veda connected with Yama as he treads the path, leading the Pandavas, holding kusha grass in his hand. When the descendants of the Kauravas have been killed in battle, the elders of the Kuru clan will chant these same hymns.'

Gandhari inhaled deeply. She could smell it in the air, the spill of blood, the charring of the flesh of corpses on funeral pyres without number; she could hear in the stillness of the air, the zing of arrows being unleashed, the clash of swords, the sounding of the conches heralding the beginning of the battle; she could feel the earth below her feet tremble with the convergence of millions of horses and elephants trampling the land, armies charging at each other.

War was thirteen years away, but it was coming.

7

It is not so easy watching your sons die. And Gandhari was not the kind to give up without a fight. She tried the easy things first. She tried to teach them how to be good. She taught them the morality parables she had learned as a child. She brought in a parade of holy men, renunciates learned in the scriptures, ascetics who had mastered their senses and conquered their minds, rid of the avarice that darkened the character of her sons. To humour her, they listened quietly. But she knew that they did not hear – she could sense their fidgeting, their restless sights. Just as her blindfold prevented her eyes from seeing, their fixation on destroying their cousins prevented them from hearing anything that would have benefited them.

Even with the Pandavas living in exile, still Duryodhana fretted about them as his father had fretted about Pandu when he had exiled himself into the mountains with Kunti and Madri. Duryodhana was tormented by obsessive curiosity, consumed by paranoia of how the Pandavas meant to usurp him. And there were indeed rumours. The Pandavas were not sitting idly, biding their time. It was Draupadi who incited them, the fury of her molestation fuelling their bloodthirst. Free of Kunti's moderating presence, Draupadi reminded them again and again of how she was shamed and humiliated, how they had been made into fools by the trickery of Duryodhana, that she would not rest until they were destroyed. She did not permit them a single contented night without whispering into their ears the constant refrain of a war that would not wait, that had become inevitable.

The rumours were incredible. That Arjuna had been dispatched to Swarga, to the heavenly realms, to win the celestial weapons. That the boisterous warrior, who enjoyed his share of wine and women, was hard at penance, meditating, standing on tiptoe with arms upraised, not moving for months on end, standing at night in chest-high freezing waters in glacial rivers, living on fruit then decayed leaves and then air alone, cultivating extraordinary endurance and forbearance. He travelled northwards, crossing the Himalayan passes, crossing Gandhamadana Parvat, until he reached Indrakila, the mountain of Indra. In his sojourn there, he won the Pashupata weapon from Shiva and the other celestial weapons from Indra.

Every day, Bhima trained in the forests, eating copiously to grow ever more massive in size and might, fighting with trees as his maces, smashing boulders, running upstream through hip-deep rivers to become stronger and faster. Nakula and Sahadeva immersed themselves in rites and scriptures, cultivating the auspicious energies that would protect and bless them. And Yudhishthira had perhaps the hardest role of all, that of the thinker, the discerner of Dharma, agonizing over philosophical questions so subtle that they exasperated his brothers and his wife. Again and again, though, he saved his brothers through his wit, through his answering the riddles posed by the *devas* in disguise come to test them and their righteousness.

This is what Gandhari and her family heard from those who passed through the forest, from the sages who travelled far and wide, carrying news of the world to all corners of the realm. Duryodhana became obsessed and paranoid, closeting himself with Karna, Shakuni and Duhshasana to plot and plan for what would happen upon the Pandavas' eventual return. He did not sit idly either. He cultivated alliances with other kingdoms, easy pickings when the Pandavas were stranded in the forest alone. He and his brothers trained with Drona and Kripa, out in the fields, duelling in mock battles from dawn until midnight. Duryodhana remembered how Arjuna had trained, giving up food, giving up sleep, and he was determined not to be outdone. He remembered Bhima's vow to break his thigh with his mace and he trained in mace fighting.

For thirteen years, day and night, Duryodhana trained in mace fighting and mace fighting alone. He was convinced that one day, the decisive battle would be between him and Bhima with the weapon of the mace. He had a statue built of Bhima, diamond hard and adamantine, bigger in frame than even the massive Bhima was in real life, and from morning to night, he thwacked that replica of Bhima with his mace, practicing blow after blow. His teacher was Balarama, the elder brother of Krishna, also teacher to Bhima. Balarama was the foremost master of mace fighting and despite himself he became fond of Duryodhana over the course of training him. He remarked once to Dhritarashthra and Gandhari that, although Bhima was the stronger of the two, Duryodhana had greater skill in mace fighting because he had worked harder at it for longer with single-minded focus. It was his opinion that if the two were to come face to face in a fair fight, Duryodhana would surely win – in a fair fight.

♋

The twelve years of exile – before the thirteenth year to be spent incognito – were drawing to a close. The great rishi Markandeya came to Hastinapur to call upon Dhritarashthra and Gandhari. After the exchange of formalities, he conveyed that he had recently seen the Pandavas, that they were suffering from heat and cold, that they were emaciated, and the years in the forest, of sleeping on the bare ground, of being exposed to the wind and rains, walking barefoot on thorns and in mud, of living off the meagre stores of food that had to serve not only them but their retinue of followers, the brahmanas who came to meet them, those wise men and their wives whom they hosted, had taken their toll.

Even Dhritarashthra was moved to pity. Gandhari was in tears. She thought of Pandu, how valiant and noble he had been, how devastated he would have been to see his sons and daughter-in-law reduced to this. She thought of Draupadi, that fierce, proud woman – now dressed in bark, leaves entwined through her thick, dishevelled hair, where the crown of a queen should have rested. She shivered in fear of the retribution that was sure to come, that would arrive soon, thirteen years in the making.

Duryodhana was gleeful. He, Duhshasana and Karna chortled to themselves over the plight of the Pandavas, tauntingly mocking them and their travails. Gandhari could hear them in the adjoining chamber, where they were eavesdropping on the conversation she and Dhritarashthra were having with the rishi. Her cheeks flamed to think of how unseemly her sons' behaviour was, how poorly the rishi must judge their uncouth, uncultured ways. Then she realized that he must already have felt that way about her sons, after the disrobing of Draupadi. There was none left but her and her husband to love Duryodhana and his brothers.

The next day, Gandhari heard the tumult as a party was being organized for an expedition. She frowned. Usually, a trip like that required a fair amount of planning and coordination, to bring together the chariots and food for one hundred of her sons, their friends and attendants. No such excursion had been planned for today. She summoned Duryodhana to inquire about what was happening.

His voice was uncomfortable, as it always was when he lied. He was fidgety and his words came out fast, tripping over themselves. 'We are going out to inspect the cattle, Mother. This is an important duty of the king, as you know, as you have taught me. We must look after the interests of our subjects, to protect our treasures, including our cattle. We are going to the *ghoshas*, the cattle stations, to inspect and brand the cattle. We shall be visiting all corners of the kingdom to ensure our subjects are prospering, as you have always bid us to do, Mother.'

Gandhari was suspicious. 'And why is Karna needed for such an excursion? He his own kingdom to tend to, the kingdom you had given him.' She reminded him pointedly.

Duryodhana's voice was wounded. 'He is my friend and companion. Wherever I go, he comes with me. Do not seek to divide us, Mother.'

Gandhari gentled her voice. 'I am not, son. But I do not think you would bring such a large party simply to inspect cattle. What are your real plans?'

Duryodhana exhaled deeply. 'If you must know, I wish very much to see the Pandavas for myself. I want to see their condition.'

Her voice sharpened: 'You want to see their suffering for yourself? Is it not enough to know they have been in exile for all of these years? Is that not enough to give you solace?'

He was peeved: 'I tell you, Mother, even if I vanquish and kill them in war, that shall not give me the satisfaction of seeing them in this state, wearing bark, eating scraps off the forest floor. Just one moment's glimpse will bring more joy to my soul than ruling over the entire earth.'

'This is beneath you, son. This is not proper regard for your cousins. This is not dharmic. It is petty and vengeful. Acting on such wrong impulses will never bring the victory or satisfaction you seek.'

Duryodhana groaned. 'You are a soft woman after all, Mother. Women cannot understand such things. You are too full of feeling. You do not understand what it is to be a king.'

Her voice stiffened. 'Is it? And what is it that your father has to say about all this?'

Duryodhana replied huffily, 'He thinks it is a very fine thing to inspect and count the cattle. It is an important duty of kings and he wholeheartedly approves of this. He understands such things. You do not!'

Gandhari snorted but could not come up with the words to dissuade him.

Duryodhana stomped out, quickly joining his brothers and Karna so they could be on their way.

They were gone for weeks. It gave Gandhari a brief respite; a palace finally at peace and in silence, days free from cooking and feeding her brood of over a hundred. She took slow walks in the gardens. In the past, she would have been joined by Ayla or Satyavati, or even, at times Kunti, but they were all gone now. Well, Kunti was nearby in Vidura's home but rarely came out. She did not miss Kunti, but she sorely missed Satyavati, and whenever she thought of Ayla, a sharp pain entered her heart, a potent poisonous mix of hurt, betrayal and a terrible longing for her companionship. It was too painful to dwell on so she concentrated on Satyavati. That was a bearable pain.

She wondered if Satyavati lived still. There was no word from the forest to which she had retired. When one lived the life of a renunciate, there was no longer the connection with the past, with one's old family, no compulsion to share or receive news. Gandhari hoped for her sake that Satyavati had passed on, that she did not run the risk of hearing about the dire state of affairs of the Kuru clan, the war threatening to break apart the dynasty, the clash of her great-grandsons against each other. She had given so much of her life to trying to protect the family she had married into; she should not have to witness its destruction. How wise Vyasa had been to send her away.

Selfishly, though, Gandhari wished Satyavati was still here. She could perhaps have accomplished what Gandhari could not. She, who had successfully controlled Shantanu and Bhishma, perhaps could have controlled Duryodhana and Karna. She perhaps would have known what to say to dissuade

Duryodhana from his foolhardy acts. She would not have stayed quiet in the assembly-hall when Draupadi had been disrobed.

Gandhari felt terribly alone. Kunti and Draupadi could call on Krishna. Satyavati could call on Dvaipayana. But Gandhari had nobody.

One day, when it was twilight, the hour of dusk, when the sacred fire was being rekindled, the scent of incense wafting through the air, and she was reflecting thus, the quiet patter of footsteps entered into her chamber, intruding upon her thoughts. She frowned.

The figure knelt in front of her hesitantly, his hulking frame blocking the orange glow of the oil lamps in the sconces in the wall. He said gently, 'Mother, I have come to ask for your help.'

Gandhari was relieved. It was Karna. So close were he and Duryodhana that he called her his mother, as if they were brothers, as if indeed what was one's was the other's, too. 'What is it, Karna?'

'Your son needs you. Duryodhana. He is threatening to commit suicide.'

'*Suicide!*' she exclaimed. It was so preposterous that she almost laughed. Duryodhana, so full of vim and vigour, so restless, so frenzied, how could that Duryodhana be given to thoughts of suicide? But Karna was not the joking type. She steadied herself. 'What has happened, Karna? Tell me at once.'

'The Gandharvas attacked us while we were inspecting the *ghoshas*. We fought a brave battle but they defeated us roundly and kidnapped us. Then the sons of Pandu, at Yudhishthira's command, fought the Gandharvas to rescue us and set us free. The Gandharvas fought against them only half-heartedly, since their commander was great friends with Arjuna. That one, Chitrasena, expressed surprise that the Pandavas were fighting them, since he had only kidnapped us to bring pleasure to the Pandavas. Arjuna told him that if he wanted to please the Pandavas, he should set his cousins, the Kauravas, free as they were still his kin. Chitrasena agreed and thus we were set free. Duryodhana is so distraught and humiliated at having to be rescued by the Pandavas that he has sat on the ground, vowing to fast unto death.'

Gandhari's heart thudded painfully. *I had told him this would end in disaster. Why does he never listen?*

'Take me to him at once.'

It took a long time to reach Duryodhana's side, and on the way, Gandhari was fervently in prayer that she would not be too late. She reached the field as evening fell, as campfires dotted the landscape, warming her body as she walked towards him, led by Karna. All her sons were there, along with their companions, soldiers, attendants and ministers. Duryodhana was sitting on the field, on a bed of darbha grass, having touched the water to solemnize the vow to fast unto death. There was a growing frenzy around him as his followers and friends realized this was not a passing moment of pique – he actually meant to do this. Gandhari heard the mutterings of some of the men, scoffing at her son's weakness, his febrility of mind. Her cheeks warmed in embarrassment. This was not good. He needed to inspire strength in his leadership now more than ever, not cause his followers to question his soundness of mind.

Suicide was a sin, and even worse, it was a sign of weakness. Gandhari sat down next to Duryodhana. She whispered to the others, 'Leave us,' and they obeyed immediately, dispersing so that only silence surrounded her and her son.

Gandhari placed a hand on his broad back, feeling the sighs heaving through his body. 'Son, you must not yield to such unmanliness.'

'It is not unmanliness, Mother! I promise you, I am not a coward. I would gladly fight the Pandavas in battle again and again if I had the chance until one of us were finally destroyed. But I never get the chance at a clean fight, Mother! Never! Again and again I plot for their demise, it is true, I do. But again and again I am thwarted, not in a clean fight with them, but through the worst kind of luck, by my own incompetence, and again they laugh at me and mock me. Like they did when I fell into that fake pool in their palace of delusions. What is intolerable, Mother, is their mockery and contempt. How Arjuna lorded it over me, when he freed us from the Gandharvas! As if we were women in need of rescue. They will not come out and fight me but they will insult my pride and humiliate me again and again. It is intolerable!

'Better I die, Mother, than suffer this kind of humiliation anymore. A kshatriya is nothing without his pride and glory intact. After today, I have lost all my glory. I have lost my pride.'

She rubbed his back, wishing she could hold him and cradle him in her lap like she did in those days of yore, when he was nothing more than an adorable baby who would contentedly cuddle with her for hours. Even then he was restless. He never slept, always pumping his fists in the air, fighting imaginary battles. But he had been hers. All hers.

'But, son, it is you who have won. You who rule over the earth. You who has defeated them in the game of dice. You who sleep in the palace while they live in the forest, dressed in deerskin. You who has won and driven them away from their ancestral home, again and again.'

Duryodhana's voice was thick, clogged with indignation. 'And yet they keep coming back, Mother. Why? They lived happily in the mountains. These sons of *devas*, students of the rishis, companions of the Gandharvas. We are mere humans. What was the need for them to come to my home, to take away my throne? Their father was not there in Hastinapur all those years. He had gone away. It was my father who ruled the kingdom, my father who stayed back home and protected the throne. It was I who was born in Hastinapur, who was trained to rule it. And even now they say, Mother, I am a good administrator, I am an able king. No one faults my reign!

They had gone away. They should have stayed away! If they got anything from us, they got it as alms, through our own generosity!'

'If you give up your life, son, they would have defeated you. Rise, Duryodhana! If you want victory, you must arise.'

He grunted: 'I am not stupid, Mother. I see how helpless it is. I am not like Father, in hiding and in denial. I see that they are protected by the *devas*. I see that they have the powers and might of the celestial ones, that they are truly the sons of the *devas*. I see that I will suffer indignity again and again when I challenge them, when I fight them. I see that the best of all those who roam this earth are supporting them and wish for my defeat. I see all this, Mother, and I no longer want to live.'

She thought about it then. She thought about letting him go. She thought about Vidura's words – that in Duryodhana's death lay the salvation of the Kuru dynasty, that his destruction was the only answer. How easy would it be to let him go now, to let him continue down the path he had chosen of suicide. She knew then it would all resolve itself; the world would set itself right, the threads of karma would harmonize and knit themselves peaceably around the hole his demise would leave in the warp of fate. The Pandavas would rule but be merciful and compassionate towards them. There would be reconciliation. She could live in such a world, a queen who no longer was. For a moment, her heart eased itself of the burden of being the mother of the sons who would cause the destruction of the lineage, of millions of lives, the entire breadth of Bharat. For a moment, the guilt, the regret, the remorse ebbed away and she was clean of the taint of her son. She could live in a world without her son. She could.

How easy it would be to not have to act, to not have to say a word. She did not have to do a thing. Only let nature take its course; only let fate lead him away into the afterlife; only indulge her son in his final wishes, as she always did.

Almost she did it. Almost.

Then, she heard it. That small, choked sob emitting out of her son's trembling lips. His pain. The intensity of his hurt. And she could not bear it. All her resolve, all her resignation melted in the fire of fierce maternal love, the determination to see her son happy, to see him live even at the cost of her soul.

She wrapped her arm around his shoulders, but his shoulders were so broad and heavily muscled, that she had to wrap her arm around his neck instead, tugging him towards her. He did not resist, resting his head on her shoulder, his long mane of hair tickling her chin. He sighed heavily. She had told her daughter-in-law, Bhanumati, the day she married Duryodhana, that her son was like a baby and that she should never be frightened of him. He may have a wicked temper and may yell and throw things, but he was like a puppy who could easily be soothed with a hug and gentle words. He was fierce to his enemies but kind to his friends. Bhanumati laughed happily, touching Gandhari's feet for her blessings before marrying her son. She was an impeccable wife, who brought a happiness to Duryodhana's life that Gandhari had not thought possible. He adored and fawned over his bride, and Gandhari could not imagine a better wife for her son. Kunti and Draupadi had their fights and tension, but Gandhari would have given the moon to Bhanumati, would defer to her on anything for the happiness she brought her son. Belatedly, Gandhari wondered why Karna had not called Bhanumati to come to her son instead of her. Perhaps he knew that it was Gandhari's iron, her strength, that Duryodhana needed at that moment, her fathomless depth of will-power.

Duryodhana pulled away, sitting up straight again. 'You do not know how I suffer, Mother. You cannot imagine. The sting of always being second, always being one step behind, always being one rung below the Pandavas, never being good enough. Always they are the best of things. I am nothing mediocre. But there is never glory for the one who is second. You do not know my pain, Mother.'

Gandhari hesitated. It was not something of which she had spoken to anybody in all those long years since, but perhaps it was the only way to save her son. She inhaled deeply and said softly, 'I do, son. I do. I, too, have suffered like you. I, too, was brought to this house as the secondary bride. I was the first of the two wives to be pregnant, but then Kunti gave birth before me. Always I was overshadowed by her. For two years, I bore you before you were born. I was haunted by nightmares of you and your brothers wanting to be born, but I was unable to give birth, to bring you into this world soon enough. Son, I thought you would never be born, that I had lost you. So lost in grief was I that I struck my belly, to end things, for myself and for you. But I did not. I lived.

'And that was the one thought that remained inside me, the one idea to which I clung to in those years of bearing you, those years of watching over you as you finally came to life. *Let him live.* Even when they tried to take you away from me later, I did not let you go, son. I held onto you. I cried out, "*Let him live!*"

'Oh, my son! I have given my life for you to live, despite all the odds, despite those who have opposed us again and again. That life that I have fought so hard for, that I protected with my own, how can you give that up so easily, so soon?'

Duryodhana's voice was choked with tears and he hugged her hard. His arms had grown so strong through the mace training; they held her in a vice-like grip. 'I swear to you, Mother, your struggles will not have been for naught. I will bring you the honour you deserve! You shall be the mother of a king without second. I promise you this, Mother! We are the ones who fight and struggle for everything we have been given. I shall win the heavens for you. I will not squander this life you fought so hard to save. You will be the queen whose name is remembered and glorified in the ages to come. I will bring you honour, Mother. I will!' He stroked her face gently. 'How beautiful you are, Mother, and you cannot even see it! There shall be no queen more regal, more graceful, more powerful than you!'

They sat together in silence for some time. The sky darkened to black all around them. In the darkness, Duryodhana asked, 'Mother, you pray so much. Who is it that you pray to? Is it the *devas*?'

Gandhari was startled. 'Well, of course it is the *devas*, Duryodhana! Who else would I pray to?'

His voice turned low and quiet. 'There are others who can be worshipped, Mother. Others who answer prayers more quickly. Have the *devas* ever answered your prayers, Mother?'

'Of course, they have, son! You were born because of the blessings of the *devas*.'

He chuckled softly. 'Shakuni Mama says that they tricked you, that they are always tricking us and our kind. But there are – others, who smile upon us, who bestow our wishes as soon as we ask it of them.'

Gandhari grew panicked and alarmed. 'You should not listen to everything your uncle says,' she admonished in a voice sharper than she had intended.

His voice was eerie in its depth of conviction. 'But he is right. He prayed to them and see how the dice responded to him. He controls the dice through the powers bestowed upon him by the demons and dark ones, the daityas. They are protecting us even now. He has taught me, too, Mother.' His voice softened to a whisper. 'I have learned how to worship the demons.'

Gandhari wanted to shake him. 'Son, this is madness! They are demons. They bring only destruction and darkness. Do not trust them!'

He was unruffled: 'Mother, before you came, I had a dream, a vision. This gorgeous creature, this demoness, came to me from the fire. There were hordes of them, the asuras, crowding the field. She told me I would fight and I would win, that I would defeat the Pandavas. She said the asuras would spread, invade the bodies of Bhishma, Drona, Kripa and the others, to bring them under our sway. She said many other things, too, Mother, but all I remember, all that has stayed with me, is that I shall fight and defeat the Pandavas.

'And then you came, Mother, and you gave me the strength I needed, the encouragement, to find my resolve. Yes, I shall arise. I will not give into cowardice and defeatism. I will fight and defeat the Pandavas. Oh, Mother! You are the one who has made the asura's words come true!'

Dread sank in her stomach like stone. A heaviness that brought with it a churning fire, roiling her innards until she feared she may empty her bowels and soil herself on this very field. She felt the presence of the asuras on the wind, the hum of their cackling voices, their grotesque forms coming towards her sons, towards them all. *I should have let him go. What have I done?*

♋

The exile of the Pandavas had ended and now began the preparations for war in earnest. The kingdoms of Bharat were being carved up into alliances. The favour of the Yadavas, the clan led by Krishna and Balarama, was still up for grabs. Balarama, who was equally partial to both of his students, Duryodhana and Bhima, did not want to take sides and urged Krishna that they stay out of this petty fratricidal dispute. But Krishna had other plans.

Gandhari urged Duryodhana to rush to Krishna's side as quickly as possible and seek his support. While Krishna naturally disdained Duryodhana and his brothers, they were still tied together by matrimonial ties as distant cousins and he could not simply disregard his familial connections to Dhritarashthra and his sons.

Gandhari sat Duryodhana down and advised him as she would a child. He was to be humble. He was not to demand anything. Listen first, and then ask. He was not to lose his temper. He was to speak in gentle tones. He was to bow down to Krishna and honour him properly. He was to remember that Krishna was not a mere mortal. He was Vishnu incarnate. He was not to invoke the asuras ever again. Again and again Gandhari repeated this to Duryodhana. He bore it patiently. Since the moment of his suicide attempt, there had grown a new bond between them. He sought her out now more than his father. He listened to her advice and in his own way tried to follow it. She had, once again, despite everything, a glimmer of hope. He had risen from the field in which he had intended to die. Surely, he was learning. Surely, he could grow. Surely, he could be salvaged.

Duryodhana set off. Gandhari waited anxiously for his return. She could not stand being alone, so she paced in Dhritarashthra's chambers, stuffy and dimly lit as usual. Dhritarashthra sighed as she fretted. 'Why do you worry so, wife? It is all in the hands of Fate. Whether or not Krishna's favour is won – only the Fates know. What can we do? Just wait and watch the roll of dice.'

Gandhari grew exasperated and left her husband's chambers. She was pacing the hallways when Shakuni approached her. He stood directly in front of her so that she had no choice but to halt her pacing. He addressed her in a reproachful tone. 'You do not need Krishna, sister, when I am here. Have I not protected your sons so far? It is because of me they won the gambling match and sent the Pandavas to exile.'

Gandhari was so on edge that she blurted out, seething with frustration and anger at this point, 'Protected? You have rather hurtled them on the path towards their destruction. As if that was not your plan anyway, to win their trust, entwine yourself with them, and then slowly push them towards their death and ruin.'

'That is a serious charge, queen.'

'It is the truth. I heard you that night itself. I have not forgotten the revenge you seek.'

'And do you not seek it as well? For what happened to our family? For what happened to you?'

Her voice was stiff and cold. 'I do not know what deluded fantasies you harbour. Neither Bhishma nor my husband would have murdered our family like that. For what purpose? They would have wanted our father's armies as their allies. Why marry me and then destroy my family? You tried to work your powers of illusion on me but I am not so stupid. Not anymore.'

He leaned into her face, his breath putrid and sour, making her wrinkle her nose in disgust. 'Still you have not heard from our parents or any of our brothers, have you, sister? You must wonder why that is, why they keep their distance or why it is they have been kept at a distance from you. You have become isolated here. Isn't that why you called me to your side?'

She gritted her teeth. 'You should leave my sons alone. You are working against the family I married into, my own sons. This is treason against the court that has given you home and harbour for so many years now.'

He chuckled softly. 'Then why not have me imprisoned, sister?'

She had thought of it. She had thought of turning against him publicly, after the gambling match, once she realized what he was capable of doing. She had thought of going to Bhishma and sharing her fears and suspicions. But her brother was already despised, by Bhishma, Vidura and all the other elders. Her saying anything could not have helped. Dhritarashthra had become dependent upon him, hanging his fantasies on her brother's shoulders. Her sons had become too caught up in his snares to extricate themselves now. And, part of her feared, had she made her sons choose, she may have been the one who lost. A woman who turned on her brother, a mother jealous of her sons' uncle whom they adored and credited with their successes – how much more vulnerable could have her position become? So, she hedged her bets, warning repeatedly but in muted ways, hoping they would turn against him without explicitly urging them to do so.

'Why do you not accuse me in the open, sister, and have me imprisoned?' Shakuni pressed again, testing her.

'You are family,' she said weakly, reluctant to name the true reasons.

He laughed. 'Oh, that is not it.' He reached out to brush her face with his cold, clammy finger. She flinched. He leaned into her face, whispering next to her lips, so close he almost kissed her. 'I think you like me here. I think you like having someone on your side and your side alone. I think you seek the same revenge I do. But I think, dear sister, your revenge will be something even more destructive, even more spectacular than mine. I simply cannot wait to see it. If I live that long.'

With that, he patted her head and left. Gandhari was left shaking. She bathed herself twice; she sat in the gardens, deeply drinking in the fresh floral air; she drank cooling and soothing cups of milk. But she could not stir off how he disturbed her, how he troubled her. *I am not my brother. I am not the one who will seek revenge. I will not become bitter and obsessed like him.*

It was a relief when the servants came to inform her of Duryodhana's imminent return. He ran straight to her chambers, exultant and exuberant. He embraced her and lifted her up off her chair, squeezing her, and putting her back down with a whoop. Gandhari could not help smiling. Even Dhritarashthra rushed in, led by Sanjaya, to hear what had happened.

Duryodhana exclaimed, 'Mother! The best possible outcome has taken place. You will be so proud!'

Gandhari beamed and urged him, 'Son, tell me what happened. Say it slowly and in detail. I want to know everything.'

'Well, Mother, I was the first to arrive. I beat Arjuna by thirty minutes at the least! Krishna was sleeping, but I went straight into his chambers and sat right next to him, so he would see me as soon as he awoke.'

'And what did Arjuna do?'

'He came in, too, but he sat at Krishna's feet, further away from me.'

Gandhari's mouth dried. She had told him to be respectful, to honour Krishna properly. He did not mean ill, but he lacked the subtlety of thought that Arjuna had, to sit at his feet humbly, placing himself in the position of a supplicant. But surely it had worked out for the best. How else could he be so happy?

Duryodhana continued: 'When Krishna woke up, his eyes fell immediately on Arjuna, of course, since he was at Krishna's feet. I told him I had reached first and therefore had the right of precedence. He acknowledged that with a nod but said since his eyes fell on Arjuna first, he had to hear him out first. And also Arjuna was the younger of the both of us, so he got first preference.'

Gandhari's lips curled downwards in annoyance. Krishna and his sly ways. She should have known that he would find a way to favour the Pandavas.

'Krishna said that he would help both sides. One of us would receive his armies and the other would receive him but he would not take up arms. He would just be on their side personally as an adviser.'

Gandhari's heart began to pound. It was a riddle. Her son had understood it, had he not? She had told him to remember who was Krishna, to be humble and respectful, to listen well, to think before speaking. Had he chosen wisely?

Duryodhana crowed with laughter. 'That foolish Arjuna! He chose an unarmed Krishna! Over his armies! That means,

Mother, I have gotten all of Krishna's armies. Surely now victory will be ours!'

Gandhari's heart fell to her stomach. The smile on her lips curled downwards bitterly. She had never forgotten that vision of Krishna, the Sudarshana chakra whirring gently around his finger, the flash of anger in his eyes, those eyes that in a blink could decimate the entire earth. She shivered. What were ten thousand armies compared to the power of Krishna? What was the point of all the weapons in the world when confronted by the wisdom of Krishna? With righteousness on their side, with the guidance of Krishna, the foremost of the *devas*, the Pandavas did not need anything else. With Krishna on the other side, even if they had everything else the Kauravas were doomed to lose.

Duryodhana stopped laughing when he realized that everyone had grown troubled and anxious. Dhritarashthra had grown sombre, too. They all saw what Duryodhana did not. That the war had been lost before it had begun.

The civilized world did not simply let itself devolve into war. There was a protocol, a process. The three arts of diplomacy – of pacifying through *sama dana* and *bheda,* through logic, enticements, and coercive diplomacy – all had to be tried before one resorted to *danda* (violence). And so the dance of the emissaries began. The Pandavas, to avoid war, offered to take only five villages from the kingdom, one for each brother, and forfeit their right to the rest of the kingdom that was rightfully theirs. Duryodhana refused to grant them even a pinpoint of land.

How easy it would have been for Gandhari to pretend that all this was the work of the asuras. But she could not rest in that fatalism so easily. In her son's obstinacy she saw writ her own failure as a mother to get through to him, to mould him into a noble lord as Kunti had moulded her sons. Finally, Krishna himself came as the envoy of the Pandavas. It was a breathtaking gesture, for Krishna, Vishnu himself, to lower himself to the status of a mere messenger – it showed how beloved the Pandavas were to Krishna, how intent he was on their wellbeing and also in avoiding the war if at all possible. He was a god who did not mind acting as their servant.

By now, Duryodhana had learned from his mistake, when he chose the armies of Krishna over Krishna himself, when he had forgotten to sit at Krishna's feet. Now he recognized the importance of honouring Krishna properly. But he did not really understand. At Dhritarashthra's insistence, he had commanded the construction of elaborate living quarters for Krishna designed to entice him, filled with all kinds of beautiful artwork and ornamentation. But Krishna was not enticed by such material things. As soon as he reached Hastinapur, he went directly not to the king and queen, not even to Bhishma, but to the lowborn Vidura, who was his great devotee.

Vidura and his wife were simple folks who always lived by truth and were in constant remembrance of Krishna. They washed his feet with their tears and fed him their simple rustic fare. Gandhari heard later that he ate with great gusto, fairly licking his fingers with delight. Gandhari felt a stab of wistfulness then. She remembered how she had looked after Dvaipayana, how devoted and meticulous she had been, how pleased he had been with her ministrations. She wished her sons would have understood that, the way the Pandavas instinctively did. Duryodhana thought that everything was showmanship, that it was the grander spectacle that won. Perhaps because he had not grown up with the rishis, like the Pandavas had, he had not understood these things. Perhaps it was because she never made him care for others when he had been young. She had always done everything herself.

Krishna was polite in Duryodhana's quarters but even in his obsequiousness, Duryodhana's smugness shone through, his expectation and impatience that Krishna could be bought off, that now that he was suitably honoured he should accede to his demands. And so it was that Krishna returned to stay with Vidura and Kunti.

There was only the gesture left, the last formality before the descent into war. Not that it made it without substance. There was meaning in that it was Krishna who was the last emissary. Even the gods were supplicating Duryodhana, giving him a chance to stop the madness. Even they tried to show him their mercy.

But Duryodhana still refused to concede even a drop of soil to the Pandavas. He would not budge. They were all assembled in court – Dhritarashthra, her sons, Bhishma, Vidura, their ministers and allies. Krishna again offered that the Pandavas would accept just five villages, and again Duryodhana refused. He stormed out of the palace after being pressed, one by one, by Vidura, Bhishma, Drona and Dhritarashthra. His brothers followed after him. All the entreaties of the allies and elders were to no avail.

It was then that Gandhari was called to court by her husband for one last chance to turn her son. It was the first time she had been asked to address the court, the first time her maternal role had morphed into an official one. She could feel the weight of the eyes of Bhishma, Vidura, the elders who had been preceptors to her sons, the ministers and priests, the brahmanas who had ceased the performance of their daily agnihotra ceremony when her sons had molested Draupadi, and she also felt the absence of Kunti, the other matriarch of Hastinapur, who remained secluded in Vidura's house. Then she felt the weight of the presence of her one hundred sons, who filed back into the palace after being summoned by

Vidura to listen to their mother. Most of all, she felt the weight of Krishna's assessing gaze.

Gandhari swallowed. Duryodhana stood before her. She remembered the fear she had felt when he had threatened suicide, when she held his life in her hands. Now she felt the weight of the lives of all the assembled kings and their kin, the lives of all those who would fight on behalf of the kingdoms of Bharat, in her trembling hands. She wished they were alone, so she could reach out and touch Duryodhana. She swallowed again.

'Son, it is the righteous who will prevail. Turn away from this path of adharma. Desist. Give the Pandavas their five villages. Still you will enjoy the earth; still you will be king. That will bring you the victory you seek. War will not end well for you or for us.' Her voice was soft but urgent.

Duryodhana said nothing.

It felt as if everyone in the palace was holding their breath, waiting to see whether her words would do their magic. Her palms sweat with their expectations, their hope. *I have to make this right somehow.* 'The true enemies of a king are greed and anger. A king becomes a conqueror when he defeats these inner enemies, not when waging war against those who have not done him ill, who do not wish him ill. Oh, son, if you conquer your own anger and greed, the whole earth shall be yours. It is the righteous who will have victory in the end. Pay heed to the word of your elders, your teachers and your ministers. They seek your welfare.'

Duryodhana still said nothing.

Her words became rapid, jostling against each other to tumble out, to try to win him over before it was too late. She racked her brain, trying to remember the lessons her father had taught her about governance and the dharma of kings. He had taught her so well. *Why have I not been able to teach Duryodhana anything?* She turned from the moral to the practical, as wily Subala would have done.

Discreetly licking her lips to keep her mouth from going dry, Gandhari pressed on. 'You are thinking that Bhishma and Drona will protect you. But, son, do not forget their fondness for the Pandavas. Their loyalty to the throne of Hastinapur will not stay their hands when the Pandavas come to take their blessings; fear of your retribution will not cease their love and wishes for the wellbeing of the Pandavas. They will fight out of duty. But it is passion, the conviction of the righteous, that wins wars. It is the Pandavas who are engulfed in the flames of revenge, seeking to avenge their wife, whom you accosted and molested, who have the one-pointed focus to win the war, to destroy you and us, they who are enraged by the indignity and injustice of what you have done to them. Oh son, greed is not enough to win the war, when you fight for what is not holy, what is not yours by right, when those who fight with you have been bought by bribes and alliances of convenience, who neither admire nor respect you, who will abandon you when your luck runs out, and surely, son, it will run out soon.

'How can you fight even with all the armies of the world when Krishna stands on the other side? Think, son! Even now, you can give away five small villages and enjoy the rest of your empire. Let them have those villages. Let them fight and win more territory for you. Let them live on your alms of five villages. You shall be the king. There is no need for destroying them now; it is like kicking a dead body. You have taken away thirteen years of their lives; you have taken their kingdom. Give them the crumbs from your throne. It does not make you any less. It shall make you great. The world shall remember you as the magnanimous king who gave away land for the peace and prosperity of all.'

Duryodhana said nothing. He did not show her the anger and rudeness he had shown to the others. He simply touched her feet in respect and walked out silently.

I have failed.

For a long time, there was silence in the palace as the inevitability of war sunk in, as plans were slowly made, dates drawn up for the commencement of war, preparations made for long marches of armies and weapons from across Bharat, the command structures drafted. After some time, a breathless Satyaki ran into the court and announced that he had overheard dastardly plans that Duryodhana and the others were putting into place to kidnap Krishna. They thought if Krishna was kidnapped and held hostage, the Pandavas would become dispirited and give up their campaign, that they would go back to the forest in despair.

Gandhari's head bowed down. Part of her could not believe her sons could be this stupid, but the other part was not surprised. Dhritarashthra once again summoned Duryodhana and admonished him, aghast. 'No hand can grasp the wind. No hand can touch the moon. No head can bear the earth. No force can grasp Krishna.' He was too distraught, too choked up to say anything more.

Duryodhana said nothing.

Krishna laughed. 'O evil-minded one, Duryodhana! You desire to overpower and capture me. Here are all the Pandavas and the Andhakas and the Vrishnis. Here are the Adityas, the Rudras, the Vasus and the maharishis.'

Even with the blindfold, Gandhari had to shield her eyes. She was grateful that she could not see, that Krishna did not reveal himself to her in a vision this time. She could feel the burning brilliance emanating out of him; it was hotter than a thousand suns, painful in its intense radiance. The sight was such a marvel that later all recited it in wonder – that thirty gods sprouted from his sides, as small as thumbs, as radiant as fire. Brahma appeared on his forehead and Rudra on his chest. The protectors of the directions were on his arms and Agni, the god of fire, rested on the tip of his tongue. He was adorned by the sacred conch, the discus, the goad, the spear and many other weapons, shining in all directions, held aloft by his many arms. Terrible flames and blindingly dark smoke emanated from his eyes, nose and ears. The sun shone out from the pores of his body. All the kings turned away their eyes in sudden fear, other than Drona, Bhishma, Vidura, Sanjaya and the rishis.

The celestial drums were sounded, reverberating through the palace, making the rafters themselves shake. It felt as if the earth itself was shaking, the oceans shivering. Finally, Krishna resumed his normal form and with a whiff of air, disappeared, leaving the denizens of Hastinapur following Duryodhana, weeping and devastated.

War had begun.

8

Women go to war, too. Not just those iconic figures like Satyabhama, the wife of Krishna, or Kaikeyi, the wife of Dasharatha, or Shikandi, Amba, the woman scorned by Bhishma, reborn to take revenge against him – those brave fierce warrior-women who ride into the field alongside the men to fight valiantly and become the heroines of epics and ballads and history. The women left behind – they go to war, too. They are the ones who nurse their men, who prepare them, who anoint them with the sacred vermilion power, who comfort them, who prod them when they are afraid, who sew and clean their uniforms, who have to wait for word on whether they die or live.

For eighteen days, the war was fought. For eighteen days, Gandhari did the most severe penance of her life. Penance was not just abstinence. Once you have given up food, sleep, the senses, bodily comforts, what is left to give up? Penance was also what you put into it, how much kindling you could gather together and ignite into an inferno of power that could alter the course of fate, that could bring down the gods to grant blessings, that could work miracles. In penance, Gandhari was unrivalled. It was not just austerity. It was her intensity, her iron will, her laser focus. The same spirit that allowed her to keep that mass of flesh within her belly for over a year, that ball of flesh that grew into her one hundred sons, whom she nursed with her own blood and marrow, whom she protected hawkishly.

For eighteen days, Gandhari poured an incessant stream of intense prayers as oblations into her internal fire of penance. She did not sleep. Hours passed between breaths, between the

passing of heartbeats. In the adjoining room, Sanjaya regaled
Dhritarashthra with news of the war, but Gandhari was
impervious to sound or sight or smell or taste. She was lost in
penance.

She could not tell you what it was that was the focus of her
penance. Did she wish to win the war for her sons? No, she was
not so foolish. Did she wish to somehow stop the war? No, she
was not so naïve. Did she wish to save herself? No, she had lost
that hope long ago. But it was her war, something she battled
for inside herself, to kill not enemy soldiers, but the barriers
and limitations on her own power. She wanted to become
stronger than iron, more powerful than the blessings and boons
that had been granted her, something better than a queen.

Gandhari remained in her meditation, impassive,
impervious to the cutting down of Bhishma, the fall of
Abhimanyu and the other great heroes, the fall of Drona,
the carnage whose screams, whose smells of blood, reached
her quarters. Her meditation did not falter as millions died,
as both armies decimated themselves against each other. The
sounds of the dialogue between Sanjaya and Dhritarashthra,
as he recounted the unfolding of the events of the battle to
Dhritarashthra, did not penetrate her ears. She was oblivious
to the devastation of the war transpiring all around her.
It was only on the seventeenth day that her penance was
interrupted.

Kunti stumbled into Gandhari's quarters. She landed at
Gandhari's feet in a wet heap, sobbing and wailing. It took a
few moments for Gandhari to come back to consciousness, to
regain the ability to speak and move and feel herself again a
part of this world. Gandhari steeled herself. *What could it mean
if Kunti was crying? Was it possible the tides had turned in favour of
Duryodhana?*

But Gandhari could feel the air, heavy with the smell of
rust and rot, the sour acrid smell of bloodshed everywhere, and

so she knew the tidings could not be good. 'Kunti, what has happened?'

Kunti's voice was choked with sobs. Gandhari had never heard her so weak. Kunti wailed, 'Karna has fallen. He has died.'

Gandhari shuddered. Immediately she wanted to go to her son, Duryodhana, to comfort him. How badly he would take the loss of his dearest friend, the one he loved even more than his blood brothers. But she had never seen Kunti like this, not even when she came back after Pandu had died. She could not leave her.

Gingerly, Gandhari sat herself on the ground, next to Kunti. They did not touch, just sat side by side. Kunti was bedraggled and wet. Had it been raining outside? Gandhari did not even know. In between choked sobs, Kunti said, 'For once, sister, we are united in grief. You have lost the general of your army, your son's dearest friend, and I have lost –' Another woman, a weaker woman untested by the travails visited upon Kunti, would have howled, but it was in a measured tone that Kunti completed the sentence '–my son.'

Even though Gandhari had always suspected, always intuited this, since the day of the tournament when Karna had first entered Hastinapur, Kunti's words made her wince. Later, there would be time for details. Later, she would hear the story of how it happened, how Kunti had come to give birth as an unmarried mother to this boy who had been born with a golden armour and earrings, bestowed by Surya, the sun god, to his son from Kunti. Before the war, Karna had given away his armour to Indra, when Indra asked it of him so that Indra could protect Arjuna, who was the son of Indra from Kunti. It was for this that Karna became famed as the most generous of men. But this was not the time for such storytelling, not at the moment a mother had lost her child.

Gandhari did not have words. Comfort had always been awkward for her; softness had never come easily for her, or compassion. She knew how to serve, how to be reverent and devotional. She knew how to care for elders. Even with her one hundred sons, when they had fallen and hurt themselves, she had tended to their injuries efficiently, pressed the wounds with her fingers to remove the pain; she had made soothing tonics and fed them; she had put them to bed; she had held them. But it was something brusque, competent, efficient. She had not cosseted them; she had never sung them lullabies or cooed to them. She had just breathed in the scent of their hair, muttered a prayer with a kiss to their forehead.

With her husband, she was even more useless as she did not have the patience to listen to his incoherent rantings, his paranoid delusions, his constant need of reassurance. She gave him concise curt words of advice, tended to his bodily needs, and left him closeted with Sanjaya, and in the old days, Kutili, who had the patience and indulgence that she lacked. She had given birth to one hundred sons but she sometimes wondered whether she had been mother to them. Should she have laughed more, played with them more, coddled them more? Should she have been softer for them? Would that have prevented all this?

This was something even worse. Gandhari reached out a hand awkwardly, intending to land it on Kunti's shoulder but instead it ended up on her head, patting her hair. Duryodhana had always loved this. This is how he had fallen asleep as a child, with her hand wrapped in his curly, tangled locks, so hot in her palm — his restlessness a palpable thing that warmed his body from hair to toe, that made his thick locks of hair perpetually unruly.

Kunti turned her face into her hands. Her body was trembling slightly. Another would not have noticed it, but Gandhari did. She pulled down a blanket and wrapped it around her. Kunti accepted it wordlessly. She sighed repeatedly, reminding Gandhari of Dhritarashthra. Then she laughed bitterly. 'Do you know, sister, before the war started, I went to meet Karna. The very first time I presented myself to my son, my eldest son, he who should have been rightfully crowned the king of Hastinapur. A fully-grown man, the king of Anga, and this was the first time I met him when I finally went to visit him right before the war started. Do you know what I said?'

Perhaps it was rhetorical. But Gandhari had too long been trained by Subala to be quizzed and expected to answer instantaneously. So, she guessed, 'You asked him to not take up arms against your other sons.' It was the obvious conclusion.

Kunti sniffled. 'That would have been one thing. Imagine, to finally be reclaimed by your mother, only so she could ask you to give yourself up for your brothers, who are also your sworn enemies. That would have been bad enough. And, I did that, too. I revealed myself to him as his mother, having done nothing for him that a mother should do for her son. But I – I went even further than that.' She swallowed hard and then whispered in a mortified voice, 'I tried to bribe him.'

Gandhari stiffened.

Kunti continued, her voice stoic now. 'I offered him the throne, his rightful place as the eldest Pandava, the one who would rule the kingdom.' It was the legally correct answer. A woman's sons belonged to her husband, even if they were born before marriage. So, Karna would indeed have been Pandu's heir. Again, Kunti's bitter laugh. 'And I offered him Draupadi. I did not think the throne would sway him, but I thought perhaps she would.'

Gandhari remembered that day in the assembly-hall when Karna had urged the disrobing of Draupadi, the tortured anger in his voice, the ferocity. Even then she had wondered if the depth of contempt in his voice had disguised something else, desire morphed into vengeance?

Gandhari kept her voice neutral and bland. 'Why did he refuse?' If he had not refused her then surely Duryodhana would have lost on the first day of war itself. Karna and Bhishma were the greatest deterrents against the Pandavas, the only counter they had to the five sons of the *devas*. Had Karna joined the Pandavas, Duryodhana's war would have been lost immediately. That they still had a chance, as remote as it was, was largely due to the threat of Karna. Gandhari knew he had sat out the war until the thirteenth day. But even knowing that he was waiting in the sidelines was enough to worry the Pandavas and their allies. He was nearly invincible.

'Loyalty to your son. He refused to abandon Duryodhana, after everything Duryodhana had done for him. Duryodhana was his friend, and he would not leave him.'

Gandhari started to cry. It twisted her heart to know that it was Kunti's eldest son who had ended up being Duryodhana's greatest supporter, his last ally, his only true friend. She remembered that day when Duryodhana had threatened suicide, the worry in Karna's voice as he had begged her to save him, how steadfast he had been even when the others around Duryodhana prepared to abandon him when they thought he would take his own life.

Gandhari cried out, 'If Duryodhana had known —' She wanted to say that if Duryodhana had known the truth about Karna, he would have set aside his claim to the throne for the sake of their friendship. She wanted to believe there was still that generosity in him, that brash impulsiveness, that rush of emotion and loyalty that made him crown Karna the king of Anga, that love for his friend would have triumphed over his jealousy of his cousins. She wanted to believe that. But she could not quite finish the thought.

Kunti took a deep breath to calm herself. 'He gave me one promise. He told me that he would spare four of my five sons and that it would only be Arjuna that he would kill. So that I would always be left with five sons, all the sons of Pandu or Karna and the four other Pandavas.' Then her sobbing began afresh. 'As a mother, I never gave him anything, not even the milk from my breasts. And yet I revealed myself to him only to ask of him a terrible promise. I am not even a mother! They say there is no such thing as a bad mother, only a bad son – they only could have said that before there existed a woman as accursed and evil as me.'

Gandhari did not know how to respond to that so she asked, 'Was it Arjuna who killed him?'

Kunti laughed softly. 'Of course, it was. Goaded by Krishna.'

Krishna was always behind everything.

Kunti whispered, 'Tonight, sister, I cannot go back to my sons. They are revelling in the defeat of Karna. They are mad with celebration and bloodlust at the death of my son. Please let me stay here, just for tonight.'

Gandhari nodded. She did not know what else to say.

After Gandhari had put her to bed, draping a blanket on her, Kunti said, 'Do you know, Gandhari, he was so beautiful as a baby. I still remember how golden and radiant he was the day he was born. He was fat and big and happy, laughing, waving his fists around, already a warrior. None of my sons could match the pure beauty and majesty of Karna. The hardest thing I ever did was put him in that basket on the river. I did not think I would ever see him again.'

Gandhari sat next to her silently. She put her hand next to Kunti's without touching it, just so she would know she was there.

The last thing Kunti told her that night, the last thing she said to her before the end of the war, before the cold dawn in which she made that lonely walk back to the Pandavas' camp on the other side of the battlefield was this: 'I wish I had never seen him again. That loss would have been more bearable than seeing my son dead. Oh, Gandhari! I have lost my son! It is a grief I cannot comprehend or survive. It is unbearable! Oh, Gandhari! We are at war but may you never suffer as I am suffering now! Gandhari, you have one hundred sons and today I wish you may never lose even one. We are at war but I cannot wish this upon you. Better we die ourselves than see our own flesh and blood die before us.'

Gandhari froze, paralysed by a fear she had never before known.

♋

Some think it is magic, this play of blessings and curses, but it is not, not really. It is only one who has never gone through the rigors of sadhana, the science and math of it, who do not realize the workings of its power. Just as a man counts the coins in his treasury and knows what it is he can buy and what he cannot afford, one trained in sadhana, one who has accumulated piety and merit, knows one's own store of powers, what it can achieve and what it cannot.

When she was a girl, Gandhari had needed the promptings of the *devas*, of rishis like Dvaipayana, to teach her what was within her abilities and what was not. But she was a woman now, beyond the prime of her life, and she had come into her own. She had spent a lifetime cultivating piety, undergoing penance. So it was natural to her that she knew in a matter-of-fact way, that night after Kunti had left, that she had the power to make her son invincible. And she knew she never wanted to go through what she had seen Kunti reduced to that day over the death of Karna – Karna, a son Kunti had never claimed, never known, never before embraced. How much deeper the pain would be to lose a son one had nursed and raised.

Gandhari sent a messenger to Duryodhana, summoning him to appear before her at dawn, bathed and naked. Totally naked, she had specified. She did not give him the reason why – that would have detracted from the power of what she intended to do. It needed to remain secret. The secrecy was like a screen that kept the power of the blessing from disintegrating diluted into the surroundings and from being contaminated by the energies of others. And then she prepared herself. Once there was an objective, all the penance, all the merit of her meditation, had to be channelled and directed towards that end. She spent the night gathering together the threads of her penance, her meditation, the strength of her vow, her merits of devotion as a wife and as a mother, the blessings bestowed upon her by the rishis once upon a time, by the *devas* once upon a time, and she concentrated them into a ball of light and heat that she fortified in those last few hours before dawn with a new fervour of prayer and outpouring of silent mantras and invocations to all the *devas*, all the celestial beings, all the forces auspicious and good in the universe, to keep her son safe.

Duryodhana appeared before her at the appointed hour, at dawn. She could sense the sky slowly turn to pink behind him, feel the auspicious rays of the sun washing the world anew. Even the sun seemed wan and sad that morning, still mourning the son he had lost the day before. Gandhari stood up slowly, standing some distance away from Duryodhana.

'Have you come bathed and naked, son, as I had told you?'

'Yes, Mother.'

'Keep standing there like that. Do not move.' She did not want to reveal the purpose of what she was doing. But he was too unpredictable, his reactions too potentially volatile if he did not understand what she was doing, so she told him, 'For a moment, I will remove my blindfold. My gaze will protect you from all weapons and keep you safe from all destruction. Do not say a word. Do not move a hair on your body.'

Duryodhana gasped in excitement and agreed immediately.

She was careful not to cheat too much. She raised the blindfold only to her eyebrows so she could immediately lower it as soon as she was finished. She looked at him as a healer would look at a patient, not as a mother would look upon her son for the first time. Sentiment and attachment got in the way of such things; they interrupted the flow of the life force, *prana*, and it was her prana that would protect him. So, she kept herself at a distance physically and psychically. She was clinical as she started with the top of his head, those curly locks of hair she had felt so often between her fingers, that had rested below her nose so many nights as she sniffed his head with affection. She did not let herself become greedy, to let her eyes linger for even a fraction of a moment as they moved downward, to his eyes, bright with hope and wide with shock at what she was doing, to his mouth, slightly agape with wonder. She took in the breadth of his shoulders, the muscled chest. He was the first person she had ever seen since the day she blindfolded herself, since she had seen Krishna. But she did not let herself become greedy for sight.

It was one thing to give up food, sleep, sex. But to give up sight itself, that was something unique. And once having given it up, to have it back but to control it, to not seize more, was excruciatingly difficult. But then the world had not known a woman of Gandhari's willpower and discipline. She controlled herself expertly. Her eyes covered every pore and follicle of his body, comprehensively and thoroughly, and she could feel his flesh become adamantine under her gaze, invincible. She could feel the power of her gaze penetrate his body, go through his skin and bones, the arteries of blood, through the heavy muscle and the skin and flesh on the other side. She could feel the strength of armour she was cloaking him in, as strong and destruction-proof as the armour Suryadeva had bestowed upon Karna. The thought niggled in the back of her mind that Karna had given away the armour, that there were limits to the parameters of parental protection, but she did not let such doubts cloud her concentration then. It was a thought that would haunt her later.

She protected his torso, his ribs, his navel, his belly. And then her eyes dropped to his waist. A piece of cloth was tied around it. She staved off the dismay, the anger at her son's disobedience! She did not let her gaze falter, to move too quickly or to skitter away. She methodically finished the scan of her son's body, covered each hair on his legs, each toe and toenail, and as soon as her eyes hit the ground, she slipped the blindfold over her eyes again.

It was then that she let herself breathe, her heart pound. It was then she allowed herself to ask in a cracked voice, 'What have you done, Duryodhana? Why did you not come naked as I said?'

'Mother, I did! But – it is just a small cloth. How could I come before you naked, Mother, without covering my waist? It would be indecent.'

Gandhari dragged a hand through her hair. Her heart was beating wildly. She was depleted and drained. All the stores of energies and inner strength that she had survived on for so many years were gone, channelled into Duryodhana. She had needed him unclothed. She could not protect him where the cloth obstructed her gaze. She had known that. That was why she had told him to come naked. Her limbs were shaking but she could not bring herself to sit down. It had all been a waste. All her penance, all her vows, all expended in futility.

She could not help repeating, 'I told you to come naked. I was very clear.'

Duryodhana approached her but then stopped, afraid to come closer perhaps. There was something awful emanating from her now; all the goodness had been distilled into her gaze as she had covered him. Now it was the residue of her psyche left behind. The inauspicious, noxious, dark waves of doubt and dismay. She started becoming unhinged. One moment she wanted to laugh wildly, the next she wanted to pound the ground with her fists in frustration, and then she wanted to run out to the battlefield and scream at everyone to stop, just stop. How many others were going to suffer as she would now, losing their sons, their husbands, their brothers?

She shook her head again and again.

Duryodhana tried to comfort her in a tumble of words. 'Mother, do not be upset with me. I did come naked as you had said. I was walking here stark naked, Mother. But then—'

Gandhari raised her head sharply.'Then what, Duryodhana?'

He confessed sheepishly, 'Then Krishna saw me and asked what I was doing. When I told him, he admonished me that it would be a sign of disrespect to come to you naked, that I should at least cover my waist.'

Then Gandhari did laugh – madly. *Of course, it was Krishna.* He had to thwart them one more time.

Duryodhana's voice was unexpectedly timid as he asked, 'Mother? What is it that I did wrong?'

Gandhari snorted. 'Foolish boy, I protected you with my eyes, everywhere your skin was visible to my gaze. But the cloth you wore blocked my vision, so your thighs are vulnerable while the rest of you has become invincible.'

Duryodhana laughed. 'Oh, is that it? But, Mother, all you have to do is remove the blindfold and do it once more. I will untie the cloth right now.'

'No. It is impossible.'The words came out before Gandhari could think about it. She instinctively knew it to be true, that the moment had passed, that her power of protection was gone. It would take decades to rebuild that store of tapasya. But even if she could do it in a matter of minutes, something more important than the quantum of tapasya required had seeped out of her. The will was gone, the desire and the intent to see her son live.

Even mothers have to give up sometimes.

She could not stop herself from reproaching him bitterly. 'You have never listened to your father or me. You have always disobeyed us. I had given you the strict command to come to me naked and again you disobeyed, unthinkingly, recklessly. There is nothing to be done for one who never learns to mend his ways. Leave it. There is nothing more I can do for you.'

At that, Duryodhana fell silent. She could imagine his head falling. Now that she knew what he looked like she could picture him perfectly. It made it hurt more. Now she could see what he would look like dead, how strong and handsome his body would be as it was consigned to the funeral pyre. She bit her tongue until it bled. She should not say anything more to demoralize or distress him. *He should go out into battle one last time with that same brash confidence he had always carried; he should go out into battle one last time still thinking there was the possibility he would win. At least that much he should have.*

Abashed, he came to her silently and knelt at her feet, lying prostrate before her. His hands and then his head touched her feet. He lay there prone. It was the deepest sign of respect that could be offered. His voice was muted and humble as he said, 'Bless me one more time, Mother. Not with your powers but as my mother. One last time as the last day of the war approaches. I shall come back to you as the crowned king and carry you back to the palace on my shoulders as the Queen Mother. Or I shall come back to you a corpse.'

Gandhari's hand brushed his hair and even though such blessings should be given while standing, she could not help it but lower herself to the ground and hold him to her one last time. Despite everything, she had wanted him to win. Not to be king but to be alive. She had wanted her one hundred sons to live. Whether in a palace or in a forest in permanent exile, she had just wanted them alive, to know her daughters-in-law would enjoy the fullness of married life, a joy she herself had never known. She was no longer capable of laughter herself but wanted to be surrounded by the sound of her grandchildren's laughter. Oh, how many grandchildren she would have had! She would have grown old with them, with her sons and daughters-in-law and her grandchildren. They would have taken care of her in her frailty. They would have fed her and looked after her as she had once looked after them. She would not have died alone – she would have died with them at her side, buoyed by their love and company. She had wanted him to win.

But even mothers have to give up sometimes.

She had always been haunted by Vidura's words, when she had proudly carried the new-born Suyodhana into her husband's chambers, how he had called for his nephew's death for the sake of the kingdom, the family, the world itself. She had wondered then how such doom could be writ in the face of an innocent baby, one that had suckled at her breast. Again and again, she and Dhritarashthra had been urged to turn their backs on him. Again and again, they had refused. She had thought it was love, the duty of a mother to always protect her son. But maybe there was a duty higher than that. And now she saw the folly of thinking blessings could protect or curses destroy when one was on the wrong side of righteousness.

For the sake of the family, the individual should be abandoned. For the sake of a village, abandon the family. For the sake of a country, abandon the village. And for the sake of your soul, abandon the world.

She let her lips and nose nuzzle the top of Duryodhana's head. Each day, before marching out to battle, her one hundred sons had filed before her for her blessings, before she began her morning meditation. She had sniffed their heads and touched their foreheads in blessing. She had blessed them with long lives and good health.

Her blessing changed today. Perhaps it was too late, to say this on the day that she knew her son would die, on the last day of the war; perhaps it was nothing more than a meaningless gesture. But it meant something to her to pronounce the death sentence on her eldest son as she whispered into his hair: 'May victory go to the righteous.'

And then she let him go from her embrace and from her life.

It was Krishna they sent to inform her of Duryodhana's death. The Pandavas, Yudhishthira especially, were too afraid to face Gandhari's wrath, afraid of the power of her curse. But they were not the ones she would curse. In their unknowing fear, they sent Krishna to inform her and placate her.

Of course, she already knew. She knew when he had left her that morning. She had smelled his death, the death of Duryodhana and all her other sons. Each morning, the wind had carried to her the smell of blood and broken entrails, of earth churned under the tread of chariot wheels. But the smell of her sons' deaths was distinctive for her. She smelled their death on the wind. It was through smell that she knew her sons. Every morning and every night, they had filed past her and she would smell their heads and bless them with a murmur for a long life, health and prosperity. So much for the power of her blessings.

She did not gasp in shock when Krishna came or let a tear fall or let her trembling lips quiver. Dhritarashthra was seated next to her, too lost in grief to say a word, for once. Even he knew the news that Krishna carried; even his blindness had fallen away. For once, Krishna was not flamboyant, not immediately mesmerizing and captivating, in his entrance. It was as if he muted his powerful magnetism so as not to intrude upon their grief. He made himself smaller to accommodate their pain.

It was Gandhari he addressed as he seated himself next to them. Almost always the king came first, but in the matters related to children, it had to be the mother who came first. Gandhari could not bear to hear the words that Duryodhana had died from Krishna's lips, so instead she asked him, 'Tell me, Krishna, how did my son die?'

At her request, Krishna told her unflinchingly of how Duryodhana had been beaten in battle and had run away to a lake to hide from the Pandavas in hot pursuit. The loss of Karna precipitated chaos and disaster for the Kauravas. The army disbanded and soldiers ran away from the battle. Duryodhana himself had retreated to the lake to conceal himself. He had been outed by the Pandavas and forced to rise from the waters. He then begged in fear of his life to retreat to the forest in exile. The Pandavas refused to accept alms from the Kauravas anymore, now that they knew how fickle the holders of the throne of Hastinapur could be. They demanded that he fight. Yudhishthira cajoled him. He offered to Duryodhana a new kind of gamble. One-on-one combat between Duryodhana and any of the Pandavas, and to the victor would go the kingdom of Hastinapur. Gandhari could imagine how displeased Krishna would have been at Yudhishthira's reckless gamble. But Krishna did not get side-tracked. He talked to them only of their son.

Of course, it was Bhima that Duryodhana had chosen to fight in one last duel. Krishna was about to skip to the end but Gandhari insisted on the details. It was what her father had taught her. A ruler must always take full account of victories and defeats in battle. He must listen to all the details and learn. It is owed to the memory of the fallen that their last encounters are recounted and heard by the ones who rule, the ones who sent them to war and to their death. It is the last duty owed to them. There would be time for the funeral pyre, for the rites of passage to the afterlife, but for now, in this moment, this was what she owed to her son as a mother, what was owed to the prince from the queen. She would hear his tale with pride.

It had been an even fight and a long one. A long-awaited combat that drew the *devas* and Gandharvas and other celestial beings to the clouds above to witness this extraordinary

battle that raged for the greater part of the day. They both
bled profusely and needed periods of rest in between bouts
of intense fighting. Everyone came to watch. Everyone was
spellbound and watched with baited breath. They had never
seen anything like this.

Krishna told Gandhari that Duryodhana had fought
valiantly, that when he had fallen the skies rained down blood
and dust, that rivers reversed their course, the air darkened all
around them and gusts of wind blew. He spared her the gory
details, which she would hear later from others, how her son's
head had been kicked by Bhima after he had died, how the
Pandavas had danced and shouted madly in glee at their final
victory. She was haunted by nightmares then, feeling again and
again in her dreams the press of Bhima's foot kicking hard
against Duryodhana's helmet – Bhima who had always been
the especial object of Duryodhana's hate. She could have
borne everything that Krishna told her but not these words
whispered into her ears by gossiping hangers-on at court after
the war had ended. Krishna had never been cruel like that.
It was Krishna who reprimanded Bhima and Yudhishthira
for their unbecoming disrespect of their cousin. She was not
capable of gratitude for that gesture yet.

In between Dhritarashthra's sobs and gasps of his son's
name, Gandhari asked abruptly, 'How did you do it?'

Krishna hesitated, clearly reluctant. 'How did I do what?'

Gandhari said sharply, 'I remember your brother's words.
Balarama had said that while Bhima was the stronger of the
two, Duryodhana was the better of the two in mace fighting
because he had practised more and worked harder. He spent
the past thirteen years solely devoted to becoming the best at
mace fighting to defeat Bhima. It must have been you who
defeated him.'

She imagined Krishna's faint smile as he said admiringly,
'Truly, you are the daughter of Subala.'

Gandhari touched her thigh. She let herself remember now, now that it could no longer hurt any more than it was hurting, how her son had looked bathed in the rosy light of dawn. How virile, how massive, how strong, how infinitely dear with his shy smile and his big broad eyes that blinked too fast. She remembered his thighs, how muscled they were, and the thin cloth that kept them from her protective gaze. She squeezed her thigh until it hurt to block out this other deeper pain. She whispered, 'Is this where Bhima struck him? Is this how Duryodhana died?'

'Yes, queen.'

She kept whispering, not trusting herself to speak in a normal voice. 'It is against the rules of combat. That was cheating.' The thigh was not a fair target in the rules of mace-fighting.

'Queen, the rules of dharma are there to protect those who take refuge in dharma. Those who have violated dharma again and again, who have shown no respect for it – they cannot hide behind the façade of dharma when it has come time to meet their fate.'

Gandhari's hand released her thigh. She hugged herself around the waist and bent over her knees as if somehow that physical pressure would suppress the grief that radiated outwards from her heart in spirals of fiery pain. 'You cheated.' She imagined how he did it. She imagined him tapping his thigh with his slender blue fingers, indicating to Bhima where to strike.

Krishna's voice remained mild and cool. 'Yes, Gandhari. There was no way for Duryodhana to be defeated in a fair fight. He had become invincible, even if the gods themselves were to fight him. It was only through cheating that he could be defeated. For the sake of dharma, he had to be defeated.'

Gandhari's lips quivered. She shook her head.

Krishna knelt before her, and he said in a voice suddenly so melodious and firm, so resonant, that the currents of his voice flowed all around and throughout her body and swept her up into the cloud of his ethos, illuminating once again his presence that he had muted earlier. The power of him could comfort her even when his words could not.

Krishna said to Gandhari in a voice so earnest, so moving, it brought tears to her eyes when her eyes had remained dry even at the news of Duryodhana's death. He said, 'O daughter of Subala! You are the one excellent in vows! There is no woman like you in the world, no wife as devoted, no woman as virtuous and noble. O queen! Remember the words that you spoke in the assembly-hall in my presence. Your words full of dharma were not able to restrain your sons. You said to Duryodhana, 'O foolish one! Victory goes to the righteous!' Now those words of yours have come true.

'Through the strength of your austerities, you are capable of burning down the earth. O queen! Do not hate the Pandavas. They shall carry out the duties of your sons who are now gone. They shall treat you as their own mother. O queen! Do not grieve.'

Gandhari could not help it. She began weeping. It would be the hand of her son's enemy who would light her funeral pyre. *This was against nature. It should be a crime to outlive your children. What kind of greed is it to keep drawing breath, clinging to life, now that all my reasons for living have died? How is it that I survive? How is that I accept this and continue to live? How can I accept inside my chambers the killer of my son and take comfort from him?*

Yet Gandhari could not stop herself from asking this last question, desperate for this small piece of consolation. She asked, 'Did he die well, Krishna? Did Duryodhana have a good death?'

'Yes, queen. When your son fell, fierce winds began to blow. The earth began to tremble at the loss of this hero. Thunder split the skies and large meteors appeared to fall from the sky. Duryodhana died a valiant hero. He fought well.'

'Suyodhana,' Gandhari whispered. Now she could say it, the name that she had chosen for him. He was no longer there to protest. How proudly she had named him, how beloved the sound of that name had been on her lips, when she first named him, carrying him proudly through the corridors of the palace in Hastinapur, the palace she had imagined would be his one day to rule over as king, how she had pressed that name into his head with her lips, as he sat cradled against her chest, as she took him to meet his father, her husband, this shell of a man who was weeping next to her now.

It was then that Krishna touched Gandhari's hand. His voice was as soft as Gandhari's baby's once was, striking softly against her cheek as she had cuddled him. 'Yes,' Krishna said in that soft, caressing voice. 'Suyodhana.'

And with that her son was gone.

9

Should it have even been called a curse? It was just the outpouring of grief, of anger, of bitter loss, of a mother. You can imagine the pain of losing a son — no, actually, hopefully you cannot imagine such a thing. Hopefully, you never have to imagine it, let alone live through it. But, this unimaginable thing, imagine that multiplied one hundredfold. You may think one hundred children is a lot, that they get jumbled sometimes in a mother's memory, that it is so extreme a number that one cannot possibly love each of one hundred sons as intensely as one would love an only child. You may think that some may get lost in the background, that one's mind, one's heart, can only hold so much.

No. Not for Gandhari. She grew one hundred and one hearts and gave one to each of her children. She could distinguish their cries from each other. She was surrounded by one hundred and one children whom she loved and who loved her, and she felt the presence and personality of each one palpably. If one was missing at mealtime, if one was not there in bed at bedtime when she went to kiss them good night, she knew. She knew their habits, their routines, their proclivities, how the touch of each one's skin differed from the next. And, yes, she felt each of their deaths individually as a death blow to herself, each moment that would ruin irrevocably and forever another woman's life, she felt a hundred times.

It was this inconceivable grief that weighed her down when the Pandavas came to take her and Dhritarashtra's blessings. They had mustered the courage to face Gandhari now. Or perhaps they had lost fear. After Duryodhana had fallen, after the war had officially ended, the sons of the Pandavas had been slaughtered in their sleep by the last remnants of Duryodhana's army, led by the son of Drona, their erstwhile teacher. They had done it with Duryodhana's blessing before he had died. Arjuna had chased Ashwatthama, the son of Drona, captured him and brought him before Draupadi for her vengeance, for the queen's justice. And then the woman who had vowed to bathe her hair in the blood of the man who had molested her, who again and again had urged war against Gandhari's sons, whose quest for justice and vengeance had catalysed the most devastating of wars – this mother who had lost her sons to murder in their sleep forgave Ashwatthama and let him go free.

Gandhari had been shaken by the story of the dastardly murder and Draupadi's grace and mercy. She felt again as she had in the assembly-hall, when Draupadi challenged the court. She felt eclipsed by the other woman's greatness. She was determined not to be outdone this time.

The Pandavas came and bowed at her feet and Dhritarashthra's feet. Yudhishthira wept at the misfortune of the war, at the loss of their cousins and vowed to look after Dhritarashthra and her as their own parents, to be the sons they no longer had. It made her lip curl. As if five could substitute for one hundred. As if she would rather have Yudhishthira's nurturing care than the absentminded, impetuous affection of Duryodhana. As if the killers of her sons could become her sons.

Yudhishthira approached her to take her blessings. She looked down at his feet. Somehow his toes came into her view through her bandaged eyes. As soon as the left toes of his foot came into her view, they suddenly blackened and deformed under her gaze. He flinched and his brothers jumped back, suddenly fearful of her.

Oops.

She had not meant to do it. There was too much of Pandu in them for her to destroy them or even wish them ill. She had loved Pandu once and she would not be the cause of the destruction of his sons. But she could not tolerate the stifling presence of the Pandavas in her chambers. It was driving her mad.

She gathered together her suddenly widowed daughters-in-law and the other wailing women of her entourage, and with the permission of Dhritarashthra, they all travelled to the battleground. It was important for her to take stock, to take inventory of the aftermath of the war, to tally up the casualties and losses. It was what her father would have done. It was the duty of a queen, of a mother who had sent her sons off to battle to die.

When they arrived, she was able to see through her bandaged eyes in a divine vision. She saw the grass fields reddened with blood, slippery with strewn guts and sinew. Vultures and other birds of prey swirled over carcasses broken in half, some bodies adjacent to heads that were not their own. The bodies were so badly gored that the widows could not identify their husbands. Gems ripped apart from golden crowns and carved scabbards littered the blood-stained ground. It was impossible to step more than a few feet without sliding in entrails. The odour of blood, of death, drew insects in droves and hungry birds lapping at the corpses.

The air was rent by the groans of men dying, of widows wailing, pitiful women trying to piece together their husbands' bodies. Some had lost sons as well and flung themselves from one corpse to the other. The orange fires of funeral pyres dotted the immense plain like torches on a foggy day. Horses and elephants trampled to death were piled in heaps. The acrid smell of burning flesh singed their nostrils.

She looked upon the field, where each of her one hundred sons lay fallen. She looked at those fools who had thought they would win the war, that the throne of Hastinapur was worth all this. She looked at those who killed her sons and those whom her sons had killed. She knew their blood was on her hands and her husband's. They could not escape the guilt of it.

Then her eyes fell upon Krishna. He had been the mastermind of the war, counsellor, advisor and strategist for the Pandavas, charioteer to Arjuna, the most valiant ruler of the times. Even in the midst of all that hair-tearing, chest-clawing, air-piercing wailing that billowed out over the battlefield, Krishna was remarkably cool, composed and calm. Even then there was the slight smile curving his lips. Even then his eyes shone like obsidian.

They approached Krishna – Gandhari, the king, the wailing widows, the Pandavas. Gandhari was overwhelmed by the spectacle of it all, the sheer number of mangled corpses, the heaps and mounds of horse carcasses, discarded armour and broken arrows strewn across the land all the way to the horizon like haphazard mountains. Jackals and vultures and other flesh-eating birds were already on the prowl, hungrily devouring freshly dead corpses. Widows had to fend off the beasts from the corpses as they were carried to the funeral pyre. The stench was so overpowering that the princesses behind Gandhari were gagging and vomiting, but Gandhari herself was impassive. She saw but she was numb to what she saw. Sight was so new to her, the sensory overload overwhelmed her consciousness. She could feel nothing after the death of Duryodhana reached her ears. She saw but she did not feel. Not yet.

She had thought it was perhaps a punishment that she was being allowed to see this, after having been deprived the gift of sight for so long. She only knew the sight of Duryodhana and if the corpses of any of her other sons fell under the scan of her eyes, she would perhaps not recognize them in death as she had never seen them in life. But later she thought that perhaps it was not a punishment. Perhaps it was given to her to see this because only she could have done what happened next.

No, not the curse. The curse itself was not as important as what happened in those hours before the curse. What mattered was the naming of the dead. With painstaking meticulousness, Gandhari pointed out the dead to Krishna. For hours, for what felt like hours, until her voice wore out from hoarseness, she named them all to him, all that she could see, all she could count, all she could recall – those who had died, the kingdoms from where they hailed, those they left behind. Her memory was pristine and precise from her girlhood days when she was trained by her father and her tutors to memorize the dynasties of the land. She was indiscriminate in naming them – whether they fought for her sons or fought for the Pandavas, she named them all. This is how warriors and soldiers were to be honoured. They were all due this dignity.

Sometimes it was difficult to identify them. Bodies were broken in half, one soldier's torso above another soldier's legs, heaped together and consigned to the flames for cremation. Sometimes it was only by the insignia of the crown that she could decipher the name, so mangled and mutilated were the corpses. Sometimes she slipped and almost fell to the ground as the puddles of blood and entrails reached up to her calves, as the wet earth opened itself and tried to drag her under. But she did not stop.

Gandhari knew the perniciousness of large numbers. There was a difference between saying she was the mother of one hundred sons and naming each son individually. There was the loss of becoming a statistic instead of an individual. She insisted on naming them, so that they would be remembered. And when her words were recorded, as they were in the minutest of details, the names of the fallen were preserved in the books of history where, without her naming, they would otherwise have been forgotten.

Krishna patiently heard it all. She tallied up the count and heaped it at his feet, this god who permitted her and her husband, all the others, to play these vile games, carry out these murderous wars. Sometimes her voice was venom; sometimes she wept inconsolably; sometimes she came close to fainting.

At the end, when she should have been spent, she was overcome. It was not anger; it was not vengeance; it was not even grief. It was the bafflement of the human in the face of the divine that permits such depravities of the humans to occur without intervention. It was the cry of the helpless, of millions of mothers melded into one. She spoke on behalf of all of them then, all the widows, all the mothers bereft of their children, all the maimed soldiers who had travelled far and wide to fight a war for a land they had never seen, all the horses and elephants decimated in battle, all those who survived who would find no peace in the victory. She spoke not as Gandhari but as something more than Gandhari.

She said, 'O Krishna! It is the way of mortals to be foolish and greedy and monstrous. But you are divine; you are Narayana himself! How could you have permitted this to happen? How could you stand by and watch these innocent women be widowed, these mothers rendered childless? Just as you have brought the ruination of our clan, just as you have left so many women widowed, so many mothers childless, so, too, in thirty-six years, your entire clan shall be destroyed from within, just as mine has been ruined from within, and you, too, shall face an inglorious death as the warriors here have found here today – a death without glory, without victory.'

It was a cry, but there was power in that cry, power that made the earth soaking in the blood of the fallen armies tremble, that shook the trees and sent birds flying away, squawking.

Krishna nodded slightly; his lips turned upwards imperceptibly in gracious acceptance even of the curse. 'O virtuous queen! O one of great vows! You are a woman of immense austerity and without doubt your words shall come true. Your words will bring to fruition that which must come to pass. So be it!'

Gandhari was nonplussed. She had expected anger, a protest, a chiding. That would have given her some satisfaction. His nonchalance robbed her of the thrill of revenge. She collapsed to the ground, spent. Krishna coaxed her, 'Arise, arise, O Gandhari, do not give in to grief! Are you not at fault, too, for this vast carnage? You who had ignored the evil committed by your son, who watched him commit unspeakable horror without stopping him. Why do you ascribe to me your own faults? Let go of this grief. Indulgence in grief only doubles it. Just as a brahmana woman bears children for the practice of austerities, a princess like you brings forth sons for slaughter!'

It was then that Gandhari fell silent, then that she felt an emptiness that would never again fill, that would leave her hollow like a coconut shell with the flesh removed. It was a foolish game, this business of curses and blessings. One hundred sons may not be equal to one good son. A son could be made invincible but not against his own stupidity. A son could be born who would become the bitter enemy of his brothers also bestowed from a boon given by a grumpy rishi. What chance was there of a curse against a god like Krishna?

How could one curse Krishna if he had not wanted the curse himself?

It was hubris to think she could bless or curse from her powers of penance alone. The workings of fate and karma were so much more intricate and subtle than that. For example, why would she have given him the grace period of thirty-six years before the curse took place? What use would it be then, when he was old, once he had wrapped up his affairs and all that he had to do in this world? No, such a thing could not have been said even through her own lips without his own intervention. *That pose of a curse, which was meant to be a demonstration of her power, instead showed only the hollowness of that power.*

One could be queen and govern the lives of millions. But if one had not mastered herself, what was the use of it? Was that not the lesson she had tried to teach Duryodhana, the day he declared the war?

And this was the last lesson she learned about curses and blessings on that battlefield with Krishna, after he had reprimanded her and she had fallen silent. It was not just about the limitations on the efficacy of curses and blessings. It was the delusion of the idea that one could do something to someone else without doing it to oneself. Yes, Gandhari was the queen who cursed a god. More importantly, though, she was the queen who had cursed herself.

There was nothing left to be done now but mourn the dead. The funeral rites were performed. Sandalwood, aloe, perfumes and costly silken robes and other cloths were piled onto large heaps of wood. Funeral pyres were lit. Broken chariots and weapons accompanied the corpses in cremation on their last journey. Torrents of clarified butter and oil were poured over the bodies so they would burn quickly. There were hundreds of thousands to be burned. Those who came from remote realms and were friendless in this foreign clime were heaped together and their rites presided over by the wise and compassionate Vidura.

There was an order to this, too. First, the bodies of Duryodhana and his brothers were burned. This was the last honour due them: their seniority among the dead, the vanquished. There was a solemnity of silence, a pause, as the first of the funerary rites were performed for Duryodhana. Even the Pandavas were in mourning. There was a wrongness in killing one's own kin, no matter how horrible they may have been, and the Pandavas felt the weight of it now, the cost of their kingdom, the cost of their justice and vengeance. It was righteous, yet not right.

Gandhari was later told how their heads were bowed, their faces etched in grief and regret as her one hundred sons' corpses burned on the pyre. Her own eyes were dry. She felt nothing. Dhritarashthra next to her was weeping. She handed him her handkerchief, but her hand did not even tremble.

Then came the others. Shikhandi, the reincarnation of Amba, the maiden whose advances Bhishma had spurned and who had been reborn to kill him in vengeance. She had succeeded. The sons of Draupadi, murdered not in battle but in their sleep. Shakuni, her brother. And so many more.

After the bodies were burned, Yudhishthira with the consent of Dhritarashthra gathered together all the mourners on both sides in a procession to the banks of the Ganga river. Yudhishthira placed Dhritarashthra at the front of the procession and followed him as the new king of Hastinapur. They gathered by the thousands, the relatives of the slain kings and princes and their priests.

It was time for the water rites, the offering of oblations of water to the departed. This was performed by the women, offering water to their fathers, grandsons, brothers, sons, husbands and other kinsmen. And for their friends. So many women marched to the shores to perform this rite that the pathway to the river became smooth, trodden down by their feet. It became like the shore of an ocean.

Suddenly, Kunti cried out, 'O sons! That great warrior and hero, Karna, who preferred glory to life, was your elder brother! O sons! Offer oblations of water unto that eldest brother of yours who was born to me by the sun god, Suryadeva, who wrapped himself in clouds of grief at the death of his son.' She fell to the ground, weeping.

It was then that Yudhishthira broke. All the Pandavas were distraught – even from a distance, Gandhari could hear their muffled cries, their hands covering their faces in shock, the bitterness of their sighs and muttered curses under their breath. But it was Yudhishthira who was especially devastated. Already reluctant to fight the war, he became totally undone at the realization that he had not even been the rightful heir to the throne. It had been Karna who should have been king.

Yudhishthira spoke out bitterly. 'O Mother! You, the mother of Karna? How is it that you have kept this a secret for so long? Because of this secret of yours, we have become undone. The grief I feel at Karna's death is a hundred times greater than the grief caused by the death of Abhimanyu and the sons of Draupadi. I am burning with grief. With Karna at our side, nothing would have been unattainable by us.' He wailed out loud. Later, he would tell Kunti that at the assembly-hall, the day when Draupadi had been disrobed, he had seen Karna's feet and felt strangely calmed by them, the feet that so uncannily resembled Kunti's. The feet he should have bowed to as the feet of his elder brother; the true heir to the throne.

Yudhishthira's bitterness was such that later, in the depths of his sorrow, he cursed all the women of the world that henceforth no woman would succeed in keeping a secret. Gandhari had smiled at that, later, much later, when she was once again capable of the semblance of a smile, at the naiveté of the king, who did not understand that a woman's secrets could never fully be revealed or understood.

Then, with full devotion, Yudhishthira offered the oblations of water unto his older brother killed by his younger brother. He called forward the wives and other members of Karna's family to join him in performing the rites for Karna. Gandhari could imagine how low Arjuna felt, that his arch nemesis, the one he hated and fought with so bitterly for so long, the one he had been able to defeat in the end only through cheating and breaking the rules of warfare, was his elder brother. Even that glory had been snatched away from him now.

It brought no comfort to Gandhari to see the Pandavas so devastated and downtrodden at the end of the war. It made the loss of her sons all the more meaningless and futile. There was not even a proper cause for which they had been sacrificed. She could not bear to be in the midst of such sorrow anymore, and she moved away quietly. There was one last visit she needed to make.

The battlefield was easier to navigate now that most of the corpses had been removed, the blood absorbed into the earth. The vultures had done the rest of the work. It was quiet now that the tumult of war had receded. Gandhari was able to pick her way to where Bhishma was resting, preparing to die. He had fallen in the early days of the war, brought down by the arrows of Arjuna with Shikhandi, Amba reborn, as the charioteer. He had been injured fatally but had the boon from his father that he would die only when he wished. Now Bhishma was waiting for the sun to change its course to Uttarayana, the phase of the solar cycle each year when the sun began its northward journey from the south. That was the most auspicious time to die.

He refused to be taken from the battlefield. Instead, he lay on a bed of arrows. After he had fallen, when Arjuna and the others rushed to his side to look after him, he had requested only one thing. A pillow for his head. The others had run off to the palace to bring him expensive cushions and soft pillows. Only Arjuna had understood what he meant. With tears streaming down his face, with great tenderness and love, Arjuna shot three arrows into the ground upon which his grandfather could rest his head.

Gandhari came alone. She did not want anyone else to intrude on this visit. She could pick out his location through the sound of his breath. No one else breathed as deeply, as calmly, as richly, as Bhishma. There was an aura that radiated from him, of wisdom, of experience, of having gone through things no one else could imagine. Gandhari could find him like a moth would find a flame.

She knelt next to him.

Bhishma chuckled. 'Ah, Gandhari! There are two women, I think, who have blamed me for their lot in life, who saw me as their enemy. One was Amba, who then took birth as Shikandi to be the charioteer for Arjuna. She knew I would not shoot at a woman (even if she was now a man) and so Arjuna was able to bring me down easily. I think that is one debt I have repaid. You are the other one. And what is it you would ask of me, queen? Let all my debts be repaid now before I leave this earth one last time.'

She did not know why she had come to Bhishma. She did not speak. It would be months, nearly a year, before she would speak again, before her brain and mouth could resume a semblance of proper functioning. He had always been larger than life for her – this heroic, otherworldly figure, the patriarch of a family to which she had always wanted but never quite managed to belong. His approval, so unforthcoming, had meant a lot to her. Always she remembered him as being the one who agreed with her to let her baby Duryodhana live. She wondered if he regretted it now.

She had always felt kinship with Satyavati, his stepmother. Bhishma had always been so aloof. But now she thought of how much more she had in common with Bhishma — their vows, their loyalty to family even at the cost of dharma, their quixotic idealism that did not allow them to deviate from their family, the constant foolish delusional attachment to their family. They both perhaps longed to be in the world of the *devas* but were stuck in the world of the mortals, trapped by the desires and ambitions of others. Except now Bhishma was leaving.

If she could, Gandhari would have touched his feet for his blessings. But one could not touch the feet of one who was lying down, who was ill, who was dying. And this was the pain that made the first tears fall from Gandhari's eyes. There was the pain of losing her sons, but this was another type of pain, the pain of losing elders, of no longer having anyone above her, no one whose feet she could touch for blessings, no one to offer guidance or advice. Her parents, her teachers, they were all dead. It was a different kind of loss.

Bhishma asked again softly, 'Gandhari, what is it that I can do for you?'

She lifted his hand and pressed her head into the bed of arrows next to where his hand was resting, turned her cheek to the side, the feathery shafts of the arrows dimpling the side of her face. She pressed her face down onto the arrows until it hurt. Bhishma understood and placed his hand on her head, on top of her hair, where the bandage was tied tight around her eyes. He kept his hand there in comfort, in affection, in blessing, as she wept silently.

He did not bless her with words. What could he possibly offer to her as a blessing now? But he kept his hand there for hours as her tears fell in a stream onto the ground. Soon she would have to get up again. Soon she would have to return to a palace now ruled over by the enemies of her sons. Soon she would have to tend once more to Dhritarashthra and soothe his pain. Soon she would have to endure the presence of Kunti, returned once again to Hastinapur as the dowager queen. She would have to return to a palace where she would be tended to not by her sons but by Yuyutsu, the last remaining son of Dhritarashthra, who had sided with the Pandavas and had therefore been spared, the son of her maid. She would have to return to a palace that would now be silent, that would not bear the footfall of her one hundred sons, that would never know her grandchildren but would instead house the alien grandchildren of Kunti. She would have to return to a life worse than death.

But for now, she could sit under the protective shadow, one last time, of Bhishma. She could bow her head to her elder, one last time. One last time, she could be in the presence of one like her who had known the path of dharma but had been trapped by familial ties and affection, one who, like her, had in his own way loved Duryodhana, too.

10

IN THE FOREST. NOW

She knew it was a dream because she could see. How fastidious she was about never casting her eyes upon the world. Even when she changed her bandage for cleaning, she screwed her eyes tightly closed so no ray of light would enter them, no taste of colour.

This was a dream she cringed from. It was late in the night, the dark before dawn, and she was in the forest, near the hermitage by the river. But the forest had turned ominous. The crickets chirped menacingly.

She clawed at her face.

She whimpered. She could smell Krishna in the air. The fragrance of sandalwood was stronger, more intense than before. He surrounded her. In between the frenzied gusts of wind, she thought she could hear his footsteps. He was coming after her. She cried out but there was no one in the world to listen. Kunti was gone. Sanjaya was gone. Dhritarashthra was gone. Only Krishna and Gandhari remained in this dark wild world.

She felt desperately afraid.

Was it a dream or was it something real?

It did not matter. It hurt to breathe, to inhale that scent of sandalwood that carried with it the smell of the death of her family, her sons and her brother (yes, she missed even him, too), the acrid scent of the battle air when she had cursed Krishna, the remorse, the guilt, the regret, the wistfulness, and the deflation of his rebuke, his judgment of her. She could not face it again.

She stumbled out of her pallet. She was weak on her feet, her legs trembled so badly. But she was desperate to escape. She began running away from Krishna. The wind whipped the leaves into a frenzy, the trees shaking their boughs at her as she tried to walk between them. The branches pushed her back, not letting her proceed. Her feet dug into the earth, and the dirt became a deep, sticky mud, sucking at her ankles and heels, drawing her under.

She tried breathing with her mouth but could not avoid the smell and taste of sandalwood, that fragrance that should have been light, soothing and cool but instead burned the insides of her nose. She pushed against the branches and tried to force her feet up and forward. The branches snapped back in her face, scratching her with thorns. The mud squelched around her feet and the more she resisted, the deeper she sank. She thought she felt worms crawling over her feet, dragging against the skin of the tops of her feet, curling around her toes.

Now she began to run. She hated running, had given it up since girlhood. A queen should never be hurried; a queen's gait should always be dignified, measured. She should never stumble. How could an old woman, nearly starved to death, run after all? It was just desperate walking, lurching from tree to tree, sometimes holding on to the trees and gasping for breath, then pushing off to the next few stumbling steps until the next tree. When her feet could no longer hold her up, she was content to crawl, using her belly to pull her forward, grabbing the branches that pierced her and using them as leverage.

But she knew Krishna was coming after her. Her hearing had become superfine. She could hear his feet dancing lightly through the forest, effortless, the trees parting to let him through, the leaves rubbing themselves on him gently, lovingly. The very forest seemed to caress him, and the owls, the crickets; making way for him to pursue her.

I will not see him. Not again. If I see him, he should be dead; if I see him, it should be to see the fulfilment of my curse.

'Madhu,' said Krishna softly, somewhere near her, and she nearly jumped out of her skin.

Madhu! How many years had it been since she had heard that name, her pet name, the name by which her father and brothers called her. Since she had turned a teenager, she was known as Gandhari, named after her kingdom, Gandhara, and that was the name her husband, Bhishma, Vidura, Satyavati and all the others had used for her. To hear that old childhood name again, the name that embodied all the affection from her family whom she had never seen again since the day she was shipped off to her marriage to the blind king, jolted her, made her shiver.

That voice. That somnolent voice roughened with a lilting laugh, sweeter and finer than the flute he played. The voice that had told her of the death of her son, that told her that women like her gave birth to sons for slaughter.

Her teeth gnashed together. She clutched her head but could not block out the sound of Krishna's voice, and it came out of her in a stream of bile and vomit and blood.

Then she was falling into spinning blackness and a pair of blue hands caught her, refusing to let her fall, refusing to let her elude him.

She woke with a jolt. *Where am I?* She was sitting on rough ground, something hard and smooth like rock. Her feet explored the ground beneath her. It was as smooth as pebbles, round stones stacked together, with dimpled indentations. She sniffed at the air. It was odourless, sterile.

She cocked her ear. The only sound was the harsh rise of her own breathing.

The bandage around her eyes had lightened to almost translucence. It made the world around her appear in a dull yellow glow. She instantly tried to close her eyes, but she could not. She could not *not* see.

Was this death then? A forced reckoning with the past? She had not needed the aid of her eyes to realize where she was. She was back in Kurukshetra, the battlefield, where she had lost her one hundred sons, where each of her daughters-in-law had been turned into a widow. Where she had cursed Krishna. She would have known Kurukshetra anywhere without the need of any her senses.

Kurukshetra. They called it Dharmakshetra, the site where Dharma, the order of righteousness and harmony, had been re-established through the holy war. It was where she had lost everything. And now here she was again. She looked at the earth below her feet and saw she sat perched on a mountain of skulls. A mountain built up of millions and millions of skulls. Streams of blood wound their way from the base of the mountain, spreading like tentacles across the barren parched brown terrain of the battlefield. The blood was coagulated, like solidified lava. The field was littered with broken armour and crowns. The corpses had disappeared, but she could count them in the skulls beneath her feet; in her memory, she knew the identity of each one and where each had lain on the ground. Once, she had witnessed their deaths; once, she had recited their names, immortalizing them in history.

There was no sun here, just this dull yellow light, the dying of the day.

She knew he was here, next to her, but she still refused to look at him.

'Here we are again,' said Krishna's voice.

Gandhari replied stiffly, 'You did not need to bring me back here. I have never forgotten.'

'No, you have not,' agreed Krishna softly.

Gandhari blinked hard. She was not like the others. Dhritarashthra was consumed by the need to expiate his past and attain the heavens. Kunti was stoic, resigned, fatalistic. But a mother never forgot, never lost her grief.

She carefully stood, securing her foothold by curling her toes into the eye sockets of two different skulls. She planted her hands on her hips and surveyed the field. Her father had taught her this. After every battle, he would take her to survey the damage. He would count the casualties, the prisoners, the dead, the survivors, not just for their side, not just their allies, but also for the enemy.

He would tell her, 'Madhu, we are responsible for all of them. Every horse, elephant, every enemy killed, every man of ours who have sacrificed their lives. We must honour their sacrifice. Their lives, the lives we have taken, are our responsibility.'

'I am responsible for all of them,' she whispered. It was as if a stone, one of the skulls, were lodged in her throat, making breath and speech impossible.

Krishna came to stand beside her. His shape was fuzzy to her, just a blur of blue skin and yellow silk clothes, a golden crown glittering atop curly black hair. She refused to look at him directly.

'You are, too,' she could not help accusing him.

Krishna inclined his head. 'I had my role, my reasons. I have already accepted your curse, my queen. That is not why we are here.'

'And why are we here, Krishna?' Gandhari snapped. 'Why have you chased me through the forest? Why can you not simply leave me alone?' Her voice cracked. She lacked the strength she had all those years ago, when she had railed against him and cursed him. She was a feeble woman now. 'I know the tally of my sins and virtues. I know that I will suffer for what I have done and I shall face it. It is not necessary for you to have come to taunt me, to punish me further. I know your judgment.'

'That is not what I have come for.' His voice was firm and brooked no argument.

'Then, why have you come, Krishna?' Gandhari pressed again, and she could not help it that there was something small in her voice, something soft, something a little desperate.

There was a tenderness in his voice that startled Gandhari as he said, 'I have come to help you die, Madhu.'

She was so taken aback that she lowered her head so he could not see the expression on her face. 'Did you help my sons die, Krishna? You brought them to their death, but did you help them die?'

'I gave them many chances, Gandhari.'

She could not deny that. She scoffed, 'I do not need your help to die. I am ready to die and suffer through my karma. I am prepared to face it. I am not afraid to die.' She swallowed hard, a faint tremor in her heart belying her words. She breathed deeply to steady her voice. 'What is so hard about dying? It is just the absence of life. I can sit here and die on my own without anyone's help.' Without her intending it, her voice became bitter and venomous. She thought of how she had helped Dhritarashthra to find peace in his last sleep, but no one had been there to do that for her.

'Why do you always choose to suffer, Gandhari? You, a woman of such immense virtue, a lady of such inconceivable strength and willpower. Why do you let that strength and virtue turn to rust? Even now you could change your future, your death. Why do you not try?'

Gandhari snorted. 'What future do I have left? I had no future left the day the war had ended. Ever since then, it has just been this wait for death. My life lost all meaning and purpose the moment I cursed you. Only a few hours are left now between me and death. It is too late for anything else.'

There was something otherworldly in Krishna's already otherworldly voice, as mellifluous and clear as the music of bells and flutes, as he pronounced, 'Even a moment can be enough to change the course of a lifetime, of many lifetimes. Someone with the power of your penance should understand that.'

Gandhari shook her head decisively and there was something jaded, cynical to that shake of her head. She was not interested in his philosophy, another of his metaphysical discourses that he gave once in a while. Arjuna was enraptured by what he had told him before the war had begun. Somehow Krishna had given him the strength to fight the war when Arjuna had been in despair, ready to walk away from battle before it had even started.

Gandhari was not interested in that; she was not interested in changing. She simply wanted to get it over with, whatever was to come. She looked away from him, back at the scene of sanitized carnage. She pictured it in her head, the way it had been back then – each mangled corpse, each amputated limb. She recalled the smell of the rotting flesh. In her nightmares, she walked through rivers of blood trying to get to her sons. The blood of the fallen reached chest-high and as much as she waded, she never made it through the entire river. She never made it to her sons, not even in her dreams.

'They say I should have been a better mother.'

Krishna shrugged. 'Perhaps. I wish you had been a better queen.'

Gandhari frowned.

'That is what Bhishma had hoped for, when he had picked you for Dhritarashthra's bride, you know.'

Gandhari harrumphed. 'No! I was an easy mark. A blind prince who would never become king – that was hardly a good marital prospect! The great princesses of the realm would not have settled for my husband. They must have thought a mountain bumpkin like me, someone from the hinterlands, would not have had a better option. They thought it would be a step up for me.' *And, then, of course, there was the boon. One hundred sons. That must have been tantalizing.* Still the bitterness of that day rankled, the realization that it was for Dhritarashthra that her hand was being sought, not Pandu.

'Tsk! I expected more of you than such simple-minded thinking. You are the daughter of Subala, that wily old king who fended off more foreign invasions and warlords than I could count. He raised you to be tough, to be shrewd. I had not expected such childishness from you.'

Gandhari was weary. 'Why dredge up the past now? What is done is done. There is no point going back over it now.'

Krishna suddenly pressed his right thumb on her forehead, exerting pressure on her third eye. 'Look again, Madhu, look again.'

He pressed harder and suddenly she was back to the beginning, where it had all begun, once again.

11

And then she was back to where she had not dared to go in her memories – and where else did she travel nowadays but through the maze of her memories – back in her father's palace, a young princess at sunrise on the day she had blindfolded herself.

She saw herself stony-faced and impassive, the petulance of a teenage girl on the cusp of hardening into iron that would not yield to softness again. She saw the right hand of the princess, neatly folded over a square of cloth hidden from the others' eyes.

She was in the past but not. The taint of the death of all one hundred of her sons hung heavy in the air. The bitterness of knowing which husband lay in wait for her at the end of the weeks-long journey from her father's house to Hastinapur slid like metal down her throat. She saw her father's face, and she knew he was dead.

The image wavered and blurred as she was about to lose herself in those other memories, the ones that called her like a siren, and then steadied again as the voice of Krishna sternly commanded her: 'No, Madhu. Stay. Look more closely.'

She wanted to look away. It was done. What point was there in looking back?

But she obeyed. She made herself look away from the princess she had been, to take in the crowd behind her. She had not seen that then. She had faced away from everybody and then had turned back only when she was blindfolded. She had deliberately shielded herself from her father's eyes. Even now, so many years later, in a vision that was not even the reality of what had happened, she feared seeing his eyes, his pain.

Her heart thudded as she began to turn her eyes sideways to meet his eyes. They were wet with sadness and hope. It was the hope that made her breath catch in her throat. Her gaze sidled past him to Bhishma, the moment before she had blindfolded herself. His eyes were gleaming with hope, too.

She steadied her gaze upon those two men, one who was the father of her childhood and the other the father figure of her womanhood, knowing she would see the grief, the disappointment, once she bandaged herself. She remained unflinching, waiting for the moment. In that pause, she caught in the corner of her eye a web of blue and gold. The colours were dazzling in the sunlight, enough to draw her forward, step by step, past all the old ministers gazing at her young self appraisingly, past her mother and cousins and brothers, who looked at her half enviously, that she would be leaving them all behind for the glamorous city of Hastinapur.

She reached the back corner of the audience chamber that opened onto the palace gardens. Her eyes were fixed on that web of blue and gold. It was Krishna, of course it was, and from his palm thousands of slender golden threads flowed, looping over the gardens, tangled in the branches of the trees, weaving intricate designs across the bright blue sky, and then doubling back to be clasped in his palm again. She approached curiously. The threads fluttered and shifted in the breeze, in the gentle wave of his palm.

She forgot that she despised him, so entrancing were the slivers of gold dancing in the sunlight. She reached out her hand and looked up at Krishna. When he nodded, she touched one thread, wanting to run it through her fingers – it was so delicate, it started to fray as soon as she touched it, splintering into broken fragments. She lightened her fingers, just hovering over the threads, and they began to twist and turn of their own volition and splayed themselves across her palm. They flattened on her palm and became wide ribbons, stringing together series of images, like strips of picture boxes, all beginning in the moment before she had tied that blindfold around her eyes. It was like a web of karma, of all the possible futures she could have had, beginning in that moment. They all rested in Krishna's hand, each alternative fate she could have earned for herself.

She spent what felt like hours wafting through them, one by one. In almost all of them, she was married to the blind prince. In some, she was miserable. In some, she was not. In some, she had the same hundred sons. In some, she had none. In some, she had only one. There was one that sparkled brighter than the others in the sunlight. As it unfolded itself before her, she saw herself as queen, clear-eyed and strong in reign. She did not have a happy marriage. But she was a good queen. Bhishma watched her with unabashed admiration and respect. She and Krishna jousted and sparred but were never enemies. Her sons, all one hundred of her sons, were born again and lived. They lived.

She flung her hands in front of her face and cried out, 'Enough, Krishna! Enough!'

And then they were back, sitting in that forlorn mountain where no wind blew, where no light of the sun shone, where she was old and bitter and brittle once again. Her breathing was the only harsh sound in the world.

Krishna remarked, 'That's the life I wanted for you. I thought, now here is a woman who deserves to be queen, of something greater than remote, backwater Gandhara. Here's someone I could lose to, and still Dharma would win. This noble, strong, independent woman born to be queen.'

'It is done. There is no going back. It cannot be undone.'

'No,' agreed Krishna.

Breath was harder and harder to latch onto; her ribs and chest ached with the effort of drawing in oxygen, and she wondered why she even bothered now as she was already at the threshold of death. 'Why did you show me that, Krishna? It is the past. It is all over now.' It hurt more to go to the palace of her childhood, to see again her father and brothers, to live again through the moment she had decided to blindfold herself, more than being here in the battlefield. This was a pain she had almost become accustomed to.

'Is it really over, Gandhari?'

Her voice grew a little desperate. 'Was it a mistake, Krishna? Is that what you want me to see? Was it wrong? Is — is what happened my fault, because of what I did then?'

That had always been her biggest fear, that she had caused the war with her darkness, with her negativity, her self-imposed blindness. She had brought up her sons in the darkness of her world and then that darkness had spread over the entire world.

Was it my fault? Had it begun with her, the war? She had been the one to give birth to the villains. Had she carried the fault within herself all along? Had she transmitted evil to her sons through her womb, through her blood tainted by the ills of her character, the anger and bitterness she had harboured inside for so long? Had it all started in that moment, when she had blindfolded herself?

Bile rose in her belly, acid burning her from within. Her limbs felt like jiggling rubber, as if she would roll right down this mountain of skulls.

She remembered how it felt, unfolding her hand, placing the square of cloth in front of her on that altar. That had made it sacred. She remembered her words, as plain and austere as that strip of cloth. She remembered the feeling of the presence Bhishma and her father behind her, knowing their displeasure and that she would never see them again. She remembered, as she tied that cloth so tightly her head hurt, that she had inside a small savage satisfaction, in hurting them as they had hurt her. That was not why she had done it, but a part of her had revelled in that feeling nevertheless.

Tears came to her eyes now. Regret and remorse, too little and too late. *Was I a bad woman? Was that why my sons lived and died as they had?*

She steeled herself. She was not a bad daughter. She was not a bad person. They had told her how pious the act of blindfolding made her, how devoted a bride, how virtuous a woman. That was the source of her power, her strength, this martyring of herself. What would she have been without it?

She had never seen her father again, her mother, her brothers, her maid, her friends, the mountains of her home. She had denied herself the sight of the sunlight, of flowers blooming on the trees, of her favourite horse. She had never seen the face of her husband, never given herself the chance to perhaps love him. She had never seen her children when they were born, never seen their faces, except as corpses or Duryodhana on the way to his death.

She fingered the white cloth bandage, that had once felt as if it were the source of her strength, the symbol of her defiance and virtue. It had grafted itself into her skin until she no longer knew what was cloth and what was flesh.

Her voice broke. 'Was it a mistake, Krishna?'

He did not reply. She knew her thoughts displeased him. She could feel his annoyance vibrate around her darkly, sizzling like lightning.

She shook her head decisively. 'It does not matter. What is done is done.' She could never go back; she could never change what she had already done, what had already happened.

Krishna's voice warmed. 'Now you begin to see.'

'See what?'

'That you were asking the wrong question. There is never a right answer to a wrong question. Do not ask whether it was a mistake. Such a thing cannot be asked or answered.'

Gandhari grew exasperated. 'Then why did you take me back there? What's the point? How can it matter now, now that I am almost dead? It is too late now.'

'Is it?'

She snorted and indicated her emaciated form, her thinning hair with streaks of bald scalp showing through, her skin that was beginning to wrinkle like an elephant's hide.

'Gandhari, what is it you saw when you were back there? Think carefully.'

Part of her wanted to ignore him, to simply die in peace. If she said nothing, if she were simply quiet, perhaps he would let her go. This was giving her a headache and an ulcer, churning up things she had kept away, far away from the surface of her consciousness.

But there was an urgency in his voice. It reminded her of the day that Draupadi was dragged into the court, when she had first seen him. How he had looked at her, challenging her to act. She had refused then. She did not want to refuse this time.

It felt like she was sitting across from him in a game, but they were not on opposite sides. It was like being trained by her father. She was wary and cautious, and now she began thinking like a queen again, not just a woman waiting to die.

She surveyed the scene again in her mind's eye. She remembered how those threads had unfurled from his hand, how many threads of possibility spun themselves across the skies all the way to the horizon and beyond, all extending forth from that one moment of her blindfolding. She said softly, 'A moment can change everything, for oneself and for the world.'

He quietly urged her. 'Do you not see? Even now, one moment could change so much.' His voice was so charming, seductive. Suddenly she yearned to see Krishna, to see his eyes, the shape of his mouth, that auspicious form. So much she had missed through the blindfold; how much more she would have seen, how much more she would have learned, if she had not done it.

She whispered, 'It is too late now, Krishna. I am almost dead.'

'Our lives never end, queen. They go on and on. We will come here again; we will play again. What you do now is just as important as what you did back then. It will shape your lives to come.'

Tears began slipping down her eyes. 'It is already done, Krishna. I ruined things already, and that will haunt me in my lives to come, too. The die is already cast.'

Softly, 'Roll again, queen. What is not yet done leaves open so many possibilities. You have this moment. Change your life in this very moment itself. Change the question you asked me earlier.'

Earlier, she had asked, was it a mistake? Gandhari frowned, wondering what he meant.

Krishna said, 'Change it only a little, Gandhari.'

She thought about it, carefully and logically, picking it up and examining it from corner to corner. Now she understood what he meant. Not: *was it a mistake then* – that was the wrong question – but: *is it a mistake now?*

She voiced the question aloud to herself. She knew it was for her to answer. The thought of removing the blindfold now terrified her. It terrified her more than losing her sons had terrified her. It terrified her existentially. What was she without the blindfold? There was a dignity in the vow, in taking refuge in austerity. She had been the most devoted of wives, the most virtuous of women, the queen who had cursed a god. To remove the blindfold would be to forsake all of that.

And yet.

Maybe I have to let go of who I was if I want to become something else. And she did want to become something else, oh, how she did. Even at the precipice of death, she could not quench the thirst for life that had been suppressed in her for so long, the eagerness for a new canvas on which to paint the colours of a new life, a new self, a new beginning.

Maybe it is not too late. She did not quite believe that, and yet, her fingers moved towards the back of the knot that she had tied every day for the past fifty-five years, brushing away the hands of her maids to do it herself – the blindfold that had embodied her devotion, her worship, her virtue, her penance, her sacrifice. It was an odd thing, to sacrifice a sacrifice. It felt a little weak, a little unheroic, a little like cheating. She was a woman who had always kept her vows. To break this vow now was tantamount to breaking herself.

And yet.

She untied the knot and set her eyes free.

Immediately, Krishna stood in front of her. He shaded her eyes, tenderly rubbing her eyelids, shielding her from the harsh light. She could not bear to meet his eyes, so blindingly bright was the world suddenly. His touch was overwhelming. His fingers were so tender, so gentle, so patient as they rubbed her eyelids. Her sons had never been so gentle. She had never been held with such affection, not since she had left her father's home.

She blinked away tears and stepped back. Even now she could not bear for him to see her weak and vulnerable.

She straightened herself and held her head up high, the queen once again.

She had forgotten what it was to see the world in colour. The blue eggshell of the sky, the glow of daylight on the beige slicked mud of the battlefield, dirt mixed with something else. Even as she tried to look away, even as she kept her eyes on the mountain of skulls on which they stood, her eyes kept getting dragged back to Krishna. Despite herself, she gazed upon him, drinking in the vision of his face like a ravenous woman. His face was dusky sapphire blue, with black sparkling eyes, shark earrings dangling from his ears. His face was like a blooming lotus yet he held himself with regal grace – the marriage of the cowherd and the prince. It had been half a century since she had been a girl but there was something about the mischief playing in his eyes, in that lurking smile in those slender lips, that made her a girl all over again. It was a wonder she had resisted his charm for as long as she had.

She waved her hand to indicate the field, the corpses that were no longer there. 'I have responsibility for them.'

Krishna said nothing.

'I do.' Just as she had been responsible for her sons, she felt responsible for every son, husband, father, every widowed woman, every childless mother, who had been on this field. Her eyes blurred. 'There is no escape from karma, Krishna. There is no way to not pay for what has been done.'

She surveyed the battlefield slowly, the way her father had trained her, pausing on each spot where once there was a corpse, one by one. She remembered their bodies, how they had appeared to her with wounds freshly bleeding, their hearts just stopped. She looked not just at her sons, but the sons of other mothers, the husbands of other wives, the fathers of children left orphaned. She looked where the sons of Draupadi were murdered in their tent, where the son of Arjuna had been trapped and killed, where Bhishma had lain fallen.

Something began to slowly unravel in her, starting in her belly, and unfurled upwards into a bloom of a new feeling, something she could not quite place.

Krishna replied, 'That is true. But it is also said that those who come to me never face ruin.'

She wanted to snort, to scoff at the easy arrogance of this playful god. But she stopped herself. She turned towards him, eyes brimming with tears, and looked at him hard. How casually he stood, his fingers lightly splayed against his hip. Those fingers that had once tapped his thigh in a command to strike Duryodhana on the thigh, where he had been unprotected and vulnerable, those fingers that in that one tap delivered the death blow to Duryodhana. That mischievous mouth with that slight smile, that mouth that had urged Arjuna to let loose the arrows against Karna, her son's staunchest defender, even when Karna was unarmed, against all the rules of war. Those eyes, the glittering black eyes that shone like the sun and the moon, those eyes that had been hard, unyielding as she had wailed before him, as she had grieved with abandon, as she had cursed him, as she had rebuked him, those eyes that condemned her coldly as a mother, a princess, who gave birth to sons for slaughter, who had gotten what she deserved.

But there was a softness in those eyes, too, a kindness, an understanding. It made a lump form in her throat, and she believed him after all, that he could do it, that he had the power to transform curses into blessings, that nothing was impossible for him. Had she not seen it – how he thwarted her sons again and again, how he protected the Pandavas against all the odds, how he had kept alive their last heir when he had been at death's door. Nothing was impossible for him.

But he killed my sons; he orchestrated the war that destroyed my family.

She tried to hold onto that thought, but it lacked the sharpness of anger and pain it once carried for her. It did not make her burn. It settled into her like a pebble into water, without ripple or turbulence. It just was.

She felt the weight of the mountain of skulls beneath her. She counted each one, just as she had once counted the leaves in the trees in the forest, wondering how many had died due to her folly. It had terrified her for so many years but dispassion stilled her now as she went through the count, rattling the names of each skull she could remember, names she had once defiantly hurled at Krishna as accusations. So often she had counted the names of her son thus, one after another, one hundred times.

She felt like the mountain would draw her into itself, that she would become the crowning skull on this heap of death minutes or hours from now. That thing which was unfurling in her belly now spread out of her encompassing each skull, each person, each thing, living and dead in the world. It embraced her sons, dead and gone, her husband, at the precipice of death; it embraced the sons of Pandu and Pandu himself, who had once been kind to her, and she wished them well, those who now sat upon the throne of Hastinapur, she wished them the peace she knew would remain elusive for them; it embraced her brother, who had betrayed her; it embraced Karna and Bhishma and her father and her mother; it embraced Ayla, whom she had abandoned, and Kunti, who had never abandoned her. It spread all across her, a warmth and sudden lightness of being, a radiance that sang under her skin and flowed through her bones; it made her raise her arms and stretch them out.

She wished peace for them and wellness but something more than that, something deeper than love, warmer than compassion. She gathered them all to herself, all these lives, all these bundles of being, and embraced them to herself. Once, her grandmother-in-law Satyavati had wished for her that she could be mother to more than one hundred sons, that she could be mother to one hundred and five. It had seemed impossible to her then. Now she felt she could be mother to millions more; she could be mother even to Krishna. She took them all into her heart and held them – their pains, their joys, their dreams, their worries and anxieties, their fear, their suffering. She felt it within herself and she did not flinch. She sent forth warmth and light, the healing touch only a mother has.

It was then that the world began changing. It was then that the world began righting itself. That small twinge of feeling shook and shattered the earth upon which she sat. And that was the last lesson she learned in her life as Gandhari about blessings and curses. Rules and conditions apply when the game is selfish, when the goal is limited to oneself. That's when Krishna and all the *devas* can and will come to trick you, to test you, to stop you, because the wellbeing of the world lies in the balance. That's when decades of penance can be spent in a moment of futility, when the results cannot be predicted, when the gods and rishis will mock you. But something small in service of the infinite, something that goes beyond the circumference of one's own self and identity, that is a power that can never be limited. That is a power beyond counting. When you bless the world, that blessing multiplies and showers itself upon you.

The earth began quaking. The skulls beneath her feet began rattling. The sun winked out in the sky. The earth began hissing and moaning as it started to break apart. The world began spinning fast, tilting on its axis. The skulls started raining down on her. The skulls fell on her, pulverized against her skin and scalp, filled her nostrils with powder of bones and death. Her toes gripped the eye sockets of the skulls below her, her arms flailing to catch onto anything solid, but there was nothing. Nothing besides Krishna, who stood upright, smiling, unaffected, calm.

A harsh wind blew, ripping against the skin of her stomach, stripping her bare, like Draupadi had been stripped by Gandhari's sons. Her mouth gasped open, and the air was acrid with the taste of blood, the smell of offal. The wind was so stinging it made her lips crack open and start bleeding. The world was spinning so fast, she was suspended mid-air. Carcasses began hitting her from all directions, splattering her with coagulated blood.

I am not afraid. I am not afraid of the hells. I am not desirous of the heavens. I can bear this. I can bear anything. There is no fear in me. You do not know my will, Krishna. Even the devas would bow to the strength of my willpower, to the power of my penance.

Krishna nodded imperceptibly, his curly locks falling over his forehead, his gem-encrusted crown tilting slightly, rakishly. *Even I bow to it, queen.*

I am not afraid, I am not weak. I will not go to you out of weakness or cowardice. I do not need rescue or pity.

Here there was no pride. It was just a statement of fact.

I do not want your fear, queen. Do not come to me out of fear. Come for something else.

This was not speech. There was no space for speech in the world anymore. It was just reverberations within skulls, communication that was all the more intense for its silence. Monsoon gusts of wind and sea spray were being spewed out of the splintering earth. The wind was one long howl of agony. The spinning of the earth off its axis was emitting a high-pitched wheezing tone that would momentarily cause her eardrums to break.

Something else.

She was afraid for a moment, suspicious, that this was yet another of his tricks, that she would be duped yet again. She almost turned away from him. But she could see now, and she could see that there was promise in Krishna's eyes. That which drew all the denizens of the world, the *devas*, the rishis, the humans, the immortals, the animals, even the plants, into his forests, into battle, into his kingdom. She had thought that hope was something for girlhood, for someone at the beginning of life. Yet she felt it now, old, emaciated, on the cusp of death. Not for the heavens, not for happiness, but simply for the game of life, for the chance to make another throw of the dice, to play once again.

She loosened her toehold on the skulls below her and they fell away. She leaned forward and leapt off the land, into the skies, into the starry night of the cosmos, and stepped into the circle of Krishna's arms, his hands gently steadying her shoulders as the world righted itself once again.

Life. At the moment of her death, she had chosen life.

12

The world had been washed anew by the time the dust settled. That towering mountain of skulls was now buried underground, forming strata of smooth rock supporting the ground beneath her feet. They never really leave, the ones who have died, the ones we have known and loved, lifetime after lifetime. We carry their bones with us, ground into the fine powder of our consciousness, impressions of love and life and connection. How many millions of lifetimes we wander the world, reincarnation after reincarnation, and how many memories of the remote past, are carried in the deepest recesses of our consciousness. They, our ancestors, our departed ones, never really leave, so long as we the living carry forth the memories and remains of the dead.

But they did not haunt her now, as she stepped out of the circle of Krishna's arms and felt the soft steady earth through her footsteps. They did not trouble her. There was peace for them and peace for her now in this new world she had created. It was a bare, barren world, clean and untainted, waiting for her to make her mark.

She turned back to face Krishna. He was so beautiful, so enchanting, so disarming as she looked at him. It was hard to remember she had once thought him her enemy. It was hard to summon the anger and distaste she had once felt for him. She smiled at him, and it felt a little strange, an unaccustomed expression, but she could not help herself.

Then she frowned. There was something important that she had to do. She met his eyes. This, too, was a farewell, her last farewell. She remembered that Kunti had asked of him a lifetime of sorrow as that was the only way she could be sure of never forgetting him, never losing his blessings.

What would she ask of him?

Gandhari thought about it. She thought about it hard. She said in a slow, steady voice, a voice full of conviction and certitude, 'O, Krishna, I may forget you. I may lose my way and leave you. But you must never let me go. You must never leave me.'

It was somewhat calculating, somewhat clever but with undercurrents of sincerity and devotion; it was queenly, to put the burden into his hands rather than her own; in short, it was quintessentially Gandhari.

Krishna laughed, a laugh of delight and approval. His eyes warmed and sparkled, and Gandhari felt as if, after so long, she had finally chosen the right boon and blessing.

'So be it,' said Krishna.

She began walking away towards her new life, a life she knew would be warmed by the touch of Krishna. She wondered who she would be this time around. She did not care if she was man or woman, queen or servant, beautiful or plain. Those were not the things that mattered. She just wanted to be good.

Once, in another lifetime, she had named all one hundred and one of her children herself. Her husband had lost interest as soon as he was certain that he had gained an heir, so she alone had named them. Even the priests had not wanted to get involved, so afraid were they of the ill omens that had surrounded her eldest son's birth. Already their names were starting to slip from her memory. Now she began thinking of naming herself. She began thinking of the vast stillness of the world, of the furthest corners of it, all the lands she wanted to explore.

'Madhu?'

It took her a few moments to respond to that name. Already everything of the past was slipping away, including her identity.

She turned back. Krishna was arching an eyebrow at her. She smiled at him again, girlishly, foolishly, wondering how she had ever harboured anything resembling a grudge against him. He was bright blue and effulgent. And she felt a twang of regret that she had been so stubborn, that she had pushed him away again and again, that she had cursed him instead of calling to him. How much time she had wasted – years, decades, a whole lifetime. And there was a river running through this world also, a river of regret and remorse, of wistfulness, because that, too, we carry with us; that, too, never leaves us.

'Aren't you forgetting something?'

She frowned.

Oh yes, I have to die.

#

In the Forest, Now

Finally, the morning came. Gandhari wandered through the forest in search of the others. The wildlife had run away, escorted by the acolytes of the ashram to safety. She found them at the edge of the river. Only Dhritarashthra and Kunti remained. Sanjaya had been dispatched to safety along with the others, to give the news of their passing. Later he would say that the forest fire had started auspiciously from the fire of the sacrificial yajna performed in the morning. That was the omen that had convinced Dhritarashthra that it was the right time for them to leave their bodies.

He and Kunti sat in meditation. His eyes were closed; he was already lost to the world. Kunti's eyes were wide open, calm. She saw Gandhari and did not say a word about the bandage missing from her eyes, for which Gandhari was grateful. Gandhari saw Kunti's face for the first time, a face worn by age, by tragedy, by the five children she had raised and the one she had abandoned. Gandhari had not dared to look at her own face, to see how time and life had ravaged what once was a beautiful face, a clean face, a face upon which so many dreams and ideals had been written and then washed away.

They looked at each silently for a long moment. No smile was exchanged between them. They had gone through too much for that, individually and together. They would never be friends but they were not enemies either. Perhaps they were just sisters, who knew each other as no one else would have known them, who understood the mysteries of each other that others, even husbands and children, could not crack.

The bards, when they started singing tales of the great war, would not sing of them. They would never be at the centre of the story of the heroic Pandavas and the wicked Kauravas. They lacked the flamboyant defiance of Draupadi. They were women of a different era, who could draw down the gods into the affairs and world of the mortals, who could stack the deck in favour of their sons, who plotted behind closed doors, whose power was no less potent for being less visible, less obvious. They had fought with the weapons at their disposal – their wit, their devotion, their virtue, their strength as mothers and wives first and foremost.

At least they each knew what the other had accomplished.

Gandhari sat between Kunti and Dhritarashthra. She wondered what it had been like for Kunti when Pandu had died, when she had walked away from the funeral pyre to look after her own children and those of her co-wife, that beautiful, flighty dim-witted woman who Gandhari had thought was no match for the steel and brains of Kunti. What it was to choose the messiness of life, responsibility, dealing with the dirt and mud of the real world, instead of martyrdom, instead of escape that was as illusory as it was alluring. To be something more than an ideal.

Gandhari sat but she did not close her eyes. When she reached out to take the hand next to her, it was not her husband's, it was her sister-in-law's. Dhritarashthra was oblivious to her presence. He was at the doorway of the heavens and no longer felt the need for her. Her work was done.

When the fire came to the edge of her sari, when the first fingers of flame licked at her hungrily, Gandhari was not in prayer, she was not in contemplation. There was only the sound of laughter, floating away as light and carefree as a scrap of cloth on a breeze.

Glossary of Names

Arjuna – Third of the Pandavas, the five sons of Pandu, rivals to the sons of Gandhari.

Ayla – A maidservant of Gandhari, who followed her from Gandhara to Hastinapur.

Bhima – Second of the Pandavas, the five sons of Pandu, rivals to the sons of Gandhari.

Bhishma – The venerated patriarch and protector of the throne of Hastinapur. He took a vow of celibacy so that his father could marry Satyavati and her descendants would inherit the throne. Despite not having his own heirs, Bhishma remained loyal to the throne and protector of the Kuru clan for the rest of his life.

Dhritarashthra – Blind at birth, destined to never be king, the husband of Gandhari.

Draupadi – Wife to the five Pandavas.

Duryodhana – Gandhari's son; the first-born of one hundred sons and one daughter born to Gandhari.

Dvaipayana Veda Vyasa – the compiler of the Vedas, the author of the Mahabharata. He was also the firstborn son of Satyavati, Gandhari's mother-in-law. Biological father through niyoga of Pandu, Dhritarashthra and Vidura. He blessed Gandhari to bear 100 sons.

Karna – Best friend and crucial ally to Duryodhana, Kunti's firstborn son.

Kunti – First wife of Pandu, sister-in-law and rival to Gandhari.

Krishna – An avatar of Lord Vishnu

Kutili – Maidservant to Dhritarashthra.

Madri – Second wife of Pandu.

Nakula – One of the Pandavas, the five sons of Pandu, rivals to the sons of Gandhari.

Pandu – Brother-in-law to Gandhari, the crowned king of Hastinapur.

Sahadeva – One of the Pandavas, the five sons of Pandu, rivals to the sons of Gandhari.

Satyavati – Grandmother-in-law to Gandhari; married to Shantanu, the king of Hastinapur, and grandmother to Pandu and Dhritarashthra.

Shakuni – Gandhari's brother.

Subala – Gandhari's father.

Vidura – Brother-in-law to Gandhari; brother of Pandu and Dhritarashthra.

Yudhishthira – First of the Pandavas, the five sons of Pandu, rivals to the sons of Gandhari.

ACKNOWLEDGEMENTS

This book would not have been possible without the blessings and guidance of my diksha guru, Bhagavat Bhaskar Krishna Chandra Sastri-ji, popularly known as Thakurji, and my siksha guru, Sri Nagendra S. Rao. One Sunday afternoon, when I was struggling with the last third of the book, Thakurji remarked to me that Gandhari was of a high stature and someone who Krishna respected tremendously. This single line inspired me to power through the rest of the manuscript with this one rasa in mind. Any knowledge that I have comes through the grace of my siksha guru, Sri Nagendra S. Rao; anything I have slightly understood about dharma, sadhana and the worldview and ethos of the Itihaasa comes from him. Any merits to be found in this book are due to their teachings and blessings; the errors are mine and mine alone.

Sri Rajiv Malhotra has been a mentor, role model and dear friend for over fifteen years. It was with his encouragement that I co-edited my first book, *Invading the Sacred: An Analysis of Hinduism Studies in America*. His wholehearted support and promotion of my story made this book possible. He devoted time and energy from his incredibly hectic schedule to help make my dream come true. His belief in me helped me believe in myself.

Jennifer Hawkins, my book coach from the Author Accelerator program, is a mentor, editor, coach, cheerleader and friend all rolled into one. She patiently guided me back every time I wrote my way into a corner or lost the thread of the story. She kept me motivated and gave me the confidence to work my way through the book. Most of all, she supported my vision of the story I wanted to tell and helped me tell that story – that unique sensitivity and empathy is really what made writing this book possible. Without her, I would not have had the will or confidence to write week after week. Without her, this book may never have come to be.

I am grateful to Nandita Aggarwal and Himanjali Sankar for their editorial vision and for transforming the raw manuscript into a proper novel.

Prof. Thomas McNeely, whose course I took through the Stanford University online creative writing program, was the one who inspired me to write this story as a novel. From my seed of an idea, he saw the story it would grow into before I did. Prof. Otis Haschemeyer, whose course I was fortunate to participate in through the support of the Indic Academy run under the auspices of Sri Hari Kiran Vadlamani, was my first writing teacher since my college days long ago, and he taught me the importance of both being a good writer and a good storyteller. His words often come back to me as I write today, years after I first took his class. Sri Hari Kiran Vadlamani and the Indic Academy, a platform and incubator for budding writers, thinkers and artists, have been instrumental in my taking the first steps as a novelist.

Although my father passed away before I even started the first draft of this story, I firmly believe it was his blessings that saw this through. The grief of his passing, the coming to face-to-face with death and one's own mortality, was the emotional backdrop for the entire story. I wanted more than anything to be able to give him a peaceful passing to a better world, and this fueled my desire to find a happy or at least redemptive ending to Gandhari's story.

My deepest gratitude and love to my family – my grandfather, who promised me that I would one day be published when I was less than ten years old; my grandparents and elders, at whose feet I heard the stories of the Mahabharata for the first time; my mother, Shubhra Banerjee, brother, Amit Banerjee, sister-in-law, Shilpa Banerjee, and twin nephews, Avi and Aneesh Banerjee, who have always been there for me and encouraged me to follow my dream.

And, last, but definitely not least, I could not have written this without Biswajit Malakar, who was my first reader and gifted me a statue of Ganesha reading a book to keep as my muse. I touched the feet of that Ganesha deity before each writing session for his blessings and to remind myself of my true audience – Ganesha, the *devas*, and most of all, my ishta devata, Sri Krishna –

Mookam karoti vachalam
Pangum langhayate girim
Yatkripa Tamaham Vande
Paramananda Madhavam

(I salute that supremely blissful Madhava, whose compassion makes the mute speak and the lame climb mountains.)

ABOUT THE AUTHOR

 Aditi Banerjee is a practicing attorney at a Fortune 500 financial services company. She is currently an executive MBA student at Columbia University. She co-edited the book, *Invading the Sacred: An Analysis of Hinduism Studies in America.* She has published several essays on Hinduism and the Hindu-American experience in publications such as *The Columbia Documentary History of Religion in America since 1945* and *Buddhists, Hindus, and Sikhs in America: A Short History* (Religion in American Life), Oxford University Press. She earned a Juris Doctor from Yale Law School and received a B.A. in International Relations from Tufts University. In her free time, she enjoys wandering the Himalayas and watching Chinese xianxia (Buddhist/Taoist influenced fantasy) dramas.